"It is the duty of nations as well as of men to owe their dependence upon the overruling power of God; to confess their sins and transgressions in humble sorrow, yet with assured hope that genuine repentance will lead to mercy and pardon; and to recognize the sublime truth, announced in the Holy Scriptures and proven by all history, that those nations are blessed whose God is the Lord...

"We have been the recipients of the choicest bounties of heaven; we have been preserved these many years in peace and prosperity; we have grown in numbers, wealth and power as no other nation has ever grown.

"But we have forgotten God. We have forgotten the gracious hand which preserved us in peace and multiplied and enriched and strengthened us, and we have vainly imagined, in the deceitfulness of our hearts, that all these blessings were produced by some superior wisdom and virtue of our own. Intoxicated with unbroken success, we have become too self-sufficient to feel the necessity of redeeming and preserving grace, too proud to pray to the God that made us..."

—Abraham Lincoln, Thanksgiving proclamation, Oct. 3, 1863

For information write:
George Colton Publishing, Inc.
PO Box 375, Orangeville,
ON. Canada   L9W 2Z7

Churches, schools, charities, and other not-for-profit organizations may acquire George Colton books by writing to the above attn: Ministerial Markets Department.

This book is a work of fiction. The characters, incidents, and dialogues are products of the author's imagination and are not to be construed as real. Any resemblance to actual events or persons, living or dead, is entirely coincidental.

Library and Archives Canada Cataloguing in Publication

Clemons, Keith, 1949-
        Angel in the Alley / Keith Clemons.

ISBN 978-0-9731048-3-7

        I. Title.

PS8605.L54A76 2007   C813'.6   C2007-902607-9

Printed and bound in Canada
First Edition

07 08 09 10 11 12 13 – 10 9 8 7 6 5 4 3 2 1

Dedicated to:
Larry & Linda Carpenter
with thanks for the encouragement and support
that enabled me to spread my wings as a fledgling author

Acknowledgements

I want to thank all those who contributed to the successful completion of this manuscript. Among them are several friends who took time out of their busy schedules to review these pages in unpublished form and provide me with comment: Brian Austin, Paul Damsma, Ruth Dinsmore, Ivy Tait, Sandra Van Binsbergen, and my loving wife and best friend, Kathryn. I'm also indebted to the manuscript's editor Anne Severance, who showed exceeding patience as we pushed hard against a tight deadline and prayed daily for God's favor and grace, and Carmenn Massa, who contributed many hours of invaluable research.

I would be remiss if I did not acknowledge the ministries of three men whose commitment to guarding our Christian heritage and worldview constantly inspires me to write: Dr. James Dobson of Focus on the Family, Chuck Colson of BreakPoint and Prison Fellowship and my own pastor, Rod Hembree of Good Friends Fellowship and Quick Study Television.

Finally, I am indebted to those great hymn writers from whose timeless songs I have borrowed a short phrase: *What a Friend we Have in Jesus,* by Joseph Scriven; *The Old Rugged Cross,* by George Bennard; *Just As I Am,* by Charlotte Elliott; *Amazing Grace,* by John Newton and *God Be with You,* by Jeremiah Rankin. It is also worth noting that two of the short poems used in this book were not written by myself: the one found on page 280, about masks, and the one on page 314 describing the heavens. Why the authors of these poems chose to remain anonymous I do not know, but I thank them nonetheless.

Cover Design: Laurie Smith

Also by Keith Clemons:

If I Should Die

Above the Stars

These Little Ones

ANGEL IN THE ALLEY

by Keith Clemons

GEORGE COLTON
PUBLISHING

"Ghost of the Future!" he exclaimed, *"I fear you more than any specter I have seen."*
—*Ebenezer Scrooge, in A Christmas Carol by Charles Dickens*

"And because iniquity shall abound, the love of many shall grow cold. But he that endures unto the end shall be saved."
—*Jesus, in the book of Matthew (24:12, 13)*

PROLOGUE

"Am I going to die, Daddy?"

"Everyone dies, honey—sooner or later. Your mother, you, me, everyone."

"You know what I mean. I heard..."

"Hush. The only one that matters is God. If God wants you with Him, it's because He loves you so much He wants to end your pain. Like the cocoon I showed you. You go to sleep an ugly old caterpillar and wake up a beautiful butterfly."

"Do you think I'm ugly, Daddy?"

"No, of course not. I think you're beautiful...it's just that you'll be even more beautiful."

"But I have no hair."

"Neither do I, honey, neither do I."

CELESTIAL VANTAGE

Outside the space/time continuum:

I am an angel.

Wait! Please, don't turn away. The spirit realm brings much confusion. Do angels have wings, are we wisps of air; do we take bodily form? How many of us can dance on the head of a pin? Trying to understand the invisible is pointless. Let it be known that in essence I'm just like you, a creation of God, young as the moment but old as time, given purpose beyond my deserving. I am light, a spirit without mass, yet I touch and feel everything.

Permit an introduction, though I must say my name in Hebrew as words spoken in the angelic tongue cannot be pronounced. Please, I'd be honored if you'd call me Mesapare—the teller of tales.

Reach out with me. Feel the expanse of time. Would that you could hold it in your hand, but time is transparent, difficult even for celestial ones to fathom. To be outside time, that is bliss. Yet time does serve a purpose. Within time, random bits of information can be positioned like pieces of a puzzle enabling the vague and abstract to become clear. One word of caution before we start. In the telling, you may ascribe my story to the future, but in the heavenlies the future is already past. Come see. Look through the window at a time on earth yet to come...

ONE

"Men who see not God in our history have surely lost sight of the fact that, from the landing of the Mayflower to this hour, the great men whose names are indissolubly associated with the colonization, rise, and progress of the Republic have borne testimony to the vital truths of Christianity."
—Henry Wilson, 1822-1885, Vice President under U.S. President Ulysses S. Grant

PETER DUFOE stared at his computer, staid, unblinking. His face turned white as the blood drained from his cheeks. He should have expected it. It was bound to happen—eventually—just not so soon. He scanned the message twice to make sure he'd read it right, then glanced at the little girl sitting in the supple leather chair with a book in her lap. Her curls were wrapped around a face of innocence, almost angelic. She tilted her head to one side, her dimples pronounced as she narrowed her eyes. "You okay, Daddy?"

Peter nodded. He glanced at the message again: *"I will look unto the mountain. Where does my help come from?"* He'd hoped to find it wasn't there—but it was. There was no mistake. He erased the text and reached into his drawer with his palm up feeling the underside of the desktop. He found the disc he'd taped there and peeled it away. The coin-sized optical memory device reflected a rainbow of colors as he stood and walked to the window overlooking Bay Street from the sixty-third floor. There were more people in the street than cars, a colony of ants hunting and gathering provisions for the coming winter. The tower across from him, made of anodized gold, glinted in the red afternoon

3

sun, although the building he was in, the Optitec building, was no less grand. It held its position beside the NeXt Digital Bank tower as a statement of financial stability. The operations of the company circled the globe, but now it was gone—just like that—everything lost in a moment. *He is no fool who gives what he cannot keep, to gain that which he cannot lose. Ouch!* The quote came from missionary Jim Elliot who was killed in Ecuador by the Huaorani Indians he'd been trying to convert.

Peter glanced around the room. The Toronto office was the hub of Optitec's international operations. He shook his head. Why arrest him here? Perhaps to take the focus off American law enforcement. Negative feedback over the continued church closures was growing.

Peter felt his pulse quicken. He bit his lip, his scalp itching as beads of sweat broke the skin. *Impossible.* No, it *was* for him. No point in panicking, but then again, he had minutes, not hours.

Police cars careened around the corner, scattering pedestrians like a brood of clucking hens. Tires screeched. Doors flew open. Officers threw themselves onto the pavement with guns pointed at the building. *All that?* A black cube van, plated like a tank, slid to a stop. A swat team in flak jackets and transparent bulletproof shields exploded from the rear.

Peter dropped the miniature disc into his inside coat pocket and held his hand against his shirt feeling a *thud, thud, thudding* against the wall of his chest. He glanced out the window one last time. He shouldn't be anxious—but how could he *not*? He reached in the drawer and scooped up the unmarked white envelope. He turned it sideways and pinched the corner feeling the RFID chips, like tiny grains of rice. He slipped the envelope into his inside coat pocket. He knew the drill. He reached for his little girl—*just seven years old and...curst cancer.* He tried to smile. "Come on, hon, it's time to go."

"Where?"

"On an adventure. Like I promised."

"What about Mommy? Shouldn't we get Mommy?"

"We will, honey, we will. I promise." He took his daughter's hand and led her to his private elevator. It was a large space, meant to hold a dozen people, though he usually rode alone. The brass plate offered only two options, one button for sending the elevator up, and another for sending it down. He pushed the down button and the paneled doors closed in front of them.

"Your hand is wet, Daddy."

"Oh...sorry." The fabric of Peter's shirt was pulsating with the thumping of his chest. He clutched the material, wanting to stop the pounding as he closed his eyes. He had sixty-three floors in which to prepare. He began running through the plan in his mind. One team of officers would be sent up, but the rest would remain at street level to guard the exits. If they knew anything about him, they would know he took a private elevator to his suite, an elevator that made no stops at other floors. Such was the privilege of the company's founder and CEO.

He pressed his fingertips against an ornate design of inlaid wood and slid back a hidden door that opened like a Chinese puzzle box. Behind the door was a third button. He pushed it and reached into the open space, groping for the sealed plastic bag. He removed a wig, which he smoothed over his bald head. It wasn't that long ago he'd shaved off his hair in support of his daughter who had lost hers during chemotherapy. Now it helped the wig fit better. He slipped a set of false buck teeth into his mouth, causing his lips to protrude, slid a non-prescription pair of glasses over his nose and applied a self-adhesive mustache.

He caught his daughter's eye and smiled. She giggled, placing her hand over her mouth. He owed much to his humble beginnings as a makeup artist. It was a skill he continued to hone in spite of the success he'd since achieved. He stared at the mirrored paneling and straightened his mustache. Not his best disguise. Deanne would be chagrined by its simplicity; she was the queen of costume. He would come home and find a monster lurking in the hall, or little Angela glowing like an angel, to which he would say: "That's no costume. You really *are* an angel!" and grab her to make her giggle just the way she was now. It was good to see her feeling better. Who knew what miracle God had in store...

5

The elevator didn't stop at the garage where his car was parked, where officers would be waiting. Instead it took him further down into the bowels of the building, opening into the labyrinth that housed the heating, cooling and ventilation system.

The door of the elevator opened. He closed the concealed box, pushed the button to send the elevator back up, and stepped out. From this side, the heavy fiberglass door was molded to look like a cement slab. When closed, it had the appearance of a concrete wall.

Still holding Angela's hand, Peter used his foot to push a mop bucket against the facade. The elevator would automatically rise one floor where it would open and be found empty. The baffled officers would be led to think he'd sent it down unoccupied, using it as a decoy. They would think he was still in the building.

Against the wall were three gunmetal gray lockers of the kind used by maintenance personnel. All three were padlocked. He spun the dial of the middle one and opened it to remove a pair of gray dungarees. He slipped out of his custom-tailored Ian Russell suit, hung it in the locker and pulled on his janitorial garb, making sure he retrieved his ID chips. Peter raised the latch and closed the metal door with a click, making sure it was locked, then turned, took his daughter's hand, and began walking through a steamy maze of groaning and hissing metal— *to freedom.*

TWO

"In framing a government which is to be administered by men over men, the great difficulty lies in this: you must first enable the government to control the governed, and next oblige it to control itself."
—James Madison, 1751-1836, 4ᵗʰ President of the United States

THE COMMAND center was a hub of activity. The room, situated in the interior of the building, was windowless and lit with low-watt bulbs to increase the illumination from the terminals. Banks of uniformed officers sat at partitioned work stations. Lights glowed from high-definition plasma screens in a matrix of colors. Overhead a fifty-two-inch flat panel monitor was cabled from the ceiling, churning with digital images that allowed the watch command to supervise all activity from a central location.

Bob McCauley paced in front of the screens, keeping his finger on the pulse of the operation. He paused long enough to glance over the shoulder of a man with sergeant's chevrons and American flags sewn on the sleeves of his midnight blue uniform. The sergeant was seated at a terminal with a headset covering one ear and a mike looped in front of his mouth.

He turned his head addressing Bob from the side. "Relax, Cap. They're coming down. The building's surrounded. In a few minutes we'll have Dufoe and his disc..." The words had barely left his mouth when a message appeared on his screen.

Bob sipped in a long, slow breath and closed his eyes. He was six foot with sandy red hair and ocean-green eyes, a burly man whose once firm chest had, over the years, slipped into his stomach. He slouched, crossing his arms while tapping his foot on the rubberized anti-static mat. He was standing too far back to read the message but the words, illuminated in red, were flashing. He felt the acid bubbling in his gut. Something was wrong.

The sergeant shook his head. "Sorry, Cap, it looks like the mouse blew the trap."

Bob clenched his jaw, his face turning red. "Print it!" he said. His fists balled into knots. *Sheeesh.* They had him! "Son of a...*urrrrrgh.* Give me that thing!" He snatched the paper from the printer.

"Target reported on site...hasn't turned up...complete search of office... all exits covered...will continue..." *Sheeesh.* Bob turned and stormed across the hall to Lou Nordstrom's office, plowing through the door without knocking.

"Unbelievable! Un-freaking-believable! The freakin' Mounties blew it." He tossed the paper onto his boss's desk. "I knew this would happen. I want the border watch doubled, make sure no one gets through without a scan. The whole works. He's probably turned that chip of his into mincemeat."

"Relax, Bob. Have a seat." Lou Nordstrom, Operations Director of Homeland Security Central, raised his chin toward an empty chair, then picked up the paper.

Bob backed up and dropped into the chair, the cushions wheezing beneath his two hundred pounds. He ran his fingers through his thinning hair. "I want charge of this operation."

Nordstrom, ever the consummate administrator, knew better than to take the bait. He swiveled in his chair, gazing reflectively out the wall of windows. No need for dim light here. The panorama before him was spectacular—the towering ziggurats of glass and gargoyles, the mustard sky, the brown haze that hid the mountains beyond the L.A. basin. Los Angeles, City of Angels. *El Pueblo de Nuestra Senora la Reina de Los Angeles.* Thirty years into the organization, with retirement close at hand, the Dufoe case would be his crowning achievement. There wasn't a cloud on the horizon and he didn't need the one Bob was bringing now.

He turned back, gently sliding the paper onto his desk. "I don't think that's a good idea"—he raised his hand to silence Bob before he could object—"and I've already told you why. You're too close to this. You've let it become personal. I think your judgment is skewed by your history with Dufoe. I don't want this thing blowing up in our faces."

Bob leaned forward interlacing his fingers, pushing on his cuticles with his thumbs. The vein at the side of his neck throbbed. He sucked in his breath trying to stem the rush of adrenalin. "Come on, Lou, I know what motivates these people, especially Dufoe. If he's broken the law, he goes to jail like anyone else. You do the crime, you do the time. This goes beyond friendship." He stopped rubbing his cuticles and folded his hands in an effort to appear calm, but the heel of his foot was bobbing up and down like it was on a spring.

Lou puckered his lips as he nodded. He leaned back, propping his hands behind his graying head, his elbows winging out. He did a quarter-turn in his chair, facing the window again. "Man, I wish I knew what drives them. Why do they make it so hard? Why can't they just get along?" He swiveled back toward his desk. "You're religious, aren't you, Bob? I mean, you go to church, holidays, things like that, right? And you're not out there trying to blow everyone up. What's with these guys?"

"That's my point. I know how they think. You've got a fanatic on the loose with a passport to the world. He's probably got access to a hundred secret organizations. If he goes underground, we'll never see him again. It was my team's investigation that nailed him, remember? I deserve to be in on the takedown. Come on, give me a break. I'm not gonna compromise my own investigation. How long have we worked together, five, ten years? Have I ever let you down?"

The wireless internet receiver beeped. Lou raised a finger, "Excuse me a second." He held the tiny device against his ear and turned away to listen. "*Uhmmmm.* All right...keep me posted." Lou signed off and paused for a moment, staring out the window as though wrestling with a thought. The brown smog was backed against the hills so thick he couldn't see beyond the city, though he knew the hills were there.

Lou spun his chair, facing the desk again. "Okay, Bob, it's confirmed, we got a runner. How soon can you get your things packed? If Dufoe's smart, he'll head straight for the border and try and beat the APB we just put out. If he isn't already across, we'll get him there. You want to bring him in, you're the man, but I want him in cuffs, pronto. I'm putting you in charge. Don't screw this one up."

THREE

"But a constitution of government once changed from freedom, can never be restored. Liberty once lost is lost forever."
—John Adams, 1735-1826, 2nd President of the United States

PETER SAT in his car with the window down, breathing hard, listening to the sounds of the underground garage. Water was dripping somewhere, *plunk, plunk, plunk.* A door slammed, echoing through the subterranean vault, followed by the sound of leather clapping on cement. Someone was racing to the elevator—or to his *car!* He heard the elevator, *ding. Whew!* He had to get moving, but...what if the parking attendant stopped him? *No, why would he?* Peter placed his finger on the ignition pad and waited the two grueling seconds it took to read his print. A digital display lit up. He touched the "start car" screen. The engine *urrrrrrrr, urrrrrrr, urrr-rooommm,* sprang to life. The transmission display appeared. He touched "drive," let his foot off the brake, and the car crept forward. He could hear the *squeeeak* of rubber on cement. The tires, after sitting in one place for months, were under-inflated.

His hands were trembling. The steel mesh gate was just ahead. He wiped the perspiration from his lip and glanced at Angela, who was leaning against the door.

"You okay?"

Angela nodded but her head was tilted toward the window. The movement was barely discernible. Her breath made a foggy circle on the glass.

Peter reached out to straighten her collar. The race to the car had weakened her. No decent father would put his child through this. He swallowed hard enough to feel the Adam's apple slide up and down in his throat. The doctors at Sick Kids Hospital didn't understand. They couldn't. *She's only got a day or two, probably less. There's no point in letting her suffer. You should release her. Best for all concerned.* Peter insisted on removing Angela claiming he wanted a second opinion. But that was before the warrant was issued for his arrest.

"Try to hang on a few more minutes, honey." He pulled up to the line at the parking attendant's booth and pushed the button to roll down his window. Peter was determined not to say anything unless asked. He didn't want the tremor in his voice giving him away. A camera read Peter's plate number and checked it against a database of authorized vehicles. He tugged on his shirt cuff. He'd installed an RFID chip in a hollow link of his watchband. The attendant stepped out with a scanner and Peter extended his arm so the device could be swiped across his sleeve verifying that his ID tag matched the car's registration and that this wasn't a heist. Who'd want to steal a nondescript ethanol-electric hybrid anyway? He took a fluttering breath. The man was only doing his job.

The gate began to rise and Peter edged forward, his foot twitching on the pedal. They'd made it—at least out of the building! Now he had to make it out of the city, then out of the country. One step at a time...

He rolled through the door leaving the darkness of the garage behind. Long shadows painted the downtown core a dingy gray, the corporate towers blocking the rays of the sun. His eyes swept the street apprehensively. They were looking for him, but not in this car. The old four-banger backfired with the sound of a cannon—*Boom! Oh man, don't do that.* The last thing he needed was to draw attention to himself. He eased forward tentatively. *That's what you get with a cold start and a sudden infusion of fuel.* He chided himself for not taking the car out on the road more often.

He actually preferred the older vehicle to the Lexel he owned, but the Lexel was a necessary part of his facade. The business section of every newspaper had him pegged as a wildcat entrepreneur, business tycoon, corporate mogul, power broker, empire-builder, master of the universe with an army of minions at his beck and call. He was anything *but*—the cars, boat, and houses were all pretense. *You can't take it with you.*

An image of his wife, Deanne, popped into his head. Deanne— standing in their sunlit conservatory, her soft brunette hair shiny and radiant. How would she respond? She was already mad about his leaving, and now this? Their mansion on the hill was a house of cards ready to topple. He didn't want it anyway. Give him a two-bedroom apartment and he'd be happy, as long as Deanne and Angela were there. He was sure they felt the same.

He was worth billions, and everyone knew it. Last thing he needed was some investigative reporter trying to uncover what he really did with his money. Life, he'd learned long ago, was all about costumes— *all the world's a stage.* His heart was pounding as he rolled into the street, looking to the left. A tangle of police cars surrounded Optitec, their bar lights painting the glass in streaks of red. He turned slowly to the right.

The car Peter was driving was an older model Electroaire with just enough dents to look like it belonged to a blue-collar worker. He kept both hands perched atop the steering wheel with his elbows knit together as he leaned forward. The trip was going to be hard on Angela. He reached down and wiped the moisture from his palms. His hands were shaking—*calm down Peter. Stick to the plan. Focus on getting across the border.*

Deanne thought he was paranoid. She'd scolded him for spending so much time planning an escape when there was no imminent danger, but all his careful preparation was about to pay off. He'd had the service station send a mechanic over once a month to start the car, juice the battery, and make sure everything was in good working order, and paid for it using the credit of a salaried employee who didn't exist except on paper. He had several such on staff, make-believe people he had hired using phony names, put on the payroll with high-paying classified jobs, and then transferred to subsidiaries of subsidiaries in remote locations where they were never seen. Their paychecks were electronically deposited into bank accounts he controlled using ID tags he'd programmed himself.

On paper, Alan Hampton owned the car, and the ID chip for the fictitious Alan Hampton was now banded to Peter's wrist. The vehicle had been parked in a building a block down from Optitec, a building that was connected underground by a shopping mall. He and Angela had exited the subterranean utilities corridor and entered the mall once he was sure they had crossed under the street. He'd had to carry her most of the way. Her frail limbs and fading strength made it impossible for her to keep up the pace.

Angela sat beside him now, her seatbelt holding her in place. She was staring listlessly out the window. He wished he could protect her from the world outside. All the beautiful dreams for a moral and just society where men, under God, governed themselves, had disappeared like a vapor in the wind. It was ugly out there. Vagrants sat on the sidewalks with their unwashed hands clawing out. "Buddy, can you spare a credit?" Prostitutes in spiked heels and stretch pants crowded corners holding the hands of hollow-eyed children, some as young as Angela, offering them for sale by the hour. Peter shook his head. This was Sodom.

The multi-layered socio-economic strata that had once defined North America had been divided in two. You were either rich or poor, with few in between. As the world moved to adopt the Euro, making it the international standard, nations dumped American currency crashing the U.S. dollar; the Federal Reserve was either unprepared or unwilling to prop it up. There were advantages to trading undervalued currency. The government was making billion-dollar loan repayments on the trillions it owed with money that was worth only a fraction of the value it had held when the loans were made. But skyrocketing inflation had left middle-class America in the lurch. Those rich enough to purchase and trade in international currencies, like the Euro, fared well, but everyone else found themselves having to pay dearly for a loaf of bread.

Those who considered themselves among the elite, the powerful rich and famous who worked in the downtown core of high-rise towers, lived in a bubble. They entered underground parking lots and stepped out of magnesium-wheeled, leather-upholstered, seven-speaker surround sound multi-media cars with their high-polished shoes clicking on the cement as they made their way to elevators that took them to their private domains. There they could avoid the riffraff in the streets below—the disease-ridden untouchables with pierced body parts, tattooed limbs, spiked hair and shaved heads. Even the most liberal of the rich were put off by the perverse language and overt sexual debauchery that were ever on display.

Most cars had to be protected with a dent-proof polymer coating and bulletproof glass. The car Peter drove wasn't shielded, but it wasn't snazzy enough to warrant the attention of the people as they brushed by. In his blue-collar disguise Peter was one of them. It was all about costumes.

He felt a tug on his sleeve and glanced down at his daughter. Angela had seemed fine when he'd picked her up from the hospital, but now the sun had dropped behind the buildings and the city lay in shadows. Her normally cherub pink cheeks were tinged with a pale green pallor. Her medication was beginning to wear off.

"I'm going to be sick, Daddy. I...I think I'm going to..."

"NO! Just take a deep breath."

Peter felt a *thump* as someone slapped the side of the car. He stood on his brakes, his arm shooting out to catch Angela as he snapped his gaze back to the road.

"Hey! Watch where you're going, Jack!" The disgruntled pedestrian staggered off but not before giving Peter a one-finger salute.

What was he supposed to do? The street was congested with people. Peter kept inching forward—*gas, roll forward, brake, gas, roll forward, brake.* "Try to hang on just a few more minutes. I can't pull over right now." The lights of the police cars blinked in his rearview mirror, painting the walls of the Optitec building a stroboscopic rouge. "We have to get out of here quickly as possible. They're after us."

"Why, Daddy?" Angela grabbed her stomach and closed her eyes. "What did we do?"

15

"Oh, honey, I didn't mean you. You haven't done anything. It's just that...they want to put me away somewhere so I can't see you anymore."

Angela held onto her stomach and grimaced. "But why?"

Peter glanced over at his daughter. The pained look on her face made him think about turning himself in—*almost*. They would take her into custody, too. They'd put her back in the hospital, and there, in the name of compassion, they'd give her a needle to put her out of her misery. It wasn't medicine, it was murder, and he couldn't let it happen.

Her doleful brown eyes pleaded with him, waiting for an answer. Why *did* they want him? There was no way to explain, no one thing he could point to and say, "That's where we went wrong." Actually, it was a whole lot of things, some so small and seemingly insignificant they were slipped in without being questioned, and others, though blatantly egregious, were carefully disguised to appear as though they were for the greater good.

Was it the 1960s? Did it really date back that far? The removal of prayer from schools and, along with it, the concerted effort to banish God. No God, no accountability. No accountability, no guilt. No guilt, no reprisal. " We can make the world a better place. Peace, love and flowers. If it feels good, do it. Join the sexual revolution. Free love. Get rid of your hang-ups, get loose, get real. You only go around once, grab all you can."

But the liberation had no limit. Pandora's box was open and men reached inside and found the forbidden fruit not only pleasing to the eye, but good to eat. No one dared ask whether it would satisfy the soul. Why be with one partner when you can have two, three, or more? Sex is sex, pure animal instinct. Can't find a woman? *Fogedaboutit.* Swing with another man, *mano a mano*.

Peter gulped, his Adam's apple sliding up and down. He used his fingertips to massage the back of his neck. His thoughts were cutting close to the bone. *Sissy!* He could throw a ball with the best of them— as long as they were *girls*—but nary a man could his limp-wristed toss impress. Testosterone-pumping, perspiration-pouring, meat-grinding jocks jeered at his ineptness. He carried a makeup bag for crying out loud, which, of course, eventually led him to a job in the studios.

They found him there, other men like himself, men rejected for their peculiar mannerisms. They welcomed him into the fraternity and also into their beds—but that's where he drew the line. He desired affirmation, not adoration. He was in limbo, scorned by straight men and censured by gays. "You'll never be happy until you stop trying to be something you're not." Everyone said it, but it fell on deaf ears. He couldn't rationalize what in his deep inner soul he recognized as a twisting of truth. He was effeminate, no question about that, but biologically he was also a man. He'd wrestled with his understanding of who and what he really was—until a crusty old bird named Ruth and a cowboy-booted man named Bill had shown him a better way. Now he was happy, truly happy, and he was straight, married to the most beautiful woman in the world, and daddy to the most wonderful child he'd ever met. He couldn't love Angela more—not even if she were his own.

Thank God for rare bursts of common sense. The mother of this precious child could have had an abortion, but instead she'd determined to save her baby's life. That took guts. The rule was, if you can't care for the infant, dispose of it. Now he was being asked to do the same. Those who occupied space on the planet without giving back—the elderly and disabled, the indigent and mentally unstable—were disposable. And especially those dependent on welfare. Taxpayers shouldn't have to shoulder the burden of keeping non-productive people alive.

Where was the voice of reason? Pastors, rabbis, and priests had decried the death of morality, but their protests were drowned out by a roar of accusation. *"Fascists, racists, anti-gay, born again bigots, go away!"* You had to tolerate everything except intolerance, that alone was not to be tolerated. Parents who used the rod of correction lost their children to the state. Better being shuffled around from foster home to foster home than abide an abuser with a belt, they reasoned. Churches that held to Scripture lost their tax exemptions and were forced out of existence or driven underground. The state couldn't extend public money to those who refused to welcome everyone—regardless of race, creed, or gender—into church leadership. Churches sanctioned by the government taught God countenanced every behavior as long as it was born of love. Sin was passé. Every vestige of Christian heritage from the Christmas tree to the Ten Commandments had been removed from the public square. All except one. Peter smiled. Five-hundred-and-fifty-five feet above ground overlooking the green fields of the nation's capital was the Washington Monument, at the top of which were carved the words, *Prase Laus Deo*, "Praise be to God." It was simply too high and too lofty to sandblast away.

Peter bit his lip. His daughter had asked him a question. Her button-brown eyes were still probing him for an answer. "I don't know, honey. All I know is they want me in jail, but not for anything I've done. I don't care what you hear—your daddy hasn't done anything wrong."

Peter pushed himself back in his seat, trying to release his tension. He let out his breath and relaxed taking in the scenery. The sky over the northwest shore of Lake Ontario was red. A sun bright as a cherry sat low on the horizon burning through the translucent haze. The air was thick as gauze. His back was to the sea with Pharaoh and his chariots closing in. His only way of escape was through the water. A cloud by day and a fire by night—*Lord show me the way.*

Peter leaned forward, used his touchpad to turn on the lights, and glanced up through the sunroof scanning for helicopters. They wouldn't be looking for a car like this, but with his Lexel parked in his driveway at home, they couldn't be sure of anything. Once they saw he'd eluded their net, they'd assume he was headed for an airport—or the border—and a run for the border would put him just about where he was right now, so he had to be careful. He wiped his forehead with his sleeve. It was always hot, but the tiny car was an oven. His gray cotton long-sleeved shirt and dungarees were like a second skin. He was a potato ripe for baking.

Angela held her stomach again and groaned. "Daddy, when will we be home?"

"You have to be patient, sweetheart. Pittsburgh's a long way." Peter gripped the wheel. His palms were moist and the hard smooth plastic felt slippery in his hands. He hadn't anticipated having his daughter with him when this day came. He had to get her home. It meant a risky detour, one that required getting back into the States, but he had a plan for that. In some ways, it was a good thing. He didn't want to leave the country without saying good-bye to Deanne. There were fences to mend. For the moment, that was his only goal. Then perhaps, by God's grace, he could escape to Mexico and find safe haven.

The tiny hybrid whined as they exited the Queen Elizabeth Way at North Shore Boulevard, turning right. It was time to initiate his plan. They'd be watching the border, and they wouldn't settle for a chip scan; they'd want biometric identification—*fingerprint, voiceprint, iris scan, and facial mapping.* Airports were also out of the question. His headlights illuminated a sign that read: La Salle Park. He pulled in. Lake Ontario was flat as a board, the red sun splitting the horizon and turning the water to blood.

He took an empty parking space and leaned toward Angela. "Okay, we're here. How's my costume?" He turned the rearview mirror, twisting it vertically, and saw a geeky imitation of himself staring back. "Remember, I have to pretend to be someone else. You can still call me Daddy, but if anyone asks, I'm going to call myself Alan and you have to go along with it. Think you can do that?"

Angela's eyes widened. Her cheeks dimpled with the look he adored, the one that made her look like a valentine cherub. "'Course, Daddy, you already said it a thousand times."

"I know, honey, I know. It's just that I have to stress how important it is, that's all. Now you and I are going to take a little boat ride. Come on, it'll be fun! I promise!"

CELESTIAL VANTAGE

Let me take you to another point in time. Not back in time or forward in time. Just somewhere else. Time is not a line upon which you travel back and forth. Time has no beginning and no end. Time always exists in the ever-present; there is no past and there is no future. There are simply different points in the eternal now.

Imagine you're standing in the center of a sphere, a bubble of pure light. You can reach out in any direction and touch a point on the surface. Infinite points, each one a different place in time, coexisting with all the others in the present forever.

As a physical property, time was called into existence, and indeed, time will one day be called to an end. Think not that He who is First and Last, Alpha and Omega, The Beginning and The End, is subject to His own creation. He was before time, and will remain when time is no more. Only created beings pass through time as you see me do. That is my mission. I have been called to disclose what has been revealed to me, the story of sentient beings, so that you might learn and, thereby, choose your course more wisely...

FOUR

"We do not need more intellectual power, we need more moral power. We do not need more knowledge, we need more character. We do not need more government, we need more culture. We do not need more law, we need more religion. We do not need more of the things that are seen, we need more of the things that are unseen. If the foundation be firm, the foundation will stand."
—*Calvin Coolidge, 1872-1933, 30th President of the United States*

BOB BOARDED American Airlines flight 3577 and dropped into his seat. His itinerary read, "Buffalo," where he was expected to oversee surveillance at the border. But he'd changed the destination—*no point in standing around watching a migration of Canadian geese.* Proffering his security clearance he'd demanded they hold the flight to Pittsburgh while he leaned on the counter, fixing his eyes in a *don't-mess-with-me* glare that had the clerk fumbling at his keyboard as he exchanged the ticket.

The engines were humming and the plane ready to roll by the time he settled himself, much to the chagrin of the already boarded passengers. He shoved his briefcase underneath his seat wondering, as he reached over his paunch, how his arms had got so short. He pulled the clasp to extend the length of the seatbelt, grumbling about the midget who had used it previously. *Auuugh.* Or maybe it was the cinnamon rolls.

He fell back against the cushions, releasing a sigh. L.A. Central wouldn't understand the last-minute change, but that was their problem. He had to do it. Customs and Immigration was screening all flights leaving Canada—*For all the good it'll do,* he thought. He was supposed to monitor land crossings but he couldn't cover every point of entry at the same time, not with so many possibilities: Lewiston, Niagara, Buffalo, Fort Erie, Sarnia. They were already using biometric scans and chip verification to identify travelers—no exceptions. Didn't matter anyway. Peter was smart enough to foil the technology. He'd get back into the U.S., and in the unlikely event they *did* catch him, Pittsburgh was only a few hours from the Canadian border. Bob could hustle up and take custody with minimal delay, but his gut told him the next time he saw Peter, it would be at his home in Pittsburgh. Peter would never desert Deanne. Not in this life. Deanne was the whole point...

The crowd went ballistic, people climbing out of their seats and pouring onto the field. They hefted Bob onto their shoulders, a chanting mob. He was being held aloft by a giant centipede. He craned his neck around to find Deanne and caught a glimpse of her in the stands. Her arms were raised with her hands locked in a champion's salute. That's my girl! Then the crowd turned heading across the field, and she was gone. The celebration in the locker room would go on for hours. But she would be his tonight.

Bob cranked his window down. The outside air rolled in thick and humid, tickling the hair on his arms. It was seventy degrees at eleven o'clock at night. The polished chrome and paint reflected the overhead streetlights as he pulled up to the front of the house. He hopped out, slammed the door—blamm—leaving the engine idling. It was late. He wasn't about to stand around wasting time with small talk. He thumped the side of the car with the flat of his hand feeling like a million bucks, his senses bursting with life and strength and vitality and...whatever they put in that juice was hot—hot, hot hot—he was hot—he could touch, taste, hear and smell everything. Hoo-raw! This was his night. He hopped onto the porch with a swagger and rang the bell.

Mrs. Anderson opened the door. Bob offered her a blazing white smile, warm enough to melt ice, but her greeting was cool as she turned, called her daughter's name, and walked away, leaving him standing on the stoop. That was to be expected owing to the hour, but she should cut him some slack—voted game MVP, for Pete's sake. He was the man.

The porch light wove golden threads into Deanne's hair as she leaned toward her parents to say good-night. The warm air, the mist of yellow light, and the quickening of his pulse as he took her hand greased his wheels—man, he was ready! But the hand he held as they strolled down the walk was stiff, like the hand of a plastic doll. He let go, bounced into the street and over to his side of the car, leaving Deanne to open her door.

She was looking straight ahead, not saying a word. Her silence settled between them like a frost, in spite of the heat. Her skin held a soft blush in the glow of the street lamps, making him want to snuggle her up close, but her focus was distant. Hadn't she seen the game? She should be climbing all over him. Her dark hair was shining and she wore a dark blue dress that seemed to flow like an oasis through the car's arid interior. He started the car, put it in gear, and eased away from the curb.

"Something wrong?" he finally said, breaking the silence at the first red light.

"Do you have a watch?"

Bob looked at his wrist and held it up, the gold band glinting.

"What does it say?"

"Come on, Deanne. I can't help it if the guys wanted to celebrate." The light turned green and he entered the intersection, using his left hand to steer while stretching his other arm across the back of the seat. He took a lock of her hair and looped it around his finger, savoring the silky feel, but she flinched and pulled away. "Hey, what's with you? You should be happy for me. I'm a hero, I saved the day! You saw what happened. We were down by three—they were twenty and goal—first down, with less than a minute on the clock. They had us. We were about to lose the freakin' playoffs. I was probably the only one who hadn't given up. I saw the snap and faded back. I knew he was going wide and, sure enough, the receiver went right for the end zone on my side and I was there. Man, you saw it. That ball came right to me. A ninety-five yard run! Man, when was the last time you saw that? Of course the guys wanted to celebrate. I tried to leave several times but they wouldn't let me..."

"You smell like beer. Have you been drinking?"

"Are you listening? I'm the MVP. Me, Bob McCauley, your boyfriend!"
He withdrew his arm resting it on the wheel. "No! I mean, some of the
other guys had a few—that must be what you smell—not me."

"Can we just skip the party? It's already eleven and I have to be home
by one. Let's just go somewhere and talk."

"But..."

"I know everyone wants to see you..."

"You got that right! I'm MVP."

"...but I hate going to parties. It's not the kind of place..."

"Come on, don't start with that again. We've been through it all before.
Christ drank wine. Look. How 'bout we stop just long enough to say hi, let
everyone know we dropped by and soon as no one's looking, we'll disappear?
I'll have you home by curfew, promise."

Deanne didn't say anything for a moment, then sighed with resignation.
She looked at Bob for the first time, her dark gaze penetrating his, even
through the dim interior of the car. "At least promise me you won't
drink."

"No problem. I wasn't planning on getting drunk."

"Promise me. Not even one."

"I just did."

Their wheels spun in the loose gravel as the car slid to a stop. The
music coming from the house—boom, dada boom, dada boom, boom,
boom—was so loud the car sitting at the curb vibrated with sound. She
opened her door and let herself out, waiting for Bob to come around and
escort her inside. Several boys were hiding in a darkened corner of the
porch sharing a hand-rolled cigarette. She wasn't naive enough to think it
was tobacco. She debated leaving but waffled, and when Bob crossed the
threshold, rationalized it was too late and followed him inside.

The music was rattling the walls. It was a wonder the windows didn't
fall out. They'd barely entered the room when they were surrounded.

"Hey, man, it's about time."

"Hey, dude, where you been?"

"Hey, everyone, look who's here! Ninety-five sweaty yards in the
blistering sun, mundo stinko. Dude, you need a shower." And then, as

if on cue, a half-dozen warm beer cans properly shaken were popped open releasing a fountain of a foamy spray over Bob and Deanne. Deanne squealed and raised her arms defensively, but the beer kept raining down.

Bob stuck out his tongue as if to lap it up, but caught the mortified look on Deanne's face and stopped. "Alright, enough, enough. Cool it!"

And the rain ceased.

Deanne was drenched. She held her elbows up, letting the foam drip onto the carpet. "Ohhhhh, look what you've done. I can't go home like this, smelling like beer. Oh, ohhhhh, this is disgusting!" She flicked her hands and stormed off in search of a restroom.

Bob's cronies surrounded him tugging on his arm. "Hey, Bob, come on, we got something to show you in back."

When Deanne finally returned from the washroom, clothes and eyes dabbed dry, she was ready to leave. There was no way to get rid of the smell without removing and soaking her dress and she wasn't about to do that. She'd just have to explain to her parents and hope they'd understand. She wove her way through the bodies clustered about the living room and kitchen looking for Bob, but she didn't see him anywhere.

She stepped through the open sliding glass door onto the patio. Under strings of colored LEDs the party in the backyard was going full tilt. A half-dozen people were splashing in an aquamarine pool that glowed like a huge horizontal nightlight. The rest were sitting or standing around consuming more alcohol and smoking those funny cigarettes. The air was filled with the smell of chlorine and lit matches.

Most of the kids she recognized from school, but she didn't see anyone old enough to buy liquor. A young man climbed out of the water and jumped back in doing a bombshell that drenched several of those sitting at the pool's edge, evoking a round of catcalls and shrieks. Now she definitely had to leave. People were starting to get crazy. She should never have come in the first place.

She forced her way through a smoke-filled hall, coughing as she squeezed between the bodies lining the wall. A short youth with curly red hair and zit-covered cheeks exhaled a cloud of blue smoke into her hair. She scrunched her nose and waved a hand in front of her face. Wasn't it bad enough she already smelled like a brewery?

That was it! She couldn't find Bob and she wasn't going to wait. She backed up and retrieved her cell phone from her purse, punching the buttons to call a cab. She didn't know the house address but she gave the dispatcher the name of the street and told him to follow the sound. He'd be sure to find it. She'd be waiting out front.

She turned and found herself facing a partially closed door. She leaned in to listen. It sounded like chanting, "Go, go, go, go, go!" She reached for the knob, opened the door—and froze.

There was Bob with his hand raised and a can of beer at his lips, guzzling, his Adam's apple bobbing up and down. The room was full of sweaty male egos but she somehow managed to catch his eye. She turned in full retreat, fighting her way down the hall through the thick tangle of teenagers and out the front door. She didn't stop until she reached the front lawn. Down the street she saw the cab approaching. She ran to meet it, waving her arms. The car door was already open by the time Bob stumbled onto the front porch.

"Hey, Deanne, slow down! Where you going?"

"Home!" she yelled, ducking inside.

"It was only one, Deanne. Just one beer..." but the door slammed. Bob could see her flicking her fingers at the driver as he pulled away. Deanne, visible in the light of the streetlamps, was glaring at him through the back window as two police cars turned the corner, their swirling cherries slicing through the night.

Bob spun toward the house and yelled into the living room. "Everybody split! We're busted!" Then he dove off the porch, took a left around the corner of the house, sprinted across the neighbor's back patio, dove over the fence into the adjoining yard, plowed on through to the front, and turned right, hightailing it down the street.

He'd never thanked her for that. Deanne had saved his unblemished butt. He should have said something. His entry into the police academy would have been harder with an arrest record on his sheet, but instead, when he saw her the next day, he railed on her for ditching him. *It was only one beer...*

Bob looked out the window. They were passing through a bank of clouds, the fog whipping by in tangled puffs. He frowned. She had no business being with Peter. It had to be the money, but money couldn't buy happiness, and Pete was history. He'd stepped over the line—used his technology for criminal purposes. They had to be at odds over that, which was probably why she never allowed herself to be seen with him in public. She had to know her marriage was a sham.

The plane broke into bright sunlight. Bob saw it as symbolic. Maybe there was a bright day ahead just above the clouds. Maybe now Deanne would see the light. Her husband was about to go to jail, probably for the rest of his life. His vast fortune would be seized. She was on the brink of becoming destitute, but Bob would be there to help her make a soft landing. Yes, indeed, things were looking up.

The flight attendant rolled her cart down the aisle, the plastic containers clattering as she bumped his seat. "Can I get you something?"

Bob looked up, raised his eyebrows and sucked in his gut as he leaned on his forearms, lifting himself out of his slouched position. He refrained from saying what he was thinking. He wouldn't be guilty of harassment, not when things were starting to go his way but, *hot dang*, she *was* a pretty thing. "Scotch on the rocks."

The stewardess reached for a plastic cup. "No problem." She scooped the ice cubes and poured amber liquid into the cup. "Scotch on the rocks, it is. Would you like a newspaper?" Her lips were full and inviting, but he held onto that thought, too, and just nodded.

She laid a copy of the *National Times* in his lap, and he offered his hand to let her scan the chip imbedded under his skin. "Add twenty percent for yourself," he offered.

She smiled again, her lipstick shiny as cellophane, her eyes blue as Caribbean water. She gave the drink a flick of her wrists, clattering the ice cubes before handing the cup to him. She unlocked the cart's brake and continued down the aisle to wait on her next customer.

Bob took a sip—cold as it refreshed his mouth, but warm as it trickled down his throat. He set his drink down and unfolded the newspaper, snapping it open. Under a headline that read, "Unity At Last," was a photograph of seven men, world leaders, patting each other on the back as they held up a document they had just signed. He smacked his lips. A whole new world was on the horizon, one that elevated man to his full potential. Imagine, all Europe uniting under one authority. One rule of law to govern all men equally without prejudice. Elections were underway, one man commissioned, perhaps even destined, to lead a perfect world. And he'd selected a super vice-counsel, a world-class preacher committed to uniting the remaining fractions of Muslims, Jews, Christians, and Hindus. Churches everywhere were agreeing. All God wanted was for men to love each other—not fight wars over what He should be called or how He should be worshiped. For the first time in history nations were beating their swords into plowshares.

Bob folded the paper and relaxed, letting his weight sink into the padding. His cheeks ballooned, his bottom lip protruding as he puffed out a breath. The U.S. was still holding out, claiming it valued its autonomy, but the nation had lost its position of power and with more and more countries abandoning the gold standard, the U.S. would soon be forced to adopt the global digital dollar, further diminishing their independence.

It was only a matter of time. Only the zealots opposed progress— bigoted, narrow-minded—what other reason did they need for putting them away? And Peter...Peter was the key to a large network of them. He had what was needed to quash the underground church. And soon Bob would have that disc. Let the purge begin.

Bob raised his cup to the memory of Deanne. *Here's to you, babe. One day you'll see I was right.*

FIVE

"I wish to have no connection with any ship that does not sail fast; for I intend to go in harm's way."
—John Paul Jones, 1747-1792, Father of the American Navy

THE SUN had disappeared into the hills behind the marina but it was still bright enough to paint the water red, reflecting the crimson sky. That had to be a good thing—*didn't it? Red sky at morning, sailor take warning—red sky at night, sailor's delight.* Standing beside the port rail taking in the expanse—the warm breeze, the wash of water, the bevies of waterfowl circling the jetty—Peter might have convinced himself all was well on planet earth, but only for a moment. *No*, this was *not* a delight.

He turned to see a dozen cement smokestacks spewing residual dust and fumes into the atmosphere, the blight of steel production. He glanced around. The marina was quiet except for one or two yachtsmen still swabbing decks. He stooped, ducking into the cabin to grab his GPS, readying for launch. Fewer people took to water than in days past; few could afford the luxury. Escaping from a world gone mad was getting harder all the time. *Too bad.* Except for the occasional pirate, the lake was one place people could relax with a relative degree of safety. At this point, he had to count the open water a blessing.

Peter hauled in his mooring lines coiling them on the deck while keeping an eye on the other boats to ensure he wasn't attracting anyone's interest. *So far, so good.* No one paid particular attention to the nondescript man holding the hand of the little girl as they made their way through the iron security gate onto the docks. He dropped the last loop and stood back to look around. Most of the craft were sailboats, but a few, like his own, were motor launches. The water lapped against the hull, the sound gurgling like liquid caught in a drain. Ducks and swans bantered loudly scooting in and out of the floating marina. The ruby light on the water splashed against the side of the boat, forming dark eddies like the petals of a rose. It was an image right out of a poem.

> *Lake, ocean, stream and pond*
> *with liquid portraits painted on*
> *in Van Gogh colors brightly done*
> *splashy strokes made by the sun.*

Peter smiled. Words were the friends that kept him company during the dark, lonely hours. He enjoyed playing with meter and rhyme and writing little ditties that expressed his thoughts. This one he called *Watercolors*. He'd written it while watching the water rolling along the hull of his friend Bill's boat.

> *Scarlet, emerald, midnight blue*
> *a restless rainbow swirling through*
> *to rearrange the world we know*
> *and welcome change within the flow.*

There was another verse too, but this wasn't the time to wax poetic, though it was a delicious evening, the kind he would have enjoyed if he weren't on the run. As he settled in, easing back the throttle of the now warm engine, Peter prayed it would not be his last as a free man. He swallowed the lump in his throat. *Please, Lord, let us be together—me, Deanne, Angela…at least let Angela see her mother one more time, even if only long enough to say good-bye.* His little girl was below deck in the cabin, where she lay on a bed covered with a blanket staying out of the wind.

Topside, the dusky air was warm. Peter had slipped into a cotton-lined nylon windbreaker that now whipped behind him like a sail in the breeze. He motored slowly out of the inlet, passing under the Burlington Skyway and keeping the smoking mill on his lee. He looked out at the early stars already visible in the east and plotted a course, thanking God for the invaluable schooling he'd received from Bill. It was a nautical lesson taught by the stars with a sextant—the old-fashioned way—charting his course as a man. *For such a time as this,* he mused. He drew in a deep lung full of air, stretching his lanky arms. He missed the briny smell of the sea. The oil-slick lake didn't compare, but the exhilaration was the same. The sound of water lapping against the hull, the smooth, steady purr of the engine, and the windswept spray stinging his face—these were the sights, smells and sounds—*of freedom.*

Bill was more than a mentor, Bill was his friend. It was Bill who showed him that, contrary to public opinion, it wasn't his peculiar mannerisms that defined who he was, it was the determination, or lack of it, to be the man God created him to be. Peter let go of the helm long enough to zip his jacket. It wasn't likely to get too cold, but he'd stored extra clothing on the boat just in case.

Darkness fell, spilling its inky blackness over the water. The sky was studded with diamonds that sparkled in the crown of heaven. He kept the boat's running lights off so he couldn't be seen. Customs and Immigration ran random patrols and had radar, but he'd purposely chosen a boat with a low profile, making it hard to track. And he'd selected dark mahogany for its construction as opposed to white fiberglass so it would be harder to see at night. Soon he would be anchored for the evening, invisible as a dark speck on a dark sheet in a dark room.

The hours passed like sleep, rolling over quietly unchanged—except for his dreams, which were never the same. Peter glanced up making sure he was still on course. The stars overhead gave him a heading. He was glad they were there, glad it wasn't cloudy. He preferred being guided by the constellations the way Bill taught him. It gave glory to God for direction; GPS inferred a dependence on man.

He passed the hours with his palm computer, using it to write encrypted e-mails to his internet church. They would want to know of his flight. He paused, looking heavenward again. Above the barrier of the star-laden sky, yet close enough to be inside his own skin, was a God who listened. The stars were a billion dots, like particles of white paint sprayed on black leather. He'd never seen so many. City light had a way of inhibiting the glow of heaven—or maybe he just didn't spend enough time looking up.

The boat sliced through the main, buffeted by an offshore wind. Peter rolled up the collar of his windbreaker and crossed his arms, shivering. It was fifty degrees on the water, cool enough to raise goosebumps. He kept his speed at five knots, puttering along at docking speed. He didn't want the roar of his motor to be heard. By his calculation the total crossing of forty-five miles was an eight-hour trip and he'd been on the water seven. He held the boat on a steady course due east, plotting their progress by the stars.

They had already crossed into U.S. waters. He was supposed to report his arrival and wait for U.S. customs to provide clearance. He had no intention of doing that. He sipped in his breath. Call it civil disobedience, but sometimes the laws of God superseded the laws of men—*"Whether it be right in the sight of God to hearken unto you more than unto God, judge ye. For we cannot but speak the things which we have seen and heard."* It was the model he was trying to live by.

The bow cut through the inky green, leaving a path of tiny white bubbles in its wake. He cut the throttle, taking his binoculars from his bag to scan the shore. He should see it by now. He brought his binoculars back around to search the shore again, making sure he hadn't missed it. *Yes, there it is.* He had the right place. The sign's reflection floated like a yellow shell on the surface of the water. He was ten miles west of the harbor.

He locked down the helm and quietly went downstairs. Angela was asleep, nestled on the small mattress alongside the hull with a blanket under her chin. The moon's light streaming through the porthole illuminated her smooth cheek, the line of her tiny nose, the upturned smile of her lips—a child innocent as morning. He swallowed, trying to keep his emotions in check as he reached out to stroke her hair.

She'd been bundled in a knitted shawl and left at their door, an infant not more than a few days old. Deanne couldn't have children, but no one else knew that. They themselves didn't know until after they were married, and they didn't tell anyone—that's how they knew Angela was from God. They'd taken the child in like Moses from the bulrushes. An appointment with destiny, that's what they'd called it.

Perhaps they should have reported the abandonment to the authorities—*perhaps*—but having a child was the desire of Deanne's heart. And whoever left that child had done so for a reason. The parents could have placed Angela with an orphanage or children's aid, but they had chosen not to. It was apparent they didn't want the child raised by the state. And Deanne needed someone to be with during the day. She suffered a condition that made it impossible for her to leave the house. Because she was never seen in public, no one could say she hadn't conceived and delivered the baby herself and, when people congratulated them on the arrival of their new one, they thought it best to keep up the facade, at least for the time being.

They kept their hearts open to the possibility that the mother might one day return and lay claim to the child and that they might be asked to give her up. They tried, however unsuccessfully, to keep from becoming attached. Angela was on loan from God—not a gift—and now, with the cancer, it seemed God wanted her back.

Is it me, God? Is who I am the reason You're taking her? Peter brushed his eyes with the back of his hand, the moisture on his cheeks glistening in the blue moonlight as he snuggled the blanket under her chin.

He went topside and resumed control of the helm, trying to keep from breaking, but the fear, pressure and pain, were too much. His shoulders began to heave. He hated it when he cried—and he cried all the time—just like a woman. *Crybaby, crybaby.* He sniffed. *Be a man.* He angled the boat toward a harbor he'd charted several months earlier, a precaution he'd taken once he found out he was being investigated. He wiped his eyes on his sleeve. Thank God for reliable sources, moles buried within government ranks who secretly worshiped in home churches. Long before the warrant for his arrest was issued, Peter had information suggesting his name had been flagged and that someone was planning a concerted dismantling of his internet church.

The lights along the shore were growing bigger. He looked at the luminous dial of his watch. *Two a.m.* He killed the engine and went to the bow to let down an anchor, then walked back to the stern where he hooked a ladder over the port side rail. Kneeling, he opened the storage compartment and removed an inflatable raft, which he unfolded and spread flat on the deck. He pulled the pin and stepped back as the rubberized boat filled with air. When it was fully inflated, he hauled it to the side, fighting to hold on when it buckled in the wind. He lowered it into the water and tied its mooring rope to the ladder.

Peter wiped the last bit of mist from his eyes, blinking to clear his vision. He removed his Rolex from his wrist and flipped the watchband inside out, snapping open the hollow link he'd paid a custom jewelry designer to fashion. He rolled the tiny chip into his hand and tossed it into the black water, picturing it drifting down to the bottom to become just another grain of sand. He shoved his hand into his pocket and found the envelope. He pinched the corner and opened it, carefully catching a new chip in his manicured fingernails, inserting it in the watchband. From this point on, he was Mike Reese.

He stepped down into the cabin to retrieve a small cloth bag he'd previously stored on the boat. It contained the things he needed for mold, makeup and mask-making. Unbuttoning his shirt, he belted the flat parcel around his waist so it would ride unnoticed against the small of his back. Then he tucked in his shirt and reached for Angela, fetching her, blanket and all, into his arms. She didn't stir. The rocking of the boat and the late hour had put her into a deep sleep.

He brought her on deck and took one last look around. The lights in the heavens were countless, shimmering with an aura of pink and blue. The Bible often referred to angels as stars. Maybe they were watching. He grunted, struggling to bring Angela up over his shoulder. She gave a muffled whimper and settled back down, instinctively looping her arms around his neck.

He turned and stepped over the side onto the ladder, lowering himself into the raft with one hand while trying to keep his balance on a floor that rocked with the tide. He leaned forward, grabbing a grommet for support and laid Angela down, making sure she was comfortable. He covered her head with the blanket to keep the wind and spray off her face, then took hold of the ladder again, reaching for the two plastic oars. He and the boat had to part company. He sat on the balloon rail, unhitched the rope, and felt the raft pull away.

Harbor patrol would find the abandoned launch, but like the car he'd left in the marina's parking lot, it was registered to Alan Hampton, and when they traced Alan to his address they would find a fully furnished, lived-in looking house with no one home. When the man failed to show up, they'd be left to assume he had gone over the side and drowned. But they'd never find a body because they'd be looking for a man who didn't exist.

Peter took hold of the oars and began pulling against the water, another skill he was proficient in, thanks to Bill. He figured they were about a mile offshore. It would take an hour or more to row in. He wanted to arrive on the beach while it was still dark. Hopefully, they would have enough time to catch a few hours sleep.

SIX

"God grant that in America true religion and civil liberty may be inseparable and that the unjust attempts to destroy the one, may in the issue tend to the support and establishment of both."
—*John Witherspoon, 1723-1794, Founding Father and signer of the Declaration of Independence*

B OB FELT the plane touch down, its wheels bouncing as they hit the runway with a screech that left black skid marks and a trail of smoke on the tarmac. He felt the back thrust of the engines, the hydraulic brakes kick in and the g-force thrusting him forward against the seatbelt, *uhhgggg—time to start that diet.*

The plane began its long slow taxi to the terminal. He looked out the window and saw pinpoints of light slipping by in the dark, then checked his watch. *Three a.m.* He'd had to change planes in Dallas adding two hours to the usual four-and-a-half-hour flight. He pushed his shoulders against the chair to relieve the pressure on his lumbar, wondering how he'd find a decent hotel at this hour without a reservation. For all their convenience, he would bypass airport accommodations. He wanted something closer to Deanne—and Peter, of course. He had to snag Peter. Odds were she wouldn't even talk to him till Peter was out of the way.

He unclipped his seatbelt, puffing out a breath as he sucked in his stomach and leaned forward to look out the window at the lights of the docking bay. Pittsburgh. *Home.* It had been a long time. Once out, he swore he'd never return, but every rule has an exception, and his was

36

Peter. This was where Peter had stiffed him; this was where he'd even the score. He could feel it in his gut. He reached under the seat to retrieve his briefcase and settled it on his lap, gripping its bottom with both hands, rubbing the stiff leather with his palms. He wanted to be wrong. Let them nab Peter at the border, then he would make his way up there, take him into custody, and escort him back to Los Angeles without any chance of Deanne becoming involved.

He slipped his hand inside his shirt rubbing the hair in circles, soothing the burn he felt in his chest. He wanted to see her, but not under these circumstances. Once Peter was on trial and Deanne saw the hopelessness of his situation, Bob would make his move. He would offer a strong arm of support and assume his place at her side. But timing was everything. God forbid she find out he was the one who'd headed up the investigation that led to her husband's arrest. She might refuse to see him. Unless, dare he hope, she had already abandoned her absurd commitment. *Then...*

But that was grist for another day. He had to focus on now. It wasn't likely Peter would be stopped at the border. He was too smart. The Canucks had bungled their only chance for an easy take-down. If they couldn't stop him at his own office when he wasn't expecting trouble, they'd never catch him at the border when he was wary and able to maneuver. Peter was headed for Pittsburgh—and Bob would be there waiting.

The plane bumped to a stop and the passengers bounced out of their seats clamoring for their carry-on bags. Bob pushed himself up, *oooff,* and stood, ducking his six-foot frame to keep from hitting the overhead compartment. He stepped into the crowded aisle and felt a tug on his arm.

"'Scuse me."

Looking down he saw a diminutive Chinese women. She was pulling on the sleeve of his coat. "Excuse me, preese, I cannot reach my bag—the red one. Could you, preese?" she asked.

Bob followed her pointing finger. He set his briefcase in the seat and reached for the bag, his coat falling open.

"Look, Mommy, that man has a gun."

It was an innocent comment and should have gone unnoticed. But the people around him froze. Purely by reflex, he slipped his hand inside his jacket, fingering the holster under his arm—and panic broke out. In a cacophony of shrieks and gasps, they scrambled in every direction, some ducking for cover, others squeezing through the knot of people trying to make it to the door. One elderly woman lost her footing and disappeared into the vortex of bodies as though sucked down a drain.

"Hold it. Settle down. Stop!" Bob screamed. He slipped his hand into his vest, produced a leather wallet, and flicking it open held it high in the air, turning it so everyone could see. "I'm Homeland Security! Law enforcement! Settle down. Please, everyone, calm down."

The crowd began to relax and Bob took a breath. He handed the little Chinese woman her bag and retrieved his briefcase. *Sheeesh. That does it. No more Mr. Nice Guy.* He smoothed the lapels of his coat. Creeps like Peter had turned the world on its ear. It was time to end the paranoia. *Techno-terrorists. Sheeesh.*

The alarm subsided and the people returned to the business of organizing their carry-on luggage. Intel reported that Peter was traveling with his little girl, as he often did. He'd checked her into Sick Kids Hospital in Toronto for a short while and pulled her out again. Bob hadn't had time to get a warrant for the hospital's records, so he didn't know the child's prognosis. But even if she was only in for a flu shot, traveling with a child was bound to slow Peter down.

See, now, didn't that indicate their marriage was pretty much on the rocks? If the child was sick, wouldn't Deanne want their daughter at home where she could keep her in bed? Something was definitely wrong. Actually, everything about the marriage was wrong. Deanne had become a recluse, rarely allowing herself to be seen in public. Every tabloid in the land had a different spin on the secret life of one of the country's richest women—everything from an alleged addiction to alcohol, antidepressants, and other emotion-elevating drugs, to being a bedridden victim of Lou Gehrig's disease with only a few months to live, to having gained so much weight she was ashamed to show herself—all with fuzzy paparazzi photos that backed up their stories.

Bob particularly liked the one that made her look obese because the airbrushed photo they'd used was a picture he himself had taken many years before when she'd been thin as a rail. There was even a theory about how she was behind the scenes quietly managing their billion-dollar empire and would one day be revealed as the power behind the throne. But whatever the reason, one thing was certain—Deanne had gone into hiding and neither the media, nor anyone else, knew why.

That left Peter to raise the little girl by himself, which meant he couldn't move as quickly. It also supported Bob's theory about Peter being headed for home. He would have to offload the child on her mother before making his escape. All Bob had to do was watch the house closely and make sure Peter never arrived.

The line stood, agitated but unmoving, a glut of smelly people crammed into the aisle of a plane. He looked around for the flight attendant but didn't see her. The line began jerking forward, people hustling to get off. Okay, maybe he didn't really wish Peter any ill. The guy was a problem, always had been, but it wasn't his fault. He couldn't be blamed for the genetic aberration that made him who he was. He was determined to show Peter every kindness. Never kick a man when he's down. He would demonstrate to Peter what it meant to be a Christian. He would refuse to carry a grudge. He was better than that.

The passengers deplaned and staggered toward the terminal. The hall was lit with pale green fluorescent tubes, adding to the three a.m. malaise. Bob couldn't help noticing how those anxious to get home passed him by with sidelong glances, giving him a wide berth. His briefcase hung heavy at his side. What did they think he was carrying—*a bomb?* Owing to the hour, the crowd of people waiting to greet family and friends was smaller than usual. There was the normal gauntlet of hookers to pass through, both male and female, preying on business travelers who needed a warm squeeze.

It was one of those points upon which he and Peter would disagree. They'd attended the same church for the better part of a year, but somehow they'd ended up worshiping different Gods. The deity Bob worshiped was a God of love, a God who understood man's frailty and weakness and would never torture men in eternal flames just for doing what came natural. The God he worshiped pointed to those living in glass houses and asked if they really thought it wise to throw stones. Think of the number of rapes that had been prevented because men no longer prowled the streets looking for relief. Surrogate love was a commodity. Anyone could afford a smooze—and thinking about Deanne...he looked around for the foxy flight attendant but she was nowhere to be seen. *Get a grip, Bob, stay focused. You can't score the touchdown if you take your eyes off the goal.*

CELESTIAL VANTAGE

The future is an arrangement of the physical property you earthbound ones call time. It is set for the playing out of life so that, by one choice upon another, man can learn and grow. Man's future is decided by the decisions he makes of his own free will; yet his future is also predetermined. Predestination and free will co-exist within the multi-dimensionality of time.

In the eternal kingdom there is no conflict between free will and predestination. Free will allows you to make your own decisions, but God knows in advance what decisions you will make, so your will is subject to predestination. Both are necessary. Both accomplish the same purpose.

Time has been created to allow all who inhabit creation an opportunity to choose. The future will not be changed by choice. The future has been predetermined. What can be changed is the person who makes the decision. And that, indeed, is what determines the future...

SEVEN

"Let the children...be carefully instructed in the principles and obligations of the Christian religion. This is the most essential part of education. The great enemy...never invented a more effectual means of extirpating Christianity from the world than by persuading mankind that it was improper to read the Bible at schools."
—*Dr. Benjamin Rush, 1745-1813, Father of American Medicine and Psychiatry*

PETER SHIVERED. The chill rattled in his bones as he sat in the wet sand with his arms wrapped around his knees. Angela lay beside him with a blanket tucked under her chin. He looked out over the purple haze, a velvet fog that draped the horizon. The dawn was encroaching. Soon it would be light enough to leave.

He knew they had to get going, but he couldn't bring himself to move, at least not yet. There were too many monsters in his head. He rubbed the goosebumps on his arms and brought his cheek down to his shoulder to wipe the moisture from his eye. If someone had told him a dozen years ago what he would be doing right now, though the prophet be of God, he would have denied it categorically. He stared out over the misty black water and saw himself paddling that stupid rubber raft, over and over and over again, seeing shadows in the deep, patrol boats with lights and sirens and megaphone voices coming at him from out of the fog.

He shivered again. The watery mist had buried him at sea. It had risen up to blind him, preventing him from seeing the lights on the shore. Hours of rowing without knowing if he was headed in the right direction, drifting out toward the middle of the lake, or simply going around in circles. It had actually taken him by surprise when the raft hit sand and ground to a halt.

He couldn't give up. Angela needed her mother and lives were at stake. But he did question why God had picked him, the most unlikely of candidates, to do what had to be done. It was God, wasn't it? What else could explain his absurd insistence that they add an extra floor to the elevator shaft when he bought the building, or the crazy idea of keeping an unused car in storage a block from his office, or his spending so much time cruising the lake to find a beach such as this upon which to land. Those ideas had to come from God, didn't they. Here he was, sitting in the wet sand, his butt soaking up water, shivering in the damp air—but he was on U.S. soil, and he was free.

Angela rolled over, bringing her knees up in a ball. He reached down and pulled the blanket taut under her chin. *But why now, God? Why with Angela here? She's dying, for crying out loud!* He sniffed and wiped his nose on his sleeve.

He could hear tiny waves lapping the shore, the sound of water splashing in a tub. What he wouldn't give for a nice warm bath. Just sit and relax and let all the problems of the day melt away. Others might criticize him for preferring the luxury of a tub to a quick in-and-out shower. So what? It was part of who he was. He'd made a vow to be the man God created him to be in spite of his quirky need to feel pretty. Bill had pointed out that if he needed proof of his manhood, all he had to do was stand in front of a mirror. So be it. Outwardly he was male, but inside he was strangely feminine, and the struggle between the two tore him apart. *God, you made me...I'm trying, Lord, trying real hard. It's just that there's only so much I can do.*

He could relate perfectly to homosexual men who claimed they were born gay, not because he was some kind of genetic freak, but because as far back as he could remember it was the way he'd seen himself. He'd been gangly and inept from birth, a latex rubber man who always walked with a swish, always spoke softly in a voice that resonated contralto, whose own mother called him a "pretty boy," but never "handsome." He rarely needed to shave and couldn't throw a ball to save his life—except underhand, like a *girl!* There was nothing he could do to change all that.

Despite his physical biology, his psychological and emotional makeup were female, and right now he was projecting all the same trauma and fear a faint-hearted woman might feel. Which begged the question why God would raise him up to head a multi-billion dollar empire, involve him in a project that required years of putting together a database of every home church ministry, and then bring the whole thing crashing down on his head and make him run for his life. He took a deep breath, the air fluttering in his chest.

He swept his hand across the cold wet sand picking up a pebble and rolling it between his fingers, admiring its smooth roundness, then flung it at the lake with all his might. There was no *plunk*, no *splash*. The tiny rock made it only a few feet before bouncing off other stones with the sound of a glass marble hitting cement. *That's it exactly, that's who I am! A gangly, inept fool who thinks he's a man but can't even muster the strength to hurl a rock into the water.*

He wiped sand from his finger and reached over to stroke Angela's cheek.

"I'm awake," she said.

"You're being awfully quiet."

"I was talking to my angel. I'm ca...ca...cold."

Peter drew in another staggered breath. "I know, but we have to get going. It's getting light."

He leaned over and wrapped himself around Angela's cocoon, pulling her into his arms. She had to be aching—her cells run amok, her lungs taking on water, the weight loss, chemical imbalance, her muscles wasting away—but she didn't complain, not a word. He nestled her against his shoulder as he stood and began trudging, his heavy work boots leaving tracks in the wet sand.

At the top of the hill he looked right and left and then spotted the yellow sign of the Shell station he'd used earlier as a beacon. He needed a phone. He turned and began the long two-block walk. The mist was thick on the ground, and Angela's breath, warm on his neck. A wireless VOIP phone was parceled with his palm computer but he couldn't risk using it. Homeland Security might have notified all carriers to triangulate calls made from his number.

He pushed on the kiosk. The accordion door popped in. The Plexiglas window was smeared with fingerprints and covered in spray-painted graffiti. He brought Angela up higher, balancing her weight on his shoulder so he could hold her with one arm. He waved the watch bearing the micro ID of Mike Reese in front of the reader letting it take credits for the call, pulling the blanket in front of Angela's nose. The phone booth smelled like someone had recently used it for a latrine. The dispatcher on the other end of the line assured him a cab would be there in a few minutes.

He stepped out into the morning mist. The breeze ruffled his collar and he felt a chill around his ears. He snuggled Angela in close. The air outside might be nippy and somewhat moist, but at least it was fresh. As promised, a small green and orange taxi appeared on the far side of the road heading their way. He raised his hand to hail the driver. The car pulled to the side.

"Daddy, are we on our way to see Mommy now?"

"Yes, sweetheart. Yes, we're on our way to see Mommy," he said, but in his mind Peter saw the road ahead. They needed a car, or at least a ride, to Pittsburgh. He would have to impose upon someone, putting them at risk of being arrested and possibly losing their own home and property.

Peter leaned in toward the cab and pulled the handle but it snapped back bruising his fingertips. *Ouch!* He waved his hand in front of his face, pouting as he glared at the man behind the wheel. The cab driver pushed a button. Peter heard a *thunk* and saw the door locks pop up. He placed Angela on the seat and then climbed in himself.

"Kind of early to be out for a walk, ain't it, bud?" The cabbie stretched his arm across the seat and looked back over his shoulder through the bulletproof glass. He wore a cap that shaded his eyes as he glanced first at Angela then at Peter. "Your little girl don't look so good. She sick or something? I don't need no germs runnin' 'round my cab."

"No, she's fine. Just tired. We had car trouble. I'll fix it later, but right now I need to get my daughter home." Peter held up a slip of paper and read the address to the cabbie who nodded and pulled onto the road.

It was a tiny car, hardly big enough for two people in back, but astronomical fuel prices made large cars rare. Peter tried to relax, holding Angela in his lap, watching as the night fled the day. It was only a poem, he reminded himself, but poetry was timeless.

> Day is day, and night is night
> they're never quite the same,
> Except within that moment when
> the dawn and dusk remain,
> For as twilight fades to darkness,
> and dawn returns to light,
> One cannot discern which one
> is day—and which is night.
>
> And distant too, are wrong and right,
> though close like night and day,
> When truth once held as black-and-white
> melds into muddled gray.
> When absolutes are compromised,
> when wrong is viewed as right,
> There's no discerning darkness from
> —the dimming of the light.

Okay, he wasn't a poet, but he wasn't a prophet either, yet the message he'd written more than a decade earlier rang true. The cab slowed at the corner and pulled to the curb. "This is the street."

They had come to an intersection. The house was still down the block a ways but this was the end of the ride. Door-to-door service was a thing of the past. Drivers kept their doors locked to keep strangers from jumping in, and, for the same reason, guarded against being lured to places where thugs could be waiting to rip them off.

Peter offered his wrist to pay and opened the door to climb out.

"Are we home, Daddy?" Angela held on, her arms wrapped around his neck.

"Uh huh." He ducked, making sure her head cleared the opening and turned to close the door.

The cabbie pulled away without waiting to be thanked. It was just as well. Peter had given the man the right street but had purposely transposed the numbers. He wasn't about to compromise the church's location. His disguise might be good, but the man might still listen to the news and put two and two together—*a fugitive from justice traveling with a sick child.*

He walked on. The neighborhood was shrouded in mystery. He'd been here before, knew several of the church members, but the white wall of fog made the homes set back from the road appear to be ghostly aberrations. He wasn't sure he could recognize the house. Clouds swirled in eddies around his feet, keeping him from seeing more than a few yards in front of him. Angela didn't weigh much, but he'd been carrying her long enough to feel the strain in his arms. He pulled her up tighter. At least they didn't have luggage.

The haze made it impossible to read street numbers. He began looking for familiar landmarks, but stopped short. A large pile rose out of the mist like the mound of a giant gopher. Something was wrong. The fog was rolling on the morning breeze. A car was parked at the curb—a vapory shadow one minute, clearly visible the next—a police car! Peter's heart began to pound. Every stick of furniture from inside the house was stacked on the front lawn.

He spun around and began walking back the other way. He felt faint, his hands growing clammy in spite of the cool air. He snuggled Angela against his chest. The church had been busted! His pace picked up as he turned the corner, disappearing into wispy clouds of gray. He hurried back to the main highway, out of breath, looking both ways. To his right a giant pink flamingo stood atop a building, blinking on and off. The words, "Flamingo Liquors," were scrolled in glowing pink neon underneath.

"Where we going now, Daddy?"

"*Shhhh*. Go to sleep, honey. Daddy's going to find us another cab."

He passed three youths skulking underneath a bare lightbulb at the side of the building. One was leaning against the wall by the door, rolling a small hard rubber ball over his knuckles. The boy had spiked bleached blond hair and tattoos and rings piercing almost every possible flange of his skin. He kept his eyes focused on the ball and without looking up said, "Yo, dude. Give you fifty credits for half an hour with your little girl."

The other two teens broke out in raspy sniggers. *Ha, ha, ha, hee, hee, hee.*

Peter's heart was pounding.

The boy flicked the ball up and brought his hand around to snag it mid-air. He pushed off the wall to confront Peter. "Hop around back. I got a bin filled with cardboard. No need to get dirty."

Peter tried to ignore him. He reached for the door but the boy moved to block his entrance.

"Please, I don't want any trouble. Can we get by?"

"I say you share the little miss with us. Ain't fair to keep her all to yourself."

Peter glanced over his shoulder. The other two had taken up positions behind him. A silhouette inside the store moved to the door, filling the frame. The three youths slunk back, disappearing into the fog.

"Don't worry about them," the man said, pushing the door outward so Peter could enter. "They're more bark than bite—basically decent kids. They've just got nowhere to go so they hang around bumming credits, and I give 'em whatever spoils I have to throw out. It's hard for kids, ya know?"

Easy for you to say. Peter crossed the threshold. "Ah, yeah, thanks. Ah, my car broke down about a mile back. I was wondering if I could call a cab."

"No problem." The man went back inside and leaned on the counter handing Peter a phone.

Peter used the keypad to scroll through the digital file until he found a cab company with an unfamiliar name. He turned his back to the proprietor so the man couldn't see him slip the tiny disc out of his pocket and insert it into his palm computer. He typed in a few letters and an address appeared on the screen, then he pushed the GPS function key to see a map. He gave the dispatcher the name of the store and its street location, and wrote the cross streets of his destination on a scrap of paper.

THE WINDOWS were either barred or boarded over, the yellow brick of the tenement covered in spray-painted hieroglyphics. It always amused Peter to think of how some future archeologist might spend decades trying to figure out what this primitive culture was trying to communicate. The building was brown around its base, like the soil from a garden that had once flourished there had stained the walls. The sidewalks were cracked, weeds poking through. The whole neighborhood was in sad disrepair The suburb, once the backbone of America, had been broken, and the pain of it was great.

The electronic lock buzzed to let Peter in. Just inside the door a sign taped to the elevator read, "Out of Service." Peter turned and crossed the lobby making his way up four flights of feces-stained stairs to room 404. He knocked and waited.

An eye appeared at a bubbled spy hole. He heard the sound of several deadbolts being released—*clunk, clunk, clunk*—and the door opened. The man looked down the hall and, careful not to disturb Angela, took hold of Peter's arm, urging them inside, shutting the door behind them. "Good to see you, Peter. Sorry to be so abrupt but there's a chance I'm being watched. Good disguise. If you hadn't called ahead, I probably wouldn't have let you in."

The room smelled musty, like mothballs in a drawer. "Sorry to have to intrude like this, Evan," Peter began, "and, ah, thanks. I...I went by the church. I saw what they did. The place was a mess. You okay?"

"It's not me you need to worry about." Evan went to the window and looked down on the hazy yellow street. The early morning clouds put a damper on the sun, but at least it was quiet. He pulled the blinds and the room grew dark. He went to a wall switch, flipping it on, and returned taking each step with a measure of patience. He was short and stooped as though age had reduced his stature, but there was a hot wire of energy in his voice. He reached out to take Angela from Peter's arms. "How's my little girl?" he said, nuzzling her cheek with his wrinkled chin.

Angela responded with a smile that gave Peter goosebumps. He needed to see more of that.

Evan stared at Peter. "You look tired. You both do. I guess you've been traveling hard." He turned his attention back to Angela. "Come on, I'm going to let you rest on my bed while your dad and I talk." He disappeared into the bedroom and returned a few minutes later.

"Your face is all over the news," he said, closing the door behind him. "They got international warrants out on you. Yesterday I heard they'd closed the border, and later the same afternoon, the church was hit."

"*Me?* You think they were routed 'cause of me? I...I didn't...They tore the place apart. Oh, God, they must have found the computer. I warned them about that. Keep the thing locked up, I said. It's the Achilles heel of e-mail. If they get their hands on an address book, all they have to do is trace the login names back to the user's ISP and force them to give up where people live." Peter raised his hand to cover his heart and began pacing the floor.

"Yes, sir, and it looks like they got everyone's name but mine." The old man's gaze followed Peter. "That's what I get for being too old and arthritic to fool with computers. No e-mails to trace."

Peter paused. He could feel the fluttering of his voice. "So...so what happened to everyone?"

Evan shook his head. "I don't know, Peter. Truth is, I just don't know."

EIGHT

Of all the dispositions and habits which lead to political prosperity, religion and morality are indispensable supports. It is impossible to rightly govern the world without God and the Bible."
—*George Washington, 1732-1799, 1ˢᵗ President of the United States*

ONE EYE popped open, then the other. Bob lay on his back staring up at a dingy stucco ceiling. It had looked better in the dark. He turned his head. Dingy wallpaper too. Looked like it was smeared with soot. The bedspread was a pastel floral design—downright cheesy. He propped himself up on his elbows. A stuffed chair sat in one corner with his pants draped over the arm. At one time the chair had been upholstered in a green knobby fabric, but was worn to the point where most of the texture was rubbed off. It was a dump, but what could he do? By the time he'd rented a car and driven out to the Dufoe estate—*a freakin' mansion, for cryin' out loud*—it was almost four in the morning and a faint purple light was starting to shadow the hills. He'd driven by in the dark, unable to see the house, knowing it was there only because his GPS said so. The rock wall surrounding the property seemed to never end. *A freaking estate.*

Homeland Security had placed operatives there—hidden somewhere in the trees; the house had been under surveillance for months. He didn't see them, but that was a good thing; covert ops weren't supposed to be *seen*. He wanted to stay in case Peter showed up, but the boys in the bushes wore night vision goggles—he didn't. There was no point

51

in sitting there blind. He was so tired he'd just fall asleep. Better to find a hotel, get some shuteye, and start fresh in the morning. So he'd driven back down the hill and taken a room in the first motel he'd come to. Yeah, a dump, but at least it was cheap. He'd probably get a pat on the back for saving the company money.

He tossed aside the covers and sat on the edge of the bed, his large hands gripping the mattress. *Uuggg*, the carpet was avocado green. The bedside table held two items—a green ceramic vase with handles that doubled as a lamp and his palm compu-phone. He reached for the phone and dialed the American Consul in Toronto.

"This is Chief Bob McCauley access code: one-four-six-zero, security clearance Alpha."

He waited a minute for his voice signature to be recognized. Homeland Security had an office in the American consulate building. He heard the operator's voice come on line. "Yes, Mr. McCauley, what can I do for you?"

"I'm spearheading the Dufoe terrorism case. Lou Nordstrom, L.A. Ops, will verify."

"No need. We received an encrypted transmission to that effect late yesterday."

"Good. I'm going to need the full cooperation of your office. First, I need the name of the person handling things at your end. Who's my chief liaison there?"

"That would be Frank Ainsworth. If you'll hold a moment, I'll put you through."

Bob looked at his watch again. *Sheeesh*. It was already ten.

The response was immediate. "Frank here."

"Hey Frank, this is...

"Bob McCauley," the voice interrupted. "I've been expecting you. Thought we'd see you last night."

"Change of plans. I'm leaving you in charge of the border, just keep me in the loop. I'm down in Pittsburgh, doing surveillance of the Dufoe residence. You can reach me at the number on your screen. Okay? Now bring me up to speed."

"Right. Well, you know we failed to apprehend Mr. Dufoe at his office. Not sure what happened, but our best guess is we had bad intel. Mr. Dufoe wasn't even there..."

"Or got through your net," Bob interjected.

"No, no way. We had every exit covered. No one left the building without a secure ID scan, fingerprint and wrist. He simply wasn't there. Anyway, there is some good news. His laptop was still sitting on his desk, and we have it. If he'd been there, he might have had a chance to wipe the drive before we got our hands on it. As it is, our guys in the tech lab are combing through the files. Nothing incriminating so far, but there's a lot of encrypted data we're working on. The list has got to be in there somewhere, and sooner or later we'll find it..."

Bob set his compu-phone on the table, scratching his head as he stood. They wouldn't find anything on *that* computer. Peter might be gamey, but he wasn't stupid. Bob leaned forward, grabbing his knees to pop the kinks out of his back and straightened himself, yawning, with his hands balled into fists behind his head.

Two doors were facing him. One was for the bathroom; the other led outside. Bob walked to the back door and opened it a crack. *Nice view.* He looked at a shabby brick wall across a dirt lot filled with dried weeds, sun-yellowed newspapers and discarded tires. The room's foundation was three feet below ground level. A brace of oil-blackened railroad ties held back the earth. A cement slab walkway ran off to his left until it met level ground again. A chain link fence overgrown with bushes prevented him from seeing the Ohio River beyond, but he could hear a boat off in the distance, sounding its horn. The sun appeared to be burning off a morning haze.

Bob closed the door and went to the chair to retrieve his pants, also grabbing the newspaper he'd picked up at the car rental desk the night before. He walked to the bathroom and flopped the newspaper open on the counter, staring at the headline.

OPTITEC CEO ELUDES STING OPERATION, SOUGHT BY POLICE.

On the front page was a full-face photo of Peter. He shook his head. *Ahhh, all right, be kind.* Bob leaned over the tub, turning on the tap until the water ran warm. The sound of air in the pipes thudded in the wall and then *shrieeeeked* through the room. He fiddled with the knob until the raspy sound stopped, and pulled on the lever to start the shower. The holes were calcium-clogged. Only half the water got through. The rest dribbled from the tub spout below. *Sheeesh.* He picked up the paper.

> Self-made billionaire, Peter Dufoe, largely credited with bringing optical computing to the world, is being sought after a failed attempt to apprehend him at Optitec's international headquarters in Toronto...

Blah, blah, blah. Bob's eyes scanned the page for something he didn't already know.

> Police aren't saying why they want to talk to Mr. Dufoe, but unconfirmed sources say he recently underwent an audit by the IRS...

No mention of Mrs. Dufoe, nor should there be, the disconnect of which Bob hoped indicated a separation. If the relationship had withstood the test of time, wouldn't Deanne want to make a statement defending her husband's innocence? There was always hope. Besides, even if she hadn't already come to her senses, she would after she saw this. Her husband—the criminal, the techno-terrorist, a fugitive from the law. She'd never stand for that!

CELESTIAL VANTAGE

Beloved of God, look up! The stars, formed in the sky by the Creator's hand, illuminate the gospel story: the Strong Man with his foot on the head of the dragon; the sting on the heel of the Serpent-Bearer as he crushes the scorpion's head; the sea serpent with its head caught under the mighty paw of the Lion, all revealing redemption written in the stars before life on earth began. The virgin holding her seed as the brightest star; the scales of Libra balancing the price that must be paid against the value of the purchase; the twins, two of one essence, God and man, coequal; the ram of sacrifice; the Lion of Judah, all painted on the nighttime sky. So it is written: "The Heavens declare the Glory of God."

But if the Bright and Morning Star had His life foretold, and the stars are as numerous as the sands of the sea, what else might be written up there? Were the acts of a billion lives yet unborn also scripted before time? Is all humanity acting out God's plan as fore-written on the cosmic stage of heaven?

It was revealed unto Daniel: "Those who sleep in the dust of the earth shall awake, some to everlasting life, and some to shame and everlasting contempt. And they that be wise shall shine like the brightness of the firmament, and they that turn many to righteousness, as the stars forever and ever."

May your star be one that shines.

NINE

D EANNE LOOKED at herself in the mirror. *Why bother?* Mirrors were just a reminder of who she was. There was a time they might have called her pretty...but now? She wouldn't look any better with two or three layers of makeup—paste it on, plaster up a whole new you, smooth wrinkles, raise cheekbones, reshape noses, lift chins, but alas...she'd tried it all before.

She had to stay away from mirrors. The only reflection she could handle was the one she saw in Peter's eyes. He had Superman's eyes, X-ray eyes that saw past the outer appearance into the heart. He'd take up a rag, polish his newly shaved bald dome like a bowling ball, and say: "See, everyone changes over time."

She grabbed her brush and ran it through her hair furiously as though trying to smooth out the tangles of her life, then paused to look at herself again. Love was a mysterious thing. It saw through defect. *Love suffers long, and is kind; Love does not envy...does not behave itself unseemly, seeks not its own, is not easily provoked, thinks no evil...Love never fails.* To the extent it was humanly possible, that was Peter. So why wasn't he there when she needed him?

She set her brush on the dresser, removed a stray hair that had fallen to her shoulder, and walked to the other side of the room. Imagine, a bedroom with a sitting area that had a wraparound bay window and a full living room suite including a divan, wing-back chairs, lamps and its own embroidered rug. It was like having a sun room big as a living room—situated in their bedroom. Their bathtub was big enough to wash an elephant, though pristine white, and their towels were so thick you could fluff and use them for mattresses. The drapes were hung on rods of anodized gold; the bed was hand-tooled with a headboard of inlaid wood; the wall paneling was carved in an intricate design, and she, a product of the suburbs, was overwhelmed.

Deanne sat on the soft cushions of the couch. She needed a Bible—*right now*—but Peter wouldn't let her have one. He said it was too dangerous. Other people had Bibles; they just kept them hidden, but not her, oh no, she'd married a paranoid—though she understood his reasoning. Bibles that spoke *"the whole truth, and nothing but the truth"* had been banned. The mental health of society depended on men being free from the guilt of sin. Peter was in a high-profile position, ever under the watchful eye of the media. Should it leak that he was planning to put unaltered copies of the Word of God on the street, they'd run the story and leave it to the authorities to confirm the facts. Homeland Security would tear the house apart looking for evidence. He had to be certain none was ever found.

She tried recalling a verse from memory. She wanted to assure herself that one day she'd be free. *So also is the resurrection of the dead. It is sown in corruption; it is raised in incorruption: It is sown in dishonor; it is raised in glory: it is sown in weakness; it is raised in power.* Now that was ultimate hope, not just for herself, but for Angela and Peter as well. Her own peculiar phobia, Angela's carnivorous cancer, and yes, even Peter's feminine foibles, would all be relegated to the dust bin of the grave, but the real inner person, the soul, would be elevated to glory and shine like the stars. *Amen, come, Lord Jesus—but please protect Peter until You do. I can't handle being alone.*

Her eyes darted around the room. It really didn't matter where they lived. One prison was good as another. She just wanted someone to talk to from time to time. She needed company. *You want to go—go, but at least leave Angela*—words said in anger, perhaps, but prison was one thing—solitary confinement was another. She was angry he'd left her alone, angry he'd ignored her wishes, and angry he'd taken Angela, too, though getting Angela's pain under control was a valid reason for leaving. She couldn't stand seeing Angela in pain, but she needed them here.

A threefold cord's not easily broken—how many times had she heard Peter quote that verse? They were three of a kind, full of laughter and mischief. And how they loved to dress up! The minute she'd heard about Peter's former life as a professional make-up artist, she'd refused to give him a moment's rest until he'd taught her everything he knew. She and Angela loved to play in the fantasy world they created as queen and princess, rulers of the realm of Hardwood Grove, with sashes and crowns and jewels. At other times they were biblical maidservants wrapped in tunics and veils, waiting upon Peter hand and foot. They would let their imaginations run wild—sometimes mundane, sometimes weird, and sometimes just plain silly—and then roll on the floor in hysterics. It made the burden of not being able to go outside bearable.

What would she do without Peter? Her refusal to leave the house was completely irrational, but it was something she couldn't change. She needed him more than she was ready to admit. She needed him there to support her. She was furious at him for leaving—not just for herself, but for Angela too. If he'd listened he might still be on the run, but at least he wouldn't be dragging their sick little girl with him. Now she might not see either of them again—*ever!*

Right now she needed Peter's particular kind of strength; though he always saw himself as weak, his "weakness" was strength to her. He never belittled her, never used intimidation or guilt to coax her outside, nor did he make her feel foolish, even though her thoughts were totally absurd. He encouraged her, but when she failed to muster the nerve to try, he let it go. "We'll be an indoor family," he said. "This house is as big as the state of Utah. It'll take years to explore."

And then Angela arrived. God knew Deanne had a deep need for company. She needed someone to talk to. Peter was always being called away on business, and she couldn't go with him, so God had provided Angela—a little waif who brought more laughs than the comedy channel. They were a circus act: the paranoid billionaire, his reclusive wife, and their death-defying daughter. God had to have a sense of humor. He may not have answered her prayer for restoration, but He had provided everything she needed to endure the pain. What would she do when Angela was gone?

It seemed God had determined their daughter's time on this earth would be short. They questioned *why*—such a pronouncement was hard to understand—and begged for healing, but so far they hadn't been able to change God's mind. At least Angela had outlived the doctor's prognosis. Based on her test results, her white cell count, her weight loss and her depleted energy, Angela should have succumbed months ago, but she was still around, still bringing smiles, still their little angel. All they could do was give her as much love as she could handle for whatever time she had left.

The sun streaming through the tall bay windows bathed Deanne in morning light. She felt the warmth on her shoulders and saw how it made the silky, striped fabric of the couch shine. She pulled herself up. She needed to get moving and do something to get her mind off her problems. Beneath her feet, she could feel the plush carpet through her soft, thin slippers. The sprawling mansion was built into the side of a hill. Just touring from one end to the other required ascending and descending several flights of stairs, which helped keep her in shape, though the house also had a courtyard with an indoor and outdoor pool and a full exercise suite.

The stairway was suspended in air as it swept down from the alcove above. She made her way to the bottom of the steps and meandered through a glass-domed conservatory filled with orchids, ferns and ivy, continued on past the tiled atrium with its hanging crystal chandelier, and on into the kitchen. The room was full of light. Six huge windows covered with hanging ferns and potted palms provided tropical illumination.

Deanne removed a non-stick frying pan from a cupboard beneath the island stove and went to the refrigerator for an egg. They had maids to clean the house, but though they could afford a cook too, Deanne ate so little she didn't feel she needed one. She would fix the breakfast she ate almost every day: one egg, over hard, served on a slice of unbuttered seven-grain toast. There might be a little extra cholesterol, but overall the fare was healthy. She needed the protein and fiber. She cracked the egg, dropped it into the pan, and stood back as it began to sizzle.

She sighed. It had finally come—the day Peter had predicted so many years ago. She took hold of the counter to brace herself and bowed her head, thanking God not only for the food but that her husband had been so wise. She opened her eyes, wiped her fingers on a towel and dropped a slice of bread into the toaster. Her husband was many things—caring and sensitive—but he was also paranoid and fearful. She took a certain satisfaction in knowing his own fears and phobias helped him understand hers. A stronger man, in seeking a cure, might have pushed her too hard and inadvertently destroyed what little self-worth remained.

That didn't mean she agreed with him. She was more than happy to point out that he was as unstable as she. If they thought she was crazy for wanting to stay inside, what would they call his obsession with escape hatches and secret doors? In every office tower he owned, he had concocted some elaborate escape plan, just in case. Of course he'd always retorted: "You're not paranoid if they're really out to get you."

She never dreamed it would come to this and, though she didn't want to admit it, she was grateful he'd taken the precautions he had. Every media outlet had reported the story, and while vilifying his actions through innuendo—*Police weren't forthcoming about why they want to talk to Mr. Dufoe, but unconfirmed sources say he recently underwent an audit by the IRS*—they were also verifying that he'd escaped. Of course he'd gotten away. He'd rehearsed the whole thing in advance.

She heard the doorbell chime and glanced across the room into the theater. A reporter with a mike up to his lips and a man right behind him with a camera over his shoulder were standing on her veranda. *Oh no*, sometimes you just have to think something and *poof*, it appears. She shook her head. The man wanted her on camera, but she had him instead. *Sorry, Charlie*. She never entertained the media and everyone knew it. He could camp on her front lawn till hell froze over but they wouldn't see her face. That wasn't going to happen.

She went to the refrigerator for a glass of orange juice. The stainless steel box was the size of a closet. They probably owned one of every major contrivance known to man. But it was worth nothing now. They'd have to leave it all behind—*easy come, easy go.*

There was a little town down in Mexico, a town Peter's friend Bill knew of, where there was a missionary who carefully watched what was going on in American politics. He had contacted Bill and assured him he would keep a place for them if it was ever needed. Bill and Peter had flown down to explore possibilities and Peter had determined on the spot to build one of the finest high-tech multi-media operations anywhere in North America. And it was all underground, surrounded by jungle, completely invisible to spy satellites, long-range listening devices and the naked eye.

That's where they would go. All Deanne had to do was summon the courage to step out the door, but she could take her time. It was Peter's safety that mattered. Angela probably wouldn't make the trip— not to Mexico anyway—*what will I do without Angela?*

The toaster popped, the smell of warm bread filling the air. She placed the single slice on a small china dish, slid the egg on top and stood looking at it, then set it down, suddenly realizing she didn't feel like eating.

She went to her computer to see if her husband had sent an e-mail. It wasn't a computer as much as a big-screen movie theater with controls for governing the environment—lighting, temperature, and humidity. Dozens of cameras were positioned both inside and outside the house. Nothing was hidden from view. From the giant screen she could see not only every room, but also zoom in on activities taking place down the street.

What she saw right now was a horde of trespassers. At least a dozen media had established a base of operation in her front yard. How had they gotten past the gate? They couldn't have climbed the wall—not that many people, not with so much equipment.

She picked up the remote and clicked off the camera. She didn't want to view the invasion. She'd call the police but they were probably out there too, hoping Peter would show up. Eventually they'd come with a warrant. She'd have to excuse herself and let a maid show them through. They could take whatever they wanted. Peter wouldn't be so careless as to leave anything incriminating in the house.

She glanced around the room, considering her options. On one side were a dozen theater chairs. They never went to the movies as a family—the movies came to them—though they rarely watched anything but older classics because everything made these days included virtual sex. On the other side of the theater was an office with a writing table, surrounded by a library. She walked over and sat down at the table, pushed a button and a screen emerged seamlessly from a surface of polished wood.

There were no new messages, nothing since his report from the lake, which was to be expected. They would be on the move. Peter had it all worked out; he had a support group committed to seeing him safely home, though he would have to figure a way to circumvent the gauntlet of reporters. She began to compose her own e-mail.

Peter,

No, I'm not going to pretend I'm not angry, but I'll try not to be emotional. You have enough to think about. I know you're all right, I think I'd feel it if you weren't, but I'm still mad at you, especially for taking Angela and leaving me here alone. So far, I'm holding up pretty good, but I miss her...and you too, I guess. I just wish you'd listened to me. We could have faced this together. You have no idea how lonely this house gets with both of you gone.

I didn't sleep well last night. I was restless. I kept waking up to pray. But when I finally did fall asleep, I had a dream. It was only a short thing, but it was very real. It was like I could smell the air and feel the wind in my hair. I saw a mountain on a distant horizon, and circling above that mountain, with their wings dappled by the sun, were two eagles. I think the eagles were you and I. I think it means one day we'll soar above the mountains, spreading our wings in the sun, and we'll be free.

It's silly perhaps, but you never know. I'll keep praying.

That's all I have for now,

Deanne

TEN

"I only look to the gracious protection of that Divine Being whose strengthening support I humbly solicit, and whom I fervently pray to look down upon us all."
—*Martin Van Buren, 1782-1862, 8th President of the United States*

THE SINGLE engine Piper zoomed in on a low approach, causing Peter to raise his arm and duck. The wind from the propeller whipped his fake hair and roared so loudly he wanted to cover his ears. He couldn't. He was holding Angela's hand.

The early morning fog had burned off, leaving a scorcher of a day. Peter scanned the asphalt. The sun bounced off in waves of corrugated heat making the surface appear wet—*the dead man's mirage*—mirrored lakes on a sun-scorched desert just out of a traveler's reach. He didn't see a sign pointing to, "Hanger Three," or even a large number "3" painted on the side of a building. He reached up with his sleeve and mopped his brow, looking back over his shoulder. The yellow cab was already through the chain link fence, kicking up a cloud of dust as it sped down the street. Within seconds it was gone. *There goes my ride. No turning back.*

He faced the airfield, his heart pounding and an uneasy feeling in his gut, almost hoping he wouldn't see what he was looking for, because finding it meant obligating himself to someone he didn't know.

"Why are we standing here, Daddy? It's hot."

Peter looked down at Angela. Her custom-tailored wig, miniaturized to fit a child's head, looked just like her own hair—light auburn, with the same luster, same wavy curls. Nothing but the best for his little girl. He let go of her hand and picked a piece of lint from the tresses. She stood beside him, refreshed from her rest, ready to try walking again. Her strength seemed to come and go in spurts, but every day on her feet was a good one.

"You see Hanger Three anywhere around?"

Angela took Peter's hand in both her own, clinging to his arm. "Uh uh," she said, shaking her head.

"Me, either. Guess we'll have to look." He took a step forward, still wearing the gray dungarees and work boots he'd acquired as part of his janitor's costume. He hoped his wig looked as good as his daughter's. He used the back of his hand to blot the perspiration around his fake hairline, smoothed his mustache and adjusted his buck teeth and glasses.

The small airport boasted only two landing strips surrounded by a half-dozen match-box hangars. Angela, for all her determination to walk, was moving slowly. Her steps seemed measured but she kept putting one foot in front of the other, trudging on. Why couldn't scientists, after so many years of research and all their accumulated knowledge, eliminate cancer? *Sin, the curse. But why Angela? She hadn't done anything wrong.*

They crossed the open tarmac and stopped in the shade of a domed hut made of corrugated steel. The door slammed back, *bang,* and a man with a clipboard stepped out.

Peter caught his eye. "I'm looking for Jerry Boyle," he said.

"Over there." The man raised his pen, pointing toward two people under the prop of a helicopter. "The one in the red baseball cap."

"Thanks."

Peter shuffled slowly, holding Angela's hand. He could have carried her and made better time, but though crossing the distance seemed to take forever, he didn't want to disparage her effort. Every step was a defiance of death—every step a celebration of the life she still lived. A stack of boxes on the ground bore large red crosses marking them as medical supplies. *If only...*all they needed were a few Opioid patches to keep her pain at bay until they got home, but that wasn't going to happen, not with a controlled substance.

The man in the baseball cap signed a piece of paper and handed it to a second man in a white medical uniform with a blue caduceus on the pocket. He turned and walked back to a waiting ambulance.

"You Jerry Boyle?" Peter asked.

"That would be me. You must be the 'package.'"

The pilot's arms were roped with muscles, his shoulders broad as an ox, and his neck, reddened by the sun, was thick as a bucket. Blond strands of curly hair flipped out from underneath his cap and his eyes were steel blue. Pete felt the man's glare drilling right through him. Why couldn't he be some *little* guy? He nodded. "I, ah...*package?* Ah, if that's what you call it. My name's..."

"Don't want to know your name." The man raised a can of pop with his finger pointed at Peter's chest. "I'm a delivery guy. That's what I do, transport medical supplies, stuff like that? I didn't ask for this piece of trouble, so don't cause me any. I'm not doing this for you, or for her"—he tipped his chin toward Angela. "I don't give diddly-squat how rich or powerful you think you are."

Peter took a step back. "Sorry, I...I thought you'd volunteered. My friend Evan said you were willing to help."

"Willing to help? Yeah. Good one. My father-in-law's got a screw loose, and that's all I'm saying about that. Now get in and climb all the way back. I don't even want to know you're here. Not a peep outta either one of you." He tilted his head back and drained his can in two gulps, then squeezed the aluminum, crushing it, and tossed it clattering into the cockpit. "I could lose my license for this. Your face is on the front page of every newspaper, and don't think that silly wig is going to fool anyone. Now saddle up. We take off in two minutes."

Peter brought a hand to his head. *Silly wig?* He used his finger to squeegee the sweat from his forehead. Maybe when the hair got wet, it looked fake. He began blotting his forehead with his sleeve. *Silly wig?* Jerry reminded him of the thugs he'd known in school, a relentless line of shoulder-pushers that regularly sent him sprawling across the grass—*You take the sissy. I don't want him on my team.* Peter stepped on the skid and set Angela inside. He tried to raise his foot high enough to climb aboard but missed the edge and his foot came crashing down, skinning his knee. *Owww!*

The pilot rolled his eyes and shook his head, the bill of his red cap rolling side to side.

Peter turned around and backed up, sitting on the lip of the door and scooted back until he was inside. Angela stood over him. He used one of the crates to push himself up and ducked under the low ceiling, reaching down to rub his kneecap before taking her hand. He limped toward the tail boom and sat down. The rotorcraft was stripped of anything designed for comfort. It was a no-frills utility vehicle. The walls were composed of vinyl pads covering an outer metal shell riveted together on a skeletal frame. Looking back through the tunnel, Peter had the feeling he'd been swallowed by a giant grasshopper.

Jerry continued loading boxes into the cabin, blocking most of Peter's view. The passenger seats had been removed, presumably to make room for more cargo. He squatted on the floor with his back against the wall. Jerry entered the cockpit from the other side and climbed aboard. He clamped a headset over his baseball cap, slipped on a pair of dark sunglasses, and positioned the mike in front of his mouth. Then he flipped the ignition and the main rotor began spinning overhead like a giant pinwheel—*whaffffump, whaffffump whaffffump*. Peter sulked in the back and swallowed the lump in his throat.

Jerry went through a preflight checklist and received clearance. The whirlybird shuddered and started to rise. Peter felt the lift and thrust, the tail rotor bringing them around, and the cockpit skewing forward. Then they were off. He pulled Angela in and held on tight, his stomach sinking as they left the ground. The liquid sloshed in his gut the way it did when he rode the Jonny Rocket at the carnival—the whirling dervish that made him want to puke. He looked at Angela. Her eyes were closed. She was resting. She didn't seem to mind being airborne in a metal spoon. The crates shifted with the vibration. He tried looking through the cockpit window but boxes were in his way and all he could see was a thin slice of hazy mustard sky.

After what seemed like an eternity, the rotorcraft began to slow. Peter looked at his watch. They'd been in the air most of an hour. He could hear the pilot talking to someone about his approach and felt a deceleration, his stomach sliding up to his throat as they started to descend. The skids hit softly as they touched down on the landing pad. Jerry cut the engine and climbed out. A few seconds later the door on Peter's side of the cabin slid open. A wave of heat filled the space, bringing with it the smell of diesel fuel. Peter heard voices, Jerry and someone else talking. He saw an arm reach in as a few cartons were removed. He pushed himself back against the wall. Then the voices trailed off. The missing boxes left a hole, allowing Peter to see better. A medical truck with a large red cross on the door sat a hundred yards in the distance. Its lights pulsated like strobes.

Angela looked at her father. Her lips were pinched; her face, drawn and white. "Daddy, I have to use the bathroom."

Jerry was walking across the tarmac with another man. He carried an ice chest while the second man rolled a two-wheeled dolly stacked with several boxes. They were heading toward the ambulance.

"Daddy, I need to go, now!"

"Can it wait?" But Peter knew even before it escaped his lips, the question was moot. They were several hours from Pittsburgh, especially with the stops the pilot had to make.

"All right, I'll see what I can do." Peter rose to his knees—"*Ouch*!"— and eased the pressure off his bruise, then wiped his clammy palms on his pants and spread his hands apart, wiggling his fingers. "Let me carry you. We have to hurry." Angela climbed into his arms. He stood clumsily, stooping over as he made his way toward the front of the helicopter. The men had their backs to him as they walked toward the ambulance. Across the asphalt he saw a small square building with pumps and tanks and a green door bearing the international stick symbol of a man.

He stepped down and feeling the pain in his knee, limped across the pavement working up a sweat that left melon slices under his arms. He entered the restroom and helped his daughter into the stall, turning to keep the door open a crack. The men were standing around the ambulance. The toilet flushed and he went to help his daughter. He picked her up and carried her back to the helicopter, moving quickly in spite of the heat, but Jerry was already waiting.

"Where the hell you been?"

"My...my little girl had to use the bathroom."

Jerry's eyes narrowed, his face flushing red. *"Gurrrrr*-get in. Son of a...don't even think about leaving again! I don't care if you have to pee your pants! Got it? Next time, I'm gone. You copy that?"

"Sorry, I..." Peter's words failed him. He helped Angela to the back and sat against the wall.

THE HELICOPTER'S blades were churning, *whump whump whump*. Peter had no idea what towns were below or where they were on a map. They could be headed back to Canada, for all he knew. What if someone had offered a reward for their return? Angela looked up. Her half-lidded eyes seemed to lack focus. She tried to smile, but it melted like butter in the sun. He snuggled her in his arms, resting his cheek on her head. They'd withheld pain treatment at the hospital. Every hospital they'd been to had refused to prescribe the painkillers she needed. Toronto was their last hope...she was being so brave.

Why, Lord? They could have come for me anytime. Why now? Why when Angela's with me? Deanne will be worried sick. Peter wiped her cheek with his thumb, her skin feeling soft and moist. *How much longer, Lord? Please give us a little more time. Don't let her die out here. Please. Help me get her to her mother. At least let her die in peace...*

Peter bowed his head to nuzzle his cheek against Angela's and then brought it back against the vinyl hull, staring into space. He felt the vibration in his skull as he listened to Jerry talking with someone on the radio.

"Negative. I'm on a tight schedule. This is life or death for some people. What's the problem?"

The pilot looked over his shoulder, narrowing his eyes. He adjusted his mike, routing it in front of his mouth. "No, just me and one very bright sun up here....

"As a matter of fact, I would. I've got a deadline to meet. The people waiting for this stuff don't have a lot of time. You'll have to take my word for it. There's no one on this bird but me....

"You've got to be kidding! All right, but I want it in writing. And it better be signed by the supervising flight controller. If somebody dies because of this, it's on your head....

"Roger that."

The helicopter turned an arc as though heading back. The man looked over his shoulder at Peter. "Sorry, partner, but I told you not to become a problem."

Peter felt the rhythm of the engines change and the helicopter began to drop. The blades overhead were churning, *whump whump whump whump whump whump. Oh, Lord, Lord, what are You doing? They're going to take Angela. What are You doing, Lord?* The chopper touched down with a soft bump and stopped.

"Okay, partner, this is where you get off. No way I'm taking you back with me. I can't afford to lose my license. Come on, move it! I don't want to be down more than thirty seconds. Don't just sit there. Get out! I'm doing you a favor."

"But..."

"You screwed up. You let 'em see you. Now move! Don't make me throw you out."

Peter pushed himself off the wall as he scooted toward the door, holding Angela. He turned, dangling his legs over the edge and slipped onto the ground. He was standing on a pile of bent corn husks. He caught his balance and stepped forward, the helicopter blades churning overhead, whipping his clothes. He put a hand to his wig, holding it in place. The man hit the throttle and the helicopter peeled away, turning as it rose in the sky.

Peter stood in the middle of a perfect circle of flattened corn with all the stalks laid over in one direction. He'd seen it somewhere before. *Uh huh*, crop circles. Proof that aliens were among us. Beyond the circle was a five-foot wall of corn, and beyond that he couldn't see a thing. He had no idea where he was. He could plow through the stalks stumbling over dirt clods for miles before coming to a road, and then what? He could hitchhike, but where would he say he was going? *Excuse me, I'm lost. Can you tell me what state I'm in.*

The sun bore down on his wig like a hot blanket. He shifted Angela to his left arm so he could straighten his hair. The beating rotors had whipped the corn silk into a frenzy. Pollen dust floated through the air, making him itch and sneeze. *Aaachoooo!* Angela clung to his neck, staring vaguely into the open sky. Peter's chest wheezed and started to tremble. His eyes filled with water. He tried to suck it in.

"Are you crying, Daddy?"

"No, dear. It's just the pollen. Daddy has allergies." He took a step forward, then another and another, disappearing into the tall rows of corn.

ELEVEN

"We have no government armed with power capable of contending with human passions unbridled by morality and religion...Our constitution was made only for a moral and religious people. It is wholly inadequate for the government of any other."
—*John Adams, 1735-1826, 2nd President of the United States*

B OB SAT in his rented car outside the stone home of Peter Dufoe, a secluded refuge that grew out of the angular rocks of the woodland like a medieval castle. A light morning rain dotted his windshield obscuring his view. He slammed his fist against the steering wheel. *Sheeesh*. He'd carefully situated the car a block from the drive to avoid being noticed. He wanted the car to appear empty, a random vehicle parked along the road by a neighbor. Turning his wipers on, even for a moment, would indicate someone was inside.

He raised his binoculars. *What a fortress*. The entire property, probably several acres, was surrounded by a six-foot stone wall with motorized steel gates. The house, set back against the hill at a higher elevation, looked big enough to be a hotel. Through gaps in tall growths of poplar, oak and pine he could see terraced lawns of luminous green, with gardens of yellow daffodils, purple iris and pink snapdragons. A house of privilege, totally out of sync with the rest of the world. His eyes followed an S-curved flagstone walk to a massive door of carved oak, capped with a rounded beveled glass top. Ostentatious, but short-lived. It was all coming down. He had no idea how far back the property went, but it didn't matter; there were no side streets. He would get his man. The only access was from the front, and the gate that allowed cars in was straight ahead, directly in his line of sight.

Bob set his binoculars down, rubbing his eyes. Agency operatives were out there somewhere, wearing camouflage to blend with the hillside foliage, but they'd been instructed to leave him alone. Last thing he needed was someone rousting his car in the middle of the street. They were good, he had to admit that. He had yet to spot anyone, even with binoculars. It made him wonder if they were really there—but that was foolish. Peter was a wanted man, and the agents well-trained experts. Bob's real concern was the glut of reporters camped out on the lawn. They might spook Peter before he got the chance to move in. He raised his binoculars again looking through the windows into the three-story mansion hoping to see Deanne, feeling a little sheepish, like a voyeur with a conscience. He didn't want to be there—he hoped she'd never learn of his part in her husband's demise—but he couldn't leave. Any chance of seeing her was worth the risk.

Sheeesh. Leo was right. He *was* unstable. He wasn't thinking about the operation. He should pull himself off the case. But didn't acknowledging his weakness mean he was still in control? At least he wasn't self-deluded. He knew what he was doing; he just didn't care.

He brought the binoculars up a level. *Look!* A ruffle of curtains. She was there, in the room. He couldn't see clearly through the rain-spotted windshield, but he didn't dare flick the wipers. He dialed the focus knob to sharpen the image. Was that Deanne in a lace nightgown, or just the curtains caught in a breeze? He pulled the binoculars down and pinched the bridge of his nose. Just a breeze, *this time*, but somewhere behind that glass was the only woman he'd ever loved. How had it come to this? He, a committed womanizer with infinite sexual prowess, reduced to a peeping Tom. *Sheeesh.* He drummed his fingers on the steering wheel. The emotion that held him there was foreign. Heck, any emotion was foreign. It'd been twenty years...but he couldn't let it go.

They were sitting in metal folding chairs grouped in a circle in the fellowship hall of the church, a square box painted white and bathed in fluorescent light. The worship songs had been sung, the guitar put away, and Bibles were now being opened with a rustling of pages. Bob hadn't brought a Bible, didn't need one. He was there for Deanne and would use hers, if needed.

He kept his gaze distant and made a point of not looking at the group leader. His arm was stretched across the back of Deanne's chair with his legs extended and crossed at the ankles. He wore a gray sweatshirt with cutoff sleeves and the words: COPS - Community Officers Protect and Serve, silk-screened on the front.

He looked up as someone walked in, tall and lanky. He nudged Deanne and leaned in to whisper, "Get a load of sweet pants in the turtleneck." Deanne gave the young man a cursory glance and turned her attention back to the teacher.

The leader stuck a finger in his Bible marking his place and stood with his hand extended toward the newcomer. "Hey, Peter, glad you could make it." He turned to the group. "This is Peter Dufoe. He's new to our town and looking for a church, so I invited him to our study. He doesn't know anyone, so let's make him feel welcome."

"Hey, Peter." "Nice to meet you." "Hey, welcome to the group." Random unidentified voices from the circle accompanied by the casual "Yep," "Uh-huh," and affirming nod.

"We haven't started yet. Maybe you can take a minute and tell us about yourself," the host said, returning to his seat.

Peter stopped and glanced around. He put his hands in his pockets and shuffled his feet on the carpet.

Bob flicked a piece of lint off his shirt, a lopsided grin on his face.

"I...I...I my...my name's Peter as...as already said. I, well, I guess I'm here because I, uh, I like to play with computers, and uh, there's a development company here that has their eye on a program I put together and, well, I guess since I hold the patent and they think they have a use for it, they wanted me here to show them how to use it, you know, work out the bugs, something like that."

He paused and appeared to be waiting for a response, but none came. The silence in the room grew until it became obvious they were expecting him to continue. *"I've been living in Oregon, staying with a friend and his daughter but he got married and then this opportunity came up, so here I am. That's about it. I...I don't want to interrupt. I'll just sit here and... and you go on with your meeting." Peter looked around for an empty chair and sat down.*

The group leader thanked him, did a quick review to bring him up to speed, and picked it up where he'd left off the week before. They were discussing the nature of sin and how it didn't matter what the sin was— lying, cheating, stealing, murder, sexual immorality. To commit one was the same as committing all. Any one sin, no matter how trifling, kept you from entering the presence of a holy God. The Apostle John pointed out that if we say we have no sin, we're liars, which of course is itself a sin. So it was as Paul said: "All have sinned and come short of the glory of God."

Deanne stole a furtive glance at the newcomer. Bob pulled his hand from the back of her chair and raised a finger, indicating he wanted to add his two cents. He waited until the leader acknowledged him and propped his elbows on his thighs, clasping his hands. Then he launched into a speech about how good it was to be a Christian, to know where you stood, because no matter how many sins were piled up against you, God forgave them all. God loved everyone, sinner and saint alike, irrespective of their sin. He spoke with the authority of a police academy graduate, a top-of- the-list candidate waiting for appointment to the Pittsburgh PD, but he pushed the thought a little further than the leader intended. He couldn't help himself. He glanced around the group. These lamebrains still believed man couldn't sin without fear of judgment.

The meeting ended in prayer. Several leaned forward, bowing their heads and folding their hands. Bob peeked at his watch, wondering how much longer this would go on. What was the big deal, anyway? If God was the All-Powerful, All-knowing, Sovereign Lord everyone claimed He was, prayer didn't mean much. If He was all-knowing, He already knew what you wanted; if He was sovereign, He'd do as He darn well pleased, and if He was the all-powerful Creator of the universe, He was too busy keeping everything from spinning out of control to pay attention to a few silly requests, so why bother? The buzzing of a billion people praying probably sounded like a mosquito in the ear of God. Point in fact: he'd watched his mother pray and petition the throne of God and his father still beat her. That's just the way it was. Besides, nowhere in the Bible did it say you had to close your eyes or prostrate yourself to pray.

He was looking at his watch again, yawning, wondering how much longer the pretense would go on, when he heard the final "Amen!" The group started to rise and head toward the kitchen where there were trays of cookies and a bowl of punch. An overweight girl in an ochre dress that reminded Bob of a plump ripe orange, was first in line. She leaned in too close, jolting the table and splashing juice onto the white linen. The offender's face turned red but she pretended she wasn't flustered and filled her glass, laid five cookies on paper china and turned around, almost bumping into Peter.

"Oh, hi! I'm Betty. Nice to meet you." She started to raise her hand juggling her drink and cookies, but ended up shrugging her shoulders. "Tee, hee, hee," she twittered.

Deanne stood and straightened her pink blouse. She brought a hand up to smooth her hair and started for the table, but Bob caught her arm. "Remember, you promised we wouldn't stay."

"Let go, Bob," she said pulling her arm free. She tucked her chin, looking at him from under her lashes. She wasn't smiling. "I said I wouldn't stay 'late.' Part of the reason we come is to fellowship. Now be good and let's get something to eat." She glanced over her shoulder assessing the lineup at the table.

"Part of the reason you come."

"Pardon?" she said, addressing Bob again.

"You said part of the reason we come is to fellowship. That's why you come, not me."

Deanne shook her head. "No one's making you stay, Bob. If you're in such a hurry, go on. I can catch a ride home." She turned, leaving him for the crowd at the punch bowl.

Bob hung back, feeling betrayed. Why not, just once, do something for me, he thought. He hated trying to socialize with this group of misfits. A bunch of Wal-Mart employee rejects—too fat, too frumpy, too greasy to belong anywhere else. A typical lonely hearts club.

Deanne approached the newcomer smiling. "Your name's Peter, is that right?" she said, holding out her hand, causing him to stumble backwards, the juice splashing up the side of his glass almost spilling. He shoved a half-eaten cookie into his mouth, wiping his fingers on his pants before taking her hand. "Pffffssd to meet yuff, Dianne," he mumbled through the wad of dough.

"Dee-anne. I know, a lot of people think it's Dianne, but it's Deanne." She reached out to retrieve a drink from the table, bringing the paper cup to lips that were the same color as the pink lemonade.

Sure enough, that's just who Deanne would target, Bob mused. Find the reject of all rejects and she's there like a magnet. He shook his head. Dang if she doesn't have an incurable thing about feeling sorry for nature's mistakes. Poor clown. She's going to do a number on him. She'll have him licking her hand like a puppy and then run off and break his heart.

Deanne turned and wiggled her finger, beckoning Bob to join them.

Sheeesh. He rolled his eyes. Why get involved with a bunch of pantywaists? But Deanne's finger kept reeling him in. He resigned himself.

"There's someone I want you to meet. Peter, this is Bob McCauley. Bob, this is Peter." She leaned in conspiratorially, her hand cupping her mouth as if divulging a secret. "He's just graduated from the police academy so if you have any parking tickets, it's probably not the best time to complain," she whispered aloud.

Bob put on a rubbery smile. "Cute, Deanne." He held out his hand and squeezed Peter's in a grip designed to hurt. "Pleasure," he said, smiling at the pained expression on Peter's face.

His phone rang. That's where it started, one simple introduction to the nerd of all nerds and his life went to hell in a handbasket. He unclipped the device from his belt and brought it to his ear. "McCauley here."

"Bob, it's Frank Ainsworth. You asked me to keep you abreast of any new developments."

"So I did. What have you got?"

"Couple things I thought you might find of interest."

"Go ahead."

"Border patrol spotted a boat with no one aboard anchored just outside Wilson, New York, and when they cruised the shore they found an abandoned life raft on the beach. It could be nothing. The boat was legally registered to an Alan Hampton. We're trying to track him down but you never know, it may be the way Dufoe got back into the States..."

The man continued on, but Bob wasn't listening. Of course it was how Dufoe got into the States. Have boat, will travel. Cross the liquid border, park it close to shore and use a rowboat to bring you in. It made perfect sense. He was dealing with numbskulls.

"...and there's one other thing. We were going through his computer. All the files are encrypted but the key is contained in a fingerprint algorithm. He probably thinks we won't be able to access it but, truth is, we just copied a print from his passport and had the lab make an identical latex copy complete with his exact minutiae. We laid it on the reader and we were in. We haven't found anything worth using yet, mostly business letters, marketing plans, you know, company stuff, but while we were busy going through everything, an e-mail came in from his wife."

Bob straightened himself, now taking note. "His wife?"

"Yep. How nice is that? I think we've got him. He'll pick it up on his palm computer and write her back. We won't see what he says unless he uses the reply button, but we'll get everything she writes, and there's bound to be something in that."

"Okay. Good, good, so what did she say?"

"Right. Well, there isn't much and it's kind of confusing. She's ticked off about his running off with their little girl, that much I gather, but it's mostly gibberish, written like poetry or a song, something about standing on a mountaintop or flying over the mountains. I'm not sure. It sounds like she's writing in code, but if she continues to use this e-mail address and we get enough information, we'll nail him."

Hot dang. "Good work, Frank. I appreciate it. Forward that e-mail to me, and do it now. I need to see what she said. I'm sitting outside her house as we speak. It may give me something I can use."

"Not a problem. You'll have it in two minutes."

TWELVE

"If any people ever had cause to render up thanks to the Supreme Being for parental care and protection extended to them in all trials and difficulties to which they have been from time to time exposed, we certainly are that people."
—*John Tyler, 1790-1862, 10ᵗʰ President of the United States*

PETER BROKE through the last two rows of corn, his head wreathed in a cloud of yellow pollen. The sun was fire in the sky. He held Angela, her hands strung around his neck like an apron. His arms were aching, his strength melting in the heat. He shifted his daughter from one arm to the other so he could wipe the sweat from his eyes and reached around to adjust the pack he wore under his shirt at the back. He scratched. The corn silk had him itching everywhere, especially under his wig where his scalp was wet. The dust was awful.

To his right stood a white house flanked by trees—an orchid surrounded by thick green leaves—or maybe just a mirage. He squinted trying to focus through the haze of his pollen-covered glasses. His thumping heart picked up speed as he began walking toward the building. It was a large Victorian structure, obviously a grand old house in its day, now fallen into disrepair. The paint peeled from the walls like autumn leaves starting to curl. There was a round spire with a bank of curved windows at one corner and out front, a large antebellum porch with a spindled rail.

"Alright, that's far enough. Stop right where you are or I'll drill ya full a holes."

Peter turned slowly, his heart accelerating into overdrive, rivulets rolling down his chest.

A small, gaunt man in soiled coveralls and a plaid blue flannel shirt buttoned at the neck moved out from behind an ancient Ford Ranger, holding a double barrel shotgun to his squinting eye. His cheeks were peppered with a day-old beard.

Peter twisted, instinctively shielding Angela behind his shoulder as he looked back toward the rows of corn. For an instant he was tempted to duck and run, but, *no*, he couldn't, not and protect his daughter...

"I said that's far enough, young fella."

Peter held out his flattened palm. "Hold it! Don't shoot, mister, don't shoot! I...I'm sorry. We're lost and my daughter's sick and we need help...please, we're not here to cause trouble."

The stooped figure lowered his weapon but kept it pointed in Peter's direction. "Best bring her in the house," he said.

Peter's legs felt like rubber as he shuffled across the porch. His head throbbed with heat. Beneath his feet, the steps sagged and the paint was scuffed to the bare wood. The old man reached for a door, smeared with muddy paw prints. He laid his rifle against a cupboard just inside. "Put her in there on the bed," he said, pointing.

Peter made his way through the dining room and on into the bedroom to lay Angela down. His fingers were shaking, his heart doing flip-flops in the hollow of his chest. He wiped his hands on his pants. The bedspread was a pink twill and the bed made with pillows stuffed into ruffled shams. Lace curtains covered the windows, and there were gold-framed floral prints on the walls. The old man had a wife somewhere. Angela curled up, squeezing her eyes shut as she grimaced and clutched her stomach.

"What's ailin' her?" The farmer disappeared down the hall without waiting for an answer. He returned a few seconds later with a small plastic bottle. "This is all I got. Good for most of what ails ya." He handed the bottle of aspirin to Peter. "There's water and a glass in the bathroom."

Peter rolled the container over to read the label, his sweaty fingers leaving prints on the plastic. He smeared them off. He didn't want proof that he'd been there in case the man was ever questioned. Aspirin was for mild pain relief, but it would help some. He snapped off the cap and poured a pile of the pills into his palm. "Thanks," he said, heading for the door.

"Name's Jake," the old-timer said.

"What's that?" Peter set a glass under the faucet and turned on the water. He glanced up and saw himself in the mirror realizing he'd forgotten to replace his buck teeth and mustache after removing them in the cornfield. A line of sweat rested where his wig met his forehead and the hair was matted and powdered with pollinated corn. He tried shaking the dust off, but ended up dislodging the glasses from his nose. He took them off and cleaned them with a tissue from a box on the sink, then reached for the drinking glass which was now overflowing. The porcelain sink was rust-stained from the drip of iron-heavy water. He cranked off the tap, tossed three of the pills into his mouth, drank them down, and headed back into the room holding six white tablets in the palm of one hand and the glass of water in the other.

"Said my name's Jake. What's the matter, you deef?"

Peter nodded. "Pleased to meet you, Jake," he said. "I'm Peter, and this is Angela," and then grimaced. The farmer's hospitality had caught him off guard. He was supposed to be Mike Reese.

A swaybacked hound waddled up, its stomach dragging the floor. It pushed against the farmer's leg and sat down, his tongue lolling from the side of his mouth. "This here's Marbles," Jake said, scratching the dog's floppy ears. "Good thing I found you first. Ol' Marble's been knowed to chew the leg offa trespassers. It ain't smart to go snoopin' around a man's property unannounced. He may not look like much, but he's a mean old cuss."

Peter eyed the dog skeptically. He doubted the animal had any bite left in him, but... "I'd watch it with that gun of yours. Someone could get hurt."

"Dern migrants come through here pickin' corn and stealing anything that ain't nailed down. I got to protect what's mine. Besides, wouldn't a hurt you none. I make my own shot. Fill the casin's with birdseed. Makes a lot a noise and peppers your tailwagger pretty good, but it don't kill nothin'."

"Uh huh, but when you pointed it at me I nearly had a heart attack, so I could have died just the same." Peter sat on the bed, the springs creaking as they took his weight. He helped Angela into a sitting position, handed her the glass and held out his palm like a dish. He waited as she took one tablet at a time in her small shaky fingers, and with tiny sips, washed them down.

"You never said what you was doing on my property in the first place. You wasn't stealing corn, was ya?"

"We most certainly were not!"

"Don't take no offense. Farm ain't mine anymore. Used to be. Used to grow a hundred acres of the finest, sweetest, most melt-in-your-mouth corn in the state, but it got to where I couldn't afford the taxes on the place, so I had to sell it. Owned by some big government Co-Op now. I made 'em let me keep the house, but when I'm gone they get that too. I wouldn't care a-tall if you took some of their corn. Not a-tall."

"Well, we didn't. We were just taking a shortcut and got turned around." Peter helped Angela lie down, stretching her feet out, and slipped a pillow under her head.

She looked at him through half-lidded eyes. "Daddy, will I see my angel again?"

Peter didn't answer. He smiled and nodded slowly, stroking her head until she closed her eyes. Within seconds her breathing grew heavy and she was asleep. He leaned over, brushing her hair aside to kiss her cheek. "Rest easy, sweetheart. I'll be in the next room if you need me."

He got up and followed his host into the living room. A large bay window was hung with sun-yellowed drapes. Fragments of misty light spilled into the room's dusky interior. There were cracks in the plaster; the paint, mottled like dry skin. The old man led Peter across a carpet that had once been stretched wall to wall, but now undulated in a series of rolling waves and threadbare patches.

A woman was standing at the kitchen door with her arms folded.

She was short and thin and wore a gingham apron over a pastel yellow dress that seemed to swallow her diminutive frame. Her hair was short, straight and gray, her cheeks crisscrossed with lines of age, and she wore a pair of thick glasses that made her eyes bug from her face. The farmer acknowledged her with a nod and made his way over to a cushioned rocking chair to sit down.

The old dog rubbed up against Peter's leg, pushing Peter's hand with his nose. Peter obliged, scratching the dog's head and crooning, "You're a good dog, aren't cha. *Gooood* dog." Marbles' brown eyes rolled up in appreciation. He lay down with his head on his legs, his black gums falling loose as he began to pant.

A newspaper was open on the coffee table. Right on the front page, large as life, was Peter's face. *And I introduced myself. Just plain dumb.*

The woman unfolded her arms and pointed. "That's you, isn't it?"

Peter removed his glasses, rubbing his nose with the back of his hand. He swallowed, his Adam's apple sticking like a wad of chewing gum in his throat. He shook his head. "It's not what you think. *Uhhemmm*, ah, I ah, I haven't done anything wrong. I just have a different view of things, that's all. I never stole anything or hurt anyone. I'm not some kind of terrorist. I'm just a regular guy with a wife and child, and I don't deserve to be put in jail."

"Says there you stole a man's boat..."

"Lulu..."

"and killed him and pushed him over the side..."

"behave yourself!"

"an' they're still looking for his body."

"Lulu, that's enough!" The old man's lips were pinched. His eyebrows buckled in a look of reproof.

The woman folded her arms, sucking in her lips till her toothless mouth disappeared. She turned and marched into the kitchen.

Jake looked at Peter, nodding. "My father fought the big war. Lost a leg paratroopin' behind enemy lines. Never complained about it, though. Not once. Thought it an honor and a privilege to serve his country. He'd roll in his grave to see what come of the sacrifice he made. A man can't hardly think for hisself anymore. Can't hardly say nothin' without offending someone and maybe even getting arrested for it. Like you. I may not agree with you, but you got the inalienable right to believe whatever you want. How you like that word? *In-alienable*. Learned it as a kid. *Whoeeeee!*" He slapped the arm of his chair sending up a puff of dust. "Makes me fightin' mad." He pushed himself up, groaning as he placed a hand on his back to straighten himself. "Can't help you much. My old truck wouldn't make it a hundred miles. But I can get you and your little girl into town and see if I can find you a bus."

Lulu was back at the door. "No, you don't. You just put that idea out of your head. This man has no business asking for our help. Makes us accomplices, aiding and abetting. He's going to get us in trouble. You get on that phone and call the police right now. Hear me? He has no business involving us. No, sir."

The farmer shook his head. "*Shush,* Lulu. Calm down. We're not callin' the police. And we're not gettin' into trouble. I'm going to give the man and his little girl a ride, that's all. We get stopped, I'll say they was hitchhiking. All I did was pull over and pick them up. No law against that."

THE OLD dog's head hung over the side of the pickup, his ears spinning like the wings of a weather-vane duck. The wind-stream blasted his face like a furnace.

Jake was at the helm, holding onto the large vibrating steering wheel, piloting his vehicle slowly down the two-lane road. He wore his flannel shirt with the sleeves rolled up, but he kept his collar buttoned at the neck. A broad-brimmed hat sat on his head soaking up perspiration.

Angela was asleep in Peter's arms. She slept a lot more now, more than ever, and for longer periods of time. Peter wanted her to fight, never give up, but she grew more listless each day. God forbid she surrender before they get home. The child didn't deserve to die, but if God was of a mind to take her, the least He could do was wait until she was resting peacefully in her own bed surrounded by those she loved—not on the road in some rickety old Ranger. Not running from

84

the law.

A yuppie in a red sports coupe, impatient with the slow crawl of the ancient truck, pulled around sounding his horn, saluting the elderly driver with an outstretched finger. Jake shook his head. He'd received a similar sign of respect from a half-dozen others. Vehicles manufactured in the eighties weren't designed to fly at the speed of light.

The air streaming through the window provided circulation, but they sweltered in the ninety-degree heat, nonetheless. Jake slapped the steering wheel. Another car was jamming up his bumper, laying on the horn. "Seems like everyone's in a hurry these days."

Peter nodded.

The car swung around and sped off in a cloud of dust. Jake pushed his hat back on his head and used a handkerchief to mop his brow. "Don't mind Lucy, that's her real name, I only call her Lulu when I'm mad, but she don't mean nothing by what she says. She's always fretting about something. She has a hard time thinking straight these days, but her heart's in the right place." His chin bunched up as he wiped his cheeks and the back of his neck. "My dad was a preacher. I tell you that?"

Peter shook his head. "No, you didn't."

"Yes sir, hellfire and brimstone. He'd preach it everyday of the week if he could, not that it did him much good. People were leavin' the church. Couldn't do anything to make 'em stay. They didn't like the message."

"Yeah, I know. What happened to him?"

"Ah, they finally had to close the church and after that he just kinda wasted away. I guess he figured he'd outlived his usefulness and one day decided life wasn't worth the effort, but he was seventy by then. He'd lived a good life."

"Well, if it means anything to you, he's probably with the Lord and has a new body with two good legs and plenty of likeminded friends. The sad truth is, even those who disagreed with him believe in hell now."

"Yeah, you would say that. Me and Lucy stopped going to church a long time ago. There wasn't anything in it for us. They was watering down what the Bible was sayin'. It got so we didn't know what to believe anymore."

"Yeah, I hear that a lot, like the Bible doesn't mean what it says. Then you see the shape the world's in and wonder why. Truth is, the Bible's been right all along. We're only reaping what we've sown."

Jake took one hand off the wheel, pulling the red handkerchief from his pocket to blot his forehead again. He dabbed the side of his cheeks and stuffed the handkerchief into his coveralls. "How's your little girl doin'?"

Peter looked down. The sun was in Angela's face. He reached up twisting the visor, but it was too short to do any good, so he cupped his hand over her eyes. "She's still asleep. That's a good thing. It's the only time she doesn't feel pain."

Under the dashboard a radio crackled to life. "Hey, Jake, this is Hank. You out there, Jake? Come on, pick up?"

Jake reached for the mike and pulled it on a coiled cord to his mouth. "Yeah, I'm here, Hank. What's your beef?"

"Ain't my beef, Jake, it's yours. I just got an all-points bulletin on the police scanner. They're looking for some guy and his little girl. Your wife called it in. Claims you got him with you. That true?"

Peter's eyes widened as they darted over to Jake. He began shaking his head, the color draining from his face. Droplets of sweat dotted his forehead.

"You know better than to believe anything Lulu says. All that was in the papers this morning. She must have read it. She makes stuff up, you know that. She can't think clear no more. Just forget about it."

"She's your wife, Jake. She reported you to the police."

"My wife's senile and everyone knows it. No one pays her any mind. She wouldn't know her own name if I didn't say it every mornin'."

"Highway Patrol believes her. They're setting up a roadblock. They plan to stop you on your way in. I suggest you get over here pronto. I'll take the man off your hands. My advice to you is don't get caught with him, and stay outside the city."

"And I think you been eatin' too many of them rum filled-cherries you like, that's what I think." Jake snapped the radio off and replaced the mike.

Peter shook his head. "I...ah...I don't want you getting into trouble. Maybe you should pull over and let us out. I don't know, what do you think?"

The truck crested the top of a hill just as a police car screamed by going the opposite direction, its lights flashing, its siren fading quickly into the distance. "Well I'll be. Looks like that one's headed to my place in one big hurry."

Peter craned his head around but the cruiser had disappeared over the rise. *Now what?* "He has to have seen your truck. He'll turn around for sure." The poor dog was buttressed against the tailgate, its ears flapping in the wind. Peter explored the open field. The crops had been plowed under leaving bits of brown stubble poking through clods of dirt. There was nowhere to hide.

"Maybe, but he don't know the farmin' roads like I do. Time for e-vasive action." Jake leaned hard on the wheel, pulling the truck *squealing* to the right. The tires lost traction in the soft shoulder, fishtailing in a plume of dust as they came around. He floored the gas pedal, tires spinning. They dropped into a shallow gully and bottomed out, launched into the field and sped off, bouncing over ruts as they plowed through the brown grass.

Angela's eyes snapped open, her whole body shaking, her teeth rattling in her mouth. "Wwwwhat're dddddoing, Ddddaddy?"

"*Shhhhh*, we're jjjjust tttaking aaa ssshortcut." He pulled Angela up and placed her over his shoulder, holding tight, but he wasn't ready when they flew up over a mound and all four wheels left the ground.

CELESTIAL VANTAGE

The ultimate destiny of those on earth must not be disclosed. If you knew the end from the beginning, you would surrender to your fate rather than use your will to change it. This must not be so. You who dabble with mystics, tinker with seers, and call upon spirits from the world beyond, do err. How can you depend on those whose medium is darkness to give you light? They are of the lower world. How, then, can they lift you to the heights? Only He whose scope is beyond measure can venture that.

Do not concern yourself with tomorrow, sufficient for today is the evil thereof. The choices that lie ahead are a blessing. Each one is an opportunity to please the Almighty, and each one a curse when not rightly made, so choose well. I know of that which I speak, for even celestial beings are forbidden to observe the future. If it were not so, I would prepare even now the conclusion of my tale, and thus save your ears the discomfort it may bring, but I dare not. There are many decisions yet to be made. Should evil over good prevail—even so, I will not forsake my mission.

THIRTEEN

"For these manifestations of His favor we owe to Him who holds our destiny in His hands the tribute of our grateful devotion."
—*Chester Arthur, 1829-1886, 21ˢᵗ President of the United States*

DUST SETTLED on the toes of Peter's boots. He was staring down the long side of a barn, or shed, or garage—something other than a house because the house was off to his right. He turned, watching as Jake pulled away. The old Ranger kicked up clouds of dirt, creaking and bumping over potholes and washboards on its way down the long dirt drive. Then it angled into the street and was gone. Peter raised a hand and waved. *Bless him, Lord, he was good to me.* He put his arm around Angela, held her close and turned toward the house, his heart pounding at the thought of facing another unknown—*tha-thump, tha-thump, tha-thump.*

The house was in better shape than Jake's, but it was also newer and a lot smaller, a one-story bungalow made of white aluminum siding. The windows were square with green shutters and the slanted roof was shingled in green asphalt tiles. Peter stepped forward. Angela, breathing softly against his chest, purred like a sleeping kitten. This was the third time he'd have to introduce himself to a total stranger, the third time he'd have to ask for help, and the third time he faced rejection—*all in one day.* He hated rejection—especially the rejection of men—*but that was because of his father.* He looked over his shoulder one last time. Jake's truck was long gone, having faded into ripples of heat on the horizon.

They had flown over a knoll and landed on the other side so hard Peter almost hit the ceiling. He barely had time to bring his shoulder around as they were thrown into the dashboard. He felt Angela fold into his chest and thought he might have crushed her, but when they bounced back, he found her wide-eyed and unharmed. There they waited, breathing heavily until the dust settled and the police car's banshee siren screamed by, heading back the other way.

Jake sat holding the wheel with both hands, his arms as stiff as broomsticks. "*Wheweeee.*" He removed his hat and wiped his forehead on his blue flannel sleeve. "Dang! Didn't know I had it in me." He leaned forward and levered the truck into gear.

Peter was shaking. He thought he felt Angela shaking too, but he couldn't be sure. They drove across the field, much slower now, bumping over ridges, rills and clods of dirt, and when they reached the other side, picked up a parallel road and turned right, going back the way they'd come. Jake zigzagged his way across the county turning right on one farm road and left on the next until they finally slowed and pulled into a drive with a mailbox that read, "Turnbull."

"You'll be safe here," he said as they climbed out. The old man went to the bed of his truck and, without lowering the tailgate, wrapped his arms around his dog hefting him over the side and depositing him on the front seat. "I don't know what Hank has in mind, but I do know he's one of you. Always preachin' the end of the world." He took hold of the steering wheel and pulled himself up, settling into the seat and slamming the door, *blamm.*

Jake tipped his hat back on his head, mopping the sweat from his brow with his handkerchief: "Maybe it ain't right, me not being so sure of things the way you are, but I got to believe God's watchin' out for you and the little girl." And with that he squared his hat on his head, wrenched the truck in gear, and sped off. The old man had explained on the way over how he felt it was best if he didn't stick around and make introductions. The sooner he got home, the sooner he could assure the police his wife got her cockamamie idea from the newspaper.

Angela clung to her father, a feather in his arms. She looked up through droopy eyes. "Are we home, Daddy? I want to go to bed. It hurts, Daddy. Make it go away, *pleeeese.*" She started to cry, tiny sobs muffled by his shirt. Peter snuggled her close letting her head rest on his shoulder. It was like holding cotton candy—so light and vaporous he felt if he squeezed, she might collapse in on herself and disappear.

He took a hesitant step toward the white shoebox, licking the inside of his gums. At least he'd had time to reinsert his phony teeth and reapply the fake mustache. What if the man was a police officer? This might be a trap. Jake had said the man could be trusted, and Jake had dodged a patrol car to get him here, so Peter put one foot in front of the other, snuggling Angela in close and staggering on. The sky in front of him was a cloudless brown and the sun, now at his back, seared his shoulders like a hot iron. The air around him smelled of parched hay. The flower gardens had gone to seed. Even the weeds were brown.

Peter stood on the stoop in front of a screen door and tried to peer inside. He pressed his nose to the wire mesh to see better, and then... *yip, yip, yip, yip, yip, yip, yip,* jumped back as a dog launched itself at the door. He might have knocked if he hadn't been holding Angela but now the door was too far to reach and besides, the dog was barking loud enough to wake the dead. He heard a voice. "Shut up, Killer, quiet down. Settle down, boy. Get back!"

The screen was pushed open. A man stood there, shorter than Peter but built like a tank with a thick chest, arms and thighs—a regular hay-baler. He had short gray hair and his face was broad with a flattened nose that looked like it had seen one too many fights. His skin, particularly around his cylinder neck, was burned red from hours in the sun. A bug-eyed Chihuahua scampered around his feet. "Well, don't just stand there, get yourself inside. They got the entire police department out looking for you."

Peter crossed the threshold licking his gums, teeth and lips to make sure his disguise was still in place. It was, but not that anyone seemed to notice. "Do you know me?"

"I know who you are. At least who *they* say you are. *They* say you're an insurgent accused of spreading religious propaganda, fomenting hatred and spreading lies about the state. I know your name is Peter

Dufoe, that you're filthy rich, and that you don't look like that. Your picture's in the paper. Anything else I'd need to know?"

The dog ventured out from behind the man's leg long enough to sniff Peter's cuff, its tail wagging like a metronome—*all that noise from something so small.* Peter stepped back lifting his foot to shake the tiny Chihuahua off and the dog backed up, turned in a circle and sat down, shivering like it had been kicked. Its tiny legs were trembling, its eyes protruding from its small face like huge brown marbles. The pointed ears that normally stood erect were laid flat. Angela dropped an arm reaching for the animal, but Peter pulled her back. Who knew, the thing's bark might *not* be worse than its bite.

The man wore a gray T-shirt covered by a red and black plaid wool jacket too warm for the weather, which explained why it was unbuttoned and hanging loose over his blue denims. The sleeves were rolled up, exposing sinewy forearms. "You and the girl sit yourselves down. I was just packing a few things, won't be a minute." He turned and clomped back toward the living room. The laces of his work boots were undone, trailing behind him on the ground. He hadn't bothered to introduce himself. He disappeared behind a door Peter presumed led to a bedroom.

"Packing?"

"Don't worry, it won't take long. I travel light, but I've been around long enough to know there are certain things you need."

Angela was squirming in Peter's arms. "I want down, Daddy, let me down." Peter smiled at her sudden burst of energy. The cowering dog didn't look so tough now, but the situation required caution. "This dog of yours bite?"

The man appeared at the door again. He flipped a pair of socks over his finger, rolling them together. "Who, Killer? Nah, not even his own fleas."

Peter put Angela down. She squatted to her haunches, reaching for the dog who popped to his feet, backing away with a whimper as he looked toward the bedroom imploring his master to come to his rescue. The dog hesitated, took a quivering step toward Angela, sniffing. He licked her hand, causing her to giggle, and then dove behind the leg of the chair.

Peter kept an eye on the animal. *Killer? What kind of name is that?* But he welcomed the spark of life it ignited in Angela. He didn't know what to think. It seemed the man was offering to help, but if the police were setting up roadblocks, it might be best to lay low for a while. Then again, Jake might cave in under pressure and reveal where they were, so maybe it was better to leave...

Peter's heart was palpitating. He was about to have a heart attack, or faint, or just fall on the floor, comatose. The odor of his perspiration rankled his nose, a smell he hadn't been aware of in the open air. He needed a bath. He needed to call Bill. He needed a pep talk. *"If God is for you, who can be against you? Greater is He that is in you than he that is in the world. Have I not commanded you be strong and courageous?"* Angela looked okay for the moment, making a new friend. He wished he could make friends that easily. He tried sucking it up, but his breath fluttered in his chest.

The man—*Jake called him Hank*—was making noises in the back of the house. Peter approached the door guardedly and peeked around the corner. It *was* a bedroom, and beyond that a second door led to a small bath. He watched as the man stuffed a toothbrush and razor into a shaving bag along with a yellow bar of soap and a blue washcloth and returned to the bedroom dropping the bag on the bed. He glanced at Peter standing at the door. Then his eyes darted around the room searching for something, and came to rest on the dresser. He went over and retrieved a gold watch with an expandable band that he snapped around a wrist thick as a two-by-four. His skin was leather. He stuffed the smaller bag into a larger duffel already lumpy with what was probably a spare change of clothes along with what looked to be a rectangular box.

"Honest truth, Mr. Dufoe, I don't know squat about you. I just know if you're guilty of half the things they say you are, I got to help. No choice of my own, just the way it is." Hank closed his dresser drawer and took a final cursory look around the room. His eyes stopped when they fell on Peter. "They think you could still be in Toronto, though they also think you may have crossed the border. Truth is, they don't know where you are, and that's a good thing." Hank pulled the drawstring on his duffel and brought the bag up under his arm. "First sighting anyone's reported came from Lulu, Jake's wife, and like her name implies, she's loony as a bird, just like one of those gold coins you have in Canada. They may try to interview her, but sooner or later she'll scream bloody murder and rant on about being abducted by aliens and that'll be the end of it. No one's going to believe her story."

He squeezed by Peter who backed out of the way and fell in behind as the man stomped off toward the kitchen. "And don't worry about Jake. We go way back. We don't always see eye to eye, but he's a good man. He won't be causing us any grief. With any luck the whole thing will blow over and we'll travel without incident. Now, where are you headed?"

A blue ice chest sat on the kitchen table alongside a cardboard box filled with cereal and other dry goods. Hank plopped his bag on the table and went to the sink where he grabbed a pot of coffee and poured it into a thermos. He raised his eyes, scrutinizing Peter again. "You didn't answer my question. Where is it you're headed? I need to map out a route. If they want you bad enough to get our entire police force activated, I have to be careful."

Peter looked around. A plaque above the sink read: *"As for me and my house, we will serve the Lord."* He examined the box-shaped lump in the duffel bag. Clearly it was the size and shape of a Bible, though, even if it was, it was likely a newer version with altered text. "You never mentioned your name. You know mine," he said, avoiding the question.

"Sorry, I thought Jake woulda told ya." He turned and held out a hand. "Henry, Henry Turnbull, though most folks call me Hank."

Peter reached out feeling his hand engulfed by fingers as hard, thick and calloused as his own were thin, soft and moist. It occurred to Peter that with his arm flapping around, the man might get a whiff of his body odor. He didn't dare propose a bath, no matter how nice it sounded. He looked over the man's shoulder. The plaque could mean... He swallowed, mustering his courage. "Excuse me, Mr. Turnbull, I hope you don't mind my asking but...are you a...a...a Christian?"

The man narrowed his eyes. "'Course I'm a Christian. Why the heck else you think I'd stick my neck out for a fella like you?" He let go, wiping his hand on his pants. "And the name's Hank."

"Sorry, Hank, but I..." Peter brought his head around looking into the other room to make sure Angela was still occupied with the dog. He lowered his voice. "My little girl in there, she's dying. I have to get her to her mother. She only has a few days, maybe less." Peter's eyes began to moisten. "They say she could go at any time. I have to get her home, one way or another. I'll do anything to make sure that happens." He stopped, a thought surfacing he hadn't considered before. "You just name your price. If you read the papers, you know I can afford it..."

Hank folded his arms, narrowing his eyes. "Keep your money, Jack. I ain't for hire."

Peter's face reddened. It felt like he'd just run into the man's fist. He backed up a step. "Well, I...okay...sorry, you never said why you're doing this." Peter wiped his cheek on his shoulder.

"I got a favorite verse, goes like this. 'He hath shown thee, oh man, what is good and what the Lord requires of thee. But to do justly, and to love mercy, and to walk humbly with thy God.' Doing justly means doing what is right, and it's *mercy*, not mercenary. Reason enough?"

Peter nodded. "Sure, okay, I mean...good. Anyway, to answer your question: Pittsburgh. That's where we're going."

Hank's surly face twisted into a pout. "That's what I was afraid of. They know you're from Pittsburgh. That's the one place they'll be looking." He screwed the lid on the thermos and walked over, setting it on the table. "You couldn't make it easy and be heading someplace nice like Florida or California."

He picked up his duffel bag, tossed it on top of his box of food, and stuffed both up under one arm. Then he stuck the tip of a finger into the hole on the lid of the thermos, reached for the ice chest, and looked straight into Peter's eyes. "Better grab your little girl. We have to get going before they get it in their head to do a more thorough sweep of the area. I doubt they'll believe anything Looney Bird says, but you never know. We don't want to be here if they come looking." With that he walked to the kitchen door. The little Chihuahua hopped out of Angela's lap and scurried across the floor, his tiny feet prancing on the tiles. The man held the door open and the dog raced outside, hopping in circles, chasing its tail.

Peter found Angela in the living room and scooped her into his arms. She leaned into his chest with her head resting on his shoulder as he made his way through the kitchen, following the man into the yard. The door closed behind him with the sound of rattling glass.

Hank disappeared into the barn and Peter, not knowing what else to do, traipsed after. It was hot and the air smelled of musty silage. Two huge front doors swung out, creaking on oxidized hinges, and light flooded the barn's interior. In front of him stood a bright blue, waxed and polished, lacquer-painted, dual chrome-piped eighteen-wheeler with a cab extension that looked big enough to be a traveling motel. A trailer was coupled behind the rig like the boxcar of a train. The words *Blue Heaven* were scrolled on the cab door over the airbrushed image of a cloud, but what Peter noticed right off was the chrome radiator with the word *Peterbilt* inside a large red oval. Peterbilt—this massive truck was built by a man named Peter, not some wimpy flake like himself, a real man's man—*Peter*—the builder of this massive hunk of chrome and steel on wheels. Peter!

"Mr. Dufoe, meet Baby. Baby, meet Mr. Dufoe." Hank dropped a calloused hand on the fender of the truck. Clearly he was proud of the unit. "I used to drive long-haul, private contractor, so me and the road are old friends, though I been retired most of five years now. There ain't much to do out here in farm country. I spend most of my time taking Killer for walks, listening to the police scanner just to see what's going on, and polishing Baby. This rig and me have seen a lot of miles together. Come on, Killer, climb aboard."

Hank opened the door and waved his arm like he was ushering his dog through a gate. The Chihuahua jumped onto the running board, then in two nimble hops, onto the seat and turned around, dancing on the cushion with its tail wagging. "Come on, man, don't stand there gawkin'. We got to get some miles between us and this place."

FOURTEEN

"When government fears the people, there is liberty. When the people fear the government, there is tyranny."
—*Thomas Jefferson, 1743-1826, 3rd President of the United States*

ANDY CLEAVER walked into the restaurant and stopped, looking out across the spacious interior for Lou. They were meeting for dinner, well, sort of—but hadn't Nordstrom called him and suggested they meet here? *Nice place.* He glanced down at his tweedy brown sports coat and then at the silk suits worn by the other restaurant clientele. He should have wore blue.

He ran his fingers through his greasy hair trying to slick it back. He'd never been here before, couldn't afford it even if he'd wanted to. The restaurant catered to an elite crowd of bankers, brokers and business executives. It was top of the tower in every sense of the word, with windows that offered generous views of the city in all directions. The waiters wore tuxedos and the servers, black dresses that resembled evening gowns. The tables were covered in white linen with place settings illuminated by candles—and the silver looked real. You could hear the wealth in the hushed tones of conversation and the polite clinking of ice cubes in cocktail glasses. No hustle and bustle here—*no beer*—this was class. And Lou had invited him, not to dinner exactly, but to provide an update on the Dufoe file.

It was worth it just to be noticed by Lou. Bob usually got the glory, but boss man Bob was out of town, so...he caught Lou rising from his chair holding a napkin in his lap. The silver-haired head of Homeland

Security flicked his hand, beckoning him over.

Andy straightened his tie and made his way through the maze of white-skirted tables. Setting the manila folder down, he took a seat opposite Lou. This was his moment to shine. He had to somehow communicate that it was he, not Bob, who had assimilated the information that would lead to Dufoe's arrest and conviction. It was he who would ultimately bring Dufoe down.

Andy bit a nail and quickly pulled his hand away hoping the action wasn't seen. *Bad habit*, but one he'd never been able to break. He wondered if the smell of the juju cigarette he'd smoked was still on his clothes. He dropped his hands to his lap and began picking at the skin around his cuticle, keeping his fingers close to the tablecloth out of sight.

A good-looking brunette with her hair rolled in a bun and lipstick the color of cherries, edged up to the table. She asked if they wanted anything to drink, but before Andy could answer, Lou dismissed her, explaining he was waiting for someone else to arrive. Andy turned his head away, fiddling with his napkin. He didn't want to be caught staring at the slim-waisted beauty. He felt Lou's eyes on him, and brought his hand up to take a sip of water.

"Thanks for coming on such short notice," Lou said. "I'm meeting the National Director in fifteen and I wanted to hear the latest. What have you got?"

Andy picked up the file and handed it to Lou. He knew the policy: don't waste a person's time with extraneous information. He'd pared his two-inch-thick file down to two thin pages, a brief outline of the entire case. It was a point of pride.

Lou opened the folder and scanned, speed-reading the first page and then the second. His lips puckered. "Well, this is everything I pretty much already know. Isn't there anything new?"

Andy felt a flush of embarrassment. This was all they had. It was all there *was*. Apparently Lou had already read the file. How could there be anything new when Bob hadn't reported in? Bob shouldn't be in the field in the first place. He was a desk jockey. "Well, sir, the thing is, we haven't heard anything from Agent McCauley. It's been awhile since he's taken a field assignment. He's probably not up to speed on our check-in procedures or the importance of keeping the office up to date. Frankly, I was surprised. Seems like kind of a demotion for a guy like him. I mean, you'd think he'd assign a subordinate...someone like me. After all, I did all the background. I personally gathered every piece of information we have. I know Dufoe better than his own mother. But Bob took it upon himself to handle this one, so I'm totally out of the loop." Andy brought his hand up and picked at a nail. "Sorry I can't be of more help. Maybe if I were there, but..."

Lou nodded. The warmth of the flickering candle turned his mane of silver hair a burnished gold. "Guess I struck a nerve," he said. He picked up a butter knife, rotating it in his hands, rubbing the smooth cool metal with his thumb. "Look, Andy, I'm the one who sent Bob into the field. If you have a problem, it's with me, not him. And I'm not trying to undermine your efforts, nor am I questioning your abilities. I had to make a decision and for all your strengths, Bob brought something to the table you didn't have. He knows Dufoe, and not just on paper; he knows how he thinks. He has a personal interest in seeing justice brought here. I had to factor all that in and make the call. But I know how you feel. I know you want to be there to see it through, and I'm sure you deserve it. If it's any consolation, I've known Bob a long time and one thing I can say for certain, he won't take any credit he isn't due. Couldn't even if he wanted to. Dismantling a network this size will be a feather in the cap of the whole department, but we're a team. No one man gets the glory. If there are any citations to be given, I'll make sure your contribution is recognized."

Andy sat fidgeting in his chair. His face held the dour look of a man of tenure who'd just been fired. He opened his mouth to rebut, but Lou raised his hand to silence him.

"I've made my decision, Andy. You're going to have to live with it."

"I know, Chief, it's just that..." he paused, trying to get his thoughts in order. It was important to carefully phrase what he wanted to say. "Bob's all alone out there. You said it yourself, we're a team. If he gets in trouble who's he going to call for backup? You don't want the local boys taking credit for the bust, not after we've worked so hard.

"And that's only one of my concerns. The real issue is what you said about Agent McCauley being close to this. He knows the people involved. What if he has a change of heart? Old friendships die hard. What if, let's just say for the sake of argument, Dufoe is able to turn him. Wait! Don't say anything, yet. Just hear me out." Andy pressed on to deter any possible objection. "You know Bob's a religious man, still goes to church and all that. In some ways he's no different than Dufoe. He hasn't come to grips with the fact that God is dead, and that could make him a liability, or at the very least it makes him vulnerable. And how's he going to arrest the husband of the woman he used to be engaged to?"

Lou raised his eyebrows. A sign of interest. That was it! The new piece of information he could offer. Andy had him.

"You didn't know? Sorry, I thought Bob would have said something. It's true, they were engaged." Andy relaxed, leaning forward, crossing his arms on the table. "I was doing background on Mrs. Dufoe and found an old article written in a high school newspaper. It was after some big game where Agent McCauley was the star and the interviewer wanted to know what the future Mrs. McCauley thought of her fiancé, only the woman in the story was Deanne Dufoe, Peter's wife. She and our own Agent McCauley were once upon a time engaged to be married. No kidding. I showed the article to Bob but he told me to forget it. Said it was a personal matter, and since we weren't after Mrs. Dufoe, it wasn't material to the case."

Andy dropped his voice, causing Lou to cock his head to the side so he could hear. "But what if, just supposing, what if she begs him to let them go? Look, I'm not saying Bob would do anything stupid, but what if he does? How's it going to look if one of our own turns on us? All I'm suggesting is that you send me in as backup. I won't get in the way. I won't even let Bob know I'm there. I'll stay out of sight and keep an eye on things, just to make sure the bust doesn't go sour."

FIFTEEN

"The Bible…is of all books in the world, that which contributes most to make men good, wise, and happy."
—*John Quincy Adams, 1746-1848, 6ᵗʰ President of the United States*

PETER WOKE with a start and for a second wondered where he was. His head was pressed against a window fogged by breath. A hillside swept by, then a road sign. He read "I-90" in a blur. The hum of the tires and the drone of the five-hundred horsepower engine vibrated through his cushioned seat. He wiped drool from his mouth and pushed himself away from the door, stretching his arms. He looked over at the driver—*what's that name again*—Hank?—riding high in the pilot's seat with a brown baseball cap clamped to his head, brown leather gloves on his hands, and a brown Chihuahua named Killer curled in his lap. His red mackinaw was hanging open, his jaw slightly raised as he listened to his CB.

"…that coup is dirty, *mi amigo*, better plan to stop. Word is they're looking for some bad hombre and his little girl. I just came through heading eastbound on a clean shot, but there's a five-mile wall at the toll to Penn State. There's a bear in the air and the Boy Scouts are checking everyone crossing the border. Okey-dokey. That's all for me. I'm backsliding down the lines. You take care of that little ankle-biter of yours. Give her a couple of forty-fours from me. I'm gone."

Peter reached over his shoulder to make sure Angela was all right.

"She's fine. Been resting all the way, just like you. You've both been asleep several hours."

"What was that about?" Peter yawned and nodded toward the radio.

"That's what you computer techno-geeks might call a primitive communications device. It's my CB rig. Not rocket science, but it gets the job done. I was just checking road conditions up ahead. Found out the state police are monitoring the toll booth just before we cross into Pennsylvania, and they're checking everyone for ID. I figure they think you made it stateside and wanna make sure you don't leave New York, which means we have to take measures that could be uncomfortable, but we'll manage."

"I didn't hear him say that."

Hank puckered his lips and stared out the window, his leather gloves twisting the rim of the wheel. "The man said 'the coup's dirty.' Chicken coup usually refers to a weigh station, but in this case he was talking about the toll booth at the border. The fact that it's dirty means law enforcement's on the scene. The bear in the air means they got a police helicopter in the sky and the Boy Scouts are state troopers. The rest was about how he was heading home with clear sailing. And he also told me to give my granddaughter a few kisses from him. I made up the part about your little girl being my granddaughter. I'll be able to hide you, but I don't think her little body can withstand the punishment, not in her condition. She'll have to stay up here with me. Don't worry, it'll work out fine. Lots of haulers take their grandkids with them on vacation."

Peter was rubbing his arm, trying to get the circulation moving. The air was tainted with the smell of diesel, though the conditioner kept the environment cool. He began eyeing the cab. They were sitting in huge bucket chairs with padded armrests. In front of him was a full-blown computer with GPS mapping. The dashboard had more dials and gauges than an airplane. "What punishment?" he said.

Hank looked over, squinting, his thick gray brows knitted. "You must have been tired. We hardly hit the road before you were out." The patch on Hank's baseball cap was a red oval with the Peterbilt logo and the words *Heavenly Body* scripted underneath.

It was an odd sensation sitting up so high, looking out over rows of steel on wheels. The road signs raced by like a picket fence. Peter nodded. "We left Toronto yesterday and traveled all night and haven't stopped to rest until now, so, yes, the last twenty-four hours have been very stressful and tiring. What did you mean by 'punishment?'"

"Nothin'. Under that bed your little girl's sleeping on is a storage compartment which is no big deal, but this one's special. It has a false bottom called a smuggler's hole. Ever since the country's economic system blew a gasket, smuggling's been a way of life for most drivers. I ain't saying it's right, mind you, but in a lot of cases the underground market's the only way for a man to make ends meet. There's a guy down in Beckley, a biker named Jack, has more ways of making secret compartments than any man alive. I had him build one for me for running cheap booze out of Mexico. Only God had a different plan, and I ended up smuggling Bibles into Canada. Politicians up north joined the New World Order before we did. But, see, it was one of those times God used the evil plans of men to bring about good. Did it for about three years. Finally had to stop because I couldn't afford going up and back with an empty trailer, not with the price of fuel. But I did use my last trip down to smuggle a man across the Canadian border into the U.S."

Peter was shaking his head. He brought his fingers up and combed his fake bangs, dreading how the wig must look. "Uh-uh, not me. I can't do that. I don't like small spaces. I'm claustrophobic. Like... don't ever close the door of a closet when I'm in it, or I'll freak. It's like a panic attack, a total meltdown, *uh-uh*, you'll have to think of something else."

"Nuts! This is God's doin', not mine. You'll be fine. That other man felt the same way. He was a preacher. They had him on a whole list of trumped-up charges, but I knew the man and I knew it was really about shutting him up 'cause they didn't like what he was sayin'. Kinda like you. So I put him in the box and drove him across the border and they never did catch him. The space is tight, but he made it, and so will you."

"No...I mean, I *really* can't. You'll have to think of something else."

"No deal, *compadre*. God's not in the 'I can't' business. 'Sides, there is nothing else. You'll do fine. Getting dropped off in Jake's cornfield wasn't bad luck. It was God's way of getting you here. And my putting that box back there was probably His way of saving your sorry butt from the start. The rest was just dress rehearsal, so don't be whining about it. Just take what God gives and say thanks." Without removing his hand from the wheel, Hank raised a gloved finger to point at the horizon. "The last exit before the toll is up ahead a few miles. I'll be stopping for fuel and putting you in the tank, so to speak. Don't worry, it'll be cramped, but they won't find you. 'Least, they never discovered it yet."

Peter looked over his shoulder into the cab. Angela lay on the mattress, still asleep. He reached back, but his arm was too short and his hand was shaking.

"Don't bother. You won't find it. Looks like a normal storage space even when it's open. Can't even tell from under the truck where the box hangs down a foot lower than it should because we lowered everything around it to match. It's pure illusion." Hank waved his hand like a magic wand, but Peter didn't smile. Peter, in fact, looked like he was about to lose his lunch. "Hey, think of it this way. You serve a big God who's promised never to leave you, so He's got to get in there too. If He can handle it, so can you."

The miles rolled by in a quilt of burned hills, dry woodlots and yellow sky. The constant smell of diesel made Peter want to upchuck as he bounced along riding shotgun. He tried severing his mind from the closet—*No, Mommy, no, I won't touch your shoes! No, please don't put me in there!* Maybe it was a magic trick, a box you climbed into and fell out the other side and disappeared, like you were never there in the first place—"pure illusion," just like Hank said. He needed to get his thoughts on something else.

He pushed himself back into the seat, feeling the comfort of the high back with extra lumbar support and padded armrests. Hank did know how to travel. Peter's stomach felt queasy. "You really smuggled booze and Bibles? I'll bet that's an interesting story," he said, lifting himself on his elbows with a discernible belch and a grimace.

Hank gave Peter a sidelong glance. His hands tightened their grip on the wheel. It *had* been a long hard road. He'd been driving since he was sixteen, though he'd told the freight company that hired him he was twenty-one. With a fake ID and a beard, he looked it too. But the road was a lonely place, filled with excess. Hardly a man he met wasn't into drugs, especially the feel-gooders like speed and rock. Some were into alcohol, because it calmed the nerves, and sex in all its depraved forms—from raunchy magazines to skirts for sale, "Hi, honey, wanna buy a dress? Comes with me in it,"—to men with kinky desires, right on down to children. Life was about filling the empty miles with any vice a man could conceive. With Hank, it was gambling. He had a line on every game going—hockey, football, rugby—didn't matter. He was up and down, always looking for the big score.

He drove alone. The only place he refused to go was home. His wife had already left him, well, technically he'd left her. Returned from a road trip a few days early and found her in bed with the busboy from the restaurant where she worked. Talk about class. He'd thrown his suitcase on the mattress and ordered them to both stay put. Should of seen 'em sitting there with the covers pulled up around their necks, whimpering like he was gonna blow their heads off. *Wrong.* He was too far gone to care. She deserved the little rat. He emptied his closet, zipped that old piece of luggage, and walked out the door—just like that. Never saw her again, though he did receive divorce papers sometime later, which he dutifully signed and sent back.

But he bottomed out after that. It kind of hit him that there wasn't one single person on the whole sorry planet that gave diddly-squat whether he lived or died, including himself. By then he was into his bookie for such a ridiculous amount, the only way out was to make one big score. The Cowboys were four and 0 for the season with a defensive line you couldn't touch, but he didn't have squat, so he put up the only thing he did have. He put his truck on the line and played it safe, betting the odds-on favorite. There was only a seven-point spread and, *yeah*, they got cut down like grass under a lawnmower. His bookie wanted his pink slip but he wasn't about to give it up, so he blew town. He knew they'd come after him, and they did, but the first guy they sent wasn't up to the job. He tried to confront him in a bar after he was half in the tank and feeling no pain. Not a good idea. He went crazy. The collector was supposed to break his legs, so he broke the collector's instead. He was lucky he got out before the police arrived, but he knew they'd send someone else. It wasn't going to stop until either they got their money, or he was dead.

Seemed the only thing he could do was keep moving so they couldn't get him in their sights, but he couldn't use his CB because it was a public band. Some other trucker in need of cash might be listening and decide to drop a dime on him. He tuned to satellite radio and was spinning the dial when, without realizing it, he found himself listening to a good-ol'-boy preacher talking about how gambling was wrecking lives, and about how Jesus came to fill the emptiness in every man, but how men try to fill it with every other kind of silly nonsense.

He had to wonder how that preacher—jawin' through his radio while he crossed the desert in the middle of southwestern nowhere—could understand a hard case like him. It wouldn't have surprised him if the preacher-man had called him by name. His eyes welled with water till he couldn't see and he had to pull over to avoid the horns that blared at him when he veered over the line. Baby thundered to a stop with half the desert pluming up around him, and there he sat behind the wheel of his truck, letting go. The man said give it all to *Jesus*. He cranked the door open and practically fell out.

He was crawling up off his hands and knees when he looked up and saw stars—billions of them. He walked out into the desert and stood beneath a canopy of constellations brighter than anything he'd ever seen. At that moment, he saw something bigger than himself—he saw *God*. He stood lost in the expanse of God's universe and realized he was nothing—a tiny little dot, a speck, as insignificant as dust—and his problems melted away. He fell to his knees, raised his hands, turned his face toward heaven, and just plain bawled his eyes out.

It may not have been a hellfire-preachin' tent revival meeting— *glory hallelujah!*—but it *was* a conversion. By the time he opened his eyes, a new light had begun to dawn. He felt rejuvenated, totally new. He pulled himself up and used his hat to dust off. A faint ribbon of sunrise was breaking on the mountains to the east, just a soft glow on the purple horizon. But the warmth he felt wasn't from the sun, it was from the illumination of his soul. He had no right to feel so good, not after being the hell-raiser he'd always been. He was light-headed. He felt drunk, but he was sober as a stone. The feeling was better than any high he'd ever known. He turned toward the truck practically dancing, kicking up the dust. He threw his hands in the air and shouted, "Praise the Lord! Praise the Lord!" without even knowing what it meant.

'Course he still owed a hundred large, and his bookie meant to get it. And he was praying, though it was more like talking to God because he never heard about closing your eyes or getting on your knees or asking in Jesus' name or anything like that. But God heard him anyway—and answered. Wasn't a month or two later he read about how the government tried to shut his bookie down and how the fool fought back and ended up getting himself shot dead—all debts cancelled.

"Naw, drivin' truck is a boring job. No story to tell." Hank raised a finger, pointing, "We're getting off here." He leaned back and tipped the bill of his cap to wipe his brow, but lifting his elbow woke Killer. The dog raised his head, his beady eyes popping from his whiskered face. He raised himself and stretched and jumped down from Hank's lap, trotting to the back of the cab where he hopped up on the bed with Angela. She pulled him in and snuggled him under her chin, her full lips curling into a dimpled smile.

To this world, she was asleep, but not in the realm that exists between this world and the next. There she visited with an angel, a glowing ball of white light who promised her pain would soon be over, but first there was something she had to do, something about the little dog and her father. She smiled as Killer began licking her face.

Peter saw the sign the instant it swept by the window. He held his stomach as they cut over to the exit, Hank hanging onto the wheel with one hand and engaging the engine brakes with the other. *Pop, pop, pop, pop, pop.* They thundered down the ramp and pulled into a Kwikfill diesel stop, sidling up alongside a half-dozen other tractor trailers parked in long parallel lines with their engines idling.

Hank pulled his hat from his head, slid his gloved fingers though his hair, and replaced the cap. "Don't get me wrong, I ain't doin' this for money, but you're gonna have to cough up for fuel. I can't afford to haul you around on my ticket, not at today's fuel prices. You're lucky I been keeping Baby plated and insured. But I do that just so me and Killer can take a spin if we get bored. So, here's what we do. You you go pay for the diesel, and then we'll get you situated below."

Peter's skin was the color of a honeydew melon. "B...b...but what about Angela?"

"Has she got an implant?"

"No."

"She can stay back there on the mattress if she wants, or she can ride up front with me. She can't be scanned for ID."

IT WAS black as ink. Even with his eyes fully dilated, Peter couldn't see a thing. He tried lifting the lid, but it wouldn't budge. He wanted to pound and scream, *Let me out! Let me out!* and prayed God would give him strength to withstand the torment. He was in a long narrow box, trying to rein in his fear, tears rolling down his cheeks. He couldn't make a sound. They were out there looking for him. His fingers pushed the top and felt the sides, exploring every crack and crevice within reach. He and Deanne were fond of watching old movies because, rather than violence and sex, they employed good acting and engaging stories to entertain, but there was one show he wished he could get out of his head—a late-night rerun of *The Twilight Zone.*

A convict paid a prison mortician to help him escape. He was to hide in the morgue and, when no one was around, crawl into a casket already occupied by a corpse. The mortician would come back later to have the coffin carried out and buried. Then, in the middle of the night, he would exhume the grave and let the prisoner out.

The suspense builds as the convict lies in the casket waiting for his release. It's pitch black and so quiet he can hear the beating of his own heart. Hours pass and he starts to panic, wondering why the mortician is taking so long. Finally, in desperation, he lights a match and finds the lifeless body he's sharing the coffin with—is none other than the mortician himself!

*I'm going to die...*Peter wanted to push the lid off that *coffin*. *Please, God, let me out.* He bit his lip. He could see the headlines, *"Philanthropist Peter Found Putrefied In Peterbilt."* He held back a laugh and squelched the urge to upchuck. Maybe the box had a false bottom. Maybe he was about to be ejected into the street where he would roll along the pavement, just another lump of road kill. He smiled, but it quickly faded. It was hot—*blazing hot*—and he was sweating like a pig. The cloth bag pressed against his back itched. He would have taken it off but he didn't want Hank knowing about it in case he needed to disappear and become someone else.

It was better when the truck was moving. He liked feeling the hum of the tires, but now they were stopped dead, moving only a few feet at a time. Hank said they'd have to wait at the toll booth until the truck was inspected. He wished they would get rolling. Air seemed to find its way into the compartment when they were on the road, but not when they were sitting still. He felt the heat rising off the pavement. *Get this thing moving!* Fresh air made him less prone to vomit. He was praying—*nonstop*—for the courage and strength to endure. He tightened every muscle in his body, squeezing his fists until he was shaking. *Gurrrrrrrrrr. Why do you think I made my elevator so big when I was the only one using it? No, Mother, no, please don't put me in the closet! I'll leave your clothes alone, I promise, pleeease, I'll die in there!*

No! He wasn't going to die. *No, no, no, no, no.* If Angela could stay alive—so could he. They both had to fight. They would see Deanne; they would be together as a family one more time. After that, come what may, but not until. He ground his teeth. *Grrrrrrrrrrr. Fight it.* He couldn't die without seeing Deanne again. He had to make amends. He couldn't let a brusque remark made rushing out the door be the last thing she had to remember him by. He had to get Angela home. The trucker couldn't do it. He didn't even know where they lived. Hank promised to let him out at a rest stop twenty miles inside the Pennsylvania border. Twenty miles, that's how far he said they had to go. *Twenty miles to freedom.* But before that, they had to get through the inspection. *Please, God, shouldn't we be there by now?*

He inhaled and exhaled, taking purposeful breaths to calm his nerves. *Mother, pleeese, not the closet, pleeese!* At least Hank had thought to roll out a foam mattress and had given him a pillow to ease the discomfort. He sipped in another long drawn-out breath. *Have I not commanded you be strong and courageous? Do not be terrified, do not be discouraged, for the Lord your God will go with you wherever you go.*

He felt the brakes hiss and the truck coming to another stop. His heart began to race, *pitter, pitter, pitter, pitter, pitter.* It was calling his name, *Peter, Peter, Peter, Peter, Peter.* They were sure to hear it. He heard the cab door open and the truck rock as Hank stepped down. He heard voices but they were muffled. It was hard to understand what was being said. He heard the words, "Had my contract cancelled so we're ridin' empty. Log book's up to date. What else you need?" His heart was pounding, beads of perspiration rolling off his forehead.

He felt more than heard the doors to the back of the trailer being opened. Someone was walking through the vault. He felt the vibration of a fist pounding the metal walls, searching for hidden compartments. A foot stomped on the floor. He could feel the echo of the empty tin room. Someone with a metal rod began tapping the bottom of the rig, sending shock waves rippling through his back. He heard the steel door open again. "She's my granddaughter. Try not to wake her, she's been carsick." Peter said a prayer for protection. His heart continued to pound. He felt someone crawling right above him as they searched the compartment and heard Killer growl and then start barking, *yip, yip, yip, yip, yip.*

"You bite me, dog, you'll feel my baton!"

The man completed his search quickly and scrambled to get out. Finally the door closed, the engine revved, and the truck lurched forward. Peter waited until it seemed they'd gone another mile before letting out the breath he'd been holding—just in case.

CELESTIAL VANTAGE

How big is God? Is there a yardstick by which man can measure the infinite? Upon what scale can be weighed that which contains the sum total of everything, and more?

Better to ask: How small is man?

Imagine: Man inhabits planet earth. Above the firmament, whirling through the black soup of space, are billions of stars woven into the galactic system that comprises man's universe. Compared to the cosmos, man is a speck.

Oh greatly beloved, think! You know that all matter in the universe is composed of atoms. If you could stand on the nucleus of an atom, you would look up and see billions of protons, neutrons and electrons whirling about, a universe of its own not unlike that which surrounds your planet; yet these finite particles combine to form the clumps of mass which become all that is known and experienced by man—from kernel of sand to brightest star, including the flesh and bone of man himself.

Speaking atomically then, it is possible that man's solar system is but a molecule in the heel of God's shoe!

SIXTEEN

"Hold fast to the Bible as the sheet anchor of your liberties; write its precepts in your hearts, and practice them in your lives."
—*Ulysses S. Grant, 1822-1885, 18th President of the United States*

FREEDOM WHISTLED in the wheels of the southbound semi breezing down interstate 79 as it faded into the waning of the day. The late afternoon sky looked like the peel of an orange. Peter tried to imagine a lemon sorbet atop a leafy salad of rolling hills. The thought of icy sherbet was a pleasant diversion. He couldn't remember the last time he'd seen green hills or blue sky. The planet was overheating. Environmentalists called it global warming. Peter didn't. What he saw was a correlation between changes in the atmosphere and men turning their backs on God. God had warned the children of Israel that as long as they followed His precepts He would bring them sun and rain and bountiful harvest. But if they turned away... Considering the future of the planet—Peter stroked Angela's cheek—leaving the earth might not be such a bad thing.

He had survived the ordeal...*Thank You, Lord.* Hank's strong hands—the kind of hands Peter wanted—had pulled him from the coffin into the bright light of day. But as he stood there sweating and shaking, leaning against the back of the seat trying to catch his breath, his one thought was to grab Angela and hold her and *hold her* and *hold her*—and *never* let go. There might not be a tomorrow. The soft beating of her heart against his chest soothed him like a pacifier. Now as he sat in his comfy co-pilot's chair, he kissed the crown of her head.

112

"I love you," he said, closing his eyes. If only Deanne were there—the three of them locked in a group hug—all the world would be right.

The miniature dog sat beside them, his bright eyes pleading. He would nuzzle Angela's hand encouraging her to continue petting his head whenever she grew weary. "*Ah, ah ha, he-he-hee*," she giggled as the dog licked her fingers. Peter smiled. Childish laughter—especially the laughter of *his* child—was the most beautiful sound on earth.

Peter looked up. The traffic was light, the road ahead clear. They were on a direct route to Pittsburgh, closing the distance with each passing mile, soon to be home together as a family. He glanced over at the driver. The man's leather gloves matched his face. His jaw churned. "I kind of lost track. Where are we?"

Hank leaned in and covered the screen of his GPS with his hand to reduce the glare. He punched in a mile marker and sat back. "Pittsburgh's still another hundred and twenty miles. Be there in about two hours."

"The marvels of technology."

Hank pursed his lips and nodded.

Peter took another deep breath and let it go just to remind himself how good it felt to be unconfined. His head fell back, bouncing off the cushion as he slid his hand into his coat to retrieve his palm computer. "Speaking of which I should probably check my e-mail."

The tiny optical disc was in the drive. Careless of him to leave it there. If they caught him with that disc, he was going to jail, but he'd probably go to jail anyway. His crime was insurrection; he wasn't worried about the murder. He'd invented the man he was accused of killing and could prove it. When the police weren't able to produce a body, the charges would be dropped, but he couldn't let them get their hands on the disc. He laid his cheek against Angela's head and stared out the window.

The parade of clouds and sun and bovine and bird and tree and farm swept by in nonstop succession. Life was passing by. He needed to drink it in. If things turned sour he might not see the light of day for many years to come.

He held the two-inch disc to the light. A myriad of rainbow

colors danced off its surface. So much fuss over something so small. He'd have to destroy it, snap it in half, break it and throw away the pieces before letting it fall into their hands. That, of course, would be a last resort. The accumulation of the data represented more than a decade of his life. The disc contained several reputable unaltered versions of the Bible, translated into more than a dozen languages, with concordances, maps, notes and study guides, as well as the complete text in Hebrew and Greek. Far as he knew, it was the single most comprehensive database of Christian Scripture, doctrine, history, and reference material in existence. One file alone contained a directory of sixteen-hundred illegal home churches, the names of group leaders, locations, and links to available teaching resources. All of it was stored on that tiny disc. The data had to be protected at all costs.

He hadn't set out to accumulate such a vast resource, nor was it his goal to become a Templar of Holy Writ. He was a computer geek, fascinated by the properties of light. The demand for greater memory capacity had spawned the development of optical storage devices, just as the need for increased speed and bandwidth had led to mass implementation of fiber-optics. His claim to fame was in patenting an algorithm that allowed information to be managed at the speed of light. The loop was complete. Data could now be stored, transmitted *and* processed, using photons rather than electrons.

Almost by happenstance he'd created what was to become known as the highly specialized field of optical computing. But to test his hypothesis required an enormous amount of data. Guttenberg had used the Bible to test his printing press; Peter was determined to do the same. So while they were still available, he'd collected every on-line Bible, workbook, study guide and commentary he could access. He could never have guessed how that information would end up being used.

The world was changing. Doctrines of the faith that for centuries had withstood attack from the outside were disintegrating from within. The first ordained homosexual priest in the Anglican Church truly believed he was liberating God's people from the shackles of narrow-minded bigotry—*How can a God of love condemn the love of anyone?*—

as did the nineteen Catholic priests in Quebec who wrote a letter to a Montreal newspaper criticizing their church's stand on homosexuality. It was a debate close to Peter's heart because, while he had never *known* a man in the biblical sense, the opportunity had presented itself often enough. He'd fought the battle and won, and God had blessed him with Deanne, but he understood the complexities of the issue and the struggle it represented for so many men. The letter read: "The Catholic Church has failed to recognize that human nature evolves." *Human nature evolves?* Human nature didn't evolve. There was nothing new under the sun. Men were guilty of committing the same old sins over and over since time began.

But the justification that made wrong seem right came easy for those who favored change. Biblical writings might underscore kingdom principles in a general sense, they argued, but specific dogmas had to be taken in context with the times. New Bibles were released, Bibles that seemed uncomfortable with masculine pronouns to the point of exchanging them for those that were gender neutral. They promised equality and fairness in the treatment of women but served to lessen the reliance on scriptural authority. Flames of debate were fanned and quickly quenched. No sooner was that fire extinguished than another new Bible found its way to market: *God's New Law*, a text proclaiming religion without doctrine. The new revelation—writings that stemmed from a prophecy given in the year 2000—forgave homosexuality and fornication, adding four new books to the old King James. Scriptural authority was heading the way of the dinosaur.

Times change, they argued. They espoused the view that laws governing primitive societies weren't designed for enlightened men. The Apostles wrote from a perspective commensurate with their own culture. Their interpretation of Christ's words were jaded by their limited view of the world. John quoted Jesus as saying, "I Am the Way, the Truth, and the Life, no man comes to the Father but by Me," but Jesus, like Moses, was sent to minister to the people of His day, wasn't He? Mohammed came with further revelation. All attempts to reach God were valid; all religions, equal. The manifold path to God was not to be obstructed by the self-serving bigotry of the narrow-minded few, and on, and on, and on.

Peter stared out the window at the rolling hills and grassy windswept plains, the sun-wrapped clouds festooned with gold-laced edges, and trees shimmering with leaves that danced on currents of air. He thought of the art inspired by God's creation, the ancient paintings of Jesus revealing God's love, the inspired music of Handel's "Messiah," the great educational institutions of Harvard and Yale dedicated to the glory of God, and he wondered where the world had gone wrong. How had they come to the place where cities inhabited by man, once themselves inspired creations, had become like Sodom of ancient times, where fulfillment was found in realizing ever lower forms of sexual gratification and where enlightenment meant a denial of truth.

In a country founded on freedom of speech and assembly, and the freedom to worship God without interference from the state, preaching Jesus had become a crime. Any ideology that held one view as supreme over others was a detriment to world peace. Hadn't virtually every war been fought in the name of religion? The new age of enlightenment was no place for prejudice and bigotry.

Churches refusing to bow to the dictates of a godless government lost their tax exemptions. Taxes were the people's money—all the people—and any organization that refused to be all-inclusive was not to be given special consideration. Moreover, any institution that disparaged one group or another—whether they be homosexuals or atheists or Buddhists or bullfrogs—were to be taxed double. Ministries that operated on shoestring budgets were forced to close their doors. And with their pastors incarcerated for preaching the Gospel, churches holding fast to the Word of God were driven underground where, without the high overhead of church buildings to maintain, they didn't need tax exemptions. The believers met the way Christ's disciples did—in homes—and the church thrived. Soon networks were formed, Bible studies were posted on websites, and blogs used to communicate.

Peter stared at the disc in his hand. He'd seen dark clouds on the horizon buffeted by the winds of change. He'd begun gathering the names and addresses of virtual churches all across the United States— churches that were now illegal. Should the government get their hands on his database, hundreds, perhaps thousands, would be arrested or held in detention centers indefinitely. He slipped the tiny disc into his pocket, where he'd be able to destroy it if he had to.

Angela and the little dog known as "Killer" drifted off to sleep. Peter smoothed his daughter's hair. The silky fibers were warm in the sunlight from the window. She had little strength to stay awake. Her eyes remained closed, opening only for scant moments. They would soon close forever—*but not for a few more hours. Please God, not until we get home.* She may never see the wonders of God's creation: the shining monolithic face of Half Dome, Sequoias big enough to drive a car through, blazing sunsets over the Grand Canyon, and the thundering mist of Niagara Falls—for her, time was running out. But she would see heaven and all its glory, the home of God, with streets of gold and gates of pearl and every precious stone sparkling with unquenchable light, where a river flowed from the throne of God to nourish the Tree of Life, and the leaves of the trees were for the healing of the nations and...and it had to make the wonders of earth pale by comparison.

He connected to the wireless network to retrieve his e-mail. Dozens of messages scrolled down the screen. Most were business-related— monthly reports, orders shipped, and software changes made—but there was a notable decrease in the number of personal messages he received. There were several from people he knew well who promised to stand with him. They questioned the accounts they'd read in the papers. They deserved a response, but telling them the truth would be incriminating and denying his complicity would be lying. Where did that leave him? Perhaps it was best to ignore them for the moment. But not this one, this one was from Deanne. He clicked to open it.

Peter,

I can't imagine what you're going through. I worry and fret, which I know is wrong, and I have to continually remind myself that you foresaw this day coming and are simply carrying out your plan. I just wish you'd listened to me and stayed home, but I also thank God you were so thorough in your preparation. It helps me believe you're okay. I've tried to put myself in your shoes. It must be strange looking over your shoulder to see if you're being followed, averting your eyes to avoid recognition. I was looking at a map trying to figure out where you are when I suddenly realized, I already know—you're in God's hands, and that's the best place you can be.

I am well. Please don't worry about me. It's lonely here. I miss Angela's giggles and the silly fun we share when we're together, but as much as I hate to say it, I have to tell you not to come home. It isn't safe. Don't even try to call. I'm sure our lines are tapped, and I refuse to answer the phone anyway, which you know if you've already tried.

I've been avoiding the media. Did I tell you they climbed our wall? They were standing right on our porch ringing the bell but I didn't answer the door. Now they're camped out on our lawn. There's no way you'll get past them. Besides, the house is being watched. There's a car parked down the street and in certain light I can see a man sitting in it. He's been there practically all day, so don't come home, it's too risky.

Deanne

Deanne??? No endearment? No, *all my love*, just...Deanne?

She was still hurt. But she had a right to be. He should have stayed. The trip to Toronto had profited nothing and now Angela was being forced to run around with him when she could be home in her own bed. It was bound to happen. He snapped the palm computer shut and let out a breathy sigh, staring out the window into the distance, his face void of expression.

Hank glanced over. "Bad news?"

"Nothing more than I expected. My wife says I shouldn't come home. They're watching our house. *Shoot*, now I don't know what to do. I need to get Angela home. I wish there was some way of sneaking her inside without being seen. If I'm going on the run, I can't take her with me." Peter looked at his daughter. The fibers of her wig shone brightly in the sun. He readjusted his arms making her more comfortable. "I've got to figure something out, even if it means getting caught. My child's health is more important than my freedom. She deserves..." His bottom lip quivered, his eyes glistening like marbles in the rain. He pulled Angela in, snuggling her up close.

Angela coughed, her shoulders heaving as she started to vomit, waking from her stupor. Peter cupped his hand under her mouth, but it quickly overflowed. *God, no! Not now—You can't, please. You've got to get us home.*

Killer jumped down and hopped into Hank's lap. Hank raised his eyebrows. "Don't worry about it, just lean her forward. We'll wash the mats later."

Angela's frail body shook as she continued to heave. Peter emptied his hand and wiped it off. He cradled her in his arms and massaged her back until the spasm passed. She opened her eyes, but her lids were heavy and weighed down. "Daddy, are we almost there? Will I see Mommy? The angel said...*ohhh*, Daddy, it hurts."

"I know, darling. I know." Turning to Hank he shrugged, slowly shaking his head. "Children's Hospital in Toronto refused to extend her pain treatment. They said it was time to let her go—but I can't. I promised to get her to her mother, but she's in so much pain...I...I... just don't know."

Hank brought his hand up and rubbed the back of his sun-reddened neck. "Okay, you can't go home and she needs a doctor, or at least she needs medication. I know a doctor in Beckley, a Christian, who might be able to help. It's about four hours south of Pittsburgh, but they won't be looking for you there, and it'll give us a place to lay low till we can figure out what to do."

SEVENTEEN

"We have this day restored the Sovereign to Whom all men ought to be obedient. He reigns in Heaven and from the rising to the setting of the sun, let His Kingdom come."
—*Samuel Adams, 1722-1803, Founding Father and signer of the Declaration of Independence*

THE PATROL unit approached so slowly you could hear gravel crunching under the tires. Two uniformed guards, commissioned by the Hilltop Homeowner's Association to keep undesirables off the streets and out of the upper echelon homes, had been apprised of the unmarked rental car. The Homeland Security operative was doing surveillance, and while the Dufoe residence was on their regularly scheduled route, they'd been cautioned not to interfere. But that didn't mean they couldn't be friendly.

The sun burning through the cloudy haze brought the humidity inside Bob's rented vehicle to pressure cooker levels. He had his coat off, his collar open, and his sleeves rolled back, and still his shirt was wet under the arms. He couldn't start the engine and turn on the air conditioner without the car's daytime lights flickering on, giving him away. So he hunkered down in the miserable heat trying to stay low and out of sight, suffering for the cause.

He was listening to all-news radio trying to pick up coverage of the Dufoe story. There was nothing new, but he couldn't say whether no news was good news...or bad news. He kept the volume low to keep anyone from noticing the car. *"Meteorologists are forecasting another turbulent season with increased tornados throughout the Midwest, flash flooding in the drought-stricken lowlands, and hurricanes along the southeastern seaboard...Another pandemic could be in the making. Doctors at the Center for Disease Control are concerned about the number of rodents found dead with this new, as yet unidentified, strain...Our city reports a five percent increase in murders over the same period last year...a record number of violent crimes has also been reported..."*

The world was coming apart at the seams. Bob had a theory. Global warming was wreaking havoc on national weather patterns and that, combined with the number of new diseases continually being introduced, was driving people mad, which accounted for the increase in crime. His pocket communicator beeped. He reached for it, saw the message icon flashing, and clicked on "receive." Another e-mail from Deanne. The boys in Toronto were making him proud. Anticipation had him scanning faster than he could read.

I have to continually remind myself that you foresaw this day coming and are simply carrying out your plan.

Bob's eyebrows furrowed. *What plan?* Was Peter's escape premeditated? How would he know they were coming? Or was there some other sinister plot in the making, an uprising of the underground—violence in the streets? They already had radical Muslims blowing up buildings, but Christ's church, for the most part, had remained passive. What if fundamentalist Muslims conspired with fundamentalist Christians to declare war on the state? Strange bedfellows. They would each believe they'd made a pact with the devil, but it *had* happened before. Communism and democracy had joined forces to defeat the Nazis.

Bob saw the car coming up on his bumper. A blazing white elephant with a full lightbar package and stripes painted down the side, rental cops imitating Pittsburgh PD. He didn't want company right now. The hair prickled on the back of his neck. His feelings were private. He wanted to be left alone to commiserate with himself.

...It's lonely here. I miss Angela's giggles and the silly fun we share when we're together...

He looked up, swallowing the lump in his throat, his eyes burning as he stared at the house. She was in there and he sat out here, pining away in the past, while she lived in the present with someone else. Someone else? *Nuts!* Another man of caliber he could understand, someone with a little backbone, but Peter? She had to be in it for the money.

He remembered a photo someone once e-mailed him. It was a picture of some hunchbacked old geezer leaning on two scantily clad, drop-dead gorgeous girls. The old miser had a wry grin on his face and a twinkle in his eye. The photo caption read: "How you know a man is rich."

Bob's gaze roamed the grounds: the rainbow-flowered gardens, the flagstone walks, the oak doors, the palatial estate. Money covered a lot of inadequacy. She put up a good front, but no one was *that* sweet. The man was nothing—*a big fat zero.*

He had his back to the bricks with his foot raised and propped against the wall. His muscle shirt stretched around his chest, emphasizing his pecs, his biceps bulging like rocks in a sock. He fished in his pocket for change. The phone clinked with the sound of the coins dropping. The dial tone was interrupted by a metallic voice asking him for the number. He heard the phone ring once, then twice, and then she answered.

"Hello?"

"Hey, Deanne, I got tickets to the Steelers game tonight. How 'bout I pick you up in, say, fifteen? We'll do hotdogs and popcorn...great seats."

"Bob? No. What? No. I mean I'd love to, but I can't."

"Why?"

"Sorry, but you caught me on my way out the door. I already have plans."

"What plans?"

I'm going to the Friday night Bible study. I promised to show the new guy Peter around. He doesn't know anyone. I wanna help him get acquainted"

"Peter? The dweeb in tight pants? You can't be serious. Come on, you go to the study every week. This is a Steelers game—Steelers butting heads with the Rams. Go with me."

"I can't Bob. I made a commitment. Why don't you come with us? Peter could use a friend."

"Right, we'll be good buddies. Say fella, how about I give you a rubdown or maybe a little squeeze?"

"Bob!"

"Look, Deanne, the guy's a fruitcake. You're making a fool of yourself. Keep it up and people will start thinking you swing both ways. Guilt by association and all that."

"Bob, sometimes you're a real jerk. I'm hanging up now before I say something I'll regret. Good-bye."

Bob heard the click and the dead air that followed. He cradled the receiver, his jaw clenched. The tickets were in his hand, he couldn't let them go to waste. He dug in his pocket for another coin. Two could play the game as well as one. Deanne wanted to spend time with someone else, so could he. There were plenty of fish in the sea. He picked up the phone and dialed.

Bob scanned the e-mail a second time.

I'm being watched. There's a car parked down the street and in certain light I can see a man sitting in it.

Oh for the love of...*she knows. How the heck did she see me from over there?* He was parked half a block away and slumped down in his seat most of the day. She must have binoculars.

There was a tap at his window. He looked up. A rent-a-cop in a blue uniform was standing there holding coffee and a little bag which he assumed held a donut. *A donut? Where do they get these guys?*

Bob reached for the handle and cranked the window down.

"Evening, sir. My partner and I were passing by and thought you might enjoy a little hot sludge." He started to hand the bag through the window, but stepped back when he saw the look on Bob's face.

"Son of a...you know what you've done? You've just blown my cover. Why not just shout it from the roof? Get that cruiser out of here. Do it now! This is supposed to be a stakeout. What do you use for brains, toilet paper? Man, oh man, I don't freakin' believe you. What's your name? You can bet this is going in my report!"

EIGHTEEN

"All who profess Christianity believe in a Savior, and that by and through Him we must be saved."
—*Andrew Jackson, 1767-1845, 7th President of the United States*

THE SEMI snaked over hill and vale bypassing the western slopes of the Allegheny Mountains, which rose to the east, spinning up dust from the shoulder of the road and sucking it up like a vacuum in their wake. The truck whooshed down the highway with the sound of wind rushing through a tunnel, its wheels thundering across a bridge eight-hundred and seventy-six feet above the New River. They couldn't see the water channeling its way through the Appalachian undergrowth below; it was too dark.

The sun dipping behind the western horizon spread purple shadows across West Virginia. In the far-off distance, lights from the town of Beckley twinkled like a billion stars on the ground—but clouds overhead were rolling in, hiding the stars above. The truck raked and rattled and rumbled and roared.

Angela lay in Peter's arms, faint as a wilting rose. She shivered as though cold, but beads of sweat dotted the edge of her wig. Peter wiped away the moisture and leaned in to kiss her forehead. She hadn't spoken in hours, lying motionless like she was slipping into a coma— or *life hereafter. Please, God, no. Just a little longer. If You don't want to heal her, at least let me get her home; that's all I ask, and maybe that You help me get this disc into safe hands, but that's all. Please, You can do what you want with me after that.* But if God was listening, if wasn't evident in Angela's recovery or in the direction of the truck. They were four hours south of Pittsburgh and moving farther away.

The Chihuahua stood on Hank's lap, his front paws pressed against the window. His mouth was open, his tongue hanging out, his little head snapping back and forth with the passing traffic like a spectator watching the volley of a tennis ball. Hank's leather gloves were wrapped around the steering wheel, his baseball cap squared on his head. His eyes were fixed on the road. He reached down to snap on the lights but the unexpected move frightened the dog, causing it to bolt. Killer ducked under Hank's elbow and scrambled back to Peter's side where he stood licking Angela's hand. But she didn't respond.

"This is the tricky part," Hank said.

"How's that?"

"Your daughter. She needs medical attention. That's why we're here, but I got to be frank, it's getting late. The doctor I told you about has a practice in town, but I doubt he'll be at his office, not at this hour, and I don't know where he lives. Heck, I only met him once, and it was a long time ago."

"Beg pardon?"

Hank grunted and cleared his throat. The sky, buzzing with electrical current, smelled of rain. "I used to stop here a lot when I was driving long haul, back when Biker Jack was customizing Babe. I was having back problems and man, let me tell you, one thing you don't need when you're driving is a bad back. Got the doc's name from a phone book."

"But you said he was a Christian. How..."

"There was a plaque on the wall in his office: 'With His stripes we are healed.' Not just anyone has a plaque like that. Sure enough, before I left we prayed and I never felt better in my life. He gave me his card but I lost it. Heck, I can't say for sure he's even still in business."

Peter nestled Angela protectively. The red taillights of passing cars streamed like fireworks as oncoming traffic snapped on their headlights, preparing for the coming night. The trees along the side of the road whipped in the wind. He glanced over at Hank, his brows raised with questions. "You mean you drove us all the way out here without even knowing if you can *find* this guy?"

"Seems to me we didn't have a choice. You couldn't take your little girl home, and she needs help. If there was a doctor in Pittsburgh you could trust, you would have said so. Besides, they'll be looking for you there. At least down here, we can hole up until we figure out what to do."

Peter nodded, but his lips flattened into a line, white and tense. He'd been toying with the idea of trying to get Deanne to join them down there, which would be a miracle in itself. Then maybe they could lay low until Angela passed on—hopefully under the care of the doctor—and figure out what to do from there. He'd have to get someone to drive her, but any hope of that required having an address. They'd *better* be able to find the doctor. Otherwise, they'd just wasted four hours driving south, and it would be another four hours going back. Angela might not have that long. He angled his daughter up so he could reach into his pocket and remove the disc. The dog jumped down, hopping up into Hank's lap again, changing places every time someone disturbed his rest.

Peter retrieved the disc, shaking his head. The man beside him was rooted in confidence, immovable as an oak. Lightning could smash the ground and he wouldn't flinch. Men like that baffled Peter—men like Bill and a few others he'd known—men with a strength that bordered on lunacy. The idea of dropping in on a doctor you hadn't seen in years was unthinkable; driving four hours without knowing if the man was still in business was absolutely insane. What happened to the script, the plan, everything he'd worked out in advance? His safety net didn't include dropping out of helicopters or touring cross country in a eighteen-wheeler.

He poked around his seat and found his handheld computer. Keeping Angela as still as possible, he brought the disc up and slipped it into the drive. "I might be able to help," he said. "Maybe he's part of a home fellowship. What's his name?"

"Dr. Philips."

"You catch a first name?"

"Adrian. Adrian Philips. I'm sure that's what he said. I remember thinking it was a funny name for a man."

Funny? Funny as in "feminine?" At least his mother had named him Peter. It was a man's name. *Peter—Peterbilt—the mighty truck.* He shifted his eyes to Hank but held his thoughts. He pressed the button to turn on his computer. It was darker in the cab than outside, making it hard to see, but he was practiced at manipulating the keys, though his fingers trembled with anticipation. He got an instant hit. The green luminous display glowed with information. Adrian Philips—leader of a cell group in Beckley, West Virginia. *Good.* He brought his hand to his mouth biting a nail. Who was this Dr. Philips? It wasn't like Hank could vouch for him. "I got your man right here. He lives on Morning Star Lane; he's the leader of a study group."

"You get that from that little box of yours?" Hank said, keeping his eyes on the road.

Hank was avoiding eye contact—*again*. There had been little since they shook hands back at the house. Maybe it was the costume, the silly mustache, the buck teeth. *Maybe.* Peter chose to let it go. "It's a prototype," he said. "Handheld digital units have been on the market for decades, but this is the first optical processor we've been able to miniaturize. The amount of information we're able to download, store and retrieve is phenomenal."

Peter slipped the disc out and held it up. "But this—this is what they're after. I started cataloging and indexing the home church movement years ago. Paid a research firm to collect most of the data back when people weren't afraid to give it out, and I've been building on it ever since. I have a record of almost every Bible-believing group in America and Canada, and even a few in Mexico and Europe, names and locations along with a huge resource of Bibles and reference material. It's one of a kind. Churches don't release this kind of information anymore."

"I knew it had to be something like that." Hank tightened his grip on the wheel. "Think I'm in there?"

"You and hundreds of thousands of others. You come up six or seven times as part of study groups in different states. One even lists you as a source for Bibles. Sorry, but I had to check. I had to know who I was dealing with. Can't be too careful these days." He slipped the disc back into his pocket.

"Ain't it the truth," Hank said. He glanced over at Angela. "How's she doin'? She don't look so good. If we're going to the doctor's house, we'll have to figure something out. You can't park an eighteen-wheeler on a residential street. Let's plug the address into my GPS and see if we can find a nearby shopping mall where I can park this baby. We may have to do some walking, but I'll get as close as I can."

Angela stirred. Her face was white, like the color of her life had been siphoned away. She had heaved until her stomach was empty, expelling food she needed for nourishment, some of which still stained Peter's shirt. She shivered. Her eyes opened, half-lidded, and when she spoke, her gums and teeth revealed traces of blood. "Daddy, it hurts."

"I know it does, sweetheart, I know." He caressed the side of her face with his fingers. As much as her coma-like sleep was near death, he was almost sorry she'd awakened. In sleep there was peace, but every waking moment brought pain. "Try to hang in a little longer. We're taking you to a doctor now."

NINETEEN

"No Christian and civilized community can afford to show a happy-go-lucky lack of concern for the youth of today; for, if so, the community will have to pay a terrible penalty of financial burden and social degradation in the tomorrow."
—*Theodore Roosevelt, 1858-1919, 26ᵗʰ President of the United States*

THE TRUCK rolled through the parking lot of a strip mall with its engine rumbling and its running lights trimming it like a Christmas tree. Hank's GPS said they were only a quarter-mile from the street where the doctor lived. Young people hung around in clusters, milling about their cars, the red tips of their cigarettes glowing in the dark. Most of the overhead lights had been either shot out or broken with rocks. They rolled past a Bob Evans restaurant spray-painted with graffiti. The McDonalds ahead was dark, closed after sundown. Hank slowed to a stop and released the hydraulics with a wheeze and a smell that reminded Peter of a bus. The engine rumbled as they sat idling. Hank tipped his baseball cap back on his head and leaned in to cut the throttle and click off the ignition. The cessation of the rumbling left Peter feeling numb in the seat of his pants.

"Them kids better not come out here, not if they know what's good for 'em. I seen more than one trailer decorated in fluorescent paint, but not Babe." He turned, looking over his shoulder. His dog was behind him on the bed. "I'm gonna leave Killer here to guard things."

"Killer?"

"Sure, why not? You know he's small, but they don't. The racket he makes puts the fear of God in most. Had you running from my house, didn't it?" Hank peeled off his leather gloves, tossing them on the dash. He took hold of the handle and winged his door open. "Well don't just sit there, get yourself out. That little girl needs to see a doctor." Hank was on the ground in two quick steps. "Come on, we got to lock up and go. We don't want Security telling us we can't park here."

Peter felt his pocket and removed the disc, tapping it on his finger. They were heading into the unknown. He took a piece of paper from a pad by the console and wrapped it like an envelope around the disc. Setting Angela on the seat, he turned and leaned toward the back of the cab, slipping his hand into the storage compartment under the bed. He got his fingers under the lip of the crawlspace, lifting just enough to toss the paper-wrapped disc inside and let go. Killer was licking his hand like he was hiding a bone. He patted the dog's head. "You're in charge. It's up to you now."

He swung back around, reaching for the door handle. The metal resting on dry hinges was heavy against his hand but the door swung open. He turned to pick up Angela.

Hank hustled around the nose of the truck to the passenger side and stood with his hands on his hips. "Come on, boy, get a move on," and then, sensing Peter's uncertainty, placed a heavy boot on the running board and climbed up. He reached out, taking Angela, and stepped down again.

Peter rolled toward the seat and eased himself back, sliding off the cushions. He reeled around and jumped down, but landed awkwardly, stumbling forward to catch his balance.

Hank shook his head grinning, his broad bent nose flattening against his face. "Man, you are one piece of work. I got an appreciation for the fact that you've made billions, but I wouldn't trade places with you for any of it."

"Beg pardon?"

Hank stood there shaking his head. "Why in the name of heaven God hooked me up with you is beyond me. It just ain't right. I'm one of those narrow-minded folk who think God made Adam and *Eve*, not

Adam and *Steve*."

"I'm not g..g..gay…" Peter stammered, his face flushing red.

"See, I been thinkin' and it all makes sense. Your little girl's adopted, which is the way you people do it, right? And that partner of yours, Deanne, no one ever sees her. De-anne, 'de man.' I get it. Now, I won't ever agree with you, but if you want to talk about it…"

"Deanne's not a *man!* She's a *woman!* She's my wife!" Water started to rim Peter's eyes.

"Oh, for crying out loud, cut it out! Here." Hank handed Angela back to Peter.

Peter wiped his cheek on his sleeve.

"What's with the crybaby?"
"Somebody snapped him with a towel."
"You take him. I don't want him on my team."
"No way!"
"Okay, here's what we'll do. We'll toss a coin and whoever loses gets the sissy, but they also get first pick of the lineup so it evens out. Fair?"

Peter sniffed and looked away. "You're wrong about me."

"I hope so. But I kinda doubt it."

A tempest was brewing in the northeastern sky. Lightning pulsated in the clouds. *Great!* Peter could feel dampness in the air. He resigned himself. At least if he had to cry—and he felt like crying a lot—the rain would wash away his tears.

They made their way across the parking lot. The few remaining lamps held an eerie glow. Youths sat in cars with their doors open, the interior lights exposing them as they tipped back bottles of beer, their vacuous lives craving nothing beyond the next high. Peter felt them glaring at him but Hank glared back and they turned away.

Peter and Hank veered to the right and walked to the corner where they stopped at the light. Cars zoomed by, dangerously close; the shoulder of the highway wasn't designed for pedestrian traffic. The light turned green. They crossed over onto Pinewood Drive and began making their way up the street. The city had given up trying to replace the streetlights shattered by vandals. The windows of every home were barred with the curtains drawn, but that was good. They didn't need nosy neighbors wondering who they were.

A car raced up from behind, engine roaring, loaded with six or seven youths yelling and hooting and slapping the sides of the doors. A beer bottle hit the street and shattered. Peter glanced around, furtively. All that ruckus was bound to draw the attention of the neighbors. He shuddered to think someone was watching, but then remembered he was wearing a disguise. There was no reason to think he was anything but a father carrying his tired child. Besides, they were just kids. He stopped.

The car had pulled to the curb, its bright red taillights turning black as the driver killed the engine. The interior light snapped on and six boys climbed out, slamming the doors behind them. They turned and headed straight for Peter and Hank. They bristled and slouched with their arms swinging, all except the tallest one, whose thumbs were hooked in his back pockets. Implements of leather and metal hung from their ears, arms, noses and necks, and their hair ran the gamut from ratted and braided to spiked and shaved.

"Better give me the little girl. They won't try to take her from me," Hank muttered, keeping his voice low.

Peter stood unmoving. "Uhhh, what?"

"Just hand her to me and keep walking. Don't look at them. If we ignore them, they'll probably pass on by."

Peter glanced at Angela, then at Hank, and heaved a sigh passing his daughter into the protective custody of a man he hardly knew. Beads of sweat were forming on his brow. Lightning flickered in the clouds to the east, brightening the sky. The wind picked up a junkmail flyer and swept it across the road.

The boys edged up, forming an arc in front of them, blocking the way. Hank leaned in to whisper. "On second thought, see if you can get that bottle." He raised his chin slightly indicating the neck of the glass bottle lying in the street, but one of the youths had the same idea and stepped off the curb to pick it up. Two others sidled in behind, cutting off a retreat, and Peter and Hank found themselves encircled.

"Hey, gramps, there's a toll on this street. Costs two hundred credits to pass." The boy pulled a wireless miniature scanner from his hip pocket and held it up, sticking his other hand up under his shirt to scratch his chest. He wore a toque with a ponytail, and pants a few sizes too big that hung from his hips by a metal-studded belt. His armless sweatshirt was cut off half-way up, exposing his navel. A pill-popping hollowed-eyed skull was emblazoned on the shirt with the words *Die High*.

Peter froze, his heart sounding like a ping pong ball *plunk, plunk, plunking* on a table. It wasn't that he didn't have the money—he had plenty of money—but if they scanned his arm they might also steal his watch, and along with it his fake ID.

"Don't be ridiculous!" Hank said. "Do we look like we have that kind of money? We're walking in the rain, for heaven's sake. We can't even afford a car."

The boy waffled in indecision, studying the gray maintenance uniform Peter wore and Hank's red mackinaw. "Okay, how 'bout the little girl? She's worth least a hundred."

Hank stiffened, his muscles tightening, his feet planted solidly on the ground. "I wouldn't recommend it."

The tall boy elbowed the guy next to him. "He wouldn't recommend it. *Ha, ha, ha*! That's a good one. You got hair, old man. Now, hand over the girl. There's no point in getting hurt."

Hank's lips clamped together, then he relaxed and smiled. "Best not try. My friend here has a black belt in tae kwon do, and I can hold my own. I ain't as old as I look."

All eyes went to Peter, who appeared to be turning white even in the darkness. *I'm going to die.* Another flash of lightning broke so close they felt the thunder shake the ground. Heads jerked up, then settled on Peter again.

The tall boy pushed the guy next to him forward. "My man Chick knows that kwon do stuff, don'cha, Chick? Show him a few of your moves."

The boy called Chick stumbled but recovered and glanced around at his peers. His thin-lipped smile screwed one corner of his mouth up and the other down, and his spiked hair stood along the ridge of his scalp like the comb of a rooster. He put his fists under his armpits and with his elbows flapping like wings began doing a chicken dance, strutting around the circle with his knees bent and pumping up and down in exaggerated movements while crying, *barrrack, cluck, cluck, cluck.* Suddenly he raised his hands and flattened them, slicing them back and forth like the blades of a hatchet. Then he wailed like a banshee—*whoeeeeeeyaaaaa!*—rushing forward, jumping into the air with his feet kicking. Peter lurched backwards and tripped landing on his butt, hands raised over his head to protect himself. But the boy stopped short and smacked his hands together, playing them on his knees like bongos. "Yeah, how's that for tae kwon do?" And the group guffawed, laughing like it was all good fun.

Angela twisted and rolled in Hank's arms, reaching for her dad, but Hank brought her up out of the way. He grabbed Peter by the collar and pulled him to his feet, ignoring the fear in his eyes. He handed Angela back. "Sorry about that. I made a bad call." He turned to address the boys again. "Care to try that on me?"

"No guts, no glory, eh old man?" The leader of the group nodded at the boy with the broken bottle. "Elgin, the old dude wants to spill his guts. I say we oblige him." The second challenger entered the ring and started circling, holding the jagged edge of the bottle up and thrusting it forward like a knife, but Hank didn't flinch. He followed the boy with his eyes but held his position until the youth tried to stab him for real. Then, as the arm came forward, Hank grabbed it and twisted till you could hear a snap and the young man screamed, dropping his weapon to the ground. Hank let go and stomped on the bottle, crunching it under his trucker's boot. The boy limped away, holding his wrist.

The leader's eyes hardened and darted around the group coming to rest on the biggest of the bunch, a boy taller and thicker in the chest than Hank. Over his bare skin he had a denim vest stitched with biker patches and his arms were covered in so many tattoos, it looked like he was wearing a shirt with blue sleeves. The exchange was quick but he nodded, acknowledging the signal, and jumped into the fray diving at

Hank from the side.

Though he pretended not to, Hank saw him coming. At the last second he stepped aside, letting the boy's momentum carry him as he raised his clenched fist and plowed it into his assailant's face. The young man crumpled like he'd run into a brick wall. The others eyed one another in disbelief.

Hank straightened, facing them. He flexed his arms, holding his fists so tight his veins turned blue and corded. His face flushed red. *Gurrrrrr.* He stomped his boot on the ground and the group panicked. They took off scattering in all directions like they were afraid if they ran for the car, Hank might catch them and tear them limb from limb. The one with the fractured arm hobbled away whimpering in pain as lightning whitened the sky making him appear one second and disappear the next.

"Hey, don't leave this one here!" Hank called, but no one stopped. Hank shook his head. "Crud." He leaned in and rolled the boy over, tweaking the kid's nose. "I smacked him in the forehead pretty hard, knocked him silly, but at least his nose ain't broken."

He took hold of the boy's arm hefting him up and stooped to get beneath him, *uurrrggggg.* He staggered forward, carrying the boy over his shoulder like a saddlebag.

Peter was breathing hard, watching. "What are you going to do with him?"

"Don't know, but I can't leave him here."

Peter scanned the bushes, the trees, the crest of the hill and beyond. He was sure it wasn't over. They would regroup and pounce when least expected. Hank was already about twenty paces ahead. He turned, looking back, swinging the boy around like a wooden yoke. "Better get a move on. We still need to get that little girl of yours to the doctor."

Peter's eyes swept the road again but the street was empty. He took a halting step forward but once he was moving, picked up his pace till he'd caught up with Hank who stopped to lay his would-be assailant on the hood of the abandoned car. The windshield was beginning to spot with drops of rain.

"He'll be alright. The rain will wake him up and even if it doesn't, they'll come back for their wheels soon as we're gone. It's their problem, not mine."

Angela clung to her father's neck as though afraid of losing him. Peter raised a hand over her face like an umbrella. "Why...why did you do that?"

"I didn't mean to hurt him." The kid lying spread-eagle on the car was bigger than Hank. His head was shaved and a crown of thorns was tattooed around his neck, and spiked leather bracelets were laced around his wrists. He'd been set on doing serious damage. "Ah heck, the kid had it comin'."

Peter shuddered. He didn't want to be around when the boy woke up. "I wish you could have found a nonviolent way to get rid of them. Violence only breeds more violence, but that's not what I meant. I meant telling them I know karate. Why did you do that? I could have been killed."

Hank balked, shifting his eyes to Peter with a look that made Peter wish, just this once, he'd turn his eyes away. "You could have faked it."

"Me?"

"Yes, you. *Awwww,* for Pete's sake, you said you're not a wuss, so be a man. You think that chicken-clucker knew karate? Heck, no. He just bluffed you into thinking he did. You could have done the same thing. Probably would a scared the pants off 'em."

"He was bigger than me."

"Nuts! So was Goliath but that didn't stop David. Besides, it ain't about size. It's about spunk. Like Killer. You reach out to pet that critter and half the time he runs behind the leg of a chair and hides. But don't come near our house or try to mess with Baby. He'll take your head off. He's got guts when it counts."

"I'm not a dog."

Hank's face went flat. He shook his head. "You could have tried."

TWENTY

"And can the liberties of a nation be thought secure when we have removed their only firm basis, a conviction in the minds of the people that these liberties are the gift of God? That they are not to be violated but with His wrath? Indeed I tremble for my country when I reflect that God is just: that his justice cannot sleep forever."
—*Thomas Jefferson, 1743-1826, 3ʳᵈ President of the United States*

PETER PEERED into the darkness, fearing a return of the gang as they trudged down the road. He held Angela in arms that were covered in goosebumps, though it wasn't particularly cold. Rain spotted the asphalt, his wig glistening with droplets of mist.

At Morning Star Lane, they made a right. The homes on the far side of the street bore signs of neighborhood reconstruction. The houses were large, many apparently built within the past few years. They sat on expansive lots that—except for the landscaping—spoke of affluence. The cost of gas was too high to waste on lawnmowers so the lawns were now overgrown. It was the kind of neighborhood Peter would have preferred for himself, comfortable, but not ostentatious. He looked at the mailbox, counting off the numbers. Only two more houses to go. He repositioned Angela to ease the pressure as he rubbed his arm.

The faint glow from a light inside—a ribbon of tungsten yellow peeking out from behind the curtains—signaled someone was home. Peter tried to calm himself. They were intruding on a stranger. *Not good*. They climbed the steps to the porch, rang the bell, and waited, but there was no answer. Hank raised his fist and pounded on the door.

Static erupted from the wall, followed by a woman's voice. "Yes, who there?"

An intercom. Hank stood back, crossed his arms and kicked a loose pebble off the porch.

Peter waited, but Hank didn't say anything. He just stared at Peter as though waiting on him. Peter saw the tiny dot of a hidden camera and looked into it, snuggling Angela against his chest while using his free hand to smooth his matted wig. "Ahh, my daughter's sick. We're traveling, but I was told a doctor lives here."

"Sorree, you caw the office. The doctor no see patients at home."

"But we..."

"The answering service make you appointment."

"No! Please. She can't wait until morning." Peter turned Angela toward the camera. "If it wasn't an emergency, we wouldn't have come."

"You have emergency, you go Raaee hospita'. They hep you."

"In the name of Jesus, I beg you to see us tonight. My little girl is dying."

There was a pause.

"Tell the doc it's Hank Turnbull. He knows me," Hank cut in.

"Just a minute, preese." The static stopped and the speaker went silent.

"I thought you said you only met him once," Peter whispered.

"Yeah, but she don't know that."

The door opened the length of a three-inch chain. A face with dark Asian eyes peeked through the crack. "You who?"

"Hank Turnbull. And this is Pet..."

"Michael Reese," Peter offered.

"We're in a desperate situation which I'll explain if you'll just let us in," Hank continued not skipping a beat.

The door closed. Peter heard the clinking of a chain, and the door opened a few inches wider. "I don't know the doctor see you." The door opened wide, revealing a short, slim woman wearing loose black slacks and a white silky blouse. Her long straight raven hair rode over her shoulders. She stared at them through lidless eyes. Her skin was the color of caramel and so smooth Peter thought at first glance she was in her thirties, but the tiny lines crinkling the corners of her mouth suggested he might be mistaken. A beauty mark the size of a grain of sand dotted the right corner of her upper lip. "We have guest tonight. You stay only few minutes, preese." As the woman walked away she appeared to glide along the carpet, her small feet barely skimming the surface.

They were standing in the vestibule of a dimly lit living room. A couch sat in front of the window, but the drapes were drawn, blocking the view of the street. Two large sofa chairs flanked a coffee table. The furniture was old and comfortable, the kind of furniture you buy and keep for life. If there were scratches on the wood or worn places on the fabric, they didn't show. Filling the spaces between the heavily padded chairs and the graceful lines of the couch were a dozen folding chairs, positioned around the room in a loose circle. Peter studied the pictures on the walls, mostly floral lithographs, but they were realistic and free of the erotic symbolism that seemed to pervade the art of the day. He appreciated *good* art.

Peter's head snapped up when the doctor entered the room. He was tall and thin, like a runner, and—*and black*. Peter wondered why the subject hadn't come up in their conversation. Not that there was anything wrong with being black, just that it caught him off guard. The man looked to be about Hank's age, perhaps even a few years older. His hair was snowy white and cut in an afro that sat on his head like a soccer ball. His cheeks were chiseled with high sharp bones, and a pair of black half-frame reading glasses perched on the tip of his nose. His eyes, dark and piercing, bore a look of concern. He was wearing a blue button-down shirt, gray slacks and a black leather belt with a silver buckle, but Peter could easily imagine him in a white lab coat rustling through the halls of a hospital with a stethoscope dangling from his neck.

"What's troubling the little one?" The doctor said as he bustled over, his voice deep, resonating with manliness.

Peter handed Angela to Hank. "I...ah, can we talk in private?"

The doctor turned and Peter followed him into the hall. "She your daughter?" he asked.

"Yes, no, not exactly...she's adopted.

Doctor Philips nodded.

"It's like I was telling the lady who answered the door, my little girl's dying. She has cancer and it's spread through her entire body. She could go at any time, or she may have a day or two...a...a week at best." Peter's eyes began to mist. He tried staring off into space so the doctor wouldn't notice. Why was he being so emotional? He hated crying.

He stood with his books under his arm, barely home from school, tears streaming down his cheeks. "Boys don't cry!" his mother shouted, but he couldn't stop. She raised her hand and slapped him. "That'll give you something to cry about." But he already had something to cry about. The names the other boys called him, hurt and...

He blinked a few times, but it was no use. The tears came anyway. The walls began to blur. "...and...and we're okay with that." He gave up the pretense and looked through watery eyes at the doctor. "My daughter...she knows what to expect. We're on our way home so we can be together as a family one last time, but she got sick and we had to stop. She needs painkillers, Doctor, that's all. If you can give her something we'll be on our way. *Whee...*" Peter flattened a hand on his chest, trying to catch his breath.

"We don't mean to intrude. It's just that...they had her on low doses of a morphine drug, some kind of Opioid something or other, but the hospital refused to give her any more. They said it was unnecessary. They...*sniff,* they wanted me to leave her there and let them end it, but I...I couldn't. I'm not God, you know. I mean, part of me wanted to, it doesn't make sense to let her suffer and I know she's in pain, but I made a promise to take her home and I...do you have anything? I'll pay for it, whatever it costs." Peter mopped his nose with the back of his hand, careful not to disturb his mustache, and wiped his cheeks on his sleeve.

"Those drugs are prescription. Not something I keep around the house," Doctor Philips said. His voice was robust, like that of a bard or an actor. He turned and walked back into the living room and Peter followed, dabbing his eyes, feeling like a scolded puppy. Angela was resting in Hank's arms. The doctor lifted her eyelids one at a time checking her pupils for dilation. Then he put the back of this hand to her cheek and felt her forehead and nodded.

Hank finally spoke up. "You don't recognize me, Doc?"

The doctor frowned, examining Hank's broad gray-eyed face, the crooked nose, and the baseball hat angled on his head. "Yes, I remember you. I recognized the name but I couldn't put a face to it. How's the back?"

"Never better. You remember what we have in common?"

"Yes, I do." The doctor's gaze shifted to Peter, eyeing him suspiciously.

"Let me ease your concern about my friend here. He's one of us. He's the one…"

"Don't…" Peter gasped, reaching out.

"in all the newspapers…"

"say…"

"the guy everyone's looking for…"

"anything!"

"The so-called insurrectionist. They got him labeled a murderer and a terrorist but he's none of those things. It's just their way of saying he's a Christian."

Peter dropped his hand to his side. His face turned white, his lips taut with cheeks sucked in.

The doctor's eyes widened in recognition. "*Ahhh,* I see. Your hair could do with some work. I saw you were wearing a wig right off, but people wear wigs for a lot of reasons." He turned to Angela taking her hand to feel her pulse. "I can't do anything for the child tonight. She's weak. She needs to get some rest."

Peter's face was glazed with a light moisture, his eyes watery and red. He wiped a cheek on his sleeve. "But..but she's hurting, Doctor. Can't you do anything? *Please?* I just want to get her home to her mother. We want to be together when she passes."

The doctor nodded. "I can give her a strong sedative. It won't kill the pain, at least not completely, but it'll help her relax and sleep through the night. That's all we can do for now. Do you have a place to stay?"

Peter shook his head.

"Ummmm, that's fine. You and Hank can be my guests tonight. I don't want you moving the little girl. We'll check her into the hospital first thing in the morning. Put her in the bedroom. A few people are coming over later on—some folks you might like to meet."

CELESTIAL VANTAGE

There are macrocosms and microcosms and cosms within cosms, worlds within worlds. You of earth look upon the heavens with telescopes and acknowledge the great amount of space between the heavenly bodies. Then you focus inward and use microscopes to observe the world of the atom and recognize that, proportionally, there's as much space between a nucleus and its electrons, as there is between a sun and its planets. When you think of solid matter, you do err. There is more space between the protons, neutrons and electrons of an atom, than the space which is taken up by the components themselves. See the Christ—Most Blessed Son—reconfigure his atomic structure so his corporal body can slip into the spaces between the atoms and pass through walls.

You, then, live in what could best be described as a digital simulation. Your cosmos is a virtual reality. Nothing is as it appears. You presume to live in three dimensions, and add time to make it four, but there are more. Those which must be inferred, cannot be seen with the physical eye. What do you think Paul, that greatly esteemed apostle, meant when he said: "We do not look at the things which are seen, but at the things which are not seen. For the things which are seen are temporary, but the things which are not seen are eternal."

Could it be your reality, that which you see with your eyes, is only an illusion, and that which is hidden in the spiritual realm, behind the curtain of earth's space and time, is real? Oh, that you could drop your mortal body, even for a moment, and peer through to the other side. I wager there would be no looking back!

TWENTY-ONE

"The religion which has introduced civil liberty, is the religion of Christ and his apostles, which enjoins humility, piety and benevolence; which acknowledges in every person a brother, or a sister, and a citizen with equal rights. This is genuine Christianity, and to this we owe our free constitutions of government."
—Noah Webster, 1758-1843, Father of the American Dictionary

THE WIND blew, picking up random objects and throwing them against the house: a patio umbrella, branches from a tree, shingles from a neighboring roof. Earlier, when their host went to answer the bell, a wild gust ripped the door from his hand. Over his shoulder Peter saw a plastic swimming pool sail by, twisting through the air like a giant yellow balloon. Latecomers clung to each other, entering with their clothes untucked and flapping, their hair looking combed with an eggbeater. *Wafffump!* Peter jumped. A sheet of cardboard slapped the window, billowing the curtains. People straightened their jackets, brushing their hair through their fingers as they found seats. At least the storm kept roving gangs from harassing the arriving guests.

Except for one small lamp, the lights in the room were off. The tension felt like piano wire stretched to the point of snapping, but not because of the weather, severe storms were common. It was because Peter was there, a stranger in their midst. He stared at the floor, trying to avoid their eyes. His stomach fizzed like a glass of a warm soda, but the air-conditioned chill in the room caused him to shiver. He brought his hand up to rub the goosebumps. The old trucker had opted out of the meeting, complaining of weariness from the long haul and the need for sleep. He was bunked down in the next room, snoring softly, leaving Peter to waver between feelings of resentment, envy, and relief.

Peter craned his neck around as a straggler entered the room. There was nothing to be nervous about. These weren't flack-vested, taser-bearing security personnel commissioned to haul him before the courts. The room was a zoological collection of oddballs and social rejects—just like him.

Two girls sat on the arms of a large chair with a man squeezed between them on the cushion. One of the girls was tall and thin, her legs stretched out in front of her. The other was plumpish with a derriere that blocked the man's view. His shoulders scrunched as he tried to reposition himself so he could see. The second padded chair was occupied by a man who sat alone. He leaned forward on his elbows, rubbing his hands together and pushing back the hair that kept flopping in front of his face to steal furtive glances at Peter. Peter looked away, his heart thumping. *Why?* He was safe in his costume— *wasn't he?* No one could breach the wall of his disguise.

On the other side of the room, two others—a man and a woman— were seated on a large over-inflated couch. The man crossed one leg over his knee and fiddled with the lace of his shoe. The woman was Doctor Philips' wife, the Asian lady who'd let them in. She held a tissue in her hands, kneading it between her fingers. Another man waddled in and sat to her right. Peter managed to keep his expression deadpan though he wanted to smile when he saw the diminutive lady rise as the gentleman sat down, squeezing the air out of the cushions. He wore a black suit and a shirt with a clerical collar that appeared to be too tight. Loose folds of skin overflowed his neck and his plate-round face was puffy and red. A pair of wire-rimmed glasses were perched on his nose reflecting the light. His hair, once wavy and thick, had thinned to where patches of his scalp showed through.

A man with rheumy eyes, unshaved cheeks and matted hair took a folding chair next to Peter and sat down. His alcoholic breath and body odor made Peter wrinkle his nose. In a society polarized by the haves and have-nots, homelessness was a problem. This guy was probably there to get out of the weather and enjoy the assortment of muffins gracing the dining room table. He was also someone who might sell his soul for another drink—not to be trusted. The rest were women: a bespectacled teacher, or perhaps secretary, or maybe stenographer, with her notepad in her lap and pencil poised over the page; a grocery cashier wearing her green uniform, and two teenage girls sitting on a piano bench holding hands. Peter gave them the benefit of the doubt, noting the similarity of their faces and eyes, and the chocolate color of their hair. They had to be sisters. Nothing unseemly. Just a strange assortment of misfits, derelicts, and wannabes.

He was sitting on his hands, sure everyone was examining him too. He was glad for the lamp's low incandescent bulb that gave off just enough light to see by, but not enough for close inspection. He looked down, shuffling his feet, then poked his glasses up as they slid forward. They were too big, but he had to wear them; otherwise, his nose and eyes were the same as the face in the newspapers. Would that give him away? *No*, it was still a good disguise. The mouth, with false-toothed overbite and mustache, was completely different and he did have the glasses to help mask his eyes. He just had to be careful not to look anyone in the face. The fake mustache tickled. He took a breath, resisting the temptation to scratch the itch. He raised his lip over his buck teeth, twisting his mouth until his nose went cockscrewy—the spittin' image of a village idiot—but the beauty of the costume was that everybody saw someone else, not him. The wall of his costume was impenetrable. Besides, he fit right in. So why was his heart pounding so fast?

Dr. Philips sauntered into the room, his dark skin shining in the dim light, his hair snowy white. He was carrying a Bible. The gold on the gilded edge was worn, the brown of the leather rubbed to a light tan, and the cover falling off, but it was the only Bible Peter had seen. This was the church the way it existed in apostolic times—meeting in houses and caves. Gone were the nostalgic stone buildings with steeple spires and bells and oak doors that opened wide to receive parishioners. Gone even were the strip-mall mega-churches catering to hippies and yuppies with their huarache sandals and Gucci shoes that had been so popular around the turn of the century. What few churches remained were state-sanctioned, sparsely attended, and preached what the Bible called, "a form of godliness but lacking the power thereof."

Peter shifted in his folding chair, crossing one leg over the other. The people in this room were his kind of people—geeks and nerds, filled with fears and phobias, and yet, they were here seeking Christ in defiance of federal regulation. "But God hath chosen the foolish things of the world to confound the wise." *Great passage*, one of Peter's personal favorites.

He brought a finger up to poke at his mustache, not scratching, but trying to push the itch away. While applying his makeup he'd suddenly realized the image in the mirror was that of his father. He wondered if putting on that particular face was a coincidence, or somehow subconsciously intentional. He'd learned long ago not to hate his father, long before he learned how to forgive. Not hating was easy. The man couldn't help who he was—a frightened puppy running away from home to escape its master's abuse. The picture of the door closing through which he never returned was imprinted on Peter's mind like the recurrence of a bad dream. His wife, Peter's own dear mother, had chased him out with a broom. She had the power.

He looked around the closet, not sure why he was there except that it was something to do and he was bored. He couldn't go outside. He was afraid of being chased and beaten up. He reached out and took hold of a long dress, wrapping himself in it, smelling the odor of her skin. He yanked the material, watching it pop from the hanger and fall into his arms, covering his head. He buried his face in the fabric, ahhhhhh, the smell of power! He slipped it on. The hem swirled around his feet. He gathered the material into his arms, looking around for her shoes. He saw a white spiked heel and dragged it back with his toe. He slipped his foot inside, elevating himself. He stood taller than ever. Let them try to come after him now! Now he had the power! He could smell it!

It had been the beginning of Peter's love affair with disguise, a love affair that would change his life, providing a means of escape. He dressed in his mother's clothes because, in spite of his gender, he was determined not to be like his father. He wanted to mimic her strength as much as disavow who he *really* was. He loved being someone else. He loved hiding behind a masquerade, keeping the real Peter invisible. He loved swishing by a table of men, beckoning their eyes to follow. He even relished the whistles and catcalls because they affirmed the brilliance of his disguise. Effeminate yes, definitely, but not gay, though friends continually told him to quit pretending and accept who he really was. After he was married, those same friends had to admit they were wrong. He couldn't possibly be gay and find happiness in a woman. But they would also have boasted of being right had he swung the other way. He now knew the only thing that determined whether or not he was gay, was his *choice*.

Gay? The lifestyle defied the meaning of the word, unless it was meant as an oxymoron. Having won the culture war, with no one left to make them feel guilty or ashamed, homosexuals were supposed to be happy. And yet, even with acceptance at every level, there was still more suicide and spousal abuse among homosexuals than any other group. There wasn't anything *gay* about *that*. History repeating itself, line by line. In some cities, the greater population was composed of same-sex and transgender couples. A straight man couldn't walk the streets at night for fear of being put upon by other men with insatiable appetites stooping to ever lower forms of depravity. Were the Sodomites who pounded on Lot's door demanding he surrender his angelic visitors, really *happy*? Were they *gay* or merely obsessed with unbridled lust? The world still suffered from the spreading of AIDS and other STDs, but legislators and bureaucrats refused to go back and revisit what they'd been led to believe. The world was a nasty place. Peter blotted his forehead on his sleeve, his chest pounding as he waited for the doctor to speak.

He needed a way to make people like Hank understand. He'd resisted the culture, refusing to become what everyone regarded him to be. He'd discarded his femme fatale wardrobe years before meeting Deanne. Maybe he wasn't able to eradicate his feminine voice, or all his emotional garbage—at least not right away—nor could he toss hoops and race the quarter mile, but at least he knew he was a man. God had used Bill to show him that. It wasn't about strength or power, it wasn't about having muscles or being able to fight—*the meek shall inherit the earth.* The two-fisted, gruff, rough-and-tumble exterior of men like Hank was only a facade, a cheap outer covering that hid the real man. It's what the world saw, because people only looked at the outer appearance—but God looked at the heart. Real men were tender and kind and self-sacrificing and giving—like Christ. That was his example, and Hank, God bless him for trying to help, was wrong. You can't resolve conflict by fighting—at least not all the time. The meek were going to inherit the earth, which somehow implied they were more godly, so loosen your fists and put 'em in your pockets, *Hank.* Might does not make right, not when the battle is the Lord's. Peter wiggled on his hands, glad to be free of all that...

The doctor sat beside the low-burning lamp in the only vacant chair and opened his Bible. "Let's pick it up where we left off in our study of the book of the Revelation," he said.

Peter loved that voice, calm and slow as a ripple of water. *God, why couldn't I have a voice like that?*

"Those of you who were here last week will remember we talked about end-time prophecy and how Jesus predicted changes in the weather. That wind out there, that's a good example of what we were talking about. Almost every day we see extremes in the temperature, blazing hot to freezing cold. It doesn't just rain, it pours. The wind doesn't blow, it howls. You recall what we were reading last week, how brother Martin Luther said, 'The devil provokes such storms, but good winds are produced by good angels.' Luther believed all wind was caused by angels in flight, those that are good and those that are bad, and when God held back the good ones, the storms created by the bad ones...well, it's kinda like what we're seeing out there.

"Today we're going to look at an unusual verse that reveals part of the reason for all these storms. Let me read it to you. It's found in the book of the Revelation of Jesus Christ, in the first verse of chapter twenty-one. 'And I saw a new heaven and a new earth, for the first heaven and the first earth were passed away, and there was no more sea.'

"Now, the question you have to ask is, 'Why no more sea?' In Genesis we saw how God created the sea and everything in it and saw it was 'good.' So why get rid of it now? Keep in mind that God declared the sea was good before the Fall. A lot of things changed after that. Looking to the future, the prophet Micah said, 'Thou wilt cast all their sins into the depths of the sea.' So, if our sins are to be dumped into the sea, maybe the sea is a good thing to get rid of.

"Also, after the fall, the prophet Nahum said, 'He *rebuketh* the sea,' and Zechariah said 'He shall *smite* the waves.' Rebuke? Smite? That's an unusual way of talking about water. The sea is made of H^2O. It's liquid. It doesn't have ears to hear or a body to smite. Why not just say, 'Peace be still,' and leave it at that? Perhaps it's because He's not really talking about the water. Maybe there's a spiritual force under the waves. I'm not saying for certain, but maybe the evil one, and also our sin, is somehow connected to the sea, and by extension, all the crazy weather we're seeing out there.

"Remember the demon-possessed man that lived the tombs of the Gadarenes? Remember when he was delivered, where those demons asked to be sent? Into a herd of pigs, *yes*, but where did they go after that? They ran into the sea and were drowned. But not the demons. I doubt the demons raced into the sea to destroy themselves. No, I think they looked to the sea as a place of refuge.

"And why do you suppose they did that? One reason might be because the sea is the home of Leviathan. We don't know much about this beast, but we do know whatever, or whoever, he is, he isn't nice, and we know he lives in the sea. The prophet Amos said, 'And though they be hid from my sight in the bottom of the sea, thence will I command the serpent, and he shall bite them.' *Ouch!* You mean to say Leviathan's a serpent? Yes, brothers and sisters, he definitely is. Let me read Isaiah twenty-seven, verse one: 'In that day the LORD with His severe sword, great and strong, will punish the fleeing serpent, Leviathan, that twisted serpent, and He will slay the reptile that is in the sea.'

"Amen! You understand what I'm saying? Who else is called a

serpent? Satan! That's right. He's called a serpent in Genesis, and also in the book of the Revelation.

"Listen to me carefully now. I'm not saying Satan and Leviathan are one and the same. I'm just speculating on the idea that maybe there's some spiritual connection. Maybe, just maybe, all this is related to the storms and winds and rain and hurricanes and floods we're seeing out there. It's just conjecture, mind you, just food for thought..."

Peter could feel someone staring at him, but he focused on the teacher, knowing he'd draw even more attention if he started looking around. The man had made some good points, a bit far-fetched perhaps but, then again, the Bible made it clear God controlled the weather. He brought the sun and rain when He wanted to bless His people, but He was also known to withhold His blessing when they chose to worship other gods, and then—all hell broke loose. They were living at a time when the whole world had turned its back on God. If inclement weather was the result, it was warranted. Every year there were more earthquakes, hurricanes, tornados, droughts, fires, and floods—*So persecute them with thy tempest, and make them afraid with thy storm...*

One thing was sure, Dr. Philips wasn't into watering down the Word. Nor did he shy away from opining difficult passages. He'd better watch his back. Peter glanced around the room. They had a right to be suspicious, even paranoid. The assembly was illegal, and all it took was one spy...and Dr. Philips would take the hardest fall. Homeland Security wouldn't care about grocery clerks and winos, just truck them off to jail, but they'd go out of their way to make an example of a doctor.

The official government position was that men were free to believe whatever they wanted. But to assemble and discuss the Bible outside a state-licensed church was, in their view, to promote hatred and intolerance, and that was strictly forbidden. Imagine, a black man accused of intolerance. Peter vowed to pray for the man, especially since he'd promised to help Angela.

TWENTY-TWO

"The foundations of our society and our government rest so much on the teachings of the Bible that it would be difficult to support them if faith in these teachings would cease to be practically universal in our country."
—Calvin Coolidge, 1872-1933, 30ᵗʰ President of the United States

BOB THREW his shoe at the hologram of Leo Nordstrom being interviewed, then grimaced as it bounced off the set, knocking it askew.

"The manhunt continues...The net is tightening...It's only a matter of time."

What a load of...*net...tightening?* Peter had disappeared, whereabouts unknown, and Leo knew it. The spin was just his way of putting pressure on Bob to get the job done. He reached for his glass and brought it to his lips, swirling the ice with a flick of his wrist before taking a drink. Lucky the set didn't break. He'd have a hard time explaining a repair bill on his expense report.

He clicked the remote, flipping through the channels. Holovision wasn't what it used to be. It was all one, *click,* man-with-man, *click,* man-with-woman, *click,* woman-with-woman orgy after another, all in lifelike, three-dimensional display with accu-fragrance and surround sound brought right into his room via wireless optical transmission, an infinite number of channels broadcast from every corner of the globe—and not a single program worth watching.

He hit the "end transmission" button, turning the set off, and dropped the remote beside him on the bed. He couldn't see his feet over the mound of his stomach. He wiggled his toes realizing how out of shape he'd become. Problem with a desk job—not enough exercise. He took another sip before flopping over to plop the drink on the table. The liquid splashed out of the glass onto his hand and puddled on the table's surface. He wiped his hand on the blanket and then pushed it under the pillow, propping his head up to stare at the water-stained stucco. Leaky pipes from the room above.

Outside, the wind howled. Inside, the room buzzed. He hated the small confining space of the shabby motel. Sweeping his legs off the bed, Bob staggered to his feet and made his way to the window. He stood to the side so he wouldn't be seen in his skivvies as he drew the curtain back with a finger, eyeballing the parking lot. A bag from a fast food restaurant tumbled by, trees and dust swirled, the cars in the lot were rocking on their wheels, but not a living soul could be seen. Where had that wind come from?

He turned and stumbled to the bed, crawling up and collapsing onto his stomach, his face buried in the sheets. His lip was hanging open and he was drooling, the smell of a thousand unwashed bodies offending his nose. He rolled onto his back staring at the ceiling again, his elbow bumping the laptop taken from Peter's office. He pulled it over to check for the thousandth time. He'd give a month's pay for another e-mail from Deanne, just to know she was alive and well, though the content of her messages made him think, at least at a subconscious level, that it might have been easier if he'd discovered she were dead. Just a hint, that's all he needed, just a clue as to where Peter might be, and then—*gotcha*—problem solved.

He spotted Deanne across the parking lot, acknowledging her with a lift of his chin. The late summer sky stretched shadows across the ground, the evening air was warm and the sky roiled with shades of purple. Deanne waved. Her hair was russet in the twilight, riding in thick curls on her shoulders. A smile broke across her face revealing her anticipation.

Bob made his way through the lot, zigzagging around the bumpers of the cars. He caught his reflection in a window and stopped long enough to admire himself. The image was exactly what he expected—one lean, mean, dream machine. He slipped three fingers into the hair above his scalp and pulled forward, letting a curl fall over his forehead. It just didn't get any better.

Peter slid up to the car from the other side and slipped a flyer under the wiper. "Hey, Bob," he said, glancing up.

"Hey, Peter." Bob leaned over and grabbed the flyer. "What trouble you mixed up in now?"

The paper was folded into three panels. The front panel read:

CHURCH, WAKE UP!

We're losing our religious freedom.

We were told that displaying the Ten Commandments contravened a separation of church and state.

We were told that killing the unborn, the elderly, the disabled and the poor was a constitutional right.

We were told that pornography was protected by the First Amendment as freedom of speech.

Now they want us to stop preaching in the name of Jesus

WAKE UP, CHURCH!

It's time to take our country back.

Bob opened the flyer. Inside was printed the date, time and place of a meeting along with a map. "Sheeesh. You guys are nuts." Bob ripped the flyer in two and tossed the pieces into the air to be carried across the parking lot by the wind.

"Hey, those cost money..."

"I'll bet they do." Bob spun on his heel and traipsed through the lot stopping at every car en route to remove the flyer. When he reached the edge of the lot, he turned to look back at Peter who stood with his hands on his hips, still holding the flyers he'd been trying to distribute.

Bob smiled, feeling a smug satisfaction. He was looking for a trash can when he felt a hand on his arm. It was Deanne.

"Oh, I see you're handing out flyers too. Isn't it great? Someone's finally doing something."

Bob ripped his arm free. "No, it ain't great! Don't you go joining these idiots. They're going to wind up in jail."

"But, I..."

"No buts. I'm starting on the force next month and I'm not having any girl of mine get mixed up in something that could be illegal. Got it?"

The pipes in the wall rattled. Happened every time someone flushed. Man, he hated this place, but he was settled in and he was too lazy to pack up and move. He'd had to abandon his stakeout of the house. There was no point. She knew he was there, and if *she* didn't tip Peter off, the reporters would. He should have left surveillance to the pros. He thought about hitting the bars, maybe even pick up a hot squeeze, but no, if he wanted to keep abreast of Deanne's e-mails, he had to stay in his room. Besides, what decent watering hole would be happening on a weeknight?

He rolled his head to look at the phone, but there was no one to call. He'd already checked with his contact in Toronto; they offered nothing new. The trail had gone cold. What he needed now was a break. He needed Deanne to look out her window and see he was gone. *Come on, baby, tell Peter it's safe to come home.*

He needed a plan, some way of luring Peter into the open. *Think*! But Jack Daniels had his mind in its grip, slowing his thoughts to a crawl. A mouse skittered across the floor, or were there two, or was he seeing double? He reached for the remote and threw it, but the rodent was long gone and the device popped open, spilling its batteries on the carpet. Where were all the cats when you needed one? *Yeah.* That's what he had to do. This was a game of cat and mouse, and he was the cat. A cat would just wait, and *wait*, and *wait*, and finally, the mouse would begin to think it was safe to come out. Then, soon as the mouse crept into the open, the cat would pounce and—*wham*—game over! He reached for his glass and took a drink without lifting his head. The liquid spilled out the corners of his mouth onto the pillow. He didn't have the patience to wait. He wanted Peter *now*.

DEANNE STOOD at the bathroom mirror removing her makeup. She put it on each morning and took it off each night. *For what?* She never went out, and with Peter and Angela away there was no one to look good for. She turned her head slowly side to side, using her fingers to trace the fine lines in her face. Too many wrinkles...

She wiped the corner of her eye where moisture was beginning to build. *Just the makeup remover,* she told herself. *Sometimes it irritates the eyes.* She brought the tissue to the other side where a drop of saline had escaped and was rushing down her cheek. She'd done her best to keep busy—tables to dust, scrapbooks to fill, clothes to put away. But when she stood in Angela's room, looking at the veritable wonderland of fuzzy pink rabbits and life-sized stuffed giraffes, it finally hit her: she was about to lose it all—everything—*gone.*

She didn't care about the house, take it, demolish it, who cares? Grandiose architecture aside, it was just a glorified jail. Maybe it was time to bust out—*tiny prickles of sweat erupted at her temples and her heart started to pound*—or not. But if she *were* forced to leave it behind, would she miss it? *Not likely.*

She needed to apologize. She hadn't been kind when they left, letting Peter kiss her cheek without kissing him back. The thought of losing Angela was already more than she could bear. Did she have to face losing Peter too? She wadded the tissue, clenching her fist. No! *No, no, no, no, no, a thousand times, no.* She threw the tissue at a trash can but it missed and went skidding across the floor. You can't thumb your nose at the government. They make the rules. It's a miracle he'd avoided them as long as he did. She blinked back the tears, determined not to cry. No point in lamenting the inevitable. She took a deep breath and straightened herself. He knew the risks. And in truth, so did she, but she had to let him do what he was determined to do. *"To him that knoweth to do good and doeth it not, to him it is sin."* He'd said it so many times, she knew it by heart.

She resumed removing her makeup with facial cleanser. *Why now, Lord? Why must you take them both at once? It's so unfair.* She stopped. Her eyes filled with tears. She gripped the edge of the white marble counter and let them flow. Peter was the strongest man she'd ever known. He never complained about having a hermit for a wife, never made her feel guilty or ashamed—*or crazy or weird*—for refusing to go outside. If they couldn't go out together, they'd have fun at home. Peter missed his calling not being an actor, she'd decided. "All the world's a stage upon which everyone plays a part," he'd pronounce with an outstretched hand. Then he'd break out his old TV costumes and they'd dress up and put on a play, reciting lines from Shakespeare, "Oh, Romeo, Romeo, wherefore art thou, Romeo?" and roll on the floor and laugh till their sides ached.

She tried to manage a smile but it was forced and faded quickly. She buried her face in a towel folded three inches thick, pampering her cheeks and eyes with its luxurious softness. Angela had been a Godsend. Whenever Peter had to travel, she had Angela to occupy her time, someone to keep her laughing, but now...

She glanced once more at the mirror and the frightful image it contained, then went to her closet. The air in her lungs fluttered as she took a breath. She found her flannel pajamas hanging between her nightgowns and negligees and a few frilly things she wore only for Peter. She lifted them from the hanger and padded back into the room. The carpet was so thick she could squeeze it between her toes.

Would her house in Mexico have a carpet? Would the floors be made of dirt? Peter was being quiet about the whole affair. They had to focus on *how* to get there, not on what they'd find.

She picked up her pajamas. Flannel seemed right. The wind outside made her feel cold. Without Peter beside her in bed, she might catch a chill. Either way, she knew she wouldn't sleep. She glanced at the window making sure the curtains were drawn. Paparazzi could still be lurking in the yard. She struggled out of her clothes laying them on the bed. The pajamas felt soft and warm as she slipped them on bringing momentary comfort, but she thought about Angela and Peter and where they might be sleeping and the feeling quickly fled. She returned to the bathroom to put her hair in a bun.

She dabbed her cheeks. In some ways, she was glad Peter wasn't there to see her. Her emotional meltdown revealed a terrible lack of faith. She went to her dresser for a book and sat down to read, taking another breath that fluttered like a butterfly in her throat. She began scanning the page but when she reached the bottom she realized she couldn't recall a single word she'd read, nor could she see. The ink on the page looked wet, the letters washed together in a blur.

Her mind kept wandering back to her husband and daughter... *Please Lord, keep them safe. Let me see them one more time.* She closed the book and reminded herself that all the stories she read, however well written, were simply that—*stories*. The word of God was the only ultimate truth. It occurred to her that she really didn't need to read another novel—her husband and daughter were in trouble. What she needed to do was pray.

BOB WAS staring at the ceiling in the darkness. He cocked an arm over his eyes. He'd drunk enough to knock down a horse, but it seemed no matter how hard he tried, he couldn't fall asleep. He'd gone to bed too early. Three outcomes bounced around in his head, only one of which was positive. Either Peter would elude his grasp and get away, or he would capture Peter and Deanne would find out and hate him for contributing to her husband's demise. Or, and this one quickened his pulse, Peter would be arrested, Deanne would never learn of his involvement, and once beyond Peter's grasp would awaken from her spell, realize her mistake, and beg him to take her back. He wanted to believe with all his heart that Deanne had only married Peter to spite him. It was the one thing that made sense. Beautiful girls like Deanne just didn't fall for guys like Peter. Not in the real world. *But the e-mails?* She couldn't know he was monitoring them—she was upset because Peter *left*. What power did he possess that held sway over her rational mind. Or maybe it wasn't Peter she loved at all. Maybe he was just a catalyst for her own narrow-minded views.

He sat up and clicked on the lamp, waiting until his eyes adjusted to the light before reaching for the drawer of the bedside table. Inside was the customary motel Bible, the NWV (New World Version) which combined Hebrew and Christian scripture, verses from the Muslim Qur'an, the wisdom of Hindu Sanskrit, and the teachings of Buddha.

The selected texts were free of finger-pointing, judgmental name-calling, and lifestyle intolerance. He flipped through the pages but knew he wouldn't find what he was looking for. The Bible he used on the job, the old one he used to check illegal copies against—that's what he needed. He scooped his briefcase from the floor and snapped the clasps open. The hardcover edition was there. He pulled it out and began skimming through what was formerly called the New Testament. His eyes fell on a verse:

> "Do you not know that the unrighteous will not inherit the kingdom of God? Do not be deceived. Neither fornicators, nor idolaters, nor adulterers, nor homosexuals, nor sodomites, nor thieves, nor covetous, nor drunkards, nor revilers, nor extortioners will inherit the kingdom of God. And such were some of you. But you were washed, but you were sanctified, but you were justified in the name of the Lord Jesus and by the Spirit of our God."

Blaa, blaa, blaa. See, that's exactly what he meant! Didn't Christ come to bring healing and forgiveness to everyone? According to this, there were a whole lot of people God didn't love enough to forgive. That's what Deanne was all hung up about—that you had to change to get right with God—but she was reading all the wrong verses. These weren't the words of Christ. Jesus didn't write the Bible. The Bible was written by men, and while it did contain some of Christ's words, Bob was convinced most of it was written by people who didn't understand God's higher purpose, or the love of Christ. According to them, a whole lot of people were going to hell.

No sir-ee, Bob, that didn't cut it, not if you wanted to call Deanne's God a God of love. Where was the part about turning the other cheek? Love was about forgiveness, not about holding your enemies feet to a flame. That was sheer torture, and you don't torture those you love. It didn't take rocket science to figure it out. Trouble was, Deanne didn't listen—at least not to him.

TWENTY-THREE

"Liberty must at all hazards be supported. We have a right to it, derived from our Maker. But if we had not, our fathers have earned and bought it for us, at the expense of their ease, their estates, their pleasure, and their blood."
—*John Adams, 1735-1826, 2nd President of the United States*

THE OUTLAW Christians pulled their coats in tight, sashing them around their waists, and burrowed in for the long windy walk. They got up to leave shortly after the closing hymn and prayer, braving the messy night to seek the safety of their homes. The vestibule was filled with dim silhouettes. They huddled in clusters of twos and threes, staggering their times of departure. It was an unnecessary precaution. Neighbors kept their drapes drawn and rarely spent time spying on hooligans and gangs. These days, keeping to oneself was a prerequisite for survival.

The gale force storm roared on, the rain pelting the ground so hard it bounced off the asphalt into their shoes as they hustled into the street. No one escaped getting wet; umbrellas were useless in the wind, and it was customary to park a good distance away. A collection of vehicles in front of the house would look suspicious. Murky clouds laced with lightning piled one upon the other—*karrracccck, brummmmble-boom!* Lightning flashed and the wind howled. It didn't appear the weather would break any time soon.

A few stragglers stayed behind, discussing the evening's study and enjoying coffee and cake in the kitchen. The doctor's wife, whom

Peter now knew as Kim Li, sat on the living room couch talking to the girl with the long legs. The girl's spindly arms, now animated in conversation, reminded Peter of a praying mantis. Peter had switched positions and now sat in one of the more comfortable chairs, but remained in the unlit living room trying to keep a low profile. He held a magazine in his lap, a medical journal, and turned the pages but the light was too poor to read and advanced techniques for in vitro cloning were repugnant, as well as beyond his ability to understand.

Occasionally he felt someone staring at him but never looked up to acknowledge a glance or stare. He remained in the shadows, but even there, he wasn't sure his costume could withstand close scrutiny.

Only one person had approached him so far, the man who smelled like a brewery, and then only because they'd bumped into each other in the hall. It was an odd encounter. Judging by his odor and appearance, Peter had assumed the man was homeless. He would have expected him to scarf the free food and look for a quiet corner in which to crash so he could ride out the storm. Instead, the man had tried to engage Peter in a normal conversation without the tongue-dragging slur or staggering gait he expected of a drunk. Peter avoided the man by excusing himself to go to the washroom, and upon his return was relieved to see he'd already left.

The lady talking to Kim Li sat on the couch poking carrot cake into her mouth with mantis-like precision. Her straight dishwater hair was cut sharply around the back of her neck. She wore huge black plastic glasses that made her eyes appear buggy. Her elbows jacked out as she spoke in low hushed tones but Peter was close enough to hear at least part of what was said.

"I have to give you my new e-mail address." She reached into her blouse and with two fingers retrieved a folded note which she poked at Kim Li. "Sorry to have to do this again so soon, but you know how it is, they screen everyone's mail and forward copies of messages with suspicious words to Homeland Security. I'm sure I've been flagged several times. Anyway, it's time to change my ISP. I really wish people understood the importance of speaking in code, but how do you tell a new believer not to say the name of Jesus when they're so excited? I just can't help it; I talk to so many people and every once in awhile a newbe slips and uses a questionable word and up goes a flag on my account. But I think as long as I keep changing my name and address I'll be okay. Did you hear they closed down two more cell groups in Pittsburgh?" She stuffed a final bite of cake into her mouth, her elbow winging out. "Those *poor* people. It's awful, just awful. I heard it's connected to that guy they're looking for, you know, the one who killed that Canadian and stole his boat. He's supposed to be from around Pittsburgh. *Ohhhh,* the whole thing's so grizzly. They haven't even found the body, just blood everywhere. They think it was weighed down and dropped overboard. Can you imagine? And we get blamed for it..."

Peter caught the furtive glance Kim Li shot in his direction but she recovered before the other woman noticed. He held his breath as the tiny but very poised Kim Li continued nodding at her friend. Her hands were neatly folded over the note in her lap and a white smile was compressed on her lips but she withheld comment. Peter exhaled slowly, shouldering the guilt. His flight to freedom was causing others to be jailed. *Must have thought they were hiding me,* he mused. His escape had precipitated their being shut down. *No.* The agent of their demise was Satan. *"Behold, the devil shall cast some of you into prison, that ye may be tried..."*

The lady's limbs flailed out. "Imagine, every time someone gets killed they blame it on a Christian. *As if!* That man's not a Christian, not if he murdered the poor guy just so he could steal his boat. He doesn't even need it! He's supposed to be some kind of billionaire. Why didn't he just go buy his own boat? But you know what they say about the rich, harder for a camel to go through the eye of a needle than for the rich to enter heaven..."

From *fear* to *guilt* to *anguish*. He *had* bought his own boat and he hadn't *killed* anyone. The name on the boat's registration was an invention. He'd made it up. You can't kill someone who doesn't exist. The lady should be defending him. Stand up for a brother. *"And ye shall be betrayed both by parents, and brethren, and kinsfolk, and friends."*

Peter felt a presence and glanced up to see the young man with floppy hair hovering over him. "Do I know you?" the boy said. His words were muffled by the piece of cake he'd just shoved into his mouth. He stood there, licking his fingers.

Peter held the young man's gaze only as long as it took to acknowledge the question. He looked back at the magazine, turning the pages with a shake of his head.

" 'Cause I'm sure I've seen you somewhere before."

Goosebumps rose on Peter's arms. At the fringe of his fake hair he felt his temples pulsating. He rolled his eyes up at the young man without lifting his chin. "I doubt it," he said. He tried to keep the magazine from shaking as he turned the page, leaving moist prints on the glossy paper. "I'm not from around here. I'm in sales, medical supplies and pharmaceuticals. I have to travel a lot. I just stopped in to say hi to my friend Dr. Philips." He used a wet finger to drag another page over while keeping his head down. "Unless you work in requisitioning at the hospital, I doubt our paths have crossed."

Peter didn't look up again. The boy, feeling dismissed, nodded at the girl on the couch and went to stand by the door. Taking her cue, the girl bent to kiss the older lady's cheek and bid her goodnight. She moved toward the entry, skating on long legs. The pair then plunged into the storm, sending papers flying as the wind *whooshed* into the house. At least two more were gone. *That leaves only Friar Tuck.*

Peter was growing antsy about Angela. He needed to check on her. Looking around, he saw Kim Li had risen from the couch and was climbing the stairs, leaving the living room empty. He eyed the kitchen. Adrian Philips and the heavyset priest were locked in conversation, totally absorbed. He pulled himself from the chair and headed down the hall as though looking for the bathroom. Passing the dining room, he overheard the doctor clear his throat. "Ahhh, slow down a minute, brother. Come on over. There's someone I'd like you to meet."

Peter stopped. The hair bristled on the back of his neck. He gave an almost indiscernible shrug and turned to join the duo. The cleric with the round face smiled as Adrian waved his hand toward the man's stout belly. "This is my friend, Father Buddy Bloom."

If Peter thought his hands were sweaty, this man's were more so.

Squeezing the priest's palm was like wringing out a sponge. The flushed rouge of his cheeks made it appear he was choking or about to explode, but beneath the circles of his wire-rimmed glasses, his small green eyes seemed to hold a perpetual smile.

Peter nodded but his expression was flat. The man appeared too young to be called "Father"—maybe late thirties, early forties—but he *was* wearing a collar, which meant he belonged to a state-sanctioned church and was sworn to uphold the tenets of the New World Doctrine, the manifesto that called for an adjunct to the first amendment of the U.S. Constitution.

> "Congress shall make no law respecting an establishment of religion, or prohibiting the free exercise thereof—*as long as the lawful assembly for the purpose of worship and promulgation of doctrine recognizes all men as equal under God, without prejudice, avowing no religious dogma or teaching to be deemed above any other.*"

A universalist by any other name would smell the same, Peter thought. There was no manifold path. Christ said, "I am the Way the Truth and the Life, no man comes to the Father but by Me," *My way or the highway, end of story, get used to it.* The Apostle Paul warned that in the last days many would depart from the faith and follow after doctrines of demons. Surely they were living in the last days. Dr. Philips just labored to prove it. So if this man was in that camp, he taught heresy. Peter dropped his hand and stood back, unsmiling.

The priest's smile also faded. He was panting like someone who'd just run the quarter-mile, "*uhhhh huh, uhhhh huh, uhhhh huh.*" He hooked a finger into his collar, pulling it forward to relieve the pressure while shaking his head, his eyes narrowing perceptibly. "My collar bothers you, doesn't it?" His voice was hoarse, like air escaping the neck of a pinched balloon. "*Uhhh huh*, no, *uhh huh*, no, *hurrumph*, I don't expect you to understand, but I'm not one of them. I keep up the pretense to help those I can, and when I do, I preach Jesus."

Peter nodded but his cheeks were flat as cardboard. "Maybe, but publicly you have to teach there are many paths to God. I know you do. They monitor your sermons."

The priest reached into his vest pocket, removed a handkerchief and began blotting his forehead. Wet puddles stained his underarms. "There is that, *uhh huh,* I admit. We don't have the freedom we once had. But don't, *uhh huh,* don't think I hide the truth on purpose. I do what I can, and I'll probably go to jail for it some day. I will, I know I will, but until then, our church will stay open."

Peter looked over the priest's shoulder at the rain rattling the windows. Hank thought he was a coward, *well, maybe he was,* but that mantis lady said he was a murderer, and *that* he wasn't. Things weren't always as they appeared. It wasn't fair to judge without knowing all the facts. *Murderer, indeed.*

Dr. Philips placed a hand on Father Bloom's shoulder. "True, a lot of churches have stayed open, and a lot of the people who go to those churches also attend Bible studies like this. Never underestimate the power of Almighty God, glory! The church is growing faster now than it ever did when there were churches on every corner. Maybe all this is a good thing. You'd know something about that, wouldn't you, son?"

Peter's eyes narrowed. His mouth undulated, his fake mustache bristling. "You'll have to excuse me," he said. "I was on my way to use the washroom."

Hank's guttural snores could be heard through the wall as Peter made his way down the hall. He silently pushed back the door to Angela's room, a fan of light sweeping across the bed where she lay. She looked like an angel, despite the purple shadows beneath her sunken eyes. Her breathing was labored and heavy and her lungs gurgled with fluid, but she seemed to be resting. It lifted his spirits to see her enjoying a moment of peace.

He knelt beside the bed, took his daughter's hand and leaned in to kiss her goodnight. Her breath was warm and moist on his cheek. She opened her eyes, looking into the face of her father, a smile growing on her lips. He realized she wasn't seeing *him,* she was seeing his comic impersonation. He didn't want her to remember him like that. He spat his fake teeth into his hand, pulled the mustache from his lip and tipped the glasses off, slipping them into his pocket. Angela giggled. If angels could laugh, this is how they would sound. He was sure of it.

"I saw him again, Daddy," she said, her voice soft as a whisper.

"Who, sweetheart? Who did you see?"

"My angel, Daddy...the one I told you about. He stood right there." Angela raised her hand and tried to point, but her arm fell back to the bed, limp as a rag doll. "He said he wants to take me to Jesus, but...but I told him I want to see Mommy first...I think it's okay with him. It must be, 'cause I'm still here...Do you think...think he'll let me wait?"

Peter took her hand in his own, fondling her fingers—*so soft, so small.* He had to duck his head and use his shoulder to wipe the moisture from his cheek. "Of course he will, sweetheart, of course he will."

"Daddy, what's it like to die?"

His grip tightened. He didn't have an answer, other than the one he'd already given. He sighed, bringing her hand to his lips. "It's like going to sleep. That's all it is. You close your eyes and shut out this ugly world of pain and wake up in a world full of light, where everything is beautiful and nothing can hurt you ever again. And you'll see the friends you made at the hospital, Andrew and Michelle, the ones you told about Jesus." He ran her hand along his cheek. "Remember how you guys talked about getting together and playing games, but couldn't because you had to stay in bed? No more of that. You'll laugh and run across fields of flowers, and share strings of balloons." He combed her wig with his fingers. "And the sun will shine on your hair...your own hair, the real..." His eyes welled up and he choked. Angela's eyes closed. A faint smile curled on her mouth as she fell into slumber at the rhythmic sound of her father's voice. He leaned in to wipe her cheek.

Her eyes opened again. "I asked my angel if you and Mommy can...come with me so you won't have to hide anymore...but he told me not to worry...that we'll be together soon. You and Mommy..."

Peter's head snapped up. He heard the sound of footsteps shuffling across the carpet, a heavy body brushing against the wall. He jerked back, looking over his shoulder. They weren't alone. The silhouette of Father Bloom filled the door. He was wheezing like a dusty furnace.

"There's, *uhh, huhhh, uh huhhh*, more to you than meets the eye, Mr. *uhh huhhh*, *ah*, I think it's Dufoe, isn't it?"

Peter let his daughter's hand slip from his own and stood.

The red-faced priest raised his hand to wave him down, a wadded white handkerchief clamped under his pudgy thumb. "It's okay. If you can't trust a priest with a confession, who can you trust? *Uhhh huh.* You look better without your disguise, *uhhh huhhh*, but even with it on, I still couldn't help, *uh huhhh*, thinking I'd seen you somewhere before."

Great! Everyone knows.

Doctor Philips walked up, standing tall over the shoulder of the shorter man. His white hair picked up light from the hallway but his dark face was in shadow. Still, his eyes were wide and bright, his gaze sweeping from Peter to the priest and back to Peter again. "Perhaps I had better explain," he said, his voice a rich base, commanding attention.

Peter shook his head. "Isn't necessary. He knows." The small round disks of the priest's glasses reflected light from the hall as he turned toward the doctor. He gasped like he was having a heart attack, like he was about to keel over dead, like he was the one who should be in bed, not Angela. But Peter's own voice was fluted as he tried to compose himself, so he had little to criticize. "I...I trust you'll honor your vow of silence, or, *ah, ah*, whatever it is you do when you take confession."

"*Uhhh huh.* Right, *uhhh huh.* Right, of course," the priest said, covering his mouth with his handkerchief.

"I'm serious. I need you to pretend you never saw us. My little girl's sick. I have to get her to the hospital, but I'm persona non grata. Dr. Philips has agreed to help. After that we'll disappear and be gone like we were never here."

The fat friar huffed and puffed, his face flaming red. He grasped for a cross that wasn't there and clawed at his vestment instead. "I think you'll need my help too," he wheezed.

Dr. Philips put a hand on the priest's hefty shoulder. "There's no point in your getting involved, Father."

"Nonsense." *Uhhhh huh.* "You take that little girl in and the first thing they'll ask is whose child is she, *uhhhh huh, wheeze, uhhhh huuuh,* then they'll want her name and medical history, none of which *you* can provide. And when you can't tell them who the child's parents are they'll bring in social services, and then *youuuuh,* you won't be able to get the little girl back to her father. *Wheeeeze, uhhhh huh.* It's better if I do it. We have an orphanage. *Uhhhh huhhh.* Our kids get sick all the time. *Wheeeeeze.* If I bring her in, they'll think she's an orphan. They won't ask about her parents. Then, once she's inside, you can take over. *Wheeeeeew!*"

An electronic version of *The Blue Danube* started to play. The doctor reached for his cell phone, pushing the button to answer. "Hello, uh huh. No, we're not. What's that? No, don't. Everything's fine. No, please, keep the police out of this. I'll tell you about it later."

Great! Praying mantis lady—Stop it!—Stop it, stop it, stop it! Making her out to be an insect's no better than Hank thinking I'm a sissy. But why couldn't she keep it shut. Has to be her, fixated on the escaped murderer and yapping to her floppy-haired friend, and he suddenly realizes where he's seen my face and—busted! Lord, please. Too many people already know!

CELESTIAL VANTAGE

What is a miracle? Is it not something supernatural? Yes, but consider this: What seems supernatural to one is common to another. A household pet may regard music from a box, or a dark room filling with light, miraculous. But to the one who tunes the radio or turns on the light, it's part of everyday life. Look around you. Miracles abound! It's a miracle every time the day dawns, a flower blooms, or a baby cries.

Why do you say, "Show me a miracle and I'll believe?" God says, "Believe and I'll show you a miracle." A closed mind cannot fathom mountains being moved, stars falling from the sky, or those who sleep rising from the dead. Open up! You wish to see the resurrection? Oh, beloved of God, people rise from the dead every day. Every soul goes to its appointed place, rising to life anew. To the Almighty, a mountain is but a handful of dust, the stars but candles in the wind, and death but a door through which man passes into life. These things are not strange, they are common. What is miraculous is that those who deserve death receive life through the power of His name.

TWENTY-FOUR

"The sacred rights of mankind are not to be rummaged for among old parchments or musty records. They are written, as with a sunbeam in the whole volume of human nature, by the hand of Divinity itself; and can never be erased or obscured by mortal power."
—Alexander Hamilton 1755-1804, 1ˢᵗ U.S. Secretary of the Treasury

ATHER BLOOM struggled, huffing and puffing, his thinning hair swirling up like a cyclone around his pink ears as he carried Angela from the parking lot into the hospital. *No, no, no, no, noooo we're not giving up, just a few more feet, I can make it, hee, hee, hee, whoo, whoo, whoo, I can make it, I can make it, uhhh-huh, uhhh-huh.* He trudged across the puddled pavement, praising God for a lull in the torrential rain, but the moisture-laden air still spit in his face.

Mounted on the wall above the entry was a sign that read, "ER/ Prompt Care Entrance." An ambulance pulled out with a gold caduceus emblazoned on its side—a snake on a winged pole symbolizing healing. *If they knew where that icon came from they wouldn't use it*, Buddy mused. *Got it all wrong thinking it's modeled after the staff of Hermes. Nonsense!* Hermes was the Greek god of commerce and cunning and invention and theft. Totally inappropriate for a symbol of medicine. *No*, it predated that. The Greeks stole the idea from Moses—that's where it originated. The children of Israel tramping through the desert, plagued by snakes and dying in droves until God told ol' Mo' to put a serpent—an effigy of Satan and sin—on a pole and lift it up for

170

everyone to see so they could be healed. And, of course, later Christ, who took the sin of the world upon Himself and likewise was lifted up so all men could look to Him and be saved. But *no*, they wouldn't admit to that—*uhhh huh, whoo, whoo, whoo, hee, hee, hee, whoo, whoo, whoo*—they were in denial.

He took a faltering breath, squeezing Angela up to his shoulder, and leaned in to push on the door. But it opened automatically, sending him stumbling through with his short legs pumping and tennis shoes *flap, flap, flapping*, trying to catch his balance. He grappled with his load—*merciful God*—struggling to hold onto Angela without crashing to his knees. The doors behind him closed, shutting out the wind and rain.

Father Buddy Bloom stood there wet and disheveled and out of breath, *uhhhh huhhh, uhhhh huhhh*, arms aching, looking for a wheelchair. There wasn't one in sight. A young man dressed in a white nylon uniform, a male nurse or intern, stood with his back to the wall reading a newspaper. Buddy waddled up with Angela half-hanging over his shoulder. "Excuse me, *huh*, excuse me, I *huh* I...the little girl needs a wheelchair."

The man glanced at his watch and without looking up said, "I'm on a break," and went back to reading his paper.

Father Bloom shifted Angela in his arms, *uhhh huh, uhhh, huh*. He wasn't asking the man to move—*heaven forbid*—just point him in the right direction. *This is an emergency. The little girl is dying. I can do this, uhhh, huh.* The nurse's station was directly ahead. Buddy wore his black suit with a black shirt and white clerical collar, but on his feet were black tennis shoes with white rubber soles. He couldn't find leather shoes that didn't pinch his toes. He slid his foot forward, the rubber *squeeeaking* on the tiles.

Angela had been briefed about what and what not to say. She wouldn't be lying when she told them she didn't know who her parents were, but best not to say anything unless asked, and then to stick only to questions about how she felt. Father Bloom reached the desk, red-faced and breathing hard, *uhhhh huhhh*, but still able to offer a smile to the nurse on the other side. His green eyes blinked behind the gold circles of his glasses.

"Hi, I *uh*..." He transferred Angela's weight to his other arm. "I don't want to be a bother, but could I get a wheelchair?" A mixture of sweat and rain dappled his forehead.

The nurse, a large dark-skinned lady, stood and grabbed the chair parked behind her. She took it by the handles and came around front, pushing the wheeled contraption. Her smile, broad and toothy, resembled a chalk drawing of a Cheshire cat on a blackboard. "Oh my, yes, honey," She took Angela from Buddy's arms and sat her in the chair. "Oh my, my, you sure don't look so good. Whatever is wrong with you, hon?" She laid a large black hand on Angela's forehead, "*Umm-um*, mercy me, but you're hot." Her eyes, white and wide, looked to the child's companion for an answer.

Father Bloom pulled a handkerchief from his vest pocket and mopped his brow. "She's not feeling well. I think she needs a doctor. She's listless and can't seem to hold her food down and complains of pain something awful. Probably just a touch of the flu, but with all the plagues going around, you never know."

The nurse returned to her place behind the counter and sat down, looking over her computer. Her hair was short and glossy and straightened with lacquer except where it curled up under her chin. "Okay, I just need a little information and we'll get her admitted. Let's start with the patient's name."

Father Bloom pulled his coat away from his burgeoning chest and stuffed his handkerchief into his pocket. "We call her Ginny."

"And her surname?"

"Ah, unfortunately, that I don't know. We run an orphanage at Saint Boniface. She was a drop-off. Never saw her parents. We just call her Ginny and leave it at that."

The nurse looked up, her eyebrows raised so that her oversized eyes looked like polished white marbles. "You know she has to be registered with the state at age thirteen. You'll need a surname before then."

"Yes, and I'm sure we'll come up with one, though I don't rightly know when that will be. She wasn't left with a birth certificate, so we don't know how old she is."

The nurse eyed Angela's arm. "How 'bout an implant? Lots of people get them early. That'd tell us what we need to know."

"Nope. No ID number, no chip. That's the first thing we look for in a drop-off. But a lot of folks are funny about getting those darn things, so they put it off till the last minute."

The nurse tapped the desktop with her fingernail, her full lips bunched into a frown. "Okay, no age or ID. You really should have taken her to the registrar and had him supply her with an identity." She began *click, click, clicking* on her keyboard.

Father Bloom popped up on his toes, leaning in to peek at what she was typing but he was too short and too round to get close enough to see. "Of course, of course...it's just that we hoped her mother, *uhhh, huh*, her mother would come back to get her. Women, *uhhh, huh*, do that sometimes, drop off children they can't afford to feed and then come back and claim them once they find work and a place to stay."

"I guess there's no point in asking about her medical history?"

Father Bloom shook his head. "Never had her to a doctor before. No reason to. She's never been sick, nope, not ever. *Uhhh, huh*. Been healthy as a head of cabbage, until now."

The nurse looked up. "You don't sound so good yourself. I hope you have an inhaler for that asthma of yours."

Father Buddy brought a hand up, patting his coat pocket. "Never leave home without it," he assured her.

The nurse went back to typing. "Symptoms are: pain and fever, lack of energy, and loss of appetite. Am I missing anything?"

The priest rocked back on his rubber heels, pink cheeks puffed out. "That 'bout sums it up."

Angela stared into the distance, gazing through half-lidded eyes into another realm at a nebulous ball of light.

I'm scared. Can we go now? I don't need to be here. I'm okay. I mean, it hurts, but I'm okay. The pain feels sort of normal, you know? Isn't there anything you can do? I want to go home, that's all. I just want to see Mommy, then I'll be ready. Are you sure they'll be all right?

A second nurse walked in, carrying a newspaper and reeking of tobacco. She gave Buddy a sidelong glance and sat down. She was thin with skin that seemed to drape from her bones like loose folds of material. Her blond hair was razor-cut and stood straight up except around the ears and back where it was so short it bristled. When she looked at him, her watery gaze seemed distant and unfocused, and the bags beneath her eyes were puffy and gray. Large hoop earrings rocked back and forth when she moved her head. Father Bloom smiled again, but she turned away, shuffling the papers at her computer.

The black nurse spoke again. "Honey, we have a problem here, *um ummm*. I'm not sure what to do in a situation like this. The computer won't accept the information without a last name. I thought I could make something up, but I tried using Smith and found too many of them. And I can't pick a name at random because everyone has their own medical history, which on your little girl's chart could lead to a wrong diagnosis. Without a name or ID number, I'm not sure she can be admitted."

"*Uhhh, huh, uhhh, huh, uhhh, huh,* I don't thinnn...I don't think you need to worry. Ca...call Dr. Philips. He's a personal friend. He'll look after her."

The nurse stared at Father Bloom, the whites of her eyes bright as twin moons on a dark night. "Just hold on, honey, I'll check. Doctor Philips, *huh*?" The nurse clicked her mouse, scrolling down a list of names. "Well, you're in luck, Dr. Philips is in today. I'll see if I can find him." She got on the phone and pushed a button, speaking into the receiver. When she hung up, she stood and said, "Let's wheel her inside. At least we can take her temperature." She pointed to a small room behind her. "Roll her in there."

She slipped a piece of paper under a clipboard and felt a tug on her sleeve. The other nurse looked past her, waiting until Buddy and Angela were out of earshot, then whispered. "You know better than to let her in. They find out you broke the regs, it'll be your job."

"Not my decision. Doctor Philips said to admit her. He'll have to assume responsibility. Besides, the little girl's sick. How can we turn her away?" She pulled back, breaking the other woman's grip.

The thin nurse scowled. "She's spoiled goods, that one, a waste of the doctor's time. She doesn't deserve hospital care, not at taxpayer expense. None of them do. They're raising children out there who are never going to fit in. Every one of them will eventually need massive reintegration. They're damaging those kids beyond repair."

"That's not the little girl's fault. Besides, that's all changed. Churches aren't allowed to teach things that hurt people anymore. They stopped doing that years ago."

The woman rolled her eyes. "And if you believe that, I got land in Florida for sale. Just be sure to wear hip waders. Wake up, girl! Don't you read the papers? These people still teach the same old crap they always have. Love your brother, *blah, blah, blah,* unless he doesn't believe in God, then it's okay to blow him away. And we let them do it. Sooner or later they're gonna blow up the whole dang planet."

"She's just a child, Ingrid. We can't blame her for what others believe." She tucked her clipboard against her breast and went to the examination room, closing the door behind her to give them privacy. "How you feeling, honey?" She reached over, touching Angela's cheek with the back of her hand.

Angela didn't say anything, but she let out a soft groan and shivered. She closed her eyes, then opened them half-mast, wrapping her arms around her shoulders.

"Think you can do something for me? I need you to climb up here." The nurse patted a chrome bed on wheels.

Angela nodded and tried to stand, but was too weak and faltered, sitting down again. Father Buddy grasped her under the arm and raised her to her feet. The nurse took her other hand and, between the two of them, they walked her to the bed and helped her lie down. The nurse went to the cabinet and retrieved a thermometer, which she placed in the child's ear. "She's definitely running a fever," she said.

The door opened and the other nurse stuck her head in. "There's a woman at the counter who says she left her glasses. I looked around but didn't see 'em. You know anything about it?"

"Yes, they're on the file cabinet, just a second." She started to leave but turned back in afterthought. "Here...I was taking the girl's temperature. Maybe you can get her blood pressure." She disappeared through the door.

Ingrid took over, wrestling Angela's arm around and wrapping it in a plastic strap. Angela grimaced with the abruptness of the procedure. The nurse pushed a button and the band tightened around the child's arm and then relaxed. She stared at Angela's face, waiting for the count, her eyes narrowing in a quizzical expression. She noted her blood pressure on the chart and walked out just as the black nurse was returning.

Ingrid grabbed her by the arm, pulling her to the side, and handed her the clipboard. "There's something funny going on here. That little girl's wearing a wig."

"A wig?"

"Yes, and her skin is *too* pale and anemic-looking. I'd bet my bottom dollar the girl's receiving chemo. I've seen it before. That child should be in a cancer ward."

The large black nurse studied the clipboard and brought her hand to her hip. "Or she could look pale and anemic because she has the flu, but that's for the doctor to decide. He'll have to do a thorough blood screen. If you're right, he'll know."

Ingrid turned and stormed back to the admissions desk. She sat down and glanced at her newspaper. The lead story told about a fugitive, an insurrectionist and murderer who had taken his daughter and fled across the Canadian border into the U.S. The little girl was reported to be dying of cancer.

TWENTY-FIVE

"My hopes of a future life are all founded upon the Gospel of Christ."
—*John Quincy Adams, 1767-1848, 6th President of the United States*

PETER PACED the floor, his heart pounding. *Where are they?* He drew the curtain back slowly and peeked out for the hundredth time. *No one coming, where is everyone?* He let the curtain drop to its original position and then picked it up and peeked out again in case the shadow he thought he saw was a person. It wasn't. *Where is she?*

He was wearing the fresh suit of clothes he'd found on the bed when he stepped out of the shower—a dark blue polo shirt with burgundy trim and a pair of gray slacks. Not a perfect fit, Dr. Philips was at least a size larger than he, but the outfit was passable. And not half bad to look at, though he would never choose a polo shirt for himself. His own clothes—the ones he'd worn through the sweaty cornfields, and in Jake's sweaty truck, and in Hank's sweaty box—were noticeably absent. He'd taken a shower before the study last night, but he'd had to put his dirty clothes back on. *Yuck!*

Didn't matter, they could give him all the new duds they wanted and he'd still feel naked. He needed a costume, a mask to hide behind. *Where is everyone?* It was time to remake himself. He couldn't let them walk in and see the real deal. He wasn't ready for that.

Still, hadn't they already seen the real Peter? And they hadn't thrown him out, at least not yet, though Hank would if he could, of that he was sure. *Get over it.* He'd seen it before. Oil and water. He

177

would always repulse people like Hank. He didn't have to *do* anything. Just being who he was set them on edge. People like Hank and... and Bob McCauley, and probably a billion others like them, couldn't tolerate weakness, no matter how tolerant they pretended to be. Half the time they overcompensated, falling all over themselves to prove how accepting they were, and the rest of the time pretending he didn't exist.

Hank was a perfect example. He was supposed to be Peter's friend, but after the fat friar and Adrian—*fat friar?* See he was guilty of the same kind of judgmental predisposition! After Father Bloom and Dr. Philips raced off to the hospital with Angela, it was like Hank couldn't get out fast enough—*gotta go, see ya later, bye-bye.* Didn't even stick around long enough for a cup of coffee—and he knew how much Hank *loved* his coffee. But if Peter were someone else, maybe then... well, he had everything he needed—*eye pencils, face putty, new hair.* The old costume had to be retired. It wasn't fooling anyone. He slid the curtains back again—*no one. Come on, guys.*

Peter resumed his pacing. At least Hank had put together a plan. The old man might not like him, but he'd proved himself worthy of trust. He made an arc around the padded chair and marched back toward the couch. It'd be a wonder if the carpet wasn't threadbare by the time Dr. Philips got home. He resisted the temptation to peek outside. He would pace the track five times before looking out again. Maybe he should make it ten, *no five*, five is enough. He looked at his watch. 5:50. Shouldn't someone be home by now? Shouldn't they at least have called? What if they'd been arrested? What if Angela was in jail? *Oh God, please, help them—help me!*

He brought a finger to his mouth, gnawing on a hangnail. *Forget the five laps.* He leaned across the back of the sofa and stole another look outside. His stomach fizzed like seltzer. He bit his nail ripping it from his cuticle and grimaced. *Anyone out there? Anyone live in this ghost town? Wait!* He thought he saw a car turn into the drive. *Was it?* The curtains were lucent, not transparent, and with the dusky light of sunset streaming in, it was hard to tell. The apparition disappeared behind the wall. *Yes, thank God!* He heard car doors slamming and the sound of voices. Angela was home.

He rushed over, flinging the door open at the sound of a key turning the lock, and there they stood, both of them—Dr. Philips and Father Bloom—but not Angela. "Where have you been? I was worried half to death." He stood on his toes, looking around the huge priest into the unlit garage. "Where's Angela? Where's my little girl?" Peter began fanning his face. "Where's Angela?"

"Slow down, son, slow down." The doctor stepped in, placing an arm around Peter's shoulders—a reed shaking in the wind. "Your little girl is fine. I had to leave her at the hospital. Got a call from your friend Hank. He has his truck in for repairs but it won't be ready until tomorrow. You can't leave before then, and Angela needs 'round-the-clock attention to keep her pain under control. She also needs rest to recover her strength."

Peter shook off the doctor's arm and resumed his pacing. "You should have called. You had me scared to death. You've been gone all day. I sat here thinking you'd been arrested and that my little girl was in jail. What's Hank doing—did he say?" Peter paused long enough to peer into the doctor's face. "We can't stay overnight. You saw her. She's dying...she'll be lucky to live long enough for me to get her home—and I promised. Do you understand? I promised and I don't intend to break my word. I couldn't live with myself." He put his finger in his mouth, clamping down on another nail. "Why did Hank start something that won't be done until tomorrow? Did he say? He knows I have to get home. I just wanted you to numb her pain, that's all. I have to get her home, understand?" Peter's eyes filled with water. He blinked, holding back the tears. "She just wants to be with her mother, but I...I can't bear to see her in pain."

"Yes, I know, but tomorrow's the best we can do. You'll have to talk to Hank. I want her in the hospital right up until you're ready to leave. I don't want the sedation wearing off. It's the only way to keep the pain under control, and the hospital has a sterile environment. That little girl's a fighter, but she doesn't need any infections right now. Running around in a truck, I'm surprised she hasn't caught every virus known to man, Lord be praised, and her white count's so high, it's a miracle she's still alive." Adrian shook his head, his brown eyes questioning Peter, but Peter refused to meet his stare. "I don't like it, but I've got to concur with your previous physician. You may not be able to get her home. Lord, have mercy. She could go any time, but that's not for me to say. She's in God's hands. Now, son, you have to start thinking about yourself. Have you heard from your wife? Any news?"

Peter wiped his cheeks on his sleeve, and lifted his head. He took a deep fluttering breath. "No, nothing. Last I heard they...they had someone watching our house. They'll follow her if she tries to leave." He looked Adrian in the eye. "Look, it's not that I don't appreciate all you're doing, but I promised to get Angela home. I have to at least try. I've been thinking, maybe I can get Hank to take Angela to her mother. If I go near the house, I'll be arrested on the spot, but...but Angela wants the family together when...I...I've given it some thought. What about this? You think if I contact the authorities and volunteer to turn myself in, they'll let me stay with Angela and her mother until she...you know, until she passes?"

THE PHONE was ringing, but not with the rude *riiiiiinnnnnnggg,* *riiiiiinnnnnnggg, riiiiiinnnnnnggg* designed to wake the dead. The sound came from Bob's cell phone, which happened to be in his pocket when he fell asleep, so the ring was muffled and purred with a soft *bleeeeeeep, bleeeeeeep, bleeeeeeep.* Bob dragged himself from his stupor and retrieved the little noisemaker so he could slam it against the wall. He looked at it, daring it to *bleeeeeeep,* again and, when it did, flipped it open and brought it to his ear.

"B*aaah*b here, *ahh-ah-yaaawwn.*"

"Bob, it's Frank Ainsworth, in Toronto. What time is it down there? You sound like you're asleep."

Bob brought the back of his hand up to stifle another yawn, glancing at his watch. "No, same time as you. I've been keeping long hours. Must have dozed off. What's up?"

"Ah, well, I'm not sure how important this is, it sounds a bit far-fetched, but we just got a call from a hospital in Beckley, West Virginia. The call was routed to me because your office thinks you're still operating at the border. By the way, you need to check in. They want a heads up as to where you're at. Anyway, here's what we got: a priest dropped a little girl off at Raleigh Hospital in Beckley. He said she'd been left at his doorstep. He didn't know her name. The lady we spoke to said the little girl's wearing a wig, and the doctor who's looking after her refuses to let anyone else see her chart. He's ordered all kinds of tests and a white cell count in particular, which might suggest her hair is falling out because she's got cancer, like she's receiving chemotherapy or something. It seems to fit the profile of Dufoe's little girl, so I thought I'd better pass it along."

Now Bob was fully awake and sitting on the edge of the bed. "You did the right thing. That's the second time you've come through, Frank. I owe you." He hung up the phone and looked at his watch. Beckley was several hours away, less if he flew. He leaned over, pulled his computer in, and launched a travel site. He checked flight schedules but the only planes that serviced Beckley from Pittsburgh were commuter aircraft, and there weren't any flights out until morning. He couldn't wait. He stole one more quick glance at his watch and started gathering his things.

BOB ROARED down the highway. He wasn't ignoring the speed limit, but he wasn't watching it either. He was on a case, and besides cops never wrote other cops tickets. He gripped the steering wheel with white-knuckled intensity. A break at last. It had to be Peter, had to be! Beckley wasn't *that* far from Pittsburgh. How many little girls with cancer weren't already in a hospital somewhere? And dropped off by a priest? A religious connection. That's just who Peter would turn to for help. And not just any priest, but a priest who refused to give the little girl's name, a little girl who coincidentally wasn't chipped. Only religious wackos refused to get their kids chipped. All that Antichrist nonsense. Bull-pucky! Bob pounded the steering wheel with his fist. *Hot dang!* It had to be Peter's little girl. There were just *too* many coincidences to be a coincidence. And where Peter's daughter was, Peter had to be close by. *Dang!* He had him!

Bob took a breath, trying to relax. His stomach buckled. He

buuurrrped and loosened his seatbelt. Being uptight wouldn't get him there any faster, and it was bad for his heart. He began drumming the wheel with his fingers. The lights on his dashboard glowed purple and green. He wasn't going cheap when it came to a rental car, *no-sir-eee, Bob.* That danged flophouse of a motel was the limit.

He looked up, admiring the view through the moon roof. The midnight stars were brilliant. It made him think of...well, okay, of God, but...he shook his head. Millions of stars and all of them placed by natural process, *the big bang,* and all of them with planets spinning around in perfect synchronization, and all of them part of the billion galaxies that composed the nighttime sky. *The Divine Watchmaker?* Sure, God was at the center of it all, keeping it all in motion. But God Himself would've had some kind of evolutionary beginning, evolving out of his own primordial stew until he became the all-powerful, all knowing wizard with a watch of His own to wind.

Bob chuckled to himself. That's what made him different from people like Peter. For a bright guy, Peter thought small. Adam and Eve and a fairy godfather who waved his magic wand and *poof* gave them life. "God, if you're there, make Deanne come to her senses. She's too good for a nutbag like..." Bob smiled. He used to call him Sweetie Petey. Boy, would that tick Deanne off.

They were sitting in a pew. He was holding Deanne's hand, but it felt stiff, like a dry sponge, not soft and warm like before. Something was happening he couldn't explain. It was like there was an invisible wall between them, but he didn't understand where the wall had come from, or why it was there.

He had to admit it was an awesome cathedral, with high-vaulted oak ceilings and light that streamed through stained-glass windows, painting rainbows on the floor. A traditional church, the way Bob liked it. It's why God made Himself temples and such. He didn't want to be worshiped at home. The pipe organ droned and the congregation sang. Bob didn't join in but that wasn't unusual; he never sang. He glanced at Deanne. She wasn't singing either. She was mouthing the words, but her heart wasn't in it. Her lips opened and closed but her breath emitted no sound. She complained that the songs lacked meaning, something about deemphasizing the name of Jesus. So what? God was God. It didn't matter what you called Him. A rose by any other name...call Him Allah, or Jehovah, or Krishna, didn't matter, it was all one and the same. He was still God.

> Now to the highest power sing,
> And fill your hearts with love.
> Receive the warmth of channeling
> All blessings from above.

She was in a particularly ugly mood, slumped down in the pew. But even as he formed the thought, she lurched forward and raised her hand, a smile breaking on her lips.

Bob followed her gaze and grimaced. Oh, no! He squirmed in his seat. She was waving at Peter, drawing attention to herself. People were watching. He cringed and leaned back, folding his arms across his chest. Peter, sweet thing that he was, swished down the aisle and squeezed into the pew climbing over the knees of people who were already seated. "'Scuse me, sorry, excuse me." He sat down beside Deanne, then leaned over and whispered something that made her smile. The guy was starting to get on Bob's nerves. Every time they went anywhere the computer geek showed up. It was becoming a bad habit.

Bob's lips knotted. It wasn't envy or jealousy or nothin' like that, the guy was a priss. You can't get down on a guy for being what he's born to be, it's just that it creeped him out. He tried to adjust his thinking. In a morally inclusive society, it wasn't right to think of gays as the limp-wristed slime they were. Push come to shove, he didn't give diddley squat about the man's sexual proclivities. What he cared about was the invasion of his turf.

> Now count your blessings as you sing,
> With great assurance know,
> That when your praises loudly ring,
> Love's goodness starts to flow.

KEITH CLEMONS

The words were psychobabble, but Bob couldn't help smiling. That was the nut of it. He had to count his blessings and love the little creep. The fact that Peter was gay was a good thing. If he were some strapping hulk of a man, he might have reason to worry, but Deanne wouldn't dump a prince to run off with a chambermaid. He threw a sidelong glance at the two of them. Their heads were together, a couple of girls passing secrets. It's just that she was giving Peter a little too much of her time.

With his thoughts focused inward and his eyes hypnotized by the long lines of taillights in front of him, Bob missed seeing the temperature gauge blinking red until the car spoke to him. "Warning! Temperature exceeding threshold limit. Warning..." It took several seconds before he realized what was happening. A white cloud of steam erupted from the hood. "Wipers!" The Speech Activated Facile Equipment program (SAFE) prompted the windshield wipers to begin clearing the glass. The car was overheating. He glanced in the rearview mirror and started pulling over. "Gas station!" His GPS analyzed his current position and let him know of a service center at the next exit, but it was coming up fast. "Right turn!" The blinker started flashing, warning drivers of his intent to change lanes.

Ignoring the blinding cloud of vapor, he cranked his head around and squeezed between bumpers and honking horns—*yeah, same to you, get out of the way*—across two lanes of traffic to zoom up the exit at a speed much too fast for the short ramp. He hit the brakes. The sign over the gas station was lit. *Still open.* His car rolled through the stop and coasted into the station.

Bob popped the latch and watched a head of steam billow out from under the hood. He clambered out, waving the mist away from his face. *Dang it all!* He doubled his fists, pounding on the hood—*blamm*—before jerking it open. *I don't need this!* He had to wait for the cloud to dissipate to see where the leak was coming from. A loose hose clamp. *Dang factories don't pay their workers enough. Brand-new car, where's the freakin' quality control?* He grabbed the hose and jerked his hand back shaking his scalded fingers. *Aaawwwwouch, dang it all!*

Looking around he spotted a piece of wet cardboard flattened on the asphalt. He picked it up and used it to wrap the hose. Air could be heard hissing as he wiggled the rubber pipe. He went to the glove box, lifting maps and rental agreements to look underneath, and then shoveled everything onto the floor in search of a screwdriver. *Sheeesh, where're the stupid tools?* He left the glove box hanging open, slammed the car door—*blamm*—and went to pop the trunk—*rats!* Not a tool to be found.

He looked up and saw a clerk staring at him through the window of the all-night convenience store. He banged the trunk and marched inside. They were separated by a shield of bullet-proof glass, but still the kid backed up as he approached. "I need a freakin' screwdriver, pair of pliers, anything to tighten a hose clamp."

"We don't have anything. We're not allowed to loan out tools."

"Only for a minute. I mean it. Come on, don't be a chump." But the kid was shaking his head. "Look, I'm a cop." He reached into his pocket and pulled out his wallet, flipping it open to display his shield. "I'm not going to steal it, I swear."

The kid put his hands up as if Bob were about to test the strength of the glass with his gun. "Sorry, mister. We don't have any tools here. Imo takes them with him at night. Keeps them locked in the trunk of his car."

"Imo?"

"Our...our mechanic. He sometimes changes tires and does small repairs but he's gone home. He doesn't come on shift till eight tomorrow morning."

"There must be something around here. Oh, for the love of... look, all I need is a screwdriver." But the kid stood there shaking his head. "Oh, for Pete's sake, I'll buy the darn thing. You must have a screwdriver somewhere."

The kid went through the motions of checking under the counter and shuffling paper like he was looking. "Sorry, it's not like I don't get asked a lot. If people would return things, we'd probably keep them around, but I heard the boss say he'd paid for his last screwdriver and there hasn't been one around since."

"Call him."

"Who?"

"Amo, Imo, Emo, whatever his name is...that mechanic of yours. Call him. Tell him I'll give him fifty credits to bring a screwdriver down here."

The kid shook his head. "No can do. It's Thursday, Imo's bowling night. There's a girl he takes with him and he always stays at her place after the game. Sorry, but I don't even know her number."

Bob spun around and marched to the door, shoving it open so hard it slammed against the building. "I don't freakin' believe it!" He looked at his watch: 1:00 a.m. Another three hours to Beckley. If the guy didn't show up until eight, he wouldn't get out of the station until nine, and that meant he wouldn't make Beckley until around noon. He dialed Security Central. The phone was picked up by a recording.

"Operations. Please give security authorization code."

"This is Agent Bob McCauley, Homeland Security, access code one, four, six, zero, security clearance Alpha, verify please."

A few seconds later the phone was picked up by a real voice. "Good evening, Agent McCauley, what can we do for you?"

"I need backup at Raleigh General in Beckley, West Virginia. There's a little girl there. Name's Ginny, no last name. She's in the care of a Dr. Philips. Apparently she has cancer. I need someone to watch the little girl."

"Slow down, Chief. Our boys are maxed out. No way I can free someone up to babysit...don't care how sick the kid is."

"It's not for the girl. I'm tailing Peter Dufoe. Read his sheet, long as your arm—international terror, insurrection, murder. I think the little girl's his, and if so, he's bound to show up there." Bob pressed the "send" key on his phone. "I just downloaded a photograph of Dufoe. I want a man on site. You can log that as priority one from L.A. Central. Nordstrom's own access. Got that? I'm in no mood to quibble. Get someone in there now, and watch that little girl. If and when Dufoe shows up, I want to be notified immediately."

TWENTY-SIX

"I have always believed in the inspiration of the Holy Scriptures, whereby they have become the expression to man of the Word and Will of God."
—Warren Harding, 1865-1923, 29th President of the United States

PETER SAT in front of a mirror dusting his makeup. Nip here, tuck there. He wiped his hands on a tissue, keeping the tips of his fingers clean. Just a little more—*there! Perfect.* He took a hand mirror from the dresser and brought it up for a closer look, pinching his chin and turning his head side to side. A credit to his many years at the "chop shop," the term he used for special effects makeup, prosthetic design and mold and mask-making. He could turn a frog into a prince without a kiss.

It felt good to be in costume again. A bit weird perhaps, this fixation on wanting to be anonymous, but a lot of weird things had happened. Besides, taking refuge behind a mask was a good way of gaining a different perspective. There was a time when he would've done it just to get the attention of the boys. He craved their acceptance. His father had left him when he was six and he'd been rejected by the muscle-bumping, iron-pumping, steroid giants of his youth, which had left him with an innate desire to garner their approval. Costumes made it possible. In a costume he could hide who he really was—someone no one liked—and become a star, a VIP, a celebrity—anyone he wanted to be...

He'd struggled with his gender identity...*forever.* Perhaps in

187

retrospect, *struggle* was too weak a word. He'd been torn apart, wanting acceptance as a man, but finding approval only when posing as a girl. It was self-emasculation. He hated himself, *no*, he loathed himself, every time they called him "pretty." He'd put the razor to his wrist so many times 911 finally stopped responding to his calls. His psychiatrist said he was out to get attention. He knew better. He was just too weak to see it through.

He rubbed a little more gray into his eyebrows. The sad truth was, he wasn't alone. For thousands like him, the love boat was a rust-pitted garbage scow—*everyone overboard, women and children first*. He could relate to the effeminate who genuinely felt they were born in the wrong body, like some kind of mistake or cruel joke. And the abused, those who as children had been molested so often they no longer had the ability to develop and sustain normal heterosexual relationships. And the disenfranchised who again, like himself, were searching for love in all the wrong places, happy to receive fleeting moments of approval because acceptance of any kind was hard to find in the straight world. He had compassion for those who hid in the dark recesses of the bar, taking what they could, moving from one lover to the next, wearing smiling masks to pretend they were happy, praying they were never exposed.

But there were also the more perverse, those who took up placards and marched in the streets, chanting—*"Racist, bigot, anti-gay, born-again Christian, go away."* They, too, were part of the scene, prowling the nightclubs to find partners for the sake of sex alone. Not gay because they believed themselves to be born that way, but gay because of what the lifestyle had to offer—*unbridled sex*. Peter had observed how they were never satisfied, always wanting more, ever touting their promiscuity, ever falling into deeper and more depraved forms of sexual behavior.

He pushed at his cheek, molding the putty to the natural contours of his face. Just a little more nip and tuck. *Right.* Plastic surgeons used nip and tuck to make people appear younger. He was striving to look old—*go figure.* Either way, it was an art, and he took pride in the mastery of it. In his search to free himself of his past, he'd given it up for a time. But after Ruth's passing, he'd realized it wasn't the makeup that was sinful, it was how it was used. Besides, Deanne had begged him to show her how it was done.

He turned his face left and right, making sure both cheeks were evenly matched. *Ruth, Ruth, Ruth, Ruth, Ruth.* My, he hadn't thought of her in years. He hoped she was looking down from Glory and could see how he'd changed. What a great old gal—like a mother to him. She was the first person to say he was a man, in spite of his feminine bent.

And Bill who, after the loss of his wife Laurie, took Peter in. Now *there* was a man's man—made Peter captain of his ship, took him fishing on the high seas, and taught him Hemingway's version of masculinity: scaling the day's catch on the gunnel, lobbing the entrails into the bounding main, and tossing the meat on the grill to roast over hot coals. He looked at himself in the mirror again. He wasn't the man Bill was, nor would he ever be, but he *was* a man.

Like Ruth, Bill refused to accept Peter's femininity. To Bill, it was black and white and no in-between. If you're a man between the legs, you're a man everywhere else. To pretend to be anything other than what God created you to be, was sin. He refused to acknowledge Peter's weakness. "People struggle with all kinds of problems," he'd said, "but you don't tell a dog it's a cow just 'cause it moos like a cow. A dog is a dog is a dog, end of story." Bill showed him where the homosexual lifestyle led according to Scripture—*"Hot enough for ya?"* So Bible drills were part of the daily routine, sitting on the deck of the boat with the sun a ball of rouge on the horizon, rocking on the tide with the wind in his hair and saltwater spraying his face.

It was there he came to know the all-powerful Creator of the universe, Jesus, the Christ, God's only begotten Son, Savior, Friend, and an all-powerful Father who loved and accepted him and promised him strength in time of trouble. The coaching may not have altered his physical appearance—the world would always see him as frail and soft-spoken, with a touch like the petal of a rose—but inside, he'd changed. He'd never forget the day Bill had pulled a jellyfish from the waves and plopped it on the deck of the boat. "That was you," he said. But then he pointed to a swordfish they'd hauled in earlier and said, "That's you now." God bless Bill for the lessons on that boat. But that was before all the Bibles were collected and replaced with revised copies.

Wheeewee! Peter fanned his face, dusting the powder away. He'd just added a couple of decades. His hair was white, his jowls saggy and his forehead, eyes and cheeks crisscrossed with lines. If only Deanne could see him now. What a hoot, to see how he would look in another twenty years, should he live so long. She'd seen him as everything else—a scare-faced monster, a Saxon king, everything but a woman— because he'd vowed never to do that again. But they had fun with it. Peter taught her everything he knew. She matched his talent, and in some ways became as good as he. He turned his head to apply another age spot—*well almost.*

Angela, too, had been part of the fun, most often dressing up—you guessed it—as an angel. But she also liked bullfrogs and butterflies and kittens and cows. They held their own costume parties, goading each other to see who could come up with the best disguise. Other families had photo albums filled with pictures of themselves enjoying the company of other people. They had photo albums filled with pictures of themselves *as* other people. Deanne used digital imaging to take them other places—*here we are in the Nairobi Desert of Kenya, standing in front of Horseshoe Falls in Canada, visiting the Great Wall of China*—trips they never took, though there was always hope...

Peter stood dusting the lapels of the dark suit he'd borrowed from Dr. Philips. It looked baggy on him, but that would be normal for an elderly man who'd lost weight and stopped taking care of himself, especially a cleric who might be under a vow of poverty. The black shirt with the white banding collar was provided by Father Bloom, borrowed, Peter was given to understand, from a much thinner colleague. Though it was still too large, that was okay—it matched the rest of his costume.

The image staring back at him from the mirror was downright scary. Not the age, though the wrinkled, ashen, hollow-eyed likeness looked almost demonic, but the costume itself, the black draping of a bought man—*me, a universalist?* It occurred to him what he was doing was no less than what Father Bloom did every day. *Ah, put on the costume and gain a different perspective, see?* The Apostle Paul said: "To the Jews I became as a Jew, that I might win Jews...to the weak I became as weak, that I might win the weak. I have become all things to all men, that I might by all means save some." Maybe Father Bloom was right. It was something to ponder, but another time. Peter turned around.

"Well, what do you think?"

"Lord, have mercy," the doctor said. "Surely this is not the same man. God be praised!"

THE CLOUDS were driven off by the wind sweeping the turbulence of thunder and rain into neighboring states, but the sun was back with a vengeance. Not a good day to wear black, Peter mused. As a supplier of optical technology, he understood solar dynamics. The sun burned at a temperature of eleven thousand degrees Fahrenheit, a yellow dwarf star that spewed gaseous fire five-hundred-thousand miles into the blackness of space. Global warming might be a farce but he wouldn't argue it now. It did seem the earth's atmospheric shield was thinning. He felt like an ant under a magnifying glass.

He kept shuffling forward, blotting his forehead with his free hand, praying he wasn't ruining his makeup, feeling the sweat under the arms. He had to get inside. This was his début. He was finally playing a part for someone other than Deanne. He should have been an actor.

He poked at the ground with his cane, a prop he specifically chose to help him remain stooped when he was tempted to stand straight. Keeping in character was imperative. Thin patches of his hair shimmered in the light, except where it was wet and stuck to his forehead. *Poke, move the cane forward, take a step, poke.* Getting inside the building would take forever at this rate. He'd be lucky if his face didn't melt in the heat. His throat waddled with latex skin, applied to imitate the sagging neck of an old man. His eyes were runny and gray with pockets of water. His eyebrows were too long, curling out every which way and his ears and nose, with their own crop of wild hairs, were larger than normal. Eyes, ears, nose and throat—maybe he should have been a doctor.

The doors slid apart, opening automatically as he approached the front of the building. He would avoid the information desk. He knew where he was going. Fourth floor. But if they did stop him and ask, he was there on church business—visiting an elderly parishioner—and had been asked to check in on the little girl, Ginny.

The plan was to stay at the hospital until Hank showed up with Killer and Babe. Then he would show them the signed release from Dr. Philips, explain that the tests had all been negative—*just a touch of flu*—and say he was taking the child back to the orphanage. He would fetch Angela, hire a taxi to drive them down the block to where the truck would be parked, and head on out with a handshake, a thank you and Godspeed. He now had plenty of pain-killers. From here on in, wherever God took them, his daughter would be free of the constant soreness in her limbs and aching bones.

He continued to shuffle across the tiles, knowing he was receiving the occasional glance, but so would any old man poking his way through the corridors. He turned left and started down a long hall. Gleaming waxed floors reflected the harsh fluorescent lights. He stopped in front of the elevator, paused for effect, tottering, squinting to look confused, and then pushed the button with a crooked finger. The doors slid open and he stepped inside. He turned around slowly to face the front again and felt the elevator lift. Four floors and just a short walk to the right and he'd see room 471—*and Angela*. He was doing it. He was there.

The doors opened with a *ding*—and three nurses leaving on break pushed in, blocking his exit. The doors started to close but he swung his cane up just in time. The doors bounced against the wooden staff, opening again. He took a step forward, suddenly realizing how that must have looked—the vigorous thrust of a cane from someone who appeared so old. Did they even notice? The door closed behind him. *Apparently not.*

Peter shuffled by the nurse's station. No one tried to stop him. It was normal visiting hours. Dr. Philips had made sure of that. He saw the number just a few doors down. *Poke, move the cane forward, take a step, poke.* He entered the room slowly, adapting to the role of the character he played. Would Angela even recognize him? She might not be able to focus. Her drug-laden thoughts would be groggy.

He leaned over the bed. Her eyes were closed, a picture of restful sleep, though not death. He glanced up. The steady *blip, blip, blip* of her pulse was registering on the monitor. Should he wake her? He wanted to, wanted to so bad, but they would be traveling soon. It was better to let her rest. He tried to set his cane down quietly, leaning it against the bed, but it was top-heavy and toppled over, clattering on the floor. Peter looked around. No one was there to see him. He stooped over, quickly picking up the cane. When he rose again, Angela's eyes were open. A smile broke across his face, but he restrained himself before his makeup cracked.

"Hi, Angela," he whispered, "how are you?" He reached out to take her hand. "It's me, Daddy, *shhhhh*, don't say anything. We don't want anyone to know." It looked like Angela was trying to smile, but her eyes were so dark and her cheeks so sallow it was hard to tell. "Hey, you look great, *really* great, ten times better than went we brought you in. I heard you were getting excellent care. So, what do you think of my getup? Pretty spiff, huh?"

He stood back, lifting both arms. "Nothin' but the best for you, kid. So, do you like it? Think I'd beat Mom in a contest? I should get extra points for how old it makes me feel just to wear this thing. And you better get used to it, because this is probably how I'll look in a few years. I'll probably walk around like this." Peter bent over and took a few tottering steps, leaning on his cane with one arm crooked up over the small of his back. He straightened himself and moved to the bed, taking her hand again.

"You look silly, Daddy." The words spoken so softly they were barely audible, but so full of life Peter wanted to scream, *Hallelujah!* He refrained, quelling his excitement. "Can we...can we play dress-up when we get home?" she asked.

He reached over, brushing the hair from her eyes. "Maybe. We'll see. Hey, I'm sorry about last night. I didn't think you'd have to stay over. Ol' Hank, he said his truck needed work...but we'll be ready to hit the road this afternoon. Good Lord willing, we'll see your mother later tonight or, worst case, tomorrow." Peter leaned in and gave Angela a butterfly kiss, then whispered in her ear. "Your daddy loves you. Don't ever forget it." Peter backed away, stooping to take on the role of an old man again in case someone walked in. He reached over and wiped the tear rolling down Angela's cheek with his finger. "You're looking good, just keep hanging in there. Hank is gonna pick us up and you and me and your mother, we'll all be together again real soon, promise."

Angela's lips trembled. "Daddy, what...what are you doing with my...I mean, who gets my toys? Make sure they go to someone who needs them?"

Peter raised his bushy, white eyebrows. He knew what she was asking. She had hundreds of toys—every doll, stuffed animal, coloring book, puzzle and game on the market—but the world was full of have-nots who didn't have any. She'd always had a heart for the less fortunate. "Let's not worry about that. You're going to need them yourself." His eyes began to mist. "But we'll see what we can do." He looked away, not wanting her to see his emotion. His head snapped up at the sound of footsteps. A nurse entered the room and marched over to the bed. She smelled toxic, like a factory spewing carcinogens.

"Who are you?" she demanded.

"Ah, er, could you repeat that?" he said, turning his face to the side. "I don't hear so good out that ear. What's that you said?"

"I said, Who are you?" the nurse repeated, only louder.

"Me? Why I'm Father Michael...Michael Reese, from the orphanage. I was in the hospital to see a friend. They asked me to look in on the little girl."

The nurse dipped into the pocket of her apron and removed a thermometer. She wiped it with an antiseptic cleanser and inserted it into Angela's ear, then fiddled with the saline drip that fed Angela through the needle in her arm. Peter could feel her glare. *Why the hostility?*

"Ingrid! What are you doing?" A second nurse stood at the door, hands on her hips, her eyebrows furrowing. "You're supposed to be in Emergency. I've already told you once, you don't belong up here. This is the second time. If I see you in here messing with my patient again, I'll have to report it."

SEATED IN a chair down the hall, reading a newspaper and looking like a bored relative waiting for news from a patient, was the agent Bob had requested. He turned his wrist, glancing at his watch, and picked up reading where he'd left off. He'd already been through the same newspaper a half-dozen times. The personal columns weren't his cup of tea, but at least they offered something new to read. A tone in his ear let him know he had a call. He brought a finger up and clicked the answer button.

"Armbruster," he said.

"This is Bob McCauley. You the one they got watching the little girl?"

"That'd be me."

"Okay, good. Listen, I'm back on the road, but I'm a few hours away. Any sign of Dufoe?"

"No, and the wife hasn't shown up either. The only ones that have been in the room so far are the doctor, a couple of nurses, and a priest."

"The doctor and nurses are probably okay, but the priest may be in cahoots with Dufoe. Did you check him out?"

"What for? I was told to keep a low profile. I don't want to start questioning people unnecessarily."

"*Hummm.* Right, okay, but keep an eye on him. He brought the child in yesterday, so he may be in contact with Dufoe. Just watch from a distance for now, but soon as I get there, I'm gonna lock him in a room and give him the third degree."

"You do what you gotta do, but I'd go easy on him. I doubt he can handle heavy interrogation. Guy's frail as dust. "

"Frail?"

"Yeah, you know, skinny, old, looks like a six-foot stalk of wheat beaten by the wind."

Skinny—not fat? Six foot? Bob's mind raced over the possibilities. *Didn't he...right!* He'd bragged about it, fooling an entire nursing home with a costume he'd done, turning a young journalist into an old lady..."That's him!" Bob practically shouted into the mouthpiece.

"Who?"

"That old man, the priest! That's Dufoe!"

"No way. I have Dufoe's photo right here. It's definitely not him. This guy's about ninety years old with wispy white hair. Not even close."

"I want that man locked in a room somewhere and I don't want you letting him out of your sight. I'll be there in a hour. Arrest him if you have to!"

"You want me to arrest a ninety-year-old priest? On what charge?"

"Make something up. You're Homeland Security; you don't need a reason. Just get that man out of that hospital and into a holding cell. And I want you to sit on him till I get there!"

CELESTIAL VANTAGE

Oh, beloved of God, are you listening? Do you hear? The Almighty's voice sounds from one end of creation to the other. It goes forth in the sound of mighty waters, in great peals of thunder, and in quiet whispers of the heart; yet upon the ear of man, so occupied with electronic noise, God's voice seldom falls.

It is written, "Men ought always to pray." Is not prayer conversation? Make known your requests, then, but take time to abide and wait upon the Lord for an answer. Samuel, that highly esteemed one of old, said "Speak, Lord, thy servant heareth." And yet you say, "Listen, Lord, thy servant speaks."

He has given us His Word. Meditate upon it. Listen and learn. Acknowledge the veracity of the Lord when He says, "My sheep hear my voice, and I know them, and they follow me, and I give to them eternal life."

TWENTY-SEVEN

"I walked the floor of the White House night after night until midnight, and I am not ashamed to tell you...that I went down on my knees and prayed to Almighty God for light and guidance more than one night."
—*William McKinley, 1843-1901, 25th President of the United States*

DEANNE TURNED, tucking a wayward strand of hair under her plastic cap. The steam shrouded her in a cloud, the shower pelting her with tiny bullets of water as she lathered her face, washing away her tears. *Why, Lord, why?* She began rubbing the back of her neck with an exfoliating sponge. She'd hustled, speed-walking the track in the gym 'round-and-around till her feet hurt, her shoulders glistened, and her lungs were raw and depleted of breath. She'd hoped the intense workout would keep her mind off the whereabouts of her husband. It hadn't. She'd said a verse and a prayer with each lap, but still she was frantic—*Where are they, Lord? Please send your angels to protect them, and give me strength to...*no, she couldn't let herself think about that. She might chicken out.

She felt the frustration of her captivity. She had to *do* something, but she was Rapunzel, locked away in a tower without a ladder made of hair to help her escape. It was all her fault. She shouldn't have let them go. All the soap and water in the world couldn't wash away her guilt. She should have gone with them. She'd *wanted* to. Angela had so little time, and she needed her mother. She'd sensed the danger. God had given her a warning, but Peter was the paranoid one and he wanted to go. Angela needed treatment. She couldn't have Angela stay home and watch her suffer. They had to do what they could. It was their only hope. How could she say no? *Why didn't you protect them?* No! That wasn't fair. You can't jump off a cliff and blame God when you hit the ground.

Oh, Lord, You let them get away. Please keep them safe. They were on the run, which was *good* news, if you could call it that, but at least they were free. If they'd stayed home, the agency would have come to the house and arrested Peter right in front of Angela and dragged him off in handcuffs. That would have been her last memory of him. Having an image like that in her head would have been worse. At least this way they were still together. She needed to be there too, like Peter said—*a threefold cord's not easily broken*. She'd spent the whole night trying to figure out how to get her husband and daughter home, a fitful night, catching sleep in fragments. But it was no use, the posse had them surrounded. Her infrared detection cameras saw even those hidden in the trees. There would be no coming home. The place was crawling with media and cops. It was too dangerous.

She turned the water off, squeegeed herself with her hands and stepped out of a glass-enclosed shower big enough to bathe a horse. The steam-filled room was wall-to-wall mirrors. She hated it, hated watching the fog lift and being exposed to the naked truth, the person that kept her confined like a bird in a cage. She'd asked Peter to get rid of those ridiculous mirrors at least a dozen times. Why couldn't she have a normal bathroom? He always said he would, but it never seemed to happen. There were always more pressing matters that required his attention. He had to divide his time between his family, the façade of chairing an international corporation, and the mission God had called him to. God had elevated him to a position of wealth and power and given him the ability to do what no one else could. Others had tried to distribute copies of God's Word over the net, even encrypted versions, but the layman's algorithms were no match for the government's super-computers. They were forever being tracked and corrupted before they could be delivered.

Using teams located in different countries, so that each worked on a part without understanding the whole, Peter had commissioned the development of an optical encryption algorithm based on random pulses of light, photons that moved so fast the government's super-computers didn't have time to generate a key before the photo-algorithm was reconfigured with an entirely new code. The Bibles he was ready to broadcast would hold their original integrity. *Please protect him, Lord? He can't serve you in jail.* Deanne reached for a towel and drew it to herself. It was thick and luxurious and heavy in her hand, but *sooooo* self-indulgent. She patted her face and wrapped herself in it to dry.

She stood in front of a mirror that looked the way she felt—foggy, an image to be grasped, yet unclear. Tears were rolling down her cheeks, still trying to wash her clean. It was a fruitless endeavor. She couldn't wash away the past, and she would *never* feel clean. All she could do was cover her scars and hope they wouldn't be seen. She continued toweling herself dry and drew in a deep breath. It wasn't something she could do in her own strength, not in a million years. *Help me, Lord, please!* She'd come to the decision while running. She had to find her husband and daughter, and if that meant leaving the house, so be it. She let her breath out slowly, dabbed her eyes with the corner of her towel, and went to her closet to dress.

Her wardrobe included fashions by Valentino, Givenchy and Yves Saint Laurent, but they were never seen by anyone but Angela and Peter. She held up a shimmering green gown, the one she'd worn to dine on bisque of crawfish and pressed duck at La Tour d'Argent overlooking the Seine in Paris. She smiled at the memory of the fun they'd had, creating sets that transformed their dining suite into the world's finest restaurants, with their own five-star chef. She put the dress away. Maybe now she'd get a taste of real restaurant food.

What does one wear for a coming-out party? She would have to travel—best to dress casual. She reached for a pair of denims and a long-sleeved pink cotton blouse. She pulled off the shower cap, removed the pins and let her hair fall, tossing her head to remove snarls and combing it through her fingers before using a brush. She tugged at her jeans, pulling them up, and buttoned her blouse, tucking it in, but refused to return to the mirror to see how she looked. It would only discourage her. She needed strength to do what she had to do.

She turned and began the long march to the door, her small white tennis shoes leaving impressions in the freshly vacuumed carpet as she walked—*Lord, give me strength*. This was the moment of truth. She stood at the top of the stairs, looking down on the conservatory, its tall elegant palms growing toward the glass-domed ceiling. She took the steps one at a time, quoting Scripture to give herself strength, and reached the bottom turning left without slowing down. She was determined to keep moving so she wouldn't have time to talk herself out of going, one foot after the other, *go, go, go, go, go,* until she entered the atrium—and there she stopped. She stood before the door, a solid oak barrier through which she had to pass to enter the outside world. Light streamed through the beveled glass panels on either side. The arched crown of leaded antique glass looked strangely purple. Her heart was pounding, her hands beginning to shake. *Strength, Lord, please.*

She had to calm herself. Maybe she should tell the maid where she was going. But how could she when she didn't *know* herself? But shouldn't she at least say something? She spun around, walking away, then stopped short. *No!* That was avoidance. She had to do this. It was now or never. She turned to face the door again, reaching for the knob, and paused letting her hand float in space for a moment. Then she withdrew it, pulling back.

She was glad her husband had taken a taxi to the airport, leaving the car, but why had he left it sitting in the drive? If he'd parked it in the garage, she wouldn't have to expose herself. She could climb into the car, lock the doors, press the button to open the garage from the inside, and simply back out and drive away. But no. She'd seen the car from the library. It was sitting smack dab in the middle of the drive, and she had to walk down a long meandering sidewalk between pink peonies and yellow snapdragons—and a gauntlet of reporters. There would be people out there ready to shove microphones and cameras in her face and...and...she turned around and ran back through the atrium to the conservatory, collapsing on a chair in front of the grand piano, her face buried in her hands and her shoulders heaving with sobs.

She raised her head, looking up through the domed glass ceiling at a broken sky filled with sun and clouds, her cheeks streaming. *Oh, God, why could You not give me strength?* She bowed her head, her whole body shuddering, but even as she wallowed in self-pity a voice, as quiet as her imagination, rose from within, letting her know what she had to do.

ARMBRUSTER looked up. The pest was after him again, the nurse who kept wanting updates. She'd fingered him from the beginning, even though he'd done his best to deny it, but he couldn't claim to be there visiting another patient when he didn't know the other patient's name. The pest let him know she was the one who'd reported the little girl. *Self-important little money-grubber.* She had her eyes fixed on the reward. She was leaning on him like he had the authority to make sure she got it. *Go away.* He tried to breathe through his mouth. How could someone who worked in close proximity with other people let herself smell so bad? She leaned in, ready to share another secret. He wrinkled his nose.

"There's something strange going on here. There's an old guy in there dressed up like a priest, but he isn't. I've never seen him before. I know the chaplains that work this hospital, and he isn't one of them."

The agent turned his head so he could breathe. He set his newspaper on the chair, nodding. *Day late and a dollar short, lady. I was already on my way, no thanks to you.*

Peter was trying to stay out of the way while the nurse recorded Angela's test results and ticked items off her checklist. A man in a dark blue suit entered, followed by the nurse with attitude, the one with yellow porcupine quills for hair. She was back, her gaze fixed on Peter. He felt a chill run down his spine. He swallowed, the lump in his throat dry as sandpaper. He could almost see the *gotcha* in the nurse's eyes. His hands began to shake. He forced himself to think positively. The man seemed pleasant enough, large, but not intimidating—maybe a hospital administrator or another doctor.

"Sir, I need to ask you to come with me for a minute, if you don't mind," the man said. "Could you step into the hall, please."

Peter's heart began to race. Jig's up, nowhere to run, nowhere to hide. He cupped his hand behind his ear and leaned on his cane, trembling, like the old man he was pretending to be. "Say again? Sorry, I don't hear so good."

"I need you to come with me," the man said, raising his voice in a controlled manner, but noticeably louder.

Peter placed both hands on top of his cane, his whole body shaking. The smooth wood was wet and slippery in his grip. "Wh...wh...why? What did I do?"

"I didn't say you *did* anything. Just come with me, please." The agent stood with his palm out, wiggling his fingers, beckoning him.

Peter turned, looking out the window.

The man, who had to be either Homeland Security or another branch of law enforcement, stepped forward. "There's no need for any trouble. Just come with me." He reached out to take Peter's arm.

"But...but...but..."

"Just come along easy. Don't make a scene." He turned Peter gently toward the door.

Peter glanced over his shoulder. Angela's face reflected worry. Her gaze followed him, but she held her tongue as her father was led away. He kept up the façade, trying to shuffle instead of walk, but he kept looking back. His cane hung from his arm, its rubber tip dragging on the ground leaving a mark on the waxed floor. He reached the door, catching her eye one last time as he turned the corner. With exaggerated facial expression he silently mouthed the words, "I love you." Then he was gone.

Ingrid glared at the nurse who, moments before, had been recording Angela's vitals. "Might as well let me finish it. They're gonna pull her plug anyway. She's taking up space, costing taxpayer money, and you're hurting her. Ending her pain's an act of kindness."

Standing in the hospital corridor, the arresting officer put his face right up next to Peter's and reached up to pinch his cheek. "Man, you're good," he said. He called for back-up and Peter was taken to the U.S. Marshall's office amid a hullabaloo of swirling lights and blaring sirens, racing down the street like they'd captured the most notorious mass-murderer on planet Earth.

PETER SAT shivering in a cold gray room. There were no plants, or pictures, or other furniture, just the cold metal chair in which he sat, a cold steel table, and a second chair used by the officer who'd questioned him, but that was now empty. He could feel the walls closing in. *Can I come out now, Mommy? I promise not to cry. Pleeeeeese, it's been two days.*

He rubbed the goosebumps on his arms, shuffling his feet, crossing them at the ankles one way and then the other. He'd been asked every conceivable question, so repetitively and so fast, he'd ended up stammering and tripping over his words until they turned into a blubbering pile of mush. *Myyyii, she, she, she, but I...I...I...* It didn't matter, they had him, and they weren't letting him go.

If he were Paul, the apostle, he'd thank God for the privilege of being locked up for the sake of the gospel—but he wasn't Paul. He found it easier to question: *Why, Lord, why leave Angela to die alone? Didn't you hear our prayers? Why give me a way of communicating Your word and stop me from using it? Why keep me from seeing Deanne? Why, why, why, why, why?*

He shuffled his feet again. It was bound to happen—sooner or later. The United States, the last bastion of religious freedom, no longer protected individual rights. The good of the masses was more important than the whims of a few. Peter shivered, rubbing his arms to ward off the chill. They'd left him alone, sitting shirtless in the empty room, staring at himself in a mirror that covered nearly half the wall. He knew they were standing on the other side, gloating. He was the prize catch of the day. *So what?* They were standing there gawking while their boat was drifting off course. If there was one thing he knew about navigation, it was that a shift of one degree, without correction, could put a vessel on the rocks.

It began with small capitulations: the purposeful misinterpretation of Jefferson's "separation of church and state," the removal of prayer from schools, the legalization of abortion on demand, the drug culture and sexual revolution, gay rights, death with dignity, and finally the idea that anyone who disagreed with such should be silenced. One small step at a time had taken a just and moral society to the point where freedom of speech and religion, constitutional guarantees granted by the founding fathers, had simply disappeared. The Church sat like a frog in a beaker on a bunsen burner. The temperature rose so slowly it didn't feel the heat until the water started to boil.

Okay, they had him, and maybe they'd put him away, but he was only one man. If God took him out, He'd replace him with another. God's Word could not be silenced. The best they could do was keep the muzzle on. And they were practiced at that—been doing it for years—even before he was born. Peter could recall the year he'd first noticed the change. A Colorado family had posted a sign on their lawn in favor of traditional marriage, something Peter applauded, but the sign was missing in the morning and was replaced with a sign that read, "This kind of thinking, this hatred based on religious belief is why terrorists attacked the United States on September eleventh. You are no better than terrorists because you displayed that sign! Take warning, your life, your government, your world is about to change!"

A short time later, European author Christopher Hitchens introduced his book, *God Is Not Great*, to a class of undergraduates at the University of Toronto and a front page story in Canada's National Post quoted him as saying, "I am absolutely convinced that the main source of hatred in the world is religion." Entertainer, Elton John, echoed the same sentiment when he said he would, "ban religion completely," because it turned people, "into really hateful lemmings." Chris Hedges, former foreign correspondent for the New York Times, and senior fellow at The Nation Institute, warned people to beware of Christian evangelicals and their, "toxic message." And on the topic of religion, Richard Dawkins, evolutionary biologist at the University of Oxford said, "It's one thing to say people should be free to believe whatever they like, but should they be free to impose their beliefs on their children? Isn't there something to be said for society stepping in?" Peter looked down, shaking his head. Where had the church been? Why hadn't there been a cry of righteous indignation? Books like *The Da Vinci Code*, and *The Jesus Papers*, cropped up everywhere along with the discovery of the Gospel of Judas and a tomb they claimed belonged to Jesus of Nazareth complete with ossuaries of His brother James and his wife Mary. *Jesus' wife???*

There was a time when such would not have found place in the media. Peter saw a distinct parallel between what he was reading in mainstream news journals and what had happened in the 1930's when German newspapers began printing a similar vilification of the Jews. Small steps on the road to Auschwitz.

Peter peered at the glass mirror, knowing his captors were staring back. They could see him, but he couldn't see them. He felt like a goldfish in a bowl—prize catch, *indeed*. If they were so good at observation, why couldn't they see truth? The world was coming apart, but instead of seeing God's judgment, men were quick to blame each other. They attributed the problem to their poor maintenance of the planet rather than their refusal to reverence the planet's Creator. Every year the oceans grew warmer creating an increase in the number of storms along with a corresponding increase in their intensity and severity. The number of category four and five hurricanes had doubled, and then tripled. The same with fires, tornadoes and earthquakes. With fewer days of cold to keep them in hibernation the number of insects overpopulated bringing an increase in the number of new diseases. Climate related deaths were estimated to be a half million a year.

God had said it all along: "If thou shalt keep the commandments of the Lord thy God, and walk in his ways...the Lord shall make thee plenteous in goods...The Lord shall open unto thee His good treasure, the heaven to give the rain unto thy land in His season, and to bless all the work of thy hand: and thou shalt lend unto many nations, and thou shalt not borrow." So it had been for two hundred years.

But God also warned of the consequence of disobedience. "The Lord shall make the pestilence cling unto thee...And thy heaven that *is* over thy head shall be brass, and the earth that is under thee *shall be* iron. The Lord shall make the rain of thy land powder and dust: from heaven shall it come down upon thee...and thou shalt not prosper in thy ways; and thou shalt be only oppressed and spoiled evermore." It was all there, but they didn't listen.

Peter quivered, though the chill he felt came more from his vulnerability than the temperature of the room. He'd been stripped of his disguise, had the watch with the fake microchip removed from his wrist, and had his finger scanned for positive ID. The pile of face putty lay in clots on the table, along with a tangle of hair. Another costume that didn't make the grade—they'd seen right through it. How could he be so stupid?

The door opened and Peter looked up to see a face he hadn't seen in years.

"Well, well, well, Peter, my old friend, I swear you bump into the strangest people in the strangest places. What a small world."

Bob McCauley? What??? How? Peter's gaze skittered away, looking for an escape. There had to be a hole somewhere he could crawl into. He glanced up, but only for a second. "Hi Bob."

Bob walked by, smacking the back of Peter's chair with a flattened palm like they were old pals, getting reacquainted. "Danged, I swear if you weren't in such a mess, I'd say it was good to see you. Boy, look at you. You sure got yourself in one heck of a spot." He sat on the end of the table and picked up a folder, skimming through the papers inside, his stomach bulging over the buckle of his belt. It wasn't the iron-man body he'd once boasted but he was still big, and still intimidating.

He looked at Peter, shaking his head. "I've got orders to bring you back to L.A. to stand trial. Always a day of reckoning, huh, Peter? Says here you're up on charges of murder, grand theft, insurrection, terrorism, and hate-mongering. They make you sound like the Ayatollah. That's not the Peter I remember. The Peter I remember was a mild kind of guy. Where'd you get all this hostility?"

The willows whispered, their boughs sweeping out over the water. The stirring of the pond with the sun sparkling on its surface formed splashes of color. Blue and yellow umbrellas dotted the lawn. It was a scene right out of a painting by Monet.

Peter would rather have sat and talked with Deanne than play Frisbee— the view was absolutely fabulous—but this was a church picnic and the program called for non-stop activity. It's just that he wasn't good at most of the games. Talking was better. They'd had so many long conversations, just talk, nothing intimate, but he couldn't deny what he felt, and he was sure she felt the same. He wished he could just get her off by herself, but Bob was monitoring the play from a picnic bench and Deanne was still officially "his girl." Bob didn't know anything about their late-night tête-à-têtes. He had his feet on the seat and his elbows propped on his thighs and his hands clasped together, watching Peter's every move. Peter wanted to relax and enjoy himself, but how could he? He felt like a bug under a magnifying glass.

The Frisbee was zooming toward him but looped away. He ran to catch it but it was just out of reach and bounced off his fingertips. He stumbled forward onto his knees. He pulled himself up and dusted the green stain on his pants. Bob leapt from the bench and loped down the grassy slope, his muscles sinuous in their coordination. He snatched the Frisbee from the ground and gave it an underhanded spin. It floated gently over to Deanne who cupped it in her hands like a butterfly. Deanne gave the Frisbee another toss, aiming at Peter, but it sailed over his head. He ran back, going long, but Bob was there, reaching out to snag the Frisbee as Peter slammed into him and crumpled to the ground.

"Sorry about that. Didn't hurt you, did I?"

Bob grabbed Peter's hand, squeezing till Peter felt the joints of his fingers popping. He tried to smile, thanking Bob for helping him up. Bob responded with a silly grin and stuffed the rim of the Frisbee into Peter's stomach hard enough to make him double over. His eyes crossed as he grasped the Frisbee for something to hold onto.

"There you go, no harm done," Bob said. He grabbed Peter's collar and held him up till he'd regained his balance, then he slapped him on the back and yelled, "Hey, guys, how 'bout a game of Frisbee football? Peter, you be the captain of one team. I'll be captain of the other."

DEANNE REACHED the door for the second time, confident now she would make it. This time she'd looked into the mirror and liked what she saw. Something Peter once said had made all the difference: "When you go outside in costume, they don't see you, they see the person you're dressed up to be."

She stood in the foyer, wearing a maid's uniform and a completely different face. She'd leave by the maid's entrance if she didn't need the car. The keys were in her hand. She had to convince them she was using her employer's vehicle to run an errand, but how could she do that when she wasn't even sure she remembered how to drive? She didn't need luggage—not even an overnight bag or change of clothes, those things could be bought—but the car was an imperative. She took a breath and extended her hand, taking the knob. The cool brass felt faintly reassuring. Ready? *Oh, Lord, give me strength.* She turned the knob and pulled the door back—and...

There on the other side with his hand raised to knock was a man in a dark suit and sunglasses, and behind him an entourage of six blue-uniformed police officers. The ruddy-faced man handed her an envelope.

"We have a warrant to search the premises," he said. "Please inform Mrs. Dufoe we're here."

TWENTY-EIGHT

"It is the duty of all nations to acknowledge the Province of Almighty God, to obey His will, to be grateful for his benefits, and humbly to implore His protection and favor..."
—*George Washington, 1732-1799, 1ˢᵗ President of the United States*

THE DAY burned with the kind of heat that softened asphalt and left ridges in the street. The Miniwheel hybrid was an older model, leaking refrigerant. The air conditioner cooled the air, but the temperature inside was far from cold. The tiny car flew down the lane kicking up dust, whining at the top of fifth gear. It was designed for a maximum of two people but barely fit one. The doctor's long legs felt like they were crammed up under his chin and his afro globe tickled the fabric liner. It was the price he paid for stewardship of the planet.

He turned into the driveway and shoved the car into park before it was completely stopped, *grrrrrrrinding* the transmission and thrusting him forward into the steering wheel, *ooofff,* his knee plowing into the dash. He grabbed his chest, released his seatbelt, and threw the door open, letting a wave of superheated air rush in. He left the door hanging as he propelled himself toward the house, limping. Kim Li wouldn't be home, she had classes to teach, but he wasn't looking for Kim Li.

Adrian pushed through the front entry, "Hank! Hank, you here?" he yelled, his deep bass echoing through the house. "Hank! *Haaank!*" He checked every room, even the bedroom upstairs, but no Hank. Holding his thigh, he hobbled downstairs and returned to the room where his guest had spent the night. A business card was propped by the phone. He picked it up: "Barnstorm Custom Truck and Haulage." He dialed the number, but it rang without answer. The company had a Beckley, West Virginia, address. Adrian flicked the card, snapping it between his fingers.

Father Bloom...or Hank? They had to be warned. Hank had brought Peter Dufoe into town, but the priest delivered Angela to the hospital. They were both at risk. Maybe he should have gone by the orphanage first; it was closer. He'd made the mistake of thinking it was best to call Father Bloom while en route. Calling Hank was out of the question. He didn't know Hank's number. Now he was here and Hank was gone so he'd failed on both counts. Not that he hadn't tried reaching Father Bloom. All the way back to the house he'd called, but he kept getting an answering machine.

Hank, where are you? He limped to the car and backed out of the drive without securely closing the door. He spun the wheel to the left. The door popped open, but he didn't wait; he hit the gas lurching forward, letting the door slam shut, *thwanng,* with the sound of a fork hitting an aluminum pie plate. Depending on traffic, it would take at least ten to fifteen minutes to get to the parish, and that might be too long.

He turned off Morning Star Lane onto Pinewood Drive, squealing rubber and scattering dust. A corrugated heat mirage rose up from the asphalt. He accelerated, keeping a sharp eye out for pedestrians. The street used to be rural but was now cluttered with houses on both sides from one end to the other. His own home had been built on a street where several smaller, older homes once stood, but they'd been torn down to make way for progress. Out with the old, in with the new. *Beckley—the metropolis? Who would have thought?* He braked and swerved for a squirrel crossing the road—*whew*. He relaxed his foot, lifting it from the gas, and clutched down to reduce his speed. It wasn't worth taking the life of someone else just to make sure Buddy and Hank were safe. *Rats! Come on, light, don't turn red. Ahhhuh.* He waited feverishly, *come on, come on.* Droplets of sweat lined his forehead. Every second an eternity.

He thumbed the wheel and scratched his ear, his white globe of hair glistening with moisture. The sun bounced off the car in waves until the light turned green. He accelerated, pulling up to the next block. *Now what? Oh, Sweet Lord Jesus, not now. I don't have time for this.* A group of teenagers had established a barricade. Their multimedia sound system was set up in the middle of the road and they were bopping up and down to the music like the street was made for dancing, not for cars. *They'll be needing treatment for sunstroke if they keep it up*, but that wouldn't stop them; they were there for the money. They would flag him down and demand a toll. It was a nuisance, a game they played for coin. Any other time, he'd pay. They never charged much, people didn't have much to give, and it was easier to oblige than to wait around for the police to come and run them off—but not now.

He began leaning on his horn—*beeeeeeppp, beeeeeeppp, beeeeeeppp*— to let them know he was coming through and wouldn't be bothering to stop. They turned to face him, but didn't move. A showdown. He kept the car moving fast enough to let them know he was serious, but slow enough to stop if he had to. They waited, daring him, but he knew they wouldn't chance getting run over for a few lousy credits. At the last possible second they stepped aside, clearing the path of all but the sound machine. The portable satellite radio was still in the road.

Too late. He ran it over, smashing the plastic into shrapnel. The main unit got caught under the car and stayed with him for several yards before becoming dislodged. *How much is that going to cost?* He heard a thump and glanced in his rearview to see a plastic bottle bounce off the side of his car. One of the boys raised his arm, his middle finger extended. *This know also, that in the last days perilous times shall come. For men shall be lovers of their own selves, covetous, boasters, proud, blasphemers, disobedient to parents...* A Clockwork Orange, if ever there were such a time.

Adrian wound through the gears, passing the hospital, resisting the urge to stop and check on Angela. He'd just have to trust she was okay, but that was the least of his worries. Thirty years of doctoring told him the child had but hours to live. It was a miracle she'd made it this far. The important thing now was to warn Buddy and Hank.

He turned right onto Sunrise Avenue. The Church of Universal Communion, formerly St. Basil's, was ahead on the left—not a church really, more of a house used for worship. Its white spire pointed to God, but the cross at the top had been removed. Dr. Philips pulled into a parking space in front and popped the door open, slower this time because his knee was aching. He turned and planted one shoe on the ground but had to pull his other leg out. So much for keeping in shape. The body was a machine, and machines could be broken. How many times had he explained to parents how kids wouldn't hurt themselves so often if they'd just slow down?

The house had been built on the backside of a hill. The front of the building faced the street, but the back followed the line of the slope descending to a second level. Entrance to the church was down a series of steps at the side where a deck had been built to receive parishioners. Dr. Philips limped down the wooden stairs, holding his leg, and went through the side door. He noted again, as always, the absence of Christian symbols. Gone were the paintings portraying Christ's birth, life, death and resurrection. Gone was the crucifix over the altar; gone were the chairs where worshippers used to sit and genuflect before God.

Instead, the room was filled with children, some huddled in groups, some screaming, running and playing, some lying on the ground, and some crying—dozens of children. A woman dressed in black was standing in the foyer holding a crying baby. Adrian was at a loss to explain why she still wore her habit. She didn't have a cross or a rosary or any other emblem to identify her Christian faith. She was twisting back and forth, rocking her arms to quiet the child. "There, there, it'll be alright, *hush, hush,* it'll be all right, *hush.*"

Adrian caught his breath and limped over. "Ahh," he hesitated. He didn't how to address her. Were they still called sisters?..."I'm looking for Father Bloom."

The woman raised a finger, pointing, but didn't take her eyes off the baby. She brought her hand back to tickle the infant's cheek. "*Tsk, tsk, tsk,*" she clucked. "Quiet down now, child."

The doctor turned and entered the throng. He stepped over a

sleeping body, at least he hoped the child was asleep. Her coat was fluffed under her head and her cheeks appeared to have some color. The floor was littered with blankets, coats, and sleeping bags. A small brown-skinned waif looked at him, his large almond eyes void of hope. He was new. Adrian looked around, realizing he hadn't seen half the faces before. Either they were multiplying, or there had been an increase in the number of mothers abandoning their children. *Please don't ask, Lord, we're already overextended—And whoever gives one of these little ones only a cup of cold water in the name of a disciple, assuredly, I say to you, he shall by no means lose his reward—Lord, by Your mercy, by Your mercy, I'll find a way.* In the meantime he'd have to schedule another vaccination for the new arrivals.

He turned sideways and squeezed through a group of kids. Over their shoulders he saw a young man holding a napkin with a pencil drawing of what appeared to be a woman. They were giggling, but the boy shoved the sketch behind them when he saw he was being watched. Adrian stopped abruptly, raising himself on his toes and lifting his hands with his elbows winging out to avoid being run over by a boy chasing his friend, weaving in and out among the other children with ear-piercing squeals. He finally made it to the other side and slipped through the door. Here children lined the hall, some sitting against the wall, others running but most just standing in groups, talking.

He turned into what was formerly a bedroom and saw his friend, seated at a desk and pecking at a keyboard. His chubby fingers were doing their best to strike just one key at a time. Variations in the paint and a dozen screw-holes in a vertical line indicated where the bookshelves used to be. The books had been confiscated by the Ministry of Faith and Religion. Father Bloom called it "a cloud with a silver lining," exchanging dusty old books on theology for more space. He looked up. His cheeks were round and rosy, like two halves of an apple, but his smile slowly turned upside down.

"What's wrong? *Uh huhh, uh huhh.* Is everything okay?"

"Homeland Security's got Peter Dufoe. They put the poor boy in handcuffs and took him away. He was saying he was from here, so you'll probably get a visit. I just thought you'd want to know."

"They *what?* They got Peter? Wa...wa...what about the little girl?"

"They'll call Children's Aid, but she won't live long enough for it to make any difference. I caught two nurses arguing about whether or not to put her down. They were talking about killing the poor child right in front of her, like she wasn't even there. Anyway, there's not much we can do."

With his shirt sleeves rolled up, the priest's arms were visible—short and thick, tubular as sausages. He pushed himself from his chair and stood, turning down his cuffs, a man in black wearing tennis shoes. "We...we have to get her out of there,"

"Lord, have mercy, listen to yourself talk. She's going to die whether they put her down or not, may be already dead. We can't get her back to her daddy. We have to focus on what we *can* do. Right now, I have to find that man, Hank, and let him know, just like I did you." The doctor turned toward the door. The priest yanked his coat from a hook and started to follow.

"You don't need to come, Father. You already have to explain how you came by the little girl. You were the one who left her at the hospital. There's no point in your getting any further involved in this."

"Uh huh, uh uh, uh uh. Not come? Nonsense, don't be silly. *Uh huh.* Of course I'm coming."

FATHER BLOOM made a habit of wearing his black coat and clerical collar. It identified him as a spiritual advisor and often led people to confide in him about struggles they were going through, creating openings to talk about God. But right now that commitment was being tested. Dr. Philips' mini-wheeler was cramped at the best of times, but was never made for a wide body like his. His right shoulder was pressed against the door so tightly he couldn't move his arm, and on his left side he was jabbed with an elbow every time the good doctor had to shift. The proverbial sardine in a can.

They were zooming down the highway in a car with an overtaxed air conditioner. The hills were scorched brown. The digital gauge read the outside temperature at a hundred-twenty degrees. Inside, the temperature had to be at least eighty.

Buddy stuck his left thumb under the seatbelt and pulled it away to breathe. He felt the heat rise off his chest. *Uh huh, Uh huh.* What in the world was going on with the weather? Birth pangs for sure, but how much more could the earth take? *Even so, come quickly, Lord Jesus.* He kept his handkerchief in the same hand, continually mopping his red face, *uh huh*, and fanning himself. *How much farther?* He was relieved when Dr. Philips flicked the turn indicator to the right, but he didn't like getting poked when the doctor tried to downshift.

"Is this it?"

"I'm taking the frontage road. According to my GPS the house is a few miles on up ahead."

They drove through the dustbowl of the farmlands until the Global Positioning System told them to turn. Buddy could remember when the hills were green and covered with fatted calves, now they were brown and cows were rarely seen. Disease had taken most of them, and those that remained were gaunt from lack of food. They passed one decaying farmhouse after another. Most were abandoned. The peeling paint, sagging porches and broken fences were a sad reminder of what befell a country when it ignored the commandments of God.

Fifteen miles down the road, in a location so far off the highway it almost didn't exist, they came to a fenced lot with an unpainted barn. A small dilapidated house sat out front supporting a roof with less than half its shingles. The only car in sight was the burned-out shell of a pickup parked on the seedy front lawn. With its windshield missing, it sat on the rims of four flat tires surrounded by thistles. The place was a clone of every abandoned farmhouse they'd already seen. But it *was* the right address and the mailbox had a set of faded stick-on letters that, if you accounted for those that had fallen off, spelled out: Barnstorm Custom Truck and Haulage. Adrian pulled the car into the long dirt driveway and rolled up to the house in a cloud of dust.

Father Bloom had to wait for the doctor to come around and open the passenger's door; he couldn't move his hand to reach the handle. His unfolding body burst from the car as the doctor took his arm and helped him to his feet. They were a pair: Dr. Philips—long, black, and skinny as a string of licorice, and Father Bloom—short, red, and round as a tomato, huffing and puffing.

They crossed a cracked sidewalk overgrown with crabgrass and stepped onto a porch made of creaky, warped boards. Dr. Philips raised a thin knuckle and rapped on the door. There was no answer. He knocked again, but no one came. He turned with a shrug. "This place is as abandoned as the rest. I'm not sure what to do now."

Father Bloom took the steps slowly. They bowed under his weight, threatening to snap. He waddled toward the car, followed by Dr. Philips. The sun was large and pale and fell on his shoulders like a warm blanket. His black tennis shoes were covered with dust. He was almost to the car when he heard a loud *claaaanggggg*. The sound was metallic, like someone had dropped a crowbar on cement. He turned, eyeing Adrian to see if he'd heard it too, raising his eyebrows over the gold rims of his steamy glasses. The doctor shrugged and the two men simultaneously turned and headed toward the barn.

Behind the house were the hulks of a dozen tractor trailers they hadn't noticed from the road. A few were on blocks, the rest looked in poor condition—a salvage yard of truck skeletons. The door at the side of the barn was open. They stepped inside. *Ah*, that's where all the nice trucks were. Three souped up eighteen-wheeler were standing side by side in diagonal lines. A man was leaning into the trailer of a fourth with sparks flying. A low-slung, polished chrome-and-lacquered, wheel-extended Harley was parked alongside.

The man, wearing bib overalls, thick leather gloves and an iron welder's mask, stood as they approached. He turned the blue flame of his torch away and cranked off the gas. Then he flipped the lid of his headgear up, looking at his visitors as he set the torch on a bench blackened with oil. His long hair extended below the rim of his helmet. His hand went to a gun lying next to a pile of tools. "State your business, and be quick about it. This is private property."

Dr. Philips felt his heartbeat quicken. It didn't surprise him to see a gun, even though guns were outlawed. Only decent, law-abiding citizens had surrendered their guns. The bad guys still had plenty. It niggled him to know the government had done a better job of confiscating Bibles than they had of collecting the guns. It showed where they thought the real danger was. But even with a reduction of guns on the street, crime was at an all-time high, because crimes weren't committed by guns, crimes were committed by people, and until you changed the heart of people, they'd continue to commit crimes.

"We're looking for a man named Hank. Drives a truck, just like that one." Adrian raised his chin indicating the huge blue machine. "He's staying with me. I found this card in his room." Dr. Philips held the card up between two fingers. "It's important that we get a message to him."

A tiny dog lay behind the truck's front wheel. It whimpered and buried its head under its paws trying to hide. A man stepped out from around behind the trailer, wiping his hands on a grease rag. "Hey there, Doc. What brings you out here?"

"They got Peter."

"Who? Who got Peter?"

"I checked on the little girl first thing this morning, and then went on my rounds. When I got back, the nurses were arguing about whether or not to let the child go. I told them to leave her alone, she's still my patient, but one of them told me the little girl wasn't who I thought she was. Then she told me how the child's daddy was some kind of criminal who tried to sneak in and visit her, and got caught in a trap."

"What happened to Angela?"

Adrian stood there, slowly shaking his head.

TWENTY-NINE

"If there were in that Book nothing but its great precept, 'All things whatsoever ye would that men should do unto you, do ye even so to them,' and if that precept were obeyed, our government might extend over the whole continent."
—Zachary Taylor, 1784-1850, 12th President of the United States

THE SUN rose from the parking lot in ribbons of heat. No one went shirtless or barefoot, not even kids. The relentless temperature drove everyone indoors. Those who could afford the luxury sat in their climate-controlled living rooms watching wall-to-wall televisions, too glassy-eyed to enjoy the thousand channel options. Only the homeless and the restless young ventured outside, ducking from one shaded haven to the next, or loitered in shopping malls until run off by the police.

Andy Cleaver sat with the engine running and the air conditioner on. It was a waste of precious fuel, but he had no choice. It was high noon, and the sky was melting. He removed his dark shades and raised his hand to block the glare as he stared out the window. *What a dump. Bob, whatever possessed you to rent a flop like this?*

The car he'd picked up at the airport didn't have audio and visual tracking like his agency unit, but he'd brought his handheld device. It would do in a pinch. The video interface looped though three-dimensional images of wanted criminals. The red bar under Dufoe's face now said, "Captured." Andy kept music playing in the background. He reached over and cranked up the volume. The recorder was plugged into the car's eleven-speaker surround sound system. The vehicle vibrated with the pathos of love—*thump, thada, dada, dada, thump, dada, thump.*

> *I love you, Mary, but you lie*
> *You kiss and tell, and say good-bye*
> *I reach to hold you, but you're gone*
> *You swore I was the only one.*

Andy swept his fingers through his dark slick hair, but it fell in front of his eyes as soon as he let go. *Ain't it just like life? Hey, Andy, we love ya but, yeah, Bob's our guy, you understand. Everybody says they love ya, but they love someone else just a little bit more.* He took a drag off his simulated cigarette, a legal blend of hemp and herbs that smoothed jangled nerves without the ill effects of nicotine. It tasted like straw. He inhaled deeply, sucking the burning paper to the butt before crushing it in the ashtray.

Prodding his lower lip with his tongue, he pinched it between his fingers and pulled it forward, examining it in the mirror. He'd landed in Pittsburgh, connected to the matrix and, when informed that Bob already had Peter Dufoe in custody, bit his lip causing it to bleed. Once again Bob was the quarterback calling the shots while he sat on the sidelines, benched. Game over. He hadn't got a chance to play. And Bob hadn't thrown the game. *Bob, you are one motherin' disappointment.* Andy sighed deeply, letting a long thin trail of smoke seep from his nose as his head bounced off the headrest to the beat of the rockajock tune—*thump, thada, dada, dada, dada, thump.*

> *...Forever Mary, I'll be true,*
> *and kill you, Mary, 'fore I'm through,*
> *Because, Sweet Mary, I love you.*

That's it, baby, killin' in the name of love. How wholesome is that? Blame it on post-traumatic stress syndrome. Blame it on kids being kids. Okay, maybe no one ever got killed because of a song—but sometimes you just got to wonder. Andy tapped the steering wheel, his thumbs keeping the beat—*thump, thada, dada, dada, thump dada, thump.* His hair, parted down the middle, flew out as he shook his head. He'd been sure Bob would defect. He was counting on it to justify his being there. He was hoping to step into the vacancy created when Bob abandoned his post, but now Dufoe was in the system and the chance of letting him go were slim to none. From here on in, the prisoner would be monitored. Andy would have a hard time justifying the expense of his being there when Bob was already bringing the suspect back in handcuffs.

With his left hand, Andy clenched the steering wheel. With his right, he pushed a cuticle back with the ball of his thumb. He was one cooked goose. *Oh well,* the best-laid plans of mice and men. And the music kept blaring—*thump, thada, dada, dada, dada, thump.*

What smarted was that Bob had been vindicated. He'd been right. Most others, including Andy himself, would have locked down the border. He was in fact on his way there when Bob called in to let them know he was in Pittsburgh. He'd been right on the money. Dufoe hadn't crossed the border, at least not by land. Bob was one step ahead of everyone. He'd positioned himself where he knew Dufoe would eventually show up. The familiarity factor. *Clever.* And that's why Lou had made Bob lead investigator. It had proved to be a good call. Only Bob knew Peter well enough to order the arrest of someone everyone else assumed was a priest. Only Bob would have known it was a disguise. He'd probably walk away with a citation.

> *We walk through life, we take a chance,*
> *We learn to run, we learn to dance,*
> *We puff and pop the needle high,*
> *We think we love, but then we die.*

Andy balled his hands into fists, shaking them in front of him like a pair of maracas. *Yeah, Baby, dance.* He turned his wrist and looked at his watch. It would be hours before they arrived. He should get a burger. He had to eat something. *I got the marijuana munchies.* He didn't dare leave, Bob might show up early. He wasn't about to miss out again. At least he'd led the team on the raid of the Dufoe house. He'd done *something,* even though they'd come away with zilch. They hadn't found anything that tied Dufoe directly to the rebellion—not a Bible, not a cross, not even Mrs. Dufoe. She was only wanted for questioning, but it would have been nice to bring her in. They'd boxed every scrap paper, every computer, and every disc for further analysis, but that was it. A regular street cop could have done as much.

He reached for his sunglasses, slipping them on as he collapsed back onto the seat exhausted, his oily hair falling forward. *Man, Bob, you really screwed me.* He slipped his fingers under the lapel of his coat and pulled a silver flask from his vest pocket. The unbearable heat was explosive, and he was on a short fuse. He had to keep the weather from getting to him. He needed a cool head. He unscrewed the cap and took a sip, the warm whisky burning his fractured lip on the way down. *Ahhhhhh.*

It was too late to fly down to Beckley. Bob was already on his way back. The manager confirmed he hadn't checked out. He'd have to stop to collect his things before heading to the airport. Andy would wait. He would be there when Bob arrived. But that's where it fell apart. Bob wouldn't believe he'd been sent to assist him with the return of the prisoner. It didn't take two men to escort Dufoe. And Andy couldn't get on a plane and head back to L.A. empty-handed. That would be admitting he was wrong, that his flying out to Pittsburgh was one lollapalooza of an expensive mistake. He needed a good plausible explanation for why he was there.

> *...I'll kill a hundred more like you*
> *I'll kill a thousand 'fore I'm through*
> *Because, Sweet Mary, I love you.*

And the music of life played on—*thump, thada, dada, dada, dada, thump.*

THE GIANT screen flickered in three-dimensional, high-definition color, but Deanne wasn't watching. She stood at the stove fixing herself an omelet. She felt her stomach roll. All her courage had fled the moment they'd entered the door. The man had said "Mrs. Dufoe" was wanted for questioning. Thank God she'd been wearing a disguise.

A piece of egg splattered on the electric coil and started to burn. She fanned the smoke and turned down the heat. She needed to eat to keep up her strength. She would try again to leave after dark. She swirled her plastic spatula around the nonstick surface of the pan. The smell of the onions and mushrooms and ham made her nauseous. The thought of any kind of food made her feel queasy. The internet newscast droned on: *"Looks like we'll see the wind picking up again over the next twenty-four hours with gusts ranging up to sixty miles an hour. It is advised that drivers..."* Okay, maybe she wouldn't leave tonight, perhaps tomorrow. She licked her thumb and wiped it on her apron. *I can't just stay here, Lord. What am I supposed to do?*

She gave the pan a flick of her wrist and flipped the omelet to brown the other side. She turned to rinse her spatula and glanced out the window into the attached greenhouse garden. Her roses were in bloom. Right in front was a huge fully opened blossom with several smaller buds on the same stem. They needed pruning. Tending her garden was one of the few accomplishments she prided herself on. Such fragile beauty. Roses were delicate, prone to wilting, but oh so lovely when properly cared for and nurtured. She made a mental note to trim a few buds. There was nothing like colorful flowers to brighten a room.

She paused at another thought. Peter enjoyed floral arrangements as much as she did. He was fond of sending her passion bouquets whenever business called him out of town. But that was likely to stop now that he was on the run. She pulled the drawer back, searching for the card. *There.* She slipped it out and read it again.

> *Bright threads adorning mountain mass*
> *tailored into meadow grass*
> *clothe the earth in vogue design*
> *buds of silk knit intertwine.*

Behind her, the pan on the stove began to *sizzzzle*. She read on, scanning quickly.

> *Pollen born on ribbon air*
> *embroiders blossoms wheresoe'er*
> *brocade garden, leaf crochet*
> *raiment rich in spring bouquet...*

She laid the card on the counter and spun around, facing the stove again. Sliding the spatula under the eggs, she lifted the pan, tilting it sideways to slide the omelet onto her dish. She turned the stove off and grabbed her meal, envisioning how a colorful floral centerpiece would look as she headed for the table. She was only half-listening to the talking head's report but—she turned with a start, dropping the plate like it was red-hot, jumping back as it shattered.

Her husband, with his head tucked between his shoulders, was being pulled out of a building, flanked by men in dark suits. They crossed the threshold and were instantly swarmed by a centipede of arms with television cameras and microphones. The broadcaster's voice droned in the background. *...after avoiding arrest in Canada, the terrorist has been captured, Peter Dufoe sought by the police for numerous crimes against...* She didn't recognize the man on Peter's left. But the other one—though it had been, what? twenty? twenty-five years? since she'd last seen his face—she recognized vividly. It was her former fiancé, Bob McCauley.

PETER SAT in the back of Bob's rented car, his wrists cuffed behind his back and his head bowed, avoiding the intrusion of the cameras. He didn't want Deanne seeing him like this. The car rolled out of the driveway and turned right. He said a silent "Amen" and turned his head to peek out the window. The buildings were breezing by. He glanced back over his shoulder. The reporters were racing for their cars to follow.

Why, Lord? I prayed for protection. Hank prayed, Dr. Philips prayed, and I know Deanne was praying. What will happen to Angela? Who'll take care of her? Peter saw an image of a veiled executioner pulling a needle from Angela's arm. *No, Lord, You can't! I have a mission to finish. You think Hank can do it? He'll find the disc, probably, at least eventually, but he can't decipher the encryption. I'm the one...Lord, I don't understand. Was all of this—for nothing? Where will they get Bibles now? And what about Deanne? Who's going to care for her?*

Peter was struggling to breathe, his shoulders trembling. At least it was over. No more running, no more hiding, no more looking over his shoulder suspicious of every passing glance. He'd made a grandiose attempt at an escape but he hadn't gotten far. Now, he'd be dumped in a cell and left to rot until dead. That's if they didn't decide his crimes were worthy of a firing squad. Either way, it wasn't likely he'd ever see Deanne or Angela again.

His hands shook, the hair on the back of his neck prickling, beads of sweat clouding his eyes. Her lips were soft and warm. His heart stopped for a moment and then fluttered in his chest. Then he froze. He took hold of her wrist and pushed her away. "Whaaaat're you doing?

"I would think that would be obvious. I'm kissing you," she said, her dark eyes wide and questioning. "Why did you stop?" She leaned forward, her lips moist, parted just enough to see the white of her teeth.

"Bu...but what about Bob?" He felt her stiffen. It was as though someone had burst the love bubble with a pin. He pressed on. "You two are supposed to be engaged, aren't you?"

Deanne took a breath, her hand sweeping the carpet as she leaned back on her arm. "Oh? Is that what he says? Of course he does. Do you know he's never even asked me?" She moved closer, her eyes chunks of obsidian piercing his soul, her lips soft as the petal of a rose as she kissed him. But he backed away and pushed himself to his feet, stumbling forward, almost knocking her over.

"I...I...I can't."

Deanne looked up, then stood, brushing off her skirt. "I'm sorry, I assumed...Bob said you were...but you're not, are you? Because I told him he was wrong. I mean...because...I mean..."

Peter held up his hand as if to ward off the question. "No...it's just that...I...no, no, it's not that."

"Then, what?"

"I...I...I..." but he somehow couldn't quite get his words to line up with his thoughts, and by then it was too late. Her face flushed red. She brought a hand up to cover her mouth, her eyes filling with tears. She turned and fled the room, leaving him standing there—alone.

THE SUN glared off glass as they passed by the storefronts of the downtown core. Most of the buildings were vacant with "Closed" signs hanging over their doors. Bob sat in front, gloating, with Peter staring at the back of his head. "Bob, I...I..."

Bob's dark sunglasses appeared in the rearview mirror. "If you're gonna ask me to cut you loose, you can forget it. I may not like the idea of arresting an old friend, but you did break the law and I'm duty bound to bring you in."

"No, no, it's not that. I'll go quietly. I won't give you any trouble." Peter wrenched his hands behind his back, feeling the cold steel bite into his wrists. "It's just that...I need to know what'll become of my little girl."

"Far as I know, we left her in the hospital. She'll be fine."

Peter shook his head. "No, no please, you can't let that happen. She's dying. Ask anyone. She only has a few days, maybe just a few hours. You can't let her die around complete strangers. Please."

Bob smiled into the mirror, but his eyes were hidden behind his dark lenses. "You should have thought of that before you got yourself into this mess, but hey, it could be worse. Like you said, the kid's going to die. The best place for her is the hospital. They'll take *good* care of her."

Bob turned his attention back to the road, but Peter understood exactly what he meant. *Revenge is sweet.*

INGRID TURNED off the lights and went to the window to close the blinds, listening as Angela struggled to breathe. She found her way back to the bed and fumbled with the saline drip. She commended herself for doing what was right. Imagine a physician not wanting to eliminate a child's suffering. Ludicrous. The medical community had done its best. Every reasonable treatment had been exhausted and death was imminent. Any competent physician would immediately order termination for that reason alone. And the child was in pain—another thing the doctor seemed willing to ignore. Historical data from other hospitals confirmed that the child had already undergone a bone marrow transplant, but it didn't take. It was only a matter of time. Why drag it out? The bed should be freed up for someone they could actually help.

Her other reason was a little more personal, but valid nonetheless. The kid was spoiled goods. She'd said it from the beginning, even before learning about the child's father. They'd never have peace in the world until they lined all these intolerant hate-mongers up against a wall and had them shot. But that wasn't why she was doing this; she was there to administer compassion. The child was going to die, with or without her assistance. To prolong that death was to add to her suffering, and that was inhumane.

Her hands followed the drip line to the child's wrist. This was ridiculous. She shouldn't have to hide. She was acting in the best interest of the child—but she *was* ignoring protocol. She had to. The doctor was refusing to order the termination himself. She increased the drip rate, felt the plastic piping, followed it up and used her fingertips to guide the needle into the top of the bag. She pressed the plunger releasing the insulin. Forty units was more than enough. The child would slowly go into shock and in her weakened condition, cardiac arrest. She removed the needle, snapped it off and slipped the syringe into her pocket, then moved quietly to the door. She flipped the lights back on and, after looking both ways to make sure the corridor was clear, slipped out. She didn't want to be there when the child went flat-line bringing a code blue team racing to the room.

Angela tried to breathe. Her chest rose and fell, gurgling on the liquid in her lungs. She didn't see the darkness, she saw a soft fuzzy light. A ball of energy standing in the corner. Her confidant and friend.

They took him away. I couldn't say good-bye. Why? Please don't leave me here alone. I'm ready now. Just, when I'm gone, promise me you'll look after Dad. He needs you more than me...

Suddenly the room burst into explosions of light. The walls danced with rainbows. It looked like a thousand prisms of color sparkling off a mirrored ball. "So beautiful..." she whispered.

CELESTIAL VANTAGE

There are things Angels earnestly desire to look into. We are creations of God, just as you. We are designed to worship, just as you. We were created to serve, just as you. Where we differ is our locale. We are not confined to the limitations of earth. We transcend space and time, appearing before the Father in heaven one moment and ministering to those on earth the next. We are not fleshly beings; we are spirit.

We sang for joy at creation when God spoke into being every planet, moon and star. Thus, we see much of what you cannot. And we are privy to the great battle that ensues daily between the minions of darkness and those who are of The Light. Ours is to draw up a defense for those who seek after things of the Spirit, to establish a guard against the wiles of the evil one.

But what we cannot know by experience and only observe through a glass darkly, is the infinite love the Father has for you who inhabit the earth. Christ, the blessed Son, could have cut Satan down with the sword of His mouth and bound him in fetters once and forever. Instead, He chose to create you, (knowing the serpent would enlist you in his rebellion) and then enter your space/time domain as a mortal, offering up His life to cancel the debt you owe. This He did that in the eons of time to come He might show the exceeding riches of His grace and kindness. Greater love hath no man than he lay down His life for a friend. Yea, rather than proving once and for all time His matchless strength, He chose instead to demonstrate His all-consuming love.

THIRTY

"The American people have always abundant cause to be thankful to Almighty God, whose watchful care and guiding hand have been manifested in every stage of their national life, guarding and protecting them in time of peril and safely leading them in the hour of darkness and of danger."
—*Grover Cleveland, 1837-1908, 22nd & 24th President of the United States*

HANK ROARED up Interstate 77, riding herd on Doctor Philips and Father Bloom. His tuned, tooled, and polished Peterbilt hung on the bumper of the little red mini-wheeler ready to blast his horn if necessary to keep them moving—come on, come on, move it—but a car with an engine the size of a peanut could only go so fast. Killer was standing in his lap with his paws on the steering wheel. His buggy eyes were wide, his tail wagging, and his nose jutted out like a hood ornament.

Hank saw the Highway 3 exit. He flipped his blinker on, squeezing into the right and slowed, allowing the doctor to ease in front of him. They flew to the end of the ramp where the doctor turned left. The little mini-wheeler skirted the curb with a puff of dust heading for Bluefield College. Hank, with his giant tractor trailer creaking and wheezing, veered to the right, going wide to make the turn. A block later he turned right again into Sunset Memorial Park.

No mistakin' this baby for a hearse—though the words *Blue Heaven* were painted over fleecy white clouds on his doors—*so you never know...* He trundled down the winding pastoral lane, weaving through tombstones and grave markers until he reached the back of the cemetery.

The single lane was narrow with turns impossible for a lesser man to negotiate, but he was no lesser man, and it was a good place to hide an eighteen-wheeler. The trees kept the truck from being seen and the looping track took him back out to the street without having to turn around—but you can't hide an elephant in a park, no matter what you do. He pulled up alongside a vacant stretch of browned grass.

Killer jumped into the passenger seat, wagging his tail, ears erect and eyes alert. "Okay, Killer, you're going to have to stay and guard Baby again." The dog backed up pawing the seat, prancing in circles as Hank reached over to scratch his ears. "Don't let anyone touch her. I won't be long."

Hank turned around, waiting for the doctor and the priest. He looked at his watch. *Shouldn't be long.* Bluefield College was just a hop, skip, and jump on the other side of the freeway. They were trading their car for Kim Li's four-door sedan. They needed more room. *What on earth possessed the doctor to buy such a ridiculous...*he looked at his dog...*that's the Chihuahua of all cars.* Hank laughed, burying the tiny dog's head in his hand like a baseball in a glove. The dog fought, wrestling and pulling back until Hank let go.

Hank grinned, but it faded quickly. He began tapping the wheel. *Too late? Phooey.* For an educated man, Adrian didn't know squat. It wouldn't be too late until they saw the child lying stone cold blue on a slab in the morgue with a tag tied to her toe. Children's services or not, she was still the doctor's patient and until he heard otherwise, Adrian was still in charge. Never, never, ever let bullies push you around without a fight. Even the priest knew that, and he was too fat to throw a punch. *Come on, guys, hurry up.*

The trees were bending in the wind. The sun bounced off the truck's blue hood, shimmering like water in its reflection. The marble gravestones looked like sun-bleached rocks in a vale. How many of the folks laying beneath those stones would be called forth at the resurrection? It was a sure bet there would be more from earlier generations than those being planted today. Grandmas used to teach their grandkids about Jesus. It was part of their Christian heritage. But that was before the stinkin' world went to hell in a handbasket.

He caught a flicker of movement and glanced in the truck's side mirror to see a silver sedan. It pulled up beside him and stopped. *Time to jet.* He threw the door open and turned around. The little dog whined and jumped into his seat to follow. "No, Killer, you stay here. Just guard Baby and be ready to go soon as I get back." And with that he slammed the door, leaving the tiny dog jumping on the window, barking, *yip, yip, yip, yip, yip.* Hank stepped down, thumping the car on the roof and climbed inside.

THE DOCTOR, truck driver, and priest pulled up in front of the hospital. For a second they sat looking at the building, a walled city, a fortress in a desert sun. There was no way to approach without being seen. Adrian killed the engine and turned to his two passengers.

"Uh, you know what to do. I'll go in first, through the side so we're not together. Father, you go around through the front. Give me about five minutes. Then, Hank, you come in five minutes after that." He swung the car door open and stepped out, closing it again. His billowy globe of snowy white hair was short around the ears, his cheeks dark and firm with only a hint of aging. He gave them a thumbs up and spun toward the hospital marching off briskly, like a doctor making his rounds, a man on a mission.

They were a curious trio—the compliant, educated doctor who could be called upon to do what was right, but had confessed misgivings about the assault they were about to enact; the obese priest who loved the Word, but was undeniably living on more than bread alone, and the hardened, two-fisted hauler who right now felt like he could use a stiff drink. Hank pursed his lips tightly, squeezing one hand into the other, rubbing his knuckles. He nodded. *The odd squad,* each somehow perfect for the job they had to do. He heard the priest breathing hard, *uh huhh, uh huhh, uhh, huhh,* and saw he was sweating a river.

"You okay?"

"*Uh huh, uh huh, uh huh,* I'm...I'm fine," Buddy said fanning his face. He reached in his pocket for his inhaler and took a puff, then exchanged it for a handkerchief and mopped his brow.

"Nervous?"

Buddy turned to address the voice coming from the back, but couldn't get his meaty shoulder around. Hank could only see a slice of his face. A bead of sweat trickled down his cheek. "Of course I'm nervous, *uh huh*, but more than that, I'm hot. Adrian should have left the engine running with the air conditioner on."

"Yep, that's why I left the truck idling. Poor Killer would'a died in this heat, but this won't take long. You ready?"

The priest looked at the building in front of him, a wall too big to climb over or go around. He nodded, then opened his door and planted a foot on the asphalt. At least the car was big enough to get in and out of without help. He pulled himself to his feet and closed the door. Hank flinched when Buddy smacked the window with his pudgy hand. All five fingers were spread out flat against the glass. He mouthed the words, "Five minutes." Hank acknowledged with a nod.

Buddy turned and huffed off, his black tennis shoes loosely tied around his thick ankles. He was still wearing his coat and collar—*on a day like this?* Hank could see he was trying to hurry, the way his arms were pumping and the way he leaned forward as though pushing against the wind, but his short legs couldn't carry him very fast. Hank was supposed to leave in five minutes, but at this rate, Buddy wouldn't even be inside by then. Buddy rounded the corner and disappeared. Hank looked at his watch. *Five minutes.*

FATHER BLOOM stepped into the air-conditioned building. His skin was moist. The cool air felt like ice water brushing against his cheek. He removed his glasses to wipe away the sweat as he approached the information desk, his face red and blotchy. "*Uh huh,* ah, I ah...I understand you had a bit of trouble. I just got a call and, uh, my uh, my office said someone came in here, *uh huh*, pretending to be from our orphanage."

The two women looked at each other. He knew them from previous visits, elderly volunteers using their time to benefit their fellow man. They were usually affable, but this time he noticed they seemed guarded.

The one on his right stared at him. She opened her mouth, but had to stop to clear her throat. *Ahhhemmmm.* "We received a memo... it was about that child you brought in. They arrested a man, her father. He said he was with you, but he was a terrorist. He had explosives on him. They say he intended to blow up the hospital."

"That so?" Buddy hooked his wire-rimmed glasses over his ears one at a time, fighting the urge to refute the absurd accusation. He stuffed his handkerchief into his pocket. "Oh, dear. *Uh huh, uh huh,* how do I explain this? We get drop-offs all the time. *Uh huh.* We never know where they're from. Of course we always try to locate the child's parents, but in this case I didn't have a clue. I think we'd, *uh huh,* we better clear this up so there's no misunderstanding."

HANK STOOD in front of the doors, waiting the two seconds it took them to open. He was churning inside, about ready to plow through the glass if they didn't hurry up and let him in. Father Bloom was keeping the ladies behind the counter occupied. The conversation looked intense but he walked by, ignoring them. He kept his eyes fixed on the wall as if looking for a patient.

He stopped at the first corridor, looking left and right for Adrian, then spun to the left. He reached down and squeezed his thigh—*get a grip, old man, aches and pains won't kill ya*—and kept walking, his truculent gait a reflection of his thoughts. *You ain't gonna keep that little girl from her mother—not if I have anything to say about it.* His fists were doubled, spoiling for a fight. His eyes swept back and forth looking for a door, a signal.

He heard his name and stopped. The hoarse whisper came from behind, but it was the Doc's voice. He spun around.

"Hank, over here."

Through a crack in the door, Hank saw the doctor waving his hand. The room beyond was dark. He thundered over. Adrian opened the door wide to let him in and closed the door behind him just as quickly. They were standing in the dark. Hank could hear the doctor fumbling for the light-switch and suddenly the room was bright.

"Here." Adrian had slipped into a white coat, with a stethoscope around his neck. He handed Hank a pair of hospital greens.

Hank pulled the garments over his street clothes as fast as his large clumsy hands would allow. When he was finished, the doctor handed him a clipboard—instant transformation—now he was an elderly orderly.

"I wrote out what you need. If anyone asks, say you're new. They all think this child should be terminated so you should get by. It's a fairly routine procedure." Adrian opened the door and stuck his head out, looking both ways before he ducked back inside. "Okay, go, you know what to do."

Hank bolted from the room and walked a few yards until he came to a pair of elevators. He pushed the button and the doors opened, *ding*. He trundled inside.

When the doors opened again he stepped out. Two heads, one auburn and one brunette, could be seen behind the barrier of the nurses' station. They turned his way as he started down the hall. He'd hoped the nurses would be attending other patients, but here they were, eyeing him suspiciously.

He stopped and leaned on the counter steeling himself to be questioned. "Can you point the way to room 471?"

The nurses glanced at each other. The one closest had her hair tucked into a net. Her eyes narrowed. "Why?"

Hank raised his scruffy eyebrows with a look that expressed impatience. He handed the nurse the clipboard. "They got the patient scheduled for termination. Doc wants her downstairs."

She nodded. Her lips looked like a bright red flower. "I thought Child Services was taking this one. Sad case. She's dying. I guess it don't much matter when, but it didn't have to be this way."

Hank looked down at her, reaching for the clipboard.

"It's because of the little girl's father. I've got a feeling he's the cause of all this."

"What?"

She lowered her voice. "They say her father murdered some man right in front of her and stole the man's boat. I heard he made her clean up the blood. Awful. I think this little girl's been abused by her old man for a long time and finally just stopped wanting to live."

Hank was shaking his head.

"Don't think so? Well let me tell you, they arrested her father right here. Took him away in handcuffs right in front of her, some kind of religious nut. Serves him right. He'd been dragging her around in that dreadful condition, shameful. Anyway, they'll give the poor little thing some rest now. Imagine carting her around like that. That man has no thought for anyone but himself. Okay," she said proffering the clipboard. "Patient's that way." She pointed a finger with a red painted nail. "Just up on your left. Might as well get it over with."

Hank rolled his eyes and took the clipboard.

"Just a second," the nurse said, hanging on a moment longer. "Who are you?"

"Name's Jim, Jim Jackson, but folks just call me Jack. I'm new here, started only yesterday, just learning my way around."

"Where's your ID badge, Jack?"

Hank didn't skip a beat. He glanced at his chest. "Right here. Why...I'll be, I guess I forgot to pin it on. I'll be sure to have it the next time I come by."

"See you do," the nurse said, letting the clipboard go. "The hospital has strict rules. They're fussy about security."

"I'll do that, thank you very much." Hank spun on his heel, lumbering down the hall to Angela's room. The place smelled sterile, like a morgue—the smell of death. He approached Angela's bed quietly. Her eyes were closed. *Asleep, or...*he placed a finger under her nose, hoping to feel her breath. *Nothing.* But his thick-skinned fingers were old and calloused so that didn't mean anything. He leaned over the bed patting the top of her head and brought his whiskered chin in close to her ear. "It's okay, Angela, we're gonna take you home now. But I need you to be real good and not say anything. Think you can do that?"

Angela lay still as a corpse. Her skin held a bluish pallor. *Hang in there, kid.* Hank cranked the bed flat, pulled the rails up, and kicked the pedal on the brakes to release the wheels. Just one more thing. She was connected to a tube fed by two plastic bags hanging from a metal rack. Hank knew what it was, he just didn't know what to do with it. Should he take it with him, or leave it behind? If she was scheduled to die, why would she need it? It made more sense to leave it behind.

He took her lithe wrist, pulled the tape away and slipped the needle out, letting the drip tube fall dangling from the rack. He turned, swinging the bed around and wheeled her out the door, down the long corridor, and past the nurses' station. The nurse he'd talked to was on the phone. She looked up as he passed and started to raise her hand, but then got pulled back into her conversation. Hank kept going and reached the elevator pushing the button. The doors opened.

"Sir, Jack, sir, could you come back for a minute?" The nurse turned to the woman seated beside her. "I checked with hospital security. There's no Jim Jackson or Jack Jackson on the hospital register, and no one has been issued a security ID in that name either."

But Hank was already inside the elevator, stabbing the button repeatedly to take it down. He saw the woman get up from her desk. *Come on.* She was heading straight for him. Her arm was extended, reaching out, her eyes wide, her red lips parted as though about to say something—and then the door closed. He felt the car lurch and start down. *Whew!* She'd probably run back to her desk, call the goon squad and have them waiting. He doubled his fists. *Better give 'em all you got fast and furious so they won't know what hit 'em.*

He was ready to fight his way out if he had to, but when the doors opened three floors below, the space was empty. He rolled out quickly turning to the right, his boots pounding the floor as he hustled down the hall to the room where he'd left the doctor.

Adrian opened the door and Hank started to wheel the bed inside but it was too big. "Leave it there. It's only for a second."

"But?"

"Come on. They do it all the time. Get in here."

Hank looked at Angela. "Okay, but you stay with her, she don't look so good." Hank pushed past Doctor Philips, who stepped into the hall. The door slammed. Hank pulled the hospital shirt over his head, his hairy stomach bristling with static as his regular shirt came up with the hospital garment. He took hold of his shirttail, dragging it down as he flung the outer shirt to the floor. Then he pulled the drawstring of the pajama pants, letting them drop around his ankles, stepping on the cuff of one leg to pull his foot out and then the other. He tucked in his shirt all the way around, used both hands to pat his hair down, and pulled the door open, stepping into the corridor, a grizzled old trucker again.

The doctor was holding Angela's wrist, feeling for a pulse. He lifted her eyelid to check for dilation. He glanced over his shoulder at Hank and picked Angela up, wrapping her in the hospital blanket. "She's in a coma. I hope we're not too late."

Adrian handed Angela over and placed the blanket so it covered her face. She was light as a bird. "I'll go out the back. You go out the way you came. Just hurry. I'll be in the car waiting."

Hank nodded and turned, hustling down the hall. *So far, so good.* At the intersection he paused and peeked around the corner. No goons in sight, just Father Bloom yapping at the nurses. One of them was on the phone; the other had turned her head away. *Time to go.* He started walking. He could hear Father Bloom's voice. He looked up and caught the priest's eye just as another nurse skidded around the corner at the far end of the hall. Whatever her mission, she was in a hurry. Her hair frizzed out like she'd just plugged her finger into an electric socket.

"*Uh huh*, I'm glad we cleared that up," Buddy said. "You should probably be thanking me. That girl was left with us, but if we hadn't brought her in, a dangerous criminal might still be on the loose. Anyway, if you've called Child Services, I guess they can take it from here..."

One of the two receptionists put down a phone and raised her hand, calling after Hank who held Angela in his arms, racing out the door. The woman stood mute; her cheeks were drawn as she tried to speak. She cleared her throat, but she was too congested to cry out. "*Sirurr auuuuggggummm.*" Father Bloom saw Hank rounding the corner, his red mackinaw shining brightly in the hot sun. "*Ahhuhumm,* I need you to come back for a moment, sir..."

Father Bloom turned to the nurse. "Do you need to speak to that man?"

The volunteer worker's head bobbed up and down. She stood pointing. "Stop him! Someone stop that man..."

Buddy looked up. The nurse he'd seen the day before was bearing down on him. *Not good.* "Hold on, I'll get him for you," he said. Buddy waddled off, huffing and puffing, unable to catch up with Hank even if he wanted to, but he did hear the sound of rubber soles squeaking on a waxed floor, and then the *flap, flap, flap* of someone running up from behind. At the last possible second he turned and—*whapppppp!*—the nurse with the spiky yellow hair crashed into his arm, stopping dead in her tracks. Her eyes crossed and filled with water. She reached for her nose with both hands as it began spurting blood.

"Oh, excuse me. I'm so sorry. Here, let me help you."

"Get away from me, you fat pervert!" she screamed, shaking him off. By now the two elderly volunteers were at her side. They took her by the elbow turning her and began walking back toward the counter with the woman bowed over, dripping blood on the shiny tiles.

Father Bloom took a step back. "I...uh...I'll go see if I can catch the man, then, if...if that's all right with you, I...uh..." but he was backing up as he spoke and turned as he reached the door, scuffling out. "Oh, dear, I didn't mean to hurt the lady." He crossed himself as he hurried away. "Forgive me, Father. Oh, what have I done?"

Hank was climbing in the back, holding Angela in his arms. "Get yourself under that blanket and lie down," the doctor said. He reached over the seat, pulling the blanket taut to make sure the fugitives were hidden. *Where's Buddy?* Then he grabbed the key, cranking the engine to life, *runnn, runnn, runnnnnnn!* He looked up to see the priest moving quickly down the sidewalk. His short arms were flailing in front of him, swinging with determined strokes. His face was beet red. He was huffing and puffing like there wasn't enough air to fill his lungs. He stopped and leaned over, planting his hands on his knees, *uh-huh, uh-huh,* then reached into his coat for his inhaler. He brought it to his mouth and pressed the button while waving his free hand at the car, and started moving again.

Come on, don't fail me now. The doctor reached over, looping a finger in the handle, snapping it back. He pushed the door open to let Buddy in. The overweight friar plopped into the seat, causing the car to tilt to the right. He scrambled to get the door closed as the car began backing out.

A security guard in a blue uniform appeared, spotted them, and took off sprinting in their direction. Doctor Philips turned and shifted into drive moving forward slower than normal due to the added weight. The guard was running after them, trying to catch the car. Adrian gunned it. The car lurched forward. The doctor stole a quick glance in his rearview mirror and saw the man standing to the side, writing down a number.

THIRTY-ONE

*"Today, prayer is still a powerful force in America, and our faith in
God is a mighty source of strength. Our Pledge of Allegiance states that we
are 'one nation under God,' and our currency bears the motto, 'In God We
Trust.' The morality and values such faith implies are deeply embedded in
our national character. Our country embraces those principles by design,
and we abandon them at our peril."*
—*Ronald Reagan, 1911-2004, 40th President of the United States*

DEANNE SAT at her computer. The whole wall was her
monitor, but she had the field of view minimized to a
quarter of the size. Peter always referred to the image as
"the writing on the wall," like it was modern technology's answer to the
way God communicated to King Belshazzar, *"You have been weighed in
the balance and found wanting."* For once she was glad the type was so
big. It was hard to see what she wrote. Her eyes were full of water. A
tear rolled down her face, spilling onto the keyboard. She brought her
palm up, wiped her cheek, and resumed typing.

> ...my heart is broken. I learned of your arrest only
> moments ago. I'm scared, Peter, really scared. The
> thought of your not being here...and what's to become
> of Angela? Will she pass into eternity without our
> being able to say good-bye?
>
> I wish I had your faith. I know God can get us
> through anything, but I don't feel Him now. I prayed

241

God would protect you, and I saw you get arrested. I prayed God would bring Angela home, but now she'll die somewhere far away and all alone. I can't stand the thought of someone's cold hands sticking a needle in her arm. I'm crying and I can't seem to stop. I want to run and hide but there's nowhere to go.

I'm supposed to forgive. Christ forgave even those who put Him on the cross. We're supposed to do the same, but right now I can't. I watched them take you away, Peter. It was Bob McCauley, wasn't it? I cannot explain what I saw in his eyes, they were filled with a kind of sadistic light. It was the look of a madman. He probably thought he was enjoying his most triumphant hour, but I think he has demons. Only the devil would be happy to see the ruin of another human being. And I'm supposed to forgive him. I want to pray he burns in hell.

I will follow the news. If they make your trial public, I'll be there. Even if it means leaving the shelter of these four walls. I'll come. I will. I promise. But pray, Peter, that I don't have to face Bob. If I do, I'm afraid what I say won't be of God. You must pray for me, as I will pray for you. And I'll try to pray that God changes my heart, and Bob's heart too, but I fear I won't be happy until that man is in his grave.

A full moon hung over the Monongahela, silver and electric, shimmering on the water. They were sitting in Bob's car, parked high up the bluff next to the incline station overlooking the Pittsburgh night. The lights of the city were twinkling, washing into ribbons of multicolored light on the dark river below.

Bob reached for Deanne's hand. She smiled faintly. She wasn't ready to admit, even to herself, the change that had taken place in her fickle heart. She needed to talk to him about it, but it was too soon to bring it up. And Bob wasn't good at listening. She'd pour out her heart and consider herself lucky if he didn't use the back of his hand to stifle a yawn.

He pulled her over, snuggling her against his side. She tried to be receptive, but her body felt stiff and awkward.

"What's the matter, Dee?"

"Nothing. I'm just tired, that's all."

He pulled her in and began nuzzling her neck, his lips caressing her skin filling her with excitement. She didn't fight; she didn't want to. She was confused. She still had feelings for Bob. She had feelings for them both. He found her lips, and she responded in kind. Even now she had to admit some part of her still wanted him. She wondered which part was stronger, because she also knew she'd grown surprisingly fond of Peter.

Right now she was caught in the moment, her heart beating in time with Bob's, their lips pressed together, supple and warm. It was something she never did with Peter. He'd never even tried to kiss her, couldn't, he said, as long as she was still with Bob. She wondered if he desired to be with her the way Bob did, or was he—dare she think it?—gay, the way Bob said. No, he'd assured her he wasn't. Bob wanted too much, and Peter too little. That's what made it hard. Bob was a man's man. He didn't just kiss her, he craved her.

But when it came to spending her life with someone, Peter was the better choice. They'd get on the phone and talk about everything from holocausts to pussycats, never pausing for breath until the dawn broke through the curtains of her bedroom window. And their beliefs were more in line. She didn't need to spend the rest of her life defending her faith. She admired Bob for his strength, but he could also be demanding and condescending. Peter would never insist she wear a particular dress, or fix her hair a certain way, or put on special perfume. That was Bob's purview. Peter accepted her the way she was. Maybe Peter didn't have the breadth of shoulders, or thickness of chest, but he was good-looking, in a demure sort of way.

Bob's hands were traveling, as they often did. She would stop him, just not yet. The spell was magic, stimulating latent emotions. She needed to slap herself—wake up girl, break the spell—but his lips were warm, aannnnd she didn't want him to stop. They were shedding so much heat the windows were beginning to fog—but...no, don't go there, she grabbed his wrist and pushed it back.

"Come on, Deanne, we've been going together a long time. You know I love you. It's time we took it to the next level."

Caught in the fervor of the moment, she could only gasp for breath. He took it as a sign of assent. His hand broke free and reached around behind her, fiddling with a button. She felt it snap open, then another. She was coming undone.

"Bob, cut it out. Stop it. I...I...don't...want...Stop it!"

But Bob just kept kissing and groping and burning with lust, his excitement out of control. She opened her eyes, but could no longer see outside. "Bob!" She forced herself up, pushing him away, suddenly realizing how far they'd gone.

Bob sat up, glaring at her. "What's with you? We don't live in the dark ages. Everybody does it. I thought you loved me."

"No! I mean, it's not that I don't, it's just...I don't know, we're not married..."

"And we're also not kids. We're two mature adults." He turned, placing his hands on the steering wheel, his back rigid against the seat of the car. "This isn't fair. Just when you get me going, you call it quits." He turned his head to look at her. "Half the time you act like you love me, and the other half like you couldn't care less, but that's not love, is it?" He paused waiting for her to respond but something in her eyes, a sadness, or the way she denied him an answer, something he couldn't quite put a finger on, made him jump to a conclusion he would never have thought possible. "You're seeing someone, aren't you? Tell me it's not that Peter creep. Please tell me it isn't."

"Peter would never..."

"Peter's gay."

Deanne slapped him, shoving the words back into his mouth. She slid over to let herself out.

"You get out now, and it's over. We're finished!"

She slammed the door.

Deanne stood alone, feeling the goosebumps building on her arms, shivering in the chill of the night. She watched as Bob punched the steering wheel, honking the horn, causing her to jump as the sharp sound echoed across the valley. He ground the engine to a start, revving it, then dropped *the stick-shift into reverse, popped the clutch, and backed away with his wheels spinning so fast, smoke rose from the pavement. He cranked the wheel and lurched forward, leaving her standing in the ghostly cloud of his exhaust.*

BOB FELT his pocket vibrating. He slipped out the palm computer and flipped it open as the tiny screen flickered to life. The notebook he'd used to read previous e-mails from Deanne lay on the seat beside him, but the smaller handheld device he'd taken from Peter was faster. Words began to appear on the screen.

You could feel the mood change. A cloud appeared on the horizon blocking the sun. *Madman? Demon? Burn in hell? She doesn't mean that. She can't. Sheeeeeesh! She wasn't supposed to know about me.* Bob tightened his grip on the steering wheel. *We have history. We were in love*—he glanced in the rearview mirror at his prisoner who, with his head tucked between his knees, looked like he was bowing his head in shame. *All I can say is, bad choice, lady.*

THIRTY-TWO

"If we and our posterity reject religious instruction and authority, violate the rules of eternal justice, trifle with the injunctions of morality, and recklessly destroy the political constitution which holds us together, no man can tell how sudden a catastrophe may overwhelm us that shall bury all our glory in profound obscurity."
—*Daniel Webster, 1782-1852, two term U. S. Secretary of State*

THE SUN looked like a yellow dab of butter melting on a slice of white toast as the silver four-door cut through the humid haze with the temperature gauge broaching red. The heat outside and the weight of four bodies put a strain on the vehicle, but not enough to slow it down. They were flying at just over the speed limit, fast enough to make maximum use of the time but slow enough to stay under the radar. Adrian checked his speed and backed off the gas. It wasn't that he wanted to avoid a ticket, though that was important too; he wanted to avoid getting arrested for smuggling Angela out of the hospital.

With her father in custody and her mother not able to be reached, the little girl was technically a ward of the state. Absconding with her probably constituted kidnapping. Not that *they* cared about her health or wanting to keep her alive, absolutely not, they'd just want to make sure her body found its way to the morgue. It was evidence. They'd require a thorough autopsy to document she'd been there. News outlets were already reporting how Homeland Security had successfully employed the daughter of international terrorist, Peter Dufoe, to lure him in.

A gust of wind rocked the car, nearly sending it into the next lane. Hank was thrown against the window, bumping his head.

"Whoa! Easy there, partner. I have a little girl back here."

Adrian struggled to keep the car on the road, tacking right when the wind pushed left, and spinning the wheel quickly to the left when the gust of wind suddenly stopped. The cemetery was just ahead, a quarter-mile up on the left. "Hang on, we're almost there. The wind is really picking up. Hank, you gonna be able to keep that truck of yours on the road?" Another blast hit the car, slowing the vehicle momentarily. The sky was the color of carpet dust. It smelled like mud and was thick and heavy to breathe. "Maybe you should wait until the wind dies down."

Hank held Angela in his arms like a mother nursing a child. He looked into her pallid face. A pale blue surrounded her whitish lips. She wasn't going to make it. "No way. It's five hours to Pittsburgh and I haven't a moment to lose. I'm getting this kid to her mother while I still can. 'Sides, takes a stronger wind than this to move a truck big as my Baby."

Adrian nodded, scratching his nose. "I understand. It's your call, but the radio's warning of severe wind conditions."

He looked at his fingers and brought them to his nose again. *What's that smell?* He'd been conscious of it ever since Hank climbed into the car, a faint medicinal odor, like old Band-Aids on a festering wound. Apparently it wasn't Hank, it was him—*or both*. What was it? He'd put on a clean examination coat. He sniffed again. It was on his fingers, but he hadn't removed any bandages or touched medicine of any kind. What else had he touched? *What?* The doorknob as he entered the consultation room? *Wouldn't be that. What?* He'd held Angela's wrist for a moment and checked her eyes. *Coma!*

"Hank! You take your coffee with sugar?" They were approaching the cemetery. Adrian had his left blinker on, braking for the turn.

Hank looked up. They weren't stopping for coffee—*not now!* "Double, double," he said. "I drink tons but I try to mellow the caffeine with loads of cream. Why?"

"Got some in your truck? Sugar, I mean. I need sugar."

The car entered the graveyard. Hank stared at the tombstones, thankful Angela couldn't see. She didn't need a glimpse of her future. *Here lies Angela, God's child. The world called her an orphan, but she was a saint.* "Yeah, probably. I usually grab a few extra. Why?"

"Just give me whatever you've got. Angela's been poisoned."

Father Bloom twisted his head around. "P...P...Poisoned?"

Adrian nodded, putting a finger to the side of his nose. "Uh huh. I smelled it when Hank got in the car but didn't think about it until now. It's insulin. That's why she's in a coma. She needs sugar." He hit the gas. "Hold on."

The car picked up speed, spinning dust like a Formula One turbo on a winding track. They almost missed a turn and fishtailed, but the doctor corrected and brought the car swinging back around. Then they were on the home stretch. He could see the big blue truck ahead. Hank had his hand on the back of the seat to brace himself. Father Bloom's toes gripped the floor. Adrian pulled to a skidding stop, the dust swirling past them on the wind. He looked over his shoulder. "Hank, get that sugar. Hurry!"

Hank peered through the settling dust at the sidewall of his truck and turned, twisting around to lay Angela down. She looked so cold, so...*dead.* He covered her with the blanket and reached behind him for the handle, backing out. Insulin poisoning—*what was that all about? Why?* She was going to die anyway. He left the door open and raced to his truck.

"And water, too, if you have any," Adrian shouted, a second before the door slammed shut in the wind.

Hank ducked behind the passenger side of the truck. He had his keys out, pointing his RF keyfob at the door. He heard the *clunk* as the locks released. He climbed the running board. Killer was *yip, yip, yipping* and jumping up on the glass. " Shut...up, it's me, ya dern fool." Hank yanked the door open. Killer backed away, trembling. "Hey, hey, sorry, boy. You're a good dog, that's a good boy." Killer rose off his haunches and approached timorously, wagging his tail.

Hank began sifting through the glovebox. "Come on, where are you? I must have a hundred of these things somewhere." He found one, two, three, and then a handful. He reached behind his seat for his thermos.

The doctor climbed out of the car and went around to the other side. He opened the door and looked in on Angela. "I'm right. I know it. I can smell it. Someone spiked her drip tube with insulin. I'd bet on it."

Hank handed him a fistful of sugar packets and the thermos. "I ain't got water. It's coffee, but it's cold."

"It'll do." Adrian pushed the thermos back into Hank's hands. "You have to fill the cup."

Father Bloom tried to get out, but Hank and Adrian were blocking the door. Hank walked to the back of the car, placing the thermos cap upside down on the trunk. He spun the lid off and poured the cold coffee. Adrian leaned over, ripping the ends off the paper packets and, using his hand to block the wind, began pouring the sugar into the cup. Buddy seized the opportunity to climb out of the car. He stood, shifting his weight from one tennis shoe to the other, his face red and sweaty. "You...you want me to hold Angela?"

Adrian looked up. A blast of wind buffeted the car, sweeping the empty sugar packets into the field. He watched as they tumbled across the dry grass. His hair flattened and the points of his collar flapped like the ears of a dog. He turned, nodding. "Uh huh, good idea, get her out of the car." He put his finger into the mix, swirling it around until the dissolved sugar had the consistency of syrup. "Lord be praised, the coffee's a good idea. The caffeine will stimulate her heart and get her blood pumping."

Father Bloom held the little girl in his arms. Adrian turned his back to the wind. "Hank, I need you to hold her mouth open. Squeeze her cheeks until her jaws come apart. Good, that's good. Just hold her like that." He dipped a finger in the thick brew and swabbed it around Angela's mouth, rubbing it along her cheeks and under her tongue. When he was through, he poured a small amount down the back of her throat, causing her to gag in reflex and swallow. He did it again, repeating the process until the brown granulated mixture was gone.

"That'll do. The sugar and coffee won't hurt her even if I'm wrong, but I don't think I am. Everything points to insulin poisoning: her eyes, the blue color of her face, the coma. She's in shock. I'm glad whoever did this injected the feeder bag instead of her arm. A large amount of insulin injected straight into her bloodstream could have killed her instantly. Whoever did this, and I have my suspicions who it was, they wanted her to die slow, probably so they could go home and not be there when it happened."

Adrian looked at his watch. "If I'm right, you'll see improvement over the next little while, though I can't say for sure. She's so weak she may not recover. Here," he said, handing a small vial of pills to Father Bloom, "It'll help with her pain if she does come around, and make sure she gets something to eat. She needs nourishment, and it will help improve her glucose levels."

Buddy brought Angela up, resting her weight on the shelf of his stomach. He let go of her legs, took the small plastic bottle of capsules and dropped them into his pocket.

Adrian laid his palm flat against Angela's forehead and used a thumb to raise her eyelid. "All I can do now is pray. I have to believe if God has kept her alive this long, there must be some powerful reason. Now, I have to be getting back to straighten things out. That security guard wrote down my plate number. Within the hour every policeman in town will be looking for me. But you needn't worry. No one saw me with the child, and I'm the one who ordered her termination. I can't be blamed if the paperwork fell into the wrong hands. Anyway, as much as I enjoy long good-byes, you two had better go."

"They'll want to question me too," Father Bloom said. The heat rising from his face was causing his glasses to steam. "*Uh huh, uh huh*, but Hank needs me to hold Angela while he drives. They won't be looking for a truck, but you need to pray we don't get pulled over. I'll be back tomorrow to explain myself. *Uh huh*. I'll call the church and tell the sisters I'm visiting a friend."

Hank slapped the side of his big blue Baby. The sound warbled like a sheet of tin hit with a hammer. "Heck, it'll be fun. You ever been in one of these?"

"No, *uh huh*, no I haven't."

"Well then, climb aboard, you're in for a real treat."

Buddy stood looking at the rig, big as a freight train and maybe twice as tall. "I...I think I'm going to need a ladder."

Hank's unshaven chin bunched up, settling his mouth in a thoughtful pout. He hustled around to the driver's side. "Ain't got one a those," he said, his voice muffled by the truck's massive wall. "But I do have sumpthin' that'll do." He came back around with a stepstool in his hand, placing it on the ground in front of the running board. "There you go, my friend, stairway to heaven." He smiled as he pointed to the words airbrushed on the door. "You're going to like it up there. Lots of room, not like them itty-bitty critters you been riding around in."

The three men stood looking at each other. There wasn't much else to say. Dr. Philips leaned over and embraced Hank, and then his friend the priest, being careful not to squeeze Angela. They felt a bond, a fellowship of brothers, the Knights Templar on crusade bound by a common cause—*keep the faith.*

Angela felt like she was floating, suspended somewhere between earth and heaven. It was like being in another world, a parallel creation in another dimension. The sky was an iridescent blue, brighter than any she'd ever seen and the atmosphere seemed to shimmer with light. It was so... perfect, not cold, not hot, just a flawless warmth that seemed to tingle her skin. If only her father could see her now, he'd see her real hair flowing, tinged yellow with the light from her friend, who now stood with his hands reaching out to receive her. She was ready to go. White clouds glowing with luminosity began to part, but she didn't see the glory of heaven. She saw a dark blue and green ball rolling across a black-tiled floor. She saw earth. "But I don't want to go back..."

THE CUTOFF rolled over the New River Gorge and wound its way through the mountains. Bob was dodging wind and clouds of dust and trucks that appeared out of nowhere, riding his bumper and blasting their horns. He had the radio on, not particularly listening, but not ready to engage Peter in conversation either. They were driving into a headwind. Considering the trouble he'd had on the road earlier that day, he wrestled with, but rejected, the notion that God might be against him. He kept the rented car riveted to the slow lane, sometimes even dropping below the speed limit, much to the annoyance of truckers who wanted him out of their way. But he was taking it slow and easy.

In spite of the contrary weather, he was relishing the drive. He wanted to stretch out every mile and savor it. He didn't like admitting it, but Deanne was right. He felt triumphant. He was a Roman centurion riding his prancing steed with a rope around the neck of his hostage, who stumbled behind him with wrists tied; he was a gladiator with a sledge-axe and net and his fallen foe at his feet; he was the marshal of Tombstone, bringing a horse thief in for hanging. He glanced in the rearview mirror. Peter's eyes were closed. Bob knew he wasn't asleep.

Bob heard the station breaking for news. "Volume up," he said to the radio, increasing the level of sound. The broadcaster spoke of traffic, a three-car pile up on Interstate 77, next the weather, high winds and more hot temperatures, and then the headline story, none other than his capture of the man he had in the backseat of the car. He started to smile—nothing like hearing your name on radio—then squinted, his lips compressing into a flat line as he realized the cost. He looked at Peter again. *What good's the victory if you can't enjoy the spoils?* His jaw tightened, grinding his teeth, his knuckles turning white as his nails dug into his palm. There'd be no consoling Deanne now, no ringing her bell to say: "Lean on me, I'm here to share your pain." He'd have to come up with a new plan. His grip tightened on the wheel. She blamed *him*. Peter did the crime, Peter had to do the time. How was that *his* fault? If he didn't bring Peter in, someone else would. Why did she hate him for *that?*

Deal with it. The question now was how to turn the situation to his advantage. The newscaster droned on. The story was about the bombing of a senator's office in Washington, D.C., thirteen people killed and dozens of others injured. *An e-mail received simultaneously by several news outlets credits the Jihadist Intifada with responsibility...*

"Volume down." Bob glanced at Peter in the mirror.

"See, that's just why I'm bringing you in. Nothin' personal, but wackos like you breed nothing but hate." He continued to stare at Peter but got no reaction. His eyes drifted back to the road. "I can't believe you. You guys think downing other religions makes the world a better place."

Peter stared out the window to his left. When he turned to look in the mirror, Bob was studying the road so he spoke to the back of Bob's head. "Excuse me, did you hear them say that was done by a Christian organization? Because, frankly, I missed that. I heard them say it was a Muslim organization calling themselves the Jihadist Intifada. Christians aren't your problem, Bob."

"Nuts! Christians are doing the same thing and you know it. Everyone's out there trying to force everybody else to believe in their God. 'My god's bigger than your god. My god can beat your god up.'" Bob whined. He wasn't sure he wanted to get into it with Peter. Policy forbade conversing with prisoners, and his gut warned against useless debate. His mouth skewed to the side at the image of Paul the apostle, yapping about Christ the whole time he was chained to a Roman guard.

"Amen to that," Peter said. "My God doesn't need my defense. He's big enough to defend Himself. But that's the point. My God *is* bigger. You think because you got Jews and Christians and Muslims and Buddhists all sharing worship centers and acknowledging one another's faith, that everyone believes and worships the same. Forget it, not going to happen, but I don't have a problem with other religions. In fact, I liked the country the way it was, based on religious freedom the way the founding fathers intended. There's just too many differences for all faiths to have communion around the same table."

Bob rolled his eyes but they were hidden behind his shades. He'd done it now, pushed Peter's button, let the horsepucky fly.

"I once heard a Muslim cleric say Islam loves death the way Christianity loves life. He meant it as an insult, like Christians are weak or something, but he was right. See, Christians do love Life. It's Satan who wants people dead. I mean, think about it, in Islam, mothers send their sons to die for god, but in Christianity, the Father sent his Son to die for man. They're complete opposites. Christians don't kill those we don't agree with. And we don't bomb office buildings. Christ came as the Prince of peace..."

Bob's sunglasses filled the mirror again. "He also said He came not to bring peace, but a sword. He came to divide children against their parents, neighbor against neighbor, and husband against wife."

"Ah, I'm surprised. You do know your Bible. Okay, point taken. It's hard getting two people to agree on anything. Even Christians are divided in what we believe, but at least we agree to disagree. You call yourself a Christian, or at least you used to. As I remember, we used to disagree on lots of things, and I'm sure we still do, but even though I think you're wrong, I wouldn't..." Peter tightened his fists and felt the cuffs chaff his wrists, "...cart you off to jail for what you believe. So who's more tolerant of whom? Just read the Bible, you'll see what I mean. Paul even stopped his jailer from killing himself."

"You're not going to jail for what you *believe*, Peter. The charges are insurrection and murder." Bob looked out over the horizon. First time he'd seen it in awhile. They'd rounded the side of the mountain exposing them to a flat stretch of farmland turned dustbowl. The wind picked up, whipping dirt against the side of the car. It sounded like a billion microscopic pellets scouring the paint. The sky was the color of sand. Bob hoped the car's insurance covered acts of God—but which *god? Yada, yada, yaaaawn.* Peter always did have diarrhea of the mouth. Bob glanced at the mirror, a genuine nerd's nerd, right down to his rosy red mouth with lips always flappin'. "Give me a break."

"No, really, go get one of the Bibles you've confiscated and look it up. Satan is the author of death. Christ came to give life. Jesus called Satan a 'murderer' from the beginning. The Bible says the sin of one man brought death into this world, not God. Death is the result of sin, and sin was introduced by Satan. In the garden."

Bob looked up, his sunglasses filling the mirror again. "Oh, for the love of...in the garden? Man-o-man, are you and Deanne still dancing around in fig leaves?" He shook his head at the mention of the church play and how ridiculous Peter had looked with his skinny torso barely filling out the leotard with all the silly leaves sewn on. Deanne as Eve he could imagine, but Peter as Adam? No way. He watched Peter for a reaction but he'd either missed the allusion, or chose to ignore it. He just kept yappin'.

"If you want to know what God to follow, figure out which one is for life, and which one is for death. God created men to live forever, but man chose the death option when he believed Satan's lie. The good news is God promised us a way out. Right? Remember, Christ on the cross, the atonement, the resurrection? It's a simple dichotomy. Satan brings death. Christ brings life. Don't ever confuse the two. Those who think they have to die to please God, are serving the wrong god."

"Yada, yada, yada, blah, blah, blah. Just keep talking,' Peter. I'll build a stronger case against you than I already have. You Christians just don't get it, you're all the same, blissfully blinded by ignorance..." Bob jumped as the truck on his bumper gave him a blast of his air horn. "Jerk!"

The truck sidled around on the left and sped by. It was about the tenth time they'd been passed that way. Too bad his rental car didn't have a cherry. He'd pull that rig over and have it impounded, though he had to admit if *he* were in a hurry and had some sightseeing tourist blocking his lane, he'd probably do the same.

He watched the truck disappearing into the dust ahead of him. *Freakin' idiot.* It wasn't his jurisdiction, but if he had the juice, that would be one truck he'd make sure was pulled off the road, permanently. Anyone dumb enough to call their truck, *Blue Heaven*, should have their license revoked.

THIRTY-THREE

"The nearer I approach to the end of my pilgrimage, the clearer is the evidence of the divine origin of the Bible, the grandeur and sublimity of God's remedy for fallen man are more appreciated, and the future is illumined with hope and joy."
—Samuel Morse, 1791-1872, Inventor of the American Telegraph

ASIDE FROM a close flyby of Mars or the pelting of a meteor shower every few millennia or so, nowhere in the memory of man had so many catastrophes happened so frequently with such severity. It was like the disease-infested planet was forever being stoned by hail, ravaged by storms, blown apart by wind, or set on fire.

The ash and smoke billowed up in a cloud, raining down on the car like gray flakes of snow. Bob hit the window with another burst of washer fluid, his windshield wipers plowing through the muck, leaving sooty streaks on the glass. Peter peered through the speckled haze and saw a sign for a service center. The turn indicator was flashing as Bob changed lanes. The sky was dark, the sun blotted out by smoke from the fires sweeping out of the Monongahela World Forest. Peter closed his eyes, shaking his head. As if the loss of his family and being in handcuffs wasn't enough. He didn't need another reminder of how messed up the world was. The designation, "world forest," was just plain wrong. It wasn't a world forest, it was a forest reserve in the United States, in the state of West Virginia, but in compliance with the United Nations World Congress directive, all forests were under the protection of the Earth Environmental Emergency Act, a measure aimed at preserving the world's dwindling natural resources, but that was just the cover story. Peter viewed it as a ploy to chip away at U.S. sovereignty. If they wanted to provide protection of the world's resources, they weren't doing a very good job. The forest was on fire—*again*. With the superheated temperatures and abnormally high winds, it seemed every forest in the world was continually burning. International governments blamed it on global warming, but Peter, and those of like mind, saw it as the consequence of ignoring God.

There was a time, school kids were taught U.S. History, Peter mused. Not anymore. Abraham Lincoln—the sixteenth U.S. president—was a name that had fallen into obscurity. Schools now touted world, instead of national, leaders. But President Lincoln once said: "All history has proved that only those nations are blessed whose God is the Lord." Even a cursory review of world history bore witness to the veracity of his statement. Peter had tracked it. When Israel followed after Jehovah, they were the most prosperous nation on earth. Under Moses, who spoke with God face to face, the twelve tribes walked out of Egypt, leaving Pharaoh smitten with plagues and drowning in the sea. Under Joshua, who affirmed his house would serve the Lord, they conquered Canaan. Under David, whom God declared a man after His own heart, they established a kingdom. Under Solomon, who acknowledged the beginning of wisdom was the fear of God, every vassal state paid tribute.

The hand of God, moving throughout history, was so obvious, Peter wondered how people could miss it. God through His prophets, warned the people to serve only Him and they didn't listen. With few exceptions, king after successive king brought in and worshiped the gods of other nations, idols of wood and stone, sending the once great nation into a downward spiral.

Before Joshua entered the land, God promised Moses if they failed to live by His precepts, He would judge them by raising up other nations to reprove His chosen. Israel ignored God and lost its position of power and influence, uprooted first by the Assyrians and then the Babylonians, and after that, a long parade of invading armies. God permitted the rise of other empires, but only as a rod of correction, and only for a season, and only to judge His own.

While under Roman rule, God sent Israel the promised Messiah. Christ came but was rejected by the nation thus engendering the great Diaspora, and God's chosen were scattered to the four corners of the globe. But the prophets foretold how Christ would be a light unto the Gentiles, so the Gentiles received Him. With Jerusalem in ruin and Constantine on the throne, Christian worship was centralized first in Constantinople and then in Rome itself, and it fell to Europe to carry God's banner and receive His blessing. For all her faults, Europe was decidedly Christian. Clawing her way out of the dark ages, Europe became the cradle of civilization, making unheard-of advances in science and medicine while creating some of the world's most notable works of art and music, all to the glory of God.

But Europe would eventually end up like Israel, abandoning the commission granted it for the furtherance of the gospel. To keep His Word alive, God sent explorers across the ocean to establish the New World, a frontier untainted by the past. The patriarchs of the United States and Canada responded by devising systems of law and justice based on Holy Writ.

Rich in industry, technology and natural resources, for two hundred years North America was the most powerful continent on earth. It was, in a word, invincible, until (sometimes the road to hell is paved with good intentions) a zeal to assist the world's beleaguered and downtrodden, and a fervent desire to see all men enjoy religious freedom, created a melting pot of gods to the point where North America could no longer be called Christian. And God did exactly what He'd done with Europe and Israel before. He took a step back and turned them over to their gods of choice.

Peter stared at the smoke billowing out of the Allegheny mountains and shook his head. If they'd only had eyes to see, they would have understood that the deities of Hinduism, Buddhism and Islam brought only poverty and death, not blessing. They should have recognized that people from underdeveloped countries, where those gods were worshiped, had migrated to North America to escape their misery.

They came to partake in the blessings of the True God but instead of worshiping Him, brought their own gods and venerated them. Satan was a liar and a murderer from the beginning. The will of the people could not be revoked so God called it "Ichabod" saying, "The Glory has departed," and Satan and his minions were given leave. Now, everywhere he looked, Peter saw a world bent on killing itself, whether through drugs, sexually transmitted diseases, murder, suicide, abortion, or euthanasia—it was a culture of death—and the planet was burning.

Ashes swirled by the window like dirty snow. Bob pulled into the service center looking over his shoulder. "As I recall, it was you Christians who didn't believe in global warming until it was too late. I guess we have *you* to thank for *this*." He gave a nod toward the window. "I'm getting off here. We're about halfway to Pittsburgh and I need a pit stop. You'd best take advantage of it too. We won't be stopping again until we're home."

The tires of the car spun on the slick fallen ash, leaving sooty tracks as they looked for a place to park. They veered to the side reserved for cars. A few trucks lined the back of the lot, but passenger vehicles were given spots toward the front.

Peter rolled his shoulders, pulling his hands up to improve his circulation. His arms ached. He had been sitting with his wrists locked behind him for two hours. The thought of leaving the car and possibly getting out of his cuffs, even if only for a moment, raised his spirits.

Except for a few cars sprinkled here and there, the lot was virtually empty. Was a time it would have been filled with families on vacation, but owing to a recessed economy, famine, and inclement weather, vacations were rare, though vagrants abounded. A dozen men crowded around the door of the restaurant waiting for a chance to hop an outbound truck to anyplace they might find work or beg leftovers from a driver. Bob released the car's interior locks and got out, opening the door on Peter's side.

Peter grimaced as he was grabbed by the elbow and pulled from the back. The sky was gunmetal gray and smelled of smoky fires. Tiny flecks of soot floated through the air, landing on Bob's shoulders and hair like pieces of lint. Bob turned and marched Peter toward a herd of unemployed transients huddled around the door. He would be escorted through the gauntlet with his head hung low—a man once written up in *Forbes* magazine as one of the richest men in the world, now prison-bound—but the thought of having his cuffs removed, if only for a minute, eclipsed his shame.

The men parted as Bob approached, a collection of gaunt unshaven faces, disheveled hair and wrinkled clothes, men who had once worn suits and ties, with manicured nails, now in baseball caps, holding out calloused hands. "Hey, buddy, got a spare credit?" "Hey, I got my wife and kids in there, we sure could use a break."

Bob held his badge up like a talisman, warding off unwanted spirits. With his other hand, he gripped Peter's arm. "Step aside, Homeland Security transporting a prisoner, step aside." Bob pushed through the doors and paused, looking for a restroom.

INSIDE THE FOOD concession, fewer than a dozen people milled about. No one waited tables providing service—with or without a smile. Everything from chocolate bars to three-course meals were purchased at a wall of vending machines that debited a customer's account with a wave of the wrist. Food was carried to tables on cardboard plates with recycled plastic forks, knifes and spoons, and thin paper napkins.

Father Bloom, Hank and Angela sat in a booth, their bowls of lukewarm soup getting cold. Angela slumped against the priest, whose bulbous side made an agreeable pillow. Buddy had managed to get a few spoonfuls into her mouth, most of which dribbled down her chin, but she had swallowed some. He hoped it was enough. He dipped a napkin into his water making it soggy, but it came apart as he tried to wipe the spot from her blouse. They had been on the road for over an hour before she opened her eyes and began mumbling incoherently about angels and heaven and something she had to do. The improvement was nothing short of a miracle, and they were thankful for it, though they did wish she could eat more. They wouldn't have stopped for themselves, but Dr. Philips insisted Angela receive food and refreshment as often as possible. The doctor did not want her becoming dehydrated.

A woman screamed. "Somebody stop that man! He took my purse! Stop him!"

Hank glanced up and saw a man in a soiled T-shirt, hoofing it down the aisle straight for him—probably not an evil man, just hungry—but right was right. As the man loped by, Hank stuck his foot out and caught the man's leg, sending him sprawling to the floor. The woman chasing him was unable to stop and hopped over his body, diving for the purse as it went sliding across the tiles. She jumped up, clutching it to her breast with both arms.

"I don't have anything. Hear me? Just memories. You can't take what I don't have!" Her hair was frazzled, her eyes red and wired like she'd been drinking coffee all night. She spun on her heel and marched away as the man scrambled to his feet and fled out the door.

The distraction caused Buddy to look the other way, but when he turned back he saw something else. Behind the circular dials of his wire-rimmed glasses his eyes widened, the rosy color leaving his face as his jaw dropped and his mouth forming the shape of an O.

Hank laid his arm over the back of the bench and turned around, looking over his shoulder. There was Peter zigzagging through the tables and chairs, being escorted by a man wearing a suit and sunglasses who looked like he was going out of his way to avoid the purse-snatching incident. *Nark. Shouldn't he have at least tried to help?* Hank started to get up, but Father Bloom grabbed his sleeve, pulling him back. The priest was shaking his head, his eyes shifting sideways to Angela, who appeared to be asleep. Hank relaxed and released his weight into the seat again.

Father Bloom's face was red and sweaty. The priest reached into his coat and removed his inhaler, taking a puff, pausing until he was breathing again, *uh-huh, uh-huh.* Hank waited, tapping his foot until Buddy put his inhaler away and took out a small address book, which he opened to expose a pen and small tablet. He wrote a quick note and slid it across the table so it couldn't be seen by Angela. The note read: "You have to let him know we're taking Angela to her mother."

Hank grunted and gave a brisk nod. He pulled the paper and pen toward himself and wrote a second note, ripping it from the pad as he got up and excused himself to go use the washroom. He entered the men's room cautiously, knowing Peter's reaction to seeing him might be a problem. He stepped in and looked around. *Peter?* He paced back and forth, walking up and down the row of urinals, going from one side to the next. Peter was nowhere in sight, but the officer was there with his back to a stall, leaning against it with his arms folded. That could only mean one thing. Hank hitched up his pants, pursed his lips and headed for the stall adjacent, but as he reached for the door, a hand came up against his chest.

"Use the next one, Bud, this one's occupied."

Hank stiffened, his eyes fixed on the cop, his jaw set. He forced himself not to grab the man's wrist. His fists doubled into knots, then relaxed. He waggled his hands like he was shaking off water. "No trouble," he said, veering over to take a seat one stall away. The smell was rank. Wet toilet paper littered the floor. *Don't they clean these things?* He had half a mind to go punch the cop's lights out and set Peter free. Futile, of course. The truckstop would have security cameras on poles throughout the parking lot. They'd ID his truck, locate him on GPS, and send a dozen more cops after him.

But how was he supposed to pass the note to Peter now? He couldn't slip it under the stall. He leaned forward, resting his chest on his knees and dropping his head down to look under the dividing walls at what he assumed were Peter's feet. He tried to recall what kind of shoes Peter was wearing. Father Bloom wore tennis shoes, but Peter? It had to be him. Who else would they have behind a door with a police guard—*the purse-snatcher?* He wadded the note into a ball and tossed it carefully. It bounced against the toe of whoever's shoe it was and stopped. For a second nothing happened. *What if he doesn't see it?* Then a hand reached down and picked up the small wad of paper. Hank smiled.

He flushed the toilet, just for sake of appearance—*thank God for privacy walls*—and went out to wait, being careful not to look at the hulking cop hanging outside Peter's door. He wandered over to the sink, not because his hands were dirty, but because he had to do something. The grimy basin needed scrubbing more than he did. His back was to the stall, but in the mirror he could see the officer still standing there with his arms folded. The man's face held an impatient frown. His skin looked green under the dim fluorescent lights.

Another toilet flushed and a minute later Peter came out—*thank you, sweet Jesus*. He looked to be his usual nervous self, his eyes darting around until they found Hank. He gave a half-smile and nodded curtly. Hank shook off the water, used an air blower to dry his hands and headed for the door, letting it close behind him. *Mission accomplished*.

The officer took Peter by the arm and led him to a washbowl. Peter pumped the soap dispenser but it was empty. He pulled on the tap, inserting his hands too close to the spout, and spurted Bob with a wayward spray of water.

Bob jumped back, raising his elbows with his hands hanging down. "Hey?" He looked for a paper towel but there weren't any. "You son of a..." He shook his head. "I swear I'll never understand what Deanne sees in you." He wiped his hands on his pants and got in Peter's face. His eyes were slits, his lips puckered white. "You are a freakin' menace to society. Soon as I get you in jail, I'm gonna personally throw away the key. And then you know what I'm gonna do? I'm gonna steal your wife. That's right, meathead, me and Deanne. Think about it—while you're rotting in a cell, she's gonna be with me." Bob rolled up his fist with his thumb pointed at his chest and a cocky grin on his face.

Peter shook the water from his fingers and looked at Bob, shaking his head. "Bob, I don't know what pills you're on, but this much I know, Deanne wouldn't touch you with a ten-foot pole."

It happened so fast, Peter would later say he didn't see it coming, but he did. The hardening of Bob's face, his squinting eyes with those pinched crow's feet, and just the flicker of movement at the wrist as he saw Bob's fist tighten, and a second later, before he could even flinch, that fist hitting him square in the side of the face. He felt like he'd been hit with a sledge hammer. For a second everything went black, then red. White pulses of electric light sparked through his brain. He went reeling, collapsing on the dirt-encrusted linoleum. He could feel the grit under his palms and his nose gushing blood. He sat dazed, wondering what had just happened, then in a flurry Bob was on him, yanking him by the collar and pulling him to his feet.

"Come on. You want a piece of me? Come on. Show me what you got, you little pussy." Bob let go of Peter and thrust his jaw out, pointing at it. "Go ahead. Give it your best shot."

Peter wiped his nose, leaving a smear of blood on the back of his hand. He shook his head. His brain sloshed like it had been knocked loose of its moorings. "I don't want to fight you, Bob."

Bob poked him in the chest, making him step back. "You're darn right you don't, you little wimp. I'll take your freakin' head off! Deanne is going to be mine. When you're laying in the cell at night trying to go to sleep, just think of her and me doin' the slow tango. Me and her, cheek to cheek. 'Cause I promise you, that's wha..."

Peter couldn't do it. He couldn't hold it in. The man was talking about his *wife*. He launched forward, plowing his head into Bob's chest, *oooooofffff*, catching him off guard. The bigger man stumbled backward, tripping over his own feet as his head snapped back, slamming into the air blower, *crrrrack*, and he was down, sliding against the wall tiles until he hit the floor.

Peter froze, his eyes widening in disbelief. *Whaaaa?* Bob would kill him now for sure. But Bob wasn't moving, and there was a faint streak of blood marring the white tiles behind his head. *Oh no.* "Bob, you okay? Bob, wake up." Peter stood and reached for the faucet. He winced, and stole a glance at the mirror—the side of his face was turning blue and his eye drooped, beginning to swell. The red splotch under his nose hid a cracked lip. He ran his hands under the water, cupping his fingers to form a bowl and ducked down to splash it in Bob's face. "Bob, wake up!" Maybe it wasn't such a good idea since dousing Bob with water was what had set him off in the first place, but it was too late.

"*Aaaaaaaooooo!*" A hand snapped up and grabbed Peter's wrist. Bob rose, dragging Peter with him and spun around, shoving him forward until his cheek was pressed flat against the wall. He pulled Peter's wrist toward him, locking it in a cuff, and then did the same with the other. "Don't think for one second you're getting away from me, you little..."

Peter grimaced. Maybe he should have made a run for it. Hank was just outside with Angela. Bob was out cold. Yet for some strange reason...*Paul stopped his jailer from killing himself.*

"You ever say anything about this, and I guarantee it'll be the last thing you ever say. Now let's go. Move it!" Bob turned Peter and pushed him, stumbling toward the door. He reached around and felt the knot at the back of his head.

HANK SAW them coming. They were waiting at the table with their spoons still sitting idle in their bowls of uneaten soup. They were hoping Angela would get one last chance to see her father.

"Whoa. Would you look at that shiner?" Hank said, laying his arm over the back of the booth, twisting himself to get a better view. "That's out-and-out police brutality. We oughta report that guy." The cop turned the corner, following Peter. His hair was parted at the back with a bloody red lump protruding through his noggin. "Well, I'll be, looky that. Looks like they were duking it out in there. Think Peter tried to escape? Dang! Boy's got more guts than I give him credit for."

THEY WERE back on the road plowing through the gray gauze. The miles of highway were never-ending, stretching out like a pastel drawing of hills, trees and open spaces marred by a dirty charcoal streak. At least the dusting of smoke and ash lessened as they drove further north. The grassy hummocks and withering woodlots were becoming a more natural shade of brown. Bob checked the mirror. Peter was staring out the window with one side of his face turning blue and a harlequin smile resting on his lips.

"What are you gawking at?"

"Huh?" Peter started to speak, but grimaced. He might have said he was enjoying the view. Just looking at the lump on the back of Bob's head was enough to bring him a smile. *I did that? Look at the size of that egg.* Knowing he'd tried to defend his wife's reputation gave him a certain amount of pride, but he didn't want to celebrate violence. And besides, that wasn't the real reason he was smiling. "Oh, ah, nothing, I guess I was just thinking about the goodness of God." *Thank You, Lord—for rescuing Angela like that—thank You!*

"Peter, you are one amazing piece of work. Truly amazing. You're sitting back there in handcuffs with a face that looks like it's been through a meat grinder, and smiling about it."

Peter licked his broken lip. *Ouch!* "Uh huh, well, given a choice I'd rather be somewhere else but...you know, St. Francis of Assisi prayed God would grant him the grace to accept the things he couldn't change. I guess I'm no different. Hey, remember when Paul and Silas were in jail? They sang hymns all night."

"You try that and I'll slap a muzzle on ya. I swear I'll put duct tape over that silly grin of yours and wipe it off your face."

"Jesus loves you too, Bob. The *only* begotten Son of the Father, with emphasis on the, '*only*.' Here's another *only* for you. There's *only* one way to God. Jesus said, 'I Am the Way, the Truth, and the Life, no one comes to the Father but by me.'"

"Peter, you are really starting to get on my nerves."

THIRTY-FOUR

"Deeply impressed with the blessings which we enjoy...my mind is irresistibly drawn to that Almighty Being, the great source from whence they proceed and to whom our most grateful acknowledgments are due."
—James Monroe, 1758-1831, 5th President of the United States

MUSIC ECHOED in the glass-domed conservatory, music that hadn't been heard in a decade filling the room with such timbre the leaves on the potted palms were dancing. Deanne was seated at her Steinway Grand. Her fingers tickled the keys, enunciating notes and chords. She hadn't played in all the time she'd been married, though Peter never grew weary of encouraging her. She didn't know why she didn't play; she wanted to play; she loved to play—she just couldn't. Satan had ripped the song from her heart and God, for whatever reason, hadn't put it back—*until now*. She'd just had an encounter with an angel. Well, maybe, she'd interrupted the experience before it could be confirmed, but that's how it felt.

She let her fingers roll across the keys, each one responding to her gentle touch. *If music be the food of love—play on.* She smiled. It wasn't right to feel so good—not with the double loss of her husband and daughter—but she did feel good, probably for the first time in years. She couldn't help it. The keys were soft, so slick and cool, each an instrument of sound, made to be combined with others to produce melody and harmony. She had a pleasant voice, not a recording voice, but on key, and the words came from her heart. *"What a friend we have in Je-sus,"* He was her Friend—had always been her Friend—even in her darkest moments of despair. She let her fingers roll across the ivories. *Music.* It came back, like riding a bike.

> *Have we trials and temptations,*
> *Is there trouble anywhere?*
> *We should never be discouraged,*
> *Take it to the Lord in prayer.*
> *Can we find a friend so faithful,*
> *Who will all our sorrows share?*
> *Jesus knows our every weakness,*
> *Thou wilt find a solace there.*

The angel hadn't actually appeared, not visibly, but she *had* felt his presence. *Who knows?* The keys of the piano were glassy, easy to glide across. Her fingers danced, building to a crescendo, the room resonating with sound. She paused, holding her fingers on the keyboard until the room was still again.

A tear fell, followed by another, and then another. She wiped them away with her finger, tiny crystalline drops on the smooth ivory. Her shoulders buckled, her chest began to heave. Why was she forever crying? Tears of joy, and tears of grief—but these were definitely tears of joy.

BOB FELT his pocket vibrating. He reached inside his coat and pulled out Peter's palm computer. Another note from Deanne.

Dear Peter,

I don't know whether you'll receive this message or not, but I had to write. I have to let you know what the Lord has done for me. I feel giddy, light as a feather, totally free...I'm getting ahead of myself. It was the most amazing thing. I couldn't eat, I couldn't sleep, my mind couldn't rest. All I could do was cry.

If ever there was a female Job—look at me, a wilted flower, and Angela, taken by those who shed innocent blood, and you, in chains on your way to prison, and when you're gone the government will step in and seize everything we own and I'll be out on the street. I know I shouldn't complain, not after all the Lord's given us, but I was angry and hurt, and I let Him know.

Why is Bob all of a sudden back in the picture? God knows how I feel. I can't handle this. If you'd been arrested by anyone else I might have understood, but seeing you manhandled by that man—I suspect he's possessed by Satan himself. After all he's done, wrecking our wedding like that—and now this. It's like he's never satisfied. Maybe what you said is true. Maybe he thought I married you just to get even, but even so, he should be over it by now. We weren't out to embarrass him. He brought that on himself.

A lofty Hammond organ began piping the "Wedding March," and down the aisle they came, six bridesmaids in lavender and lace, holding baskets of white flowers, keeping perfect time with the music. All eyes were focused on the rear of the chapel. There flowed Deanne, soft and lovely as the petal of a white rose. They couldn't see the strain on her veiled face. Peter, already positioned at the front in a dark tuxedo, stood his ground, patiently waiting.

Deanne took the steps, her long train trailing behind, to all the world a picture of enchanted beauty. They faced each other, ready to take their vows. Dressed in satin and white lace like a fairytale princess—she was the picture of purity—but it was a lie. She couldn't feel good about getting married, not at all, though she loved Peter and knew marrying him was right. All her dreams had been shattered. They discussed postponing—under the circumstances it was probably the right thing to do—but the guests were already invited and Peter promised never to speak of it or hold it against her. He was determined to forgive and forget.

The minister went through a recital that culminated with his encouraging them to enter into a covenant with the Divine Being. That itself was an affront. How could they ask the blessing of God when they couldn't even mention His name? The church had changed with the times and, though they'd considered the option of leaving, their friends were there, so they remained.

But it was also the church Bob attended. He now sat, uninvited, all the way back in the last pew with his arms crossed. No one thought it strange to see him there.

Deanne's hands were quivering, but so were Peter's. She couldn't tell who was shaking more. She was glad she wore a veil because she found it impossible to look Peter in the eye. He deserved so much better.

"If there is anyone who has any reason why this man and this woman should not be united in the bonds of matrimony, speak now, or forever hold your peace."

There was a moment of silence, then a loud voice rang out from the back, "I do!" The room rippled with commotion, the shuffling of feet, murmurs and gasps.

Bob stood, squinting, his finger pointed accusingly at Peter. "There's no way these two should be married. Deanne, you don't know what you're doing. Come with me, right now, before it's too late. I forgive you."

A hush fell over the room as Bob waited for an answer. No one moved. "I'm warning you. This is your last chance." He held out his hand, beckoning her to come.

Deanne stared at Bob, but behind her veil her face was pale and though she struggled to hold back the tears, her eyes flooded and then overflowed. She tore her hands free from Peter's and fled the stage running past the flower-laden altar, down the steps, past the flickering candelabras, across the carpeted floor and into the pastor's study. Peter looked at the minister, then at the door as it closed. He stumbled down the steps and ran after her. The congregation turned to Bob again. His face resembled an explosion, his eyes practically bursting from their sockets, his cheeks blood red. He stormed out of the church, hitting the door loudly as he burst through—blamm—slamming it closed behind him.

If he feels any embarrassment at all, it's because of

what he did, yet he's still bent on hurting us. Now here's the part where the Lord did something I can't explain. He changed my heart toward Bob. I want to hate him—but I can't. I don't want to be like him, so I prayed, "Lord help me forgive Bob even as You have forgiven me." I think that was the first time I'd ever really meant it. I mean, you know, I'd said it before, hundreds of times, but not with my heart. And as I pleaded for forgiveness, I felt the back of my neck growing hot, the hairs on my arms standing on end and goosebumps rising on my skin.

Then I felt this awesome Presence. Honestly! If I'd turned, I know I would have seen a huge angel standing behind me, one of those beings we used to read about, you know, clothed in light, shining like the sun, with sword drawn. That's what I mean. It was so overpowering I cried out, "No, Lord!" And just as fast as it came, the Presence left. But when it was gone, so was my fear. The room was suddenly calm. It felt like the sun was shining and I was sitting by a brook in an open field with a breeze combing through my hair. You know what I did? I went to that old piano of ours and I sat down and played. I played and prayed, and played some more, and I sang. Yes, that's right—I sang.

I know this may be difficult to understand, but somehow I believe everything is going to be all right. I have this assurance, this thing we used to call a "perfect peace." And I've been singing ever since. I wish I had a Bible. There's a passage I want to look up, but I think I remember how it goes:

"For I am persuaded, that neither death, nor life, nor angels, nor principalities, nor powers, nor things present, nor things to come, nor height, nor depth, nor any other creature, shall be able to separate us from the love of God, which is in Christ Jesus our Lord."

I want you to know I've added Bob to that list.

I can't explain it, Peter, but I know beyond any shadow of doubt, everything is going to be fine. You and I will one day soar over the mountains like eagles, just the way I dreamed. Now I just have to pray the day will come soon.

Your loving wife,

Deanne

Because of what I did? Bob gripped the steering wheel, squeezing until his knuckles turned white. His face flushed red. He looked at Peter, still smiling like the village idiot. They were both smiling. He could feel it. They were laughing at him!

CELESTIAL VANTAGE

What happens when you die? When the body takes its last breath, the heart ceases to pump, and neuron pulses stop transmitting signals to the brain, is that all there is? Think it not. The body is a vessel, a container. It holds the essence of life, but it is not life itself. Life is in the nephesh, or soul. Life is not composed of matter, life is composed of data—the information that makes you all that you are.

Permit an illustration. A computer is hardware. It is made of physical elements, or matter, but it is a just a box. It is useless without software. Software, or the program, enables the computer to accomplish the tasks it was created for. Software cannot evolve. It is information. It requires a designer with knowledge to place the information inside the computer, thus enabling the computer to compute. Software gives the computer life.

But software is not composed of matter. Weigh a computer, then add more hardware, and the weight of the computer increases. But weigh a memory device and then fill it with gigabytes of information, the weight of the memory device stays the same. Software, the part of a computer that is information, cannot be weighed. It has no mass.

This massless data can be transported through the air using radio waves. In like manner, your body is hardware, but the real you is software. Someday, you will die and your hardware will become so much rust. But the massless part of you, all the information that makes you who you are, will go on. The real you, once free of your body, will be transported to another dimension. If blessed, you'll be on a frequency that transmits you to the heavenlies. If not, your address will be somewhere else. You cannot kill the soul, only whatever chance the soul has of changing its final destination.

THIRTY-FIVE

"The chief security and glory of the United States of America has been, is now, and will be forever, the prevalence and domination of the Christian Faith."
—*B. F. Morris, 1839-1899, U.S. historian*

HANK TUGGED at the brim of his baseball cap. He was hunched over the steering wheel pumping the petals and grinding the gears, hell bent for leather and willing his tooled-up semi to move even faster. If things worked out, they might still have a chance to let Angela see her father. All they had to do was catch up to the green car.

The brown fur muff known as Killer sensed his master's tension. He hopped between Hank and Buddy, the nails of his tiny paws clicking as he danced on the console between the leather seats. The air conditioner was on, but the priest was pouring sweat. He slipped a finger into his collar and pulled it away, venting his body heat, and took another puff off his inhaler. Angela lay across his lap, her wig slightly askew. Buddy tried to straighten it but it was tucked against his arm and wouldn't move. Her eyes were closed, but he couldn't say she was asleep. Every time he started to think she'd dozed off, she mumbled something, letting him know she was still awake. He always strained to listen, but he couldn't make out what she said.

Except when her eyes were open, Angela seemed to dwell inside the light now. It was a warm embryonic sack that completely surrounded her, though it was a light only she could see. Whenever she opened

274

her eyes she reentered this mortal plane, a place she now felt strangely disconnected from, so she kept her eyes closed most of the time, yearning for a return to the netherworld. For one brief moment, in that place somewhere between this life and the next, the light had taken almost human form, masculine, with hands held out to receive her and feet of bronze to carry her home, but now, as before, the glowing ball had no shape. Or perhaps behind that orb of white there was a shape, but its intensity was too dazzlingly brilliant for earthen eyes to grasp. Either way, the light had a voice. It was the sound of many waters, soft as a trickling brook and loud as the ocean's roar. But this too, was a voice only she could hear.

Will it hurt? Death, I mean. I don't remember it hurting before, but what you're asking is different. And I wasn't actually dead before, you know, was I? I do want to see Mommy again. I miss her and I want to say good-bye, so I guess...are you sure this is the only way to help my dad? I mean, it's okay to say I'll have courage when the time comes, but I'm scared.

Hank figured Bob to have at least a five-mile head start. It had taken Hank several minutes to warm up his rig and get it moving. Big machines weren't made for quick starts. He prayed Bob wouldn't get it in his head to hit the fast lane and take off. So far, he'd been driving like he had time to kill.

The once waxed and polished blue eighteen-wheeler was now buried under a thin coat of gray soot, increasing Hank's anxiety. He'd just finished detailing Baby till she sparkled, and now this? He hated seeing her dirty. He put the hammer down, shifting his thoughts to more pressing matters. He was running full bore in a race to catch Peter. He grabbed his CB and brought it to his chin, the handset bristling against the nubs of his two-day-old beard.

"Breaker, breaker, this is Blue Heaven. I'm northbound looking for a green late-model car with two men on board, one driving, and one ridin' in back. I just passed marker 118 and I suspect the car isn't far ahead. Anyone seen it? Come back."

There was a momentary pause and then a voice broke through the static. "Hey there, Blue Heaven, this is White Lightning coming back atcha. I think I got your vehicle. Driving in lane number one. Looks like the dude in the backseat is in the pokey with smoky, but the plates aren't government issue. Penn State. Sportin' a rental sticker on the back lid."

Father Bloom spritzed himself with a fresh puff of air, looking over at Hank, nodding excitedly. *Uh-huh, uh-huh, uh-huh,* "That's it. I didn't get the number, but it was a Pennsylvania plate, *uh huh, uh-huh,* the blue, yellow and white one, and the car was definitely green."

"Big ten four. I think that's the one, White Lightning. What's your twenty?"

"I'm ridin' his bumper. This lane lover's a dead pedal. Hold on a minute, he's a-blinkin'. He's heading for the rest stop at marker 123. Want me to tail 'em?"

"Negative. I've got my toenails in the radiator. We're there in five. I'm gone."

Father Bloom pulled at his collar and looked at Hank with a sheepish grin. "Now that's what I call speaking in tongues."

Hank's buckskin gloves gripped the wheel as he looked over. His gray eyes were hard as steel but his grizzled face held an impish smile. "He said the car he was following was blocking the lane and going too slow, but it was getting off at the rest stop at mile marker 123. That's only a few miles from here. I told him we're running pedal to the metal and that we'll be there in five minutes."

Buddy's face looked like a red clay plate pulled from a dishwasher before it was dry. "Isn't that just like the Lord, to have our friend pull over and wait for us to catch up?"

BOB ROLLED into the parking space. The rest stop used to provide travelers with an oasis of manicured lawns, bouquets of flowers and green-leafed trees. Now it was seedy and overgrown. The grass was tall and unkempt and the trees bore scant few leaves. Those still clinging to the branches were bug-infested, twisting in the breeze.

Bob stepped out into the blazing heat and opened the rear door letting a rush of hot air into the car. He reached for Peter's wrists and yanked them back, jerking Peter around until he faced the other way. He raised Peter's hands, causing him to duck and groan, and inserted the key into one of the cuffs. Peter felt a sigh of relief. He turned to face the front again, anticipating another moment's freedom. Bob probably wanted him to wash his face, get some of the crusty blood off. He raised his foot to climb out.

"Lean forward."

"Huh?"

"Do it!"

Peter bowed submissively. Bob grabbed his neck and pushed his head down. "Hold yourself there," he said. He fished around under the seat, found a bracket and slipped the empty cuff around it, leaving the other around Peter's wrist. He pulled the chain through and brought it back, locking it around Peter's free hand again. Peter found himself cuffed to the bottom brace of the front seat.

"No questions. I want you to keep your head down. Don't even think about looking up. I don't want you bothering the tourists. There are kids around here, families. Your picture's in all the newspapers. I don't want anyone getting nervous about your being in the car. Got it?"

Bob slammed the door and Peter jumped, his head exploding with the sound. He realized he was sitting hunched over in a very uncomfortable position and would have to remain that way until Bob returned. His face throbbed as the blood rushed to his head. *What's got into him? At least he was civil before.* This was a punishment worthy of his mother, but even she was never *this* cruel to him. *"You're a dirty little boy, dirty, dirty, dirty. You stand in that closet until I say you can come out and, so help me, I'd better not hear you cry."*

BOB HOOFED it up a sidewalk bordered on both sides by gardens of weeds. The sky was on fire. It felt like the earth's orbit had somehow shrunk, bringing them closer to the sun. Old Sol looked swollen, like a water balloon filled with yellow paint about to burst. Everything was a ubiquitous shade of yellow. At first morning light the sky was red, then orange, fading to peach, then yellow at noon, back to peach, and orange and red again before nightfall. It had been years since he'd seen a blue sky, though there were photographs in old magazines, collector pieces and in museums, that proved the sky used to be blue. He wore shades to block the sun's glare, the dark lenses offering a facade of coolness, but the sun beat down on his head and shoulders, and his temples pulsated with the headache he was starting to feel. He was determined to set things right. He would offer Deanne a chance to redeem herself. It was the least he could do.

He pushed through the doors and paused, letting his eyes adjust to the dim interior. Only half the fluorescent lights were working. He removed his sunglasses, wiping the back of his hand across his forehead. It was as warm inside the building as out. He spotted the phone and marched over, waving his wrist in front of the scanner to be recognized. He picked up the receiver. The Dufoe number was unlisted, but not to Homeland Security. There wasn't a phone number in the world he couldn't access, or put a tap on.

He dialed the Central Intelligence database and punched in his PIN. Then he spoke the first and last names, spelling them out, plus the city and street address and upon receiving confirmation, requested a connection. The line was busy. He asked for an intercept and listen-in and found she wasn't on the line—the receiver was off the hook. Intercept took over and put the call through. Deanne picked up on the third ring. Her voice—a reminder of all things good, but also of things beyond his reach—sent a titillating shiver down his spine. She seemed anxious.

"Peter? Is that you?"

"You want Peter? I've got him. If you want him back, I'm willing to trade."

"Bob?"

"Yeah, Bob. The man you love to hate. Evil incarnate"—he longed to be civil, a calm voice, thoughtful, caring, but it was too late—"the man you begged *God* to forgive." He felt her hesitation. He envisioned her standing there in tight jeans and a white cotton blouse, her dark hair curling around her shoulders, her forehead furrowed as her mind ran through the possibilities. "Your e-mails, Deanne. That's right, I've got your husband's computer. I've got his palm computer too, and I've got him. Now let's talk. Here's the deal, Deanne. I want what belongs to me. You know what that is?"

There was a long silence.

"That's right, think about it. *Sheeesh!* Use the old noggin'. What in the freakin' world could your old boyfriend want?"

There was a buzz, like static on the line. "Come on, it's not that hard. I'll give you a hint. It's something you promised to give me, and then gave to someone else."

But the silence continued.

"Sheeesh, it's *you,* Deanne, I want *you.* I want what Peter stole from me. I'm about three hours outside of Pittsburgh. I'm going to take your husband to the lockup, and then I'm going to my motel. I'm staying just down the hill in Avalon, in a sleazy little fleabag called the Alva Motel right on Ohio River Boulevard. I'm going to call the manager and tell him a woman will be by to pick up a spare key. Her name will be Deanne..."

"You're not serious?"

"Oh, but I am. If you're there when I get there, I'm going to make sure that somewhere en route to California your husband escapes. That's the deal. I want you for one whole night. You do that and I'll make sure your husband is returned to you. But if you're not there, you can kiss your husband good-bye!"

"What..."

Bob slammed the receiver into the cradle, emphasizing his words. He yanked the phone from the hook a second time and made one more quick call to his motel. Then he spun on his heel and walked outside into the blinding sun. He slipped his shades on to shield his eyes from the glare. He had no intention of letting Peter go. But throwing Peter in jail would only even the score with one of *two* people who were jerking him around. This way, he'd get both. It was perfect.

PETER WAS sweltering. Being doubled over in the back of the car was one thing, but leaving a man with his nose clotted with blood, forcing him to breathe through his mouth, with the windows closed and without the air conditioner running was just plain inhumane. The sun beat down on the thin metal roof, turning the vehicle into a furnace. Bob would be arrested for leaving a dog like this. Peter drew in a breath, but his lungs were pressed against his legs, making it hard to inhale deeply. Sweat poured from his forehead, down his cheeks and under his nose to his chin, mingling with his blood as it dripped onto the carpeted floor. He felt delirious. His head was pounding from the beating he'd taken. The buzzing in his skull was so loud it felt like he was going to pass out.

It didn't figure. Bob didn't give a fig who saw him the last time they stopped. Where was the costume? It had to be around somewhere. It was evidence. If Bob didn't want him recognized, all he had to do to was let him put on a disguise. *He, he, he, ohooo!* Peter's split lip pulled apart. *Ooouch!* Laughter ached. The air was hot enough to sear his lungs. But that was a good one—let him become someone else and walk right out of there, *he, he, he, ughhh*! Laughter may hurt, but it helped. It took his mind off his misery.

He shuddered, trying to draw in another harsh breath. He didn't want to be someone else. He wanted to be Peter, the man God made him, but that was the most difficult task he'd ever been called to do. Some years ago, he'd come across a poem that said it all. It had been signed Anonymous, and he could understand why.

> *I keep my mask right with me, everywhere I go,*
> *In case I need to wear it, so the real me doesn't show.*
> *They say mean things, and laugh at me. It's what they like to do.*
> *So I'm afraid to show you me, afraid you'll hurt me too.*
>
> *I'd like to take my mask off, to let you look at me,*
> *Try not to argue when I say, there's more than what you see.*
> *If you're patient, close your eyes, I'll pull it off real slow,*
> *Please understand how much it hurts, to let the real me show.*

The problem for Peter was, living in the many costumes of a

multiple personality meant, when he stripped them off, he didn't know for sure who he really was.

HANK EXITED to the ramp using his engine brakes to slow the truck—*pop, pop, pop, pop, pop*—as he coasted into the rest area. They were facing away from the sun, looking across the yellow-tinted grass to the other side. Right there in front was the green car Buddy had seen, but it appeared to be empty. The arresting officer must've taken Peter inside. No, wait, there he was, plowing through the doors like a bull wearing sunglasses, snorting like he was anxious to get somewhere fast. Peter wasn't with him.

"That the guy we saw in the restaurant?"

"Yes, definitely. I'm sure of it. And that's the car."

Hank brought a gloved hand up, tipping the bill of his baseball cap forward to avoid being recognized. "Okay, I'm going to follow him out and ride his tail all the way to Pittsburgh. Hopefully, we can give Peter a last chance to see his daughter, but we'll break it off if we have to. Our first priority is to get this child to her mother."

"But where *is* Peter?"

The man reached the car, opening the back door. He stooped in, rustling around with a flurry of activity, and then, as if by magic, someone else was sitting there that hadn't been there a moment before. Peter must have been sleeping. The man climbed in front, pulling the door closed. He cranked the engine.

Hank didn't have time to stop. They were still rolling through the lot. He tipped his hat as they passed the War Veterans Memorial and, when he looked back, the car was already pulling out.

THIRTY-SIX

"Rely on our dear Savior. He will be the father to the fatherless and husband to the widow. Trust in the mercy and goodness of Christ, and always be ready to say with heartfelt resignation, 'May the Lord's will be done.'"
— *Andrew Jackson, 1767-1845, 7ᵗʰ President of the United States*

BOB DISAPPEARED into a cloud of dust like smoke from a magician's wand. One minute Hank was sitting on his bumper close enough to read his plates; the next, he was gone. He'd been a dead pedal up till now, hogging the slow lane and blocking traffic. But something had changed. Bob immediately moved into the fast lane and took off. Hank rolled onto the highway, checking traffic on the left, looking for a place to squeeze in but, by the time he got Baby up to speed, Bob was nowhere in sight.

The little dog was dancing on the console, turning in circles. "It just ain't right," Hank said. "This little girl shouldn't be denied the chance to see her daddy one last time, and that poor man should be allowed to see his little girl's in good hands. Father, I think it's time you started to pray."

Buddy was holding Angela in his lap. He glanced at Hank. "*Uh-huh, uh-huh*, what do you think I've been doing? You want me to ask God to slow him down?"

"Naw, I'll take care of that. Just ask God to kinda blind him so when we pull up alongside, he won't see us. Okay, here goes." Hank reached for his CB. His lips were the color of red clay surrounded by the gray stubble of his beard. "Breaker, breaker, this is Blue Heaven. I'm trying to catch a green passenger vehicle northbound on I-79. We're just north of the rest area at Exit 123. Anybody ID the vehicle, come back."

"Hey there, Blue Heaven, this is Lumberjack in the saddle with a load of sticks. I see the car, ridin' my tail and wantin' to pass but, hey, if you don't mind my asking, what's the deal with this fella? This call went out half an hour ago. I thought you already caught up with him."

"That's affirmative, caught up to him at the rest stop, but he was pulling out as we rolled in. The dude's an undercover Bear, and the guy he's got in back's a personal friend up on a false charge. I ain't trying to take him down, but I got my friend's little girl ridin' shotgun with me, and she wants a chance to wave to her daddy. 'Ol Smokey's hauling him to the pokey and he'll be gone a long time. She deserves one last good-bye."

"Say no more, Blue Heaven. I got this bucket of bolts right in front of him. We'll put him in a box and clamp down the lid."

Hank clipped his handset back on the dashboard and looked over at Father Bloom, his lips pressed together. "That's all she wrote for that Homeland Security narc until I say otherwise. Right about now, a rig hauling logs is slowing down in front of him. The cop will blinker on and try to go around on the right, but they'll be another rig just ahead of him in the slow lane and my friend will speed up so he can't squeeze through and pass. Then a third rig will pull up behind and, with a truck in front of him, one behind, and one to his left, they'll have him locked in a cage with no way out. Now hang on. We're putting pedal to the metal. That little blockade they just formed will hold up a lot of traffic so we have to get there ASAP. We don't want to cause a major jam."

"Tha...that's called interfering with an officer, and...and you got complete strangers helping you."

Hank nodded, leaning on the wheel. "Truckers are kinda like family. We get more done when we work together. Besides, the car has rental tags, remember? He can't light 'em, couldn't pull 'em over if he tried. On the road, the bear's a predator. They're just putting him in a cage where he belongs. Heck, they'll get a kick out of causing him some grief."

It wasn't five minutes before they caught up to the three trucks. Hank couldn't see the car they had cordoned off, but he knew it was there. He could hear it. The cop was audibly upset, *bleeeeping* his horn over and over and over. Hank pulled up behind the truck on the left, a trailer with a long float of logs. He snuggled up to his bumper and grabbed his CB. "We're on your tail, Lumberjack. If you'll just slide on up, we'll take it from here. Thank you, boys, so much. And I got a little girl here who thanks you as well."

"No problemo, Blue Heaven. Glad for the chance to serve. Good luck. I'm clear." And with that the log hauler hit the gas and pulled ahead, letting Hank take the slot.

Buddy nudged Angela, trying to awaken her from her sleep. "Angela, try to wake up, honey. Angela, wake up. Your daddy wants to see you now, wake up."

Angela felt a hand on her chest, shaking her. She could hear a voice, but it wasn't the voice of her angel. She resisted answering. They'd already eaten. She'd gagged most of it up. *Leave me alone.* She equated opening her eyes with the feeling of being born. She didn't want to enter the world again. She kept her eyes closed.

"Angela, Angela, wake up. Don't you want to see your daddy?"

Daddy? Yes. She had to rescue him. She tried opening her eyes, but her lashes were glued shut. She tried again, breaking free. She was looking up at the windshield, large yellow clouds overhead. Then she saw the pudgy red face of the priest. She tried to smile. She wasn't sure if her lips actually moved or not.

"Hi, there. Hey, I want you to see something. Come on, let me lift you up to the window. Look, look down there, ah, see, we have a special treat for you. It's your daddy." Father Bloom held Angela under the arms, letting her look down on the car. He could see Peter in the back, but Peter wasn't looking at him. "He doesn't see us, Hank."

"I got just the thing for that." Hank reached up and a second later the *blllaaaannnkkkk bllaaaannnkkkk* overbearing sound of his air horn drowned out the car's honking and the insistent cursings of the driver.

Peter's head jerked up. Two smiles linked across the space of a dozen feet. The connection was pure light. Angela's hands pressed against the window. She put her lips to the glass and gave it a kiss. Peter kissed the air in reply. Angela started waving, but Peter, with his hands locked behind him, couldn't respond, and Hank couldn't hold the traffic up any longer. He gave his air horn another blast, *bl-laaaannnkkkkk,* and hit the gas.

"'Bye, Daddy," Angela whispered.

DEANNE MADE a loop around the grand piano, dragging her fingers across its slick surface, leaving tracks in the wax. A few minutes later she found herself at the potted palm, fingering its fronds, so smooth and slippery, wondering why she'd never noticed how tall it had become. How could she *not* notice? Maybe because her eyes were filled with water. Her vision was impaired, but *no,* that palm was there long before that. She'd just never looked at it before, not really. She felt an ache and turned to lean against the wall, bringing her leg up to rub her knee. *Ouch!* She didn't know which hurt worse, her knee or her upset stomach. She set her foot down, tapping the carpet, and resumed her stride.

The sun pouring through the glass-domed ceiling was bright, but darkness overwhelmed her soul. She continued pacing, back and forth, back and forth, limping. She'd been on her knees so long they hurt. She'd finally dragged herself from the carpet, straightened the cuff of a sleeve wet with tears, and returned to the conservatory to find solace at the piano, but it wasn't there. Satan had ripped the song from her heart and thrust her headlong from the mountain, and once again her tears of joy had become tears of anguish—so *many* tears. *What would you have me do, Lord; what would You have me do?*

As a child, whenever she felt discouraged, Deanne would turn to the Bible, but she didn't have a Bible, and in this case it probably wouldn't help because a Bible would only tell her not to do what she was being constrained to do and already knew was wrong. *I can't do it, Lord. I can't.* Was subjecting herself to rape the same as adultery? If—*and it was a big if*—she were to muster the courage to submit to Bob's demands, it would be by coercion, not by choice. Were victims of rape guilty of sin? *'Course not!*

Ohoooo! she paused, placed a hand on the back of a chair and brought the other to her waist—just thinking of Bob made her stomach curl. She took a deep breath, feeling the tremor in her lungs. The children of Israel were forbidden to marry outside the nation, but Esther, a Jewish maiden, pure of mind and heart, was conscripted to marry Ahasuerus, the pagan king of Babylon. She must have felt the same kind of loathing when called to his bedchamber, being forced to give her virginity to a despot. Yet, because of her willingness to lay it all down, she was able to save Israel. Did God make exceptions?

Deanne wanted to drop to her knees and ask, but thought about her rug burns and the hour she'd already spent before God's throne without receiving an answer. She looked up, closing her eyes. *God, You can't possibly want me to do this—greater love hath no man than he lay down his life for a friend—is that it? Is that what You're asking, that I sacrifice myself? Peter can't finish the work You called him to do if he's in jail, is that what it is? Will I be able to look Bob in the eye and say, "You meant it for evil, but God meant it for good?" Why me, Lord? Why? It will be the end of me. I can't live with that...Bob in my head—not again—not ever. Is that what You're asking? To lay down my life for a friend?*

How do you justify evil? Prostitution was evil, but God told the prophet Hosea to marry a prostitute. Never mind, there was a point to be made. God made the rules, He alone could break them. Weren't there prostitutes in the line of Christ—*Tamar and Rahab?* Deanne hooked her thumbs around her waist, squeezing her tummy with her fingers as she leaned over. *Ahhhhhooohh!* Her stomach was being wrung like a towel. She straightened herself and took a tentative step. There were plenty of examples of people who had done something bad to achieve something good—what about Jacob's deception? He disguised himself to steal his birthright and ended up being blessed—but that didn't mean she could justify doing what Bob required of her. Maybe saving her husband was a noble cause—she stopped and put her hand to her stomach again—but she couldn't imagine God placing His seal of approval on such a repulsive act.

So much confusion. Hadn't God assured her everything would be all right? How could she think of being unfaithful to her husband with the very man she'd petitioned God to pardon for having destroyed their lives.

She found her way to the bathroom and stood in front of the medicine cabinet. The image in the mirror said, *Look at me. Haven't I suffered enough?* She opened the cabinet door, her hands fumbling through the plastic containers, turning them to read the labels. It would be so easy—just swallow a handful and lie down and die. She couldn't bear to live, knowing her husband was in jail when she could have prevented it—or live with the guilt that would surely come if she gave in to Bob's demands. But she didn't have those kinds of drugs. And suicide was a sin—*wasn't it?* She swept the bottles aside and grabbed a bottle of antacids pushing up on the cap, but it failed to open adding to her frustration. She tried again, this time succeeding. Two of the white tabs tumbled into her hand and she popped them into her mouth. Maybe it was a joke; maybe he had no intention of going through with it; maybe he just wanted to see how far she'd go to prove she loved Peter. But if he was serious, it would be impossible to forgive. *Never again. This heart is stone.* She looked at her watch but the numbers were blurry. Another tear fell, splashing against the lens. She placed both hands on the sink to support herself, her lungs fluttering as she wiped her eyes on her sleeve.

Deanne glanced at her watch again. He'd said he was three hours away, two hours ago. She felt her stomach tighten—*ahhhhooooo*—and pressed her hand against her waist again, grinding the chalky pills with her teeth. He was almost there. She had to make up her mind!

THIRTY-SEVEN

"The highest glory of the American Revolution was this: it connected, in one indissoluble bond, the principles of civil government with the principles of Christianity."
—*John Quincy Adams, 1746-1848, 6ᵗʰ President of the United States*

THE SEMI churned up road dust as it thundered up the hill. They wound through the homes of the rich and famous, situated on palatial lots, hidden behind trees and shrubs and trimmed terraced lawns, but for all their grandeur, Hank grumbled that he'd rather live in a truck where there weren't any lawns to mow. They chugged steadily uphill in low gear, taxing the engine till it rumbled and wheezed and hissed and creaked, the setting sun a crimson drop of blood in the sky.

Hank brought a gloved hand down to rub the head of the tiny dog in his lap. It would not surprise him to learn that there were zoning laws forbidding trucks like Baby from traveling these streets. The well-to-do wouldn't abide the noise. His head swiveled back and forth, taking it all in. Pretty fancy digs for a fainthearted ne'er-do-well. Peter was full of surprises. He puckered his lips, squinting as he called to mind the lump on the officer's head. Full of surprises, indeed.

"'Cordin' to my GPS, their house is up ahead on the left."

Father Bloom kept his chubby arms wrapped around Angela, trying to contain her soul. Her eyes no longer opened, but when he dangled his handkerchief under her nose, it would vibrate with her breath. She was still alive, but just barely. "We're almost there, honey, *uh-huh,* almost there." He wished she'd give him some kind of response, just some indication that she heard his voice. He gave her a gentle squeeze, his warm breath flicking the curls around her ears as he whispered, "We'll have you in your mother's arms in a few minutes." Angela's eyelids tightened, her lashes fluttering ever so slightly. Buddy smiled.

Now the all-consuming light enveloped Angela. She was embraced by it, nestled in its warm comfort like a baby in her mother's womb. She heard the voice. It was melodic, soft, the way a mother's song traveling through the wall of her uterus sounds in the ears of her unborn child.

I don't understand. I thought you said Mommy and Daddy have to stay here. Now you say they might come with us? Might?

The twilight sky burned yellow-orange, casting warm ochre on the lush lawns. Rainbows of refracted light showered from the sprinklers, swirling like dancers in an ethereal ballet.

In a world where an apple cost an hour's wage, it was hard to believe anyone still lived in such opulence. Hank scanned the road ahead. "I'm not going to be able to park this rig on the street. Maybe I should let you out and have you take the little girl to the door. I'll keep looping around and pick you up on my way back."

"Wa...wa...what if she invites me in?"

"She won't. Peter said she doesn't like visitors. Never sees anyone for any reason. But don't worry about it. If she does, we'll think of something."

Father Buddy was patting Angela's back, rocking her as though burping a baby. "Bu...bu...but what, *uh-huh, uh-huh*, what if she doesn't open the door?"

"She may not. But that's a chance we have to take. You got knuckles. Pound hard enough to wake the dead. Or try screaming. Just make sure she knows you're there. Besides, they probably got maids that answer the door, or cameras on the porch. Once she sees you've got Angela, she'll come running. That's it right there." Hank raised his chin to point.

The house loomed like a monolithic slab of granite surrounded by trees, an island refuge set into the side of the hill, shining in the waning rays of sun. "Would you look at that? *Uh huh*. Wonder how many orphans I could feed with what it costs to air-condition that place, *uh huh, uh huh*."

"A lot, but it makes no difference now. It's in the system. Peter's an accused criminal. His assets will be frozen and when he's convicted—and he will be—everything's gonna be sold and the money used to pay for his trial and the restitution of his crimes. It's what I call legalized theft. Dang it all! We got a problem. How we gonna get you through that gate?"

Hank grappled with the engine brakes, the exhaust pipes rattling in a loud popping staccato as he slowed his magnificent metal machine—though it niggled him that the metallic blue hood was covered in charcoal dust. Killer hopped onto the console, turning circles with his tiny toes tapping on the plastic. He backed up, wagging his tail in anticipation of getting out. The rig had almost come to a full stop when the gate in front of the driveway began to move, swinging out on motorized hinges.

A woman in a late-model, jet-black luxury Lexel backed into the street full throttle with the wheel cranked so hard she almost did a complete circle, running up over the curb behind her before slamming on the brakes. The car stood for a moment gathering dust. Then the engine revved and the wheels spun, chewing up the grass as it bounced off the curb, hitting the pavement and fishtailing before squealing off down the road.

"What was that?"

"Beats me. *Uh huh*. Think it was her?"

"Don't know! Peter said she never leaves the house." Hank doubled his gloved fist and pounded the steering wheel, easing off the brakes. "Crud! Okay, we got two choices. We can chase that person, or wait here and hope Mrs. Dufoe is still inside. If we wait, and that was her, we'll lose her for good. If we chase that lady and it's not her, we can always come back." The truck was already moving. "What do you think?"

A gaggle of news reporters ran into the street, pointing their microphones and cameras at the car as it raced away.

Father Bloom eased Angela onto his arm and raised a pudgy finger. "I say, follow that car." He giggled and covered his mouth. "I've always wanted to say that."

Hank hit the gas.

There was no way to take the hill fast, not in a car, and especially not in an eighteen-wheeler. The road was too narrow and there were too many steep grades and tight turns. The lady was in a hurry, there was no denying that, but Hank was determined not to lose her. A lesser man wouldn't have been able to keep the car in sight, but as Hank was fond of reminding himself, he was no lesser man.

At the bottom of the hill the road straightened and the homes became notably smaller and closer together. They trundled down the narrow streets, following the car as it blew through stop signs— *crazy lady*—knowing if they didn't, they'd lose the driver. A gang of bohemian teenagers in braided spiked hair and brad-studded pants tried flagging the car over to collect a toll, but it flew by without slowing. Someone launched a rotten piece of fruit and it found the car's rear window—*splat*. They didn't bother trying to stop Hank. Occasionally, an unwitting car would sneak between them. Hank would ride the intruder's bumper and release a blast of Baby's air horn, forcing them to move. But the truck lacked acceleration and the lady was gaining distance. If the highway hadn't been piled with traffic, she might have gotten away. The raised cab afforded him a view over the tops of the cars so he could keep her in view, though she remained a dozen lengths ahead.

Her blinker snapped on as she eased over. At least she was driving more sanely now, staying within the speed limit and stopping for lights. Her head kept floating to the right, looking for an address. She hit the brakes and swung into the parking lot of a motel.

Hank pulled up short, cranking the wheel and bouncing the truck into a vacant dirt lot where it would be hidden behind the building. "I can't park in front. It'd be too obvious."

Father Bloom turned, looking over his shoulder. "But I can't see her now. We'll lose her."

DUSK OVERTOOK the city. The dark silhouettes of the office towers with their lights popping against the backdrop of a deep orange sky were magnificent. Bob smiled, his fingers tapping the wheel. Moments of beauty could still be found even with the mess the world was in—and Deanne was one of those moments. His heart's rhythm increased. He was almost there, so close he could smell her hair and feel the coolness of her skin. It was Peter's turn to cry.

They had traveled the miles in silence, which was good because, right or wrong, the preaching was getting on his nerves. He removed his shades and examined Peter in the rearview mirror. His face resting against the window was dark, but he could see the socket around Peter's eye had turned a deep purple and his lip was cut and swollen. Chalk it up to the heat—tempers flare—but now he had the air conditioner to help him think clearly. He had scripted out what he wanted to say, rehearsed it over and over in his mind. He looked up and saw the motel's neon sign glowing in the developing darkness. It was now, or never.

"*Ouch!* Man, you look a mess," he said to the shadow in the mirror.

Peter's eyes snapped away from the window and fixed on Bob's.

"Hey, look, I'm sorry about that. It's just that...you know, back there you said something that wasn't true and, what with the heat and all, I just kinda lost it. But what goes down between Deanne and me is our business. I shouldn't rub it in just 'cause you're going to jail."

Peter shook his head. "Bob—*ouch!*" His lip split apart. He licked the blood with his tongue. "Get a life."

"No, see, Deanne doesn't want you to know but I don't think it's fair to send you up river and have you pine away, waiting for love letters that never come. Truth is, Peter, your wife is leaving you. She and I..."

"Bob, you are so full of it."

"See, I was right. I told her you wouldn't believe it. I said let's just tell him and be done with it, and if he doesn't believe us, it's his problem. At least now we don't have to feel like we were sneaking around behind your back, if you catch my drift."

Peter closed his eyes but the swelling made him wince. He opened them again. *Not possible.* It wasn't like he'd never thought about it. He *was* gone a lot; Angela needed treatment, and she had to have the best doctors, regardless of geographical location, and Deanne always refused to come, though she never complained and...maybe things like that did happen, but not between Deanne and Bob, *no way.* "Forget it Bob, she hates your guts. I'll believe she's with you the day they discover icebergs on the sun."

Bob turned, glaring at Peter over the seat.

Peter flinched, expecting a backhand across the face but Bob swung back around. "Okay, fine." The car turned and bounced up a driveway jostling Peter, his head throbbing. "I'm not asking you to believe me. I'm going to let you see for yourself. We have a little love nest in this shoddy old motel. It isn't pretty, but it *is* discreet..."

But Peter had stopped listening. His eyes were locked on a car parked a few spaces away. *His* car.

THE TRUCK sat hissing and wheezing. Hank let the engine idle. Judging by what he saw of the motel's backside—the peeling paint and sun-bleached curtains in the windows—he'd say the motel rented rooms by the hour, not the day. *What a dump.*

Hank pulled his gloves off, tossing them on the dash. Killer jumped into his lap bouncing up and down licking his neck. Hank placed a mitt over the dog's knobby head flattening its ears. "Easy, boy." The dog whimpered. "Oh, okay, but just for a minute." He opened the door and Killer hopped down, running through the alley between the buildings on either side, sniffing trash cans and rubber tires. Hank grabbed his chin, scratching the granulated stubble. "*Humm.* Kinda makes you wonder. From riches to rags in minutes. Anyway, if it's her, and she's got a room in this hotel, it'll be under hers or Peter's name. I'll lean on the manager for the room number."

"But..."

"Don't worry, he'll give it up. I can be persuasive when I have to."

293

"But...but what do we do then?" Father Bloom settled Angela in his arms. The feather-light child didn't move. So little life. He lifted her head, straightening her wig so she'd look her best for her mom.

"Don't know exactly. Guess I'll bring her out to get her little girl."

"I'M LEAVING you here and going inside," Bob said. "Yes, Deanne's in there waiting. I won't close the drapes until you've had a chance to see her, but there's no need for you to see what comes after that. That would be cruel, and you'll see enough. At least you'll know the truth, and, well, you know what they say, Petee my man, the truth will set you free."

CELESTIAL VANTAGE

Is there a heaven to which souls can go when they depart the earth? Praise be to the glorious redemption of Christ, it is so. If man can overcome his pride long enough to acknowledge his sin, and if he believes in his heart and confesses with his mouth that the eternal Son of the Father came and shed His own blood to provide a way of salvation, he is assured a place with Christ our Lord in the eternal kingdom.

A darker question must be asked by those who refuse God's plan. Is there a hell? Sadly, it is so. It's a matter of free will. God will not force His creation to serve Him. The adoration of angels and men must be offered freely. The evil one, swelled with vanity and pride, rose up to overthrow the King to whom he owed allegiance. From the moment Lucifer proclaimed in his hellish voice, "I will ascend unto the heavens, I will make myself like the Most High," war was declared and the battle enjoined, and continues to this day, though the end is in sight and the outcome foreordained.

What, then, is to become of those who rebel? The soul is eternal. Once created, it cannot die. It must exist somewhere. God has prepared a place to be inhabited for all eternity by Satan and all those who come after him—a pit of fire where the flame is not quenched—forever.

The purpose of hell is twofold: to punish, yes, but also to deter. Think not that those who abide with their Creator for eternity will lose their free will. God would not have it so. He desires men and angels to love him of their own volition. The freedom to choose or deny God will ever be before our eyes.

If angels, who existed in the presence of God for eons before the world began, could choose to oppose their Maker, think not that humans, though glorified in body and pure in heart, but possessing free will over thousands of millennia, will somehow escape the same temptation. As long as men and angels are free to worship, they are also free to rebel.

But if the smoke of hell ascends for all eternity, will it not serve as a constant reminder that God has the power to thwart rebellion? Does it not demonstrate God's ever-abiding love when He keeps us from that which leads to certain damnation?

THIRTY-EIGHT

"The fundamental basis of this nation's laws was given to Moses on the Mount...I don't think we emphasize that enough these days."
—Harry S. Truman, 1884-1972, 33ʳᵈ President of the United States

BOB CLIMBED out of the car, his big frame hulking over the metal roof, patting it with his hand, *thump, thump, thump.* The evening had grown dark but electrical current snapped in the sky, providing pops of stroboscopic light. The air smelled warm and sultry. He stooped down, leaning in. "Get ready, the show's about to begin." He slammed the door and backed up leaving Peter inside wrestling with his restraints—*that's my car.*

Bob pulled his wireless keyfob from his pocket and leveled it at the door, engaging the locks, a smug grin on his face. He spun on his heel, facing the motel. A dim canopy light exposed the pitted metal numbers on the door. He took a breath. Now was the moment of truth. Either Deanne was there and he'd win, or he'd end up back-peddling with Peter, making excuses about why she didn't show. But she'd be there. *Yes-sir-ee Bob.* He hadn't given her a choice.

HANK TRUNDLED around the corner with his dog prancing around his boots. It looked like there were only three cars in the lot. One was sitting in the shadows at the far end, the second was the vehicle he'd been chasing, the black Lexel, and the third was green—and looked a lot like the one driven by the narc. He approached cautiously. It was hard to see, but it looked like someone was sitting in back? Yes, he was sure of it. *Peter?*

PETER PUSHED against the seat, raising himself to get a better view. His heart stopped—it was her—*Deanne!* His wife was in a sleazy motel having a secret tête-à-tête with her ex! She said she *never* left the house. Every emotion that ever seized a man jealous of a wife ran through Peter in that moment. *What? Nooooooo. No, no, no, no, no, no, no!* He erupted in a fit of rage, pounding his shoulder against the door—*again and again*—willing it to burst open. He was twisting his wrists, trying to break free of his cuffs, but only succeeded in having them cut into his flesh.

ANDY CLEAVER sat in the third car parked at the opposite end of the lot, his head banging side to side with the beat of the music. He took a drag of his hemp-laced cigarette. He smoked to calm his nerves and popped pills to stay awake. He had the stereo down to a low rumble, but now clicked it off and reached into his pocket for his pillbox, rolling two of the small white tabs into his hand. He tossed them into his mouth. *Um, um, good.* His eyes sizzled with electrical current. He was trying to focus on what he was seeing, but it was Wonderland—talking rabbits and Cheshire cats—nothing made sense.

First a woman pulls up, parks, and goes to the manager's office and gets someone to follow her back and let her into Bob's room. Bob's evening consort—*no biggie.* Then Bob shows up with Dufoe in the back of his car, and Bob goes into the room and shuts the drapes. Imagine, getting a quickie with a prisoner chained in the car.

Andy wanted to peek though the window—everyone's a voyeur at heart—but that was over the top. Better to lay low and stay on guard. Bob should have placed Peter in lockup, but he didn't, which might mean he still planned to help him escape, and if so, interrupting him now would be premature. He had to catch him in the act. *Wait a minute...who's the old dude with the dog?*

HANK TAPPED his knuckles on the window and Peter jumped.

His face was a red onion. It had to burn his eyes. They were brimming with tears. "Get me out of here!" he screamed, but his words were muffled by the glass. He began butting the door with his shoulder again. Hank tried pulling the handle, but it didn't open. His fingers were pinched as it snapped back. He circled the car with his dog nipping at his heels, trying each of the other doors, but they were all locked. He grabbed his fist and used his elbow to smash the glass but it refused to break. He cradled his arm rubbing it as he put his face to the window and spoke in a loud whisper. "Just a second. I'll be right back." His breath fogged the glass. He turned and ran around the building heading for his truck, leaving Peter dying inside.

NOW ANDY was thoroughly confused. He'd either smoked too much, drunk too much, or taken too many pills. This was bazaaro. His stoned eyes were playing tricks on him. Who was that guy? Andy went for his gun. He pulled it from his jacket and fumbled it onto the seat, scrambling to get it back.

DEANNE STOOD opposite Bob with her head turned away, hiding everything but her profile. His heart was thumping in his chest. It was the most beautiful profile he had ever seen, her flowing dark hair wrapping around her neck. To nuzzle that silky hair was something he desired more than life itself. And he would too—even if she didn't like it. He opened his mouth wanting to say something nice—*It's good to see you, Deanne. You look really great*—but all that came out was: "You ready?" He slipped out of his jacket, tossing it on the bed, and slid a finger under the knot of his tie, tugging it loose.

ALL PETER saw behind the curtains was Bob's silhouette, but it was enough to let him know he was getting undressed. *"Nooooooo! God please, nooooooo!"* His voice was deadened by the glass and, with respect to mortals, went unheard.

DEANNE KEPT her head averted and covered her mouth with her fingers. Bob could hear the tremor in her voice when she began to speak. "Bob, please, don't do this. It isn't worth it. It's not what you want."

Bob was unbuckling his shoulder holster. "You know, Deanne, I don't think you care at all about what I want. Now get going. You know the deal. You're mine for one night and tomorrow Peter's a free man."

Deanne turned to him and for the first time Bob saw the face he'd dreamed of, but... *"Whaaaaaa?"*

She *sniffed* and wiped her eyes on the back of her hand. "Disappointed?" She shook her head, a lone tear rolling down her cheek. "I'm sorry, Bob. I tried to warn you."

Bob took a half-step back, incredulous. The left side of Deanne's face was a wad of misshapen tissue. *"Whaaaaat?"*

"It was a grease fire. I was deep-frying shrimp and oil splattered and I knocked the pan off the stove and when I dove for it, the grease flew into my face." The tears broke and went streaming down a twisted rope of lumpy skin. "It's why I never go out. I can't stand the stares." She sniffed.

Bob's chest burned. *Cheated again? No! Not going to happen. Not in this life.* It was hideous, but—*so what?* This wasn't about love; it was about getting even. One side was still beautiful. Just have her look the other way. He squared his shoulders, sucked in his stomach and took a stride in her direction, reaching out to grab her arm and pull her in. "You know, I don't really care. Come here." He grabbed the back of her neck, closed his eyes, and planted his lips on hers, choking her.

Deanne gagged and pushed him away, breaking free. She stumbled backward, wiping her mouth with the back of her hand, and then spat and straightened herself, glaring at him. She raised her hand and slapped him hard enough to leave a welt on his cheek.

Bob reacted instinctively, slapping her back, *hard,* only her face felt malleable, like soft clay. Then part of her cheek fell away. He jumped back, startled. Her skin was hanging off her jaw like a chunk of decomposed flesh.

Deanne's hand went to her face. "Enough! Wasn't raping me once enough? Are you really going to do it again?"

"What is this?" Bob reached out and grabbed a wad of putty, letting it fall to the ground. *"Whaaaa?"* A costume? "Rape, what are you talking about? I never raped you." He shook his head, but the color left his face—*I didn't...*

Bob tipped the bottle back, emptying it in a few quick gulps, teetering backwards.

"Please stop drinking, Bob. I'm sorry, I really am. I didn't think you'd take it so hard. You have to let me explain. Please. That's why I called... don't you see? You don't need me. There are plenty of girls..."

Bob sent the empty bottle looping across the park into the bushes. He turned to face Deanne. "No! You caaan't. No, no, I won' lesh you. Not with him..."

Deanne reached out, taking Bob's arm. "Bob, you've had too much. You're drunk. Come on, I'll help you walk it off."

But Bob turned on her thrusting his arms around her waist, molding her body into his.

"Stop it!" she cried. "What do you think you're doing? I'm getting married. I told you. Let go!" She tried to reach around and grab his hands but when she did, he grabbed her wrists and leaned on her. He stumbled forward, tripping and taking her with him as he fell, nearly crushing her beneath his weight.

Oooofff.

She stopped for a moment, catching her breath. She struggled to free her hands but they were pinned. She began wiggling to twist free. "Stop it! This isn't funny. Get off me. Stop, or I'll scream!" She started to call for help but he brought a hand around and cupped it over her mouth, muzzling her. "Shhhhhh."

"Pleaff, mmmff! I begff you," but her cries were muffled, and Bob wasn't listening. His eyes were glazed. They were cold vacuous eyes, void of compassion. He looked...dead.

In a few short minutes, it was over. He tried to stand, swaying as he tucked himself in and buckled his belt. "Shhyou okay? I didn't..." Bob found himself wobbling and reached out to steady himself. "I didn't hurt you, did I?"

But Deanne didn't answer.

"No hard feelings, sssokay? Come on, get up. We don't have all night. Come on, let's go." He turned and wobbled, teetering off across the moonlit park. He stopped, dizzy, trying to catch his balance. He reached for a tree but was too far away. He crashed to the ground and struggled to his feet again, resting his hands on his knees. Then he straightened himself and staggered off under the cloak of night.

Deanne licked a saline tear from her mouth, *sniffed*, and blotted her eyes with the heel of her hand, *sniff*. "You don't remember, do you? I always wondered...I mean your eyes, they were weird, like it wasn't really you."

Bob leaned over, yanking his jacket off the bed—*remember?* What he remembered was waking up in his own vomit with the sun beating on his head like a wooden spoon. He remembered crawling from the bushes, wondering how he got there, and staggering home. He remembered being slapped. He remembered the pain...but not of the slap...the pain of rejection—but the rest, that was just a nightmare, flashes of anxiety that haunted him as he lay awake at night unable to sleep—*wasn't it? No way! It'd been a dream, not real*—he held up his coat, hiding behind it. He turned his back, slipping it on, and began buckling his holster again. He reached for the door.

It was dark outside. A yellow light burned overhead. He pulled the keyfob from his pocket, pointing it at the car to unsnap the locks and nearly ripped the door from its hinges as he jerked it open.

"Get out!"

Peter's swollen eyes were red and welled up, but he blinked back his tears. His lips, pinched together, started to bleed. He raised his foot but he wasn't quick enough. Bob reached in and grabbed him by the collar, tearing his shirt as he pulled him from the car, bumping his head against the metal frame. *Ouch!*

"Move!"

Peter tucked his shoulder and lunged at Bob, hitting him in the chest but, with his hands cuffed behind him, the assault had little effect. Bob spun him around and shoved him toward the motel.

THIRTY-NINE

"Democracy is the outgrowth of the religious conviction of the sacredness of every human life. On the religious side, its highest embodiment is the Bible; on the political side, the Constitution."
—*Herbert Hoover, 1874-1964, 31ᵗʰ President of the United States*

LIGHTNING SPARKED in the dry heat, brightening clouds that roiled overhead laden with thunder, dark and ominous. Hank kept off the sidewalk, avoiding the motel's illuminated passageways, but the shadows could not hide him from the electrical discharge. His bulky figure was fixed in frames the way the flash of a camera captures pictures in the dark. He approached from the far side of the building with a crowbar in hand, ready to smash the window of the car—but he was too late. The bear was already taking the fish into its cave. The door slammed. *Crud!* Hank inched up to the window and peeked through a crack in the drapes.

AT THE OPPOSITE end of the lot, Andy tipped back his silver pocket flask, but found it empty. He plunged his tongue into the throat of the bottle, licking the last drop, *bahhh,* and threw it on the floor, grinding his teeth. There had to be an easier way to make a living. What a menagerie, a full-blown circus—bring on the clowns. Bob had just dragged a prisoner into his room to share his hooker, and the old man was watching through the window, a real peephole pervert—which Andy himself wanted to do, but found disgusting nonetheless. He was trapped in a car, watching from the sidelines—*again.* He had to get in the game. *I'm ready, Coach, send me in!* But he remained on the bench waiting for a chance to play. His hand went to his gun. He brought it up, sliding his fingers along the short smooth barrel, and touched it to his cheek, taking comfort in the feel of the cold hard steel.

BOB SHOVED Peter toward Deanne. "Here! You two deserve each other."

Deanne's eyes swept from Bob to Peter, the color leaving her face. Her hands went up, clawing at the rest of the putty, brushing the residue with her palms and washing her cheeks with her tears. She swept back strands of wet hair and wiped her hands on her skirt. She stood waiting, but uncertain, and then ran to Peter, circling him in her arms.

Peter's hands were cuffed behind him. He couldn't reciprocate, nor did he seem to want to. He kept his wounded head down as though searching for something lost in the pile of the carpet. He rotated his shoulders, twisting free, and backed away.

Bob reached out and spun Peter around, shoving him forward and smashing his bruised cheek flat against the wall as he grabbed the chain, lifting Peter's wrists to remove the manacles. He inserted the key and yanked the cuffs off as they popped open. "Wise up, Peter. There's nothing going on. She's only here to negotiate your release. I made the rest up just to tick you off." He slid the key into his pocket and turned Peter around. "I'm crazy, okay? Totally off my rocker. You've got about a minute to get the heck out of here, before I change my mind."

Peter began rubbing his wrists, looking at Deanne. It had taken less than a minute to leap to a false conclusion—all the way from trust to misgiving. He'd been so easily swayed. And Bob—his nemesis— letting him go? Things were changing too fast to keep track. Where was Hank? Did he still have Angela? He turned and glanced over his shoulder. He could hear a truck engine rumbling outside, a sound that to anyone else meant a trucker was stopping for the night, but to him meant God had everything in place. He looked at Bob, knowing what he had to say, but hating the thought. "Come with us, Bob. It's not too late."

Bob slipped his hand into his jacket, fingering the gun holstered under his arm. "Thirty seconds. If you're not out of here by then, I'll blow your brains out myself."

Peter nodded. His eyes shifted to Deanne, but she was looking at the door. Her voice trembled. "I don't know if I can."

Peter took her hand and turned her, making sure she was looking at him. Her eyes were puffy and red but what he saw in the mirror of her soul was a reflection of himself. "I'm scared too," he said, "but we can lean on each other for strength. Together, Deanne. You made it this far by yourself, but we'll go the rest of the way together." He smiled. "Come on, we'll go out the back so no one sees us."

HANK SAW Deanne and Peter moving toward a door on the other side of the room. *Rats.* He turned and began trotting around the building again, hoping to catch them on the other side, his footfalls accented by peals of thunder.

ANDY SHOOK his head, flinging his hair wildly and spraying the car with droplets of perspiration. *Yaaahooooo!* he exclaimed, exhaling the smoke he'd just driven deep into his lungs, his eyes watering. He looked up and saw the old man running back the way he'd come. *Now what?*

BOB GRABBED Peter by the collar, pulling him back. "Wait!" He spun him around, looking at the head of purple cabbage. He cringed—all that damage from a single punch. That temper of his would be his undoing. *Deanne?* The dream wasn't alcohol-induced after all; it was a certainty he could no longer deny. *She could have ratted him out.* He'd jailed miscreants for less and felt good about it.

Peter took a breath, his shoulders rising with resignation. Deanne snatched his arm, holding on like a drowning soul in desperate need of life support.

"Deanne, I wan...I should say..." Bob looked down, searching for a thought. He brought his eyes up, putting his hand to his cheek.

"There's no scar. You're just...you. Why *are* you afraid to go out? If it wasn't that...I mean if it wasn't an accident, what?"

Deanne looked like an animal caught in a trap. Her eyes darted from Peter to Bob, and back to Peter again, but her tongue was stuck. She grabbed Peter's arm and in spite of her fear, pulled him toward the door, hoping to ignore the question and just go. But Peter refused to budge.

He wrenched his arm free. "He asked a question, Deanne. A fair one. This is the first time you've been out in what, twenty years? And he got you here. He deserves an answer." He turned to face Bob. "She has an illness. Doctors call it agoraphobia, or the fear of open spaces. But in her case, it's more than that. It's a fear of being seen." He paused, looking back at Deanne. Her expression pleaded with him, urging him to stop, but he kept going. "She was raped. Somebody accosted her two days before our wedding. That's the way it's been ever since. At least until now. There's some part of her that makes her think she caused the incident. She's afraid if she goes out, it'll happen again."

Bob's eyes narrowed, like he was working on a complex problem or trying to bring clarity to an obtuse thought.

Deanne gave her head a quick, almost imperceptible, shake, and then grabbed Peter by the elbow, tugging on him until he stumbled in her direction.

Bob watched Peter being pulled from the room. *He doesn't know,* Bob thought. *She never told him.*

FATHER BLOOM saw Peter and Deanne step outside. *Peter? So that's why she raced over here.* He could see they were holding hands, but it looked like they were standing in a hole. The building's foundation was three feet lower than ground level, with the dirt being held back by a retaining wall. The light from the open door illuminated their backs. At least Peter's hands were free. They turned and walked along the side of the building. *Praise the Lord!*

BUDDY LAY Angela on the seat and opened the door. "Oh, God,

help me," he whispered. He was still two feet off the ground and he couldn't jump, nor could his pudgy little legs step down, not if he had to carry Angela. The truck was parked in a vacant lot. He scanned the yard looking...*yes*, he could do this.

He took hold of the chrome handle and eased himself down, using his hands as much as his feet. On his left he could see the discarded tire half buried in the dirt, probably too heavy to carry. *Lord, give me strength.* He stooped, barely able to reach it over his massive stomach, feeling the stiff rubber. Gripping the edge he pulled back, lifting it just a few inches, but enough to pull it from the ground. He began dragging it back to the truck, where he let it fall—*whaffump*—in front of the door. *There!* The perfect step. *Praise the Lord!*

He rubbed his fingers and, taking hold of the chrome rail, carefully ascended the stair. Then, with Angela tucked in his arms, he turned and retraced his steps until he was on the ground. *Hallelujah!* "Come on, little lady. Your mommy and daddy are waiting."

Buddy waddled as fast as his little legs could carry him, huffing and puffing, *uh-huh, uh-huh*, his cheeks flushing red. Heat lightning blazed across the sky in electric shades of green. He was almost there, *uh-huh*.

Peter took Deanne by the hand, captured like a wedding photo in the stroboscopic lights. The thunder boomed. *Kapow!*

They turned and practically collided, *ooffff!* The priest backed up and smiled, his face glowing like a cherub. He handed Peter his little girl and waited, watching Peter and Deanne's expressions change from angst to joy—two tearful parents reunited with a daughter they thought was lost to them forever.

Only one thing made the moment less than perfect. The fragile child lay in Peter's arms, limp as a rag doll. *Angela needs to see them too, please, Lord. Kaaaaaboooom!* The thunder exploded and her eyes popped open. Father Bloom looked up. A surge of wind sent his hair dancing like a red flame on top of his head. *Thank You, Lord, thank You!* He looked at the couple holding their child. Sometimes a miracle is simply something too good to be true.

What the heck's all this? Bob slipped his hand inside his coat and wrapped it around the handle of his gun. A priest and a little girl—their little girl—and a truck, one he'd already seen a couple of times. "That your daughter?" he questioned.

Deanne's eyes were red and fractured. She felt her stomach tighten. She took Angela from Peter and steeled herself, trying to smile. The man was to be loathed, or perhaps pitied, but he *had* released them. The most peaceful part of her day had been the moment she'd offered him forgiveness—but that was before he'd suggested trading favors for her husband's release. Forgiving someone in prayer was so much easier than in person. She swept the hair off Angela's face and leaned in to kiss her cheek. She looked at Bob—and nodded. "Our *adopted* daughter. The thing that happened, it...I...I can't have children."

Hank came stomping up. He held the crowbar in both hands as he leaned over and placed it across his knees, *whew!* "What's going on?" There were flashes of lightning and cracks of thunder. "What did I miss?"

SWEAT ROLLED down Andy's face, but whether from the heat, or stress, or both, he couldn't say. He pulled his shirt away from his chest, fanning himself. Oh, to have the air conditioner on! But he couldn't, not without drawing attention to himself, so he waited in the dark shadows of a car that reeked with the heat of his own body, wondering what to do next. He could no longer see movement behind the curtains. The room had gone quiet. His mind replayed the old man running from the window. Where had he gone in such a hurry? It hit him. There must be a back door.

He fired up the engine, burning rubber as he bounced into the street. He continued peeling around the corner, coming at the building from the other side. The tires squealed as his car slid, barely making the turn. His lights swept across the alley, revealing several people huddled together. He'd caught them like rabbits, frozen in the yellow beams.

Hot dang! Andy's euphoria bordered on lunacy. "That son of a...he *is* letting them go." He'd been right all along! Now he could prove it!

A CAR BOUNCED into the alley and screeched to a stop. The door flew open. Bob raised his hand to shield his eyes. It looked like someone was climbing out, pointing something at them. In the glare of the headlights it was hard to tell. Bob went for his gun, reacting to the unknown threat.

"Daddy," Angela said. "Mommy." Her eyes rolled back and forth from one to the other. "You did it. You're here. My angel said, a*hhhh,* oh, I'm sooo tired. I'm going home now? My angel wants to take me home." Her breast rose as she gasped for a breath, a*hhhh uuuhhhh.* "Please stop hurting each other...*please.* I can't sleep when you're angry. Promise me..." And then a smile stole across her face. "Hey, I don't hurt anymore." A soft breath escaped her lips and the eyes slipped closed.

FORTY

"It's hard to see how a great man can be an atheist."
—*Calvin Coolidge, 1872-1933, 30th President of the United States*

THE CLOUDS split apart and for one brief moment a moonbeam settled on Angela's face, a perfect face, filled with light. Peter leaned in and tried taking Angela from Deanne, but she held on. He pursed his lips, nodding. *The Lord giveth, and the Lord taketh away, so be it.* She would never hold her child again. His own cheeks were wet, his tears rolling freely, and for once he didn't care what *anyone* thought. He brought his face down to give her a butterfly kiss. "Thank you, thank you, thank you," he whispered, his tears spotting her smooth lifeless cheek.

ANGELA STOOD in the presence of her angel. Light emanated from the man who reached out to take her hand but this was not light as she knew it, this was effulgent light, she was caught in prisms of color. It was a strange sensation. She felt like she was outside her body, but she could still feel her mother stroking her face, and could hear her words: "We will, I promise, we will. Your daddy and I love you..." The soft touch of her mother's fingers warmed her. She put her hand to her cheek, looking at the man standing there, clothed in white.

"Are you my angel? Are you going to take me home now?"
"At your request."
"What's going to happen to Mommy and Daddy?" She looked over

310

her shoulder. Her parents were caught between two seconds, frozen in a moment of time. Or perhaps she had stepped outside time where mass, gravity and motion were no longer relevant.

"You have done well. But the future is not ours to know. We must wait and see."

THE CLOUDS closed, leaving the group in the dark, and then a burst of light. A *pop* sounding small, hollow, and distant, like a rock hitting a metal cookie sheet.

Bob stepped in front of Peter. A second shot rang out. And then another.

Killer leapt forward. His short legs scampered toward the man behind the lights. *Yip, yip, yip, yip, yip.* He bounded onto the hood of the car and jumped into the air, his teeth sinking into the wrist of the man with the gun. *"Owwww!"* Lightning flared across the sky. The man danced about, trying to take aim but unable to do so with a dog attached to his arm. Shots rang out, sparks igniting like little firecrackers at both ends of the alley. Bullets shattered the windshield, others splintered the fiberglass grill. *Hey, don't shoot me; I'm one of the good guys!*

Andy tore the dog from his arm and threw it against the wall. Killer *yelped* and disappeared, sinking behind the retaining wall, out of sight. Andy dove into the front seat. He ducked, held the brake, slammed the car into reverse, and hit the gas with his tires spinning as he backed out. He straightened himself and cranked the wheels to the right, shoving the car into drive, and was gone.

Bob was in church praying for his mother. An organ in the background churned out The Old Rugged Cross—"For 'twas on that old cross, Jesus suffered and died, to pardon and sanctify me." He prayed that his dad would die. No one has a right to hurt someone like that. But his dad didn't die, and the abuse went on. What did die, he realized, was his faith. How can a God of love let such evil exist? And the anger grew. He was in high school. He was abusive. He was his father, controlled by anger, a hurt person, hurting others. He went to church, because that's what his mother wanted, but he no longer believed—miracles and angels and Santa Claus—and later because Deanne continued to drag him with her. And the choir sang, "Just as I am, without one plea, but that Thy blood was shed for me, and that Thou bidd'st me come to Thee." And Peter became the target of his anger. Anger breeding anger. Hurt upon hurt. And not one single good thing had ever come of it—not one. He wondered if one day he would stand at the edge of eternity, awestruck before his Creator, and sing, "I did it my way," as if a life spent serving self was a life that could be offered to God...and he wondered why he was thinking all these things at such a time as this...

Peter saw a gun extended in Bob's hands. Bob slowly lowered the weapon. He coughed and grabbed his chest.

"Bob?"

It took a moment to react. Bob looked down and saw a spot of inky red beginning to spread. He pulled his fingers back to examine the blood and collapsed to his knees. His dark eyes were open but dimming fast; his teeth were locked in a painful smile. He teetered for a moment, and fell to the side.

"Noooooo!" Peter thrust himself forward. He slid his hand under Bob's head, keeping it from hitting the ground. *No, please God, not this way.*

Bob's eyes were glazing over but he looked up in time to recognize the face hovering above him. "Peter, good to see youuush...*Oh, my*... oh, *that hurts*." Bob grimaced, reaching a feeble hand up to grasp Peter's arm. "Oh, God, how could I..."

Peter looked at the dying man. All the machismo that was formerly Bob was gone, all the bravado, all the hype. Bob was just a man, like all men, as he himself was a man. All men are born and all men die. Peter wanted to say something profound, but there was nothing to say. He began quoting Scripture: "For all have sinned and come short of the glory of God...If we confess our sins He is faithful and just to forgive us our sins and cleanse us from all unrighteousness...For God so loved the world that He gave His only begotten Son that whosoever believeth on Him should not perish but have everlasting life...For whosoever shall call upon the name of the Lord shall be saved."

Bob nodded and closed his eyes. "*Jesusssss.*" His grip tightened on Peter's arm. "*Jesusssss*...Hey, Pete...do me a favor? Next time you see Deanne, tell her I'm, *uuggh*, I'm...I'm sorryyyeeeee..." His hand fell away and through the cavity that had once been his mouth came a sound, like wind whistling through a cave. Peter recognized it as the long, slow, gurgling exhale of death.

The wind sweeping down the Ohio River whistled, "*Amazing grace, how sweet the sound, that saved a wretch like me.*" Lightning flashed and Bob was momentarily blinded.

He got to his feet, bewildered. Beside him stood the little girl who had just died, smiling at him.

CELESTIAL VANTAGE

King David said "man is but a flower fading in the grass." We come from seed, we grow, we wither, and we die. And all too often we are plucked out unexpectedly. Thank God, with joy unspeakable, for the marvelous restoration of His creation.

The wages of sin is death but the gift of God is eternal life, through Jesus Christ our Lord!

My story draws to a close. There are souls to deliver, and I must now depart. You whom I leave behind, behave well, for the time is short. Better to be absent in the body and present with the Lord, but it is needful that you remain. Your story has yet to be written.

Seek inspiration. "The heavens declare the glory of God?" Look up. See it? Enjoy the wonders of creation, the dwelling place of the lightbearer, the home of the constellations. Glorify God through your painting and sculpture, your songs and your words.

> *Field of glories! spacious field,*
> *And worthy of the Master: He whose hand*
> *With hieroglyphics, older than the Nile,*
> *Inscribed the mystic tablet; hung on high*
> *To public gaze, and said, Adore, O man!*
> *The finger of thy God.*

Let the Spirit now record that I have spoken well. My mission is complete. What few words remain, require little from me. Should we meet some star-laden night, on some distant celestial plane or future place in time, know if you reach out to me and speak bold the name of Jesus, I will take your hand.

Until then, I remain your humble servant Mesapare the teller of tales. Now I must finish my story. Then I must beg my leave...

FORTY-ONE

LIGHTNING PULSED on that ill-fated night. You could almost see Christ's return in the spark and rumble of the sky—*For as the lightning cometh out of the east, and shineth even unto the west; so shall also the coming of the Son of man be.* Father Bloom wrestled Angela's still warm body from Deanne, nudging her toward the truck. Hank's gloved hand was beckoning. In a few minutes the entire block would be crawling with police summoned by the man who fled when Bob opened fire. Any chance they had of getting away required their immediate departure. They would have to leave Angela behind. Difficult as it was to let go, Deanne relinquished the empty vessel that had once held her daughter's spirit. Father Bloom made a solemn vow to see she got a proper *Christian* burial.

They entered the highway passed en route by police cars with their lights flashing, screaming off toward the motel. Hank monitored the police band expecting them to put out a description of Baby, but no one mentioned seeing a truck parked in the alley that night. It was like God had "dropped a great big ol' cloaking device down on that puppy," or maybe it was just that the truck was so big and so commonplace the officer saw it but, in the heat of dodging bullets, it somehow didn't register.

They dropped the priest at a motel several miles away where Hank secured him a room. Buddy called Doctor Philips to pick him up. A doctor could always explain the death and transportation of a body if they were stopped, but they never were. They'd taken Angela back to Sunset Memorial Park in Beckley to make arrangements for her funeral—just another orphan who died that nobody wanted to know.

Peter and Deanne rode in a space less than two feet wide, hidden the way Corrie Ten boom had sheltered Jews behind a façade in their family clock shop in Holland. Biker Jack provided the trailer with the fake wall, a real work of art, completely undetectable. It had been built for someone else who'd left him a deposit but never returned to pick it up. He was more than happy to switch trailers with Hank for the balance owing, a cost which Peter, of course, covered after the fact. Access to the compartment was through a door underneath the trailer next to the fifth wheel. By standing between the two pairs of dual tires at the back of the tractor, Peter and Deanne were able to squeeze between the rails through a hatch that, when closed, fit seamlessly and looked just like the rest of the floor.

Bouncing along in the dark made the journey miserably long and arduous—but so was life—and it gave Peter time to ponder the faithfulness of God. He felt undeserving, and yet God's hand was upon him—protecting both himself and Deanne—to bring them safely home. *Why?* He himself had been so unfaithful. His wife had risked everything, facing her fears and leaving the safety of their home to brave the worst kind of degradation at the hand of a man she passionately disdained. She did it willingly—*for him*—while he was sitting in Bob's car buying into Bob's lie and fomenting a jealous rage based on false accusation. He didn't deserve her, he didn't deserve Angela, and he certainly didn't deserve God. But that was the thing. God's favor was unmerited. He'd heard it in church, read it in books, seen it preached on TV and radio, but he'd never experienced the total absolute unmerited favor of God, until now.

No, that wasn't true. He had actually experienced God's undeserved favor his whole life. There was no other way to explain Ruth and Bill, two people who each, in their own way, had shown him how to lean on Christ for strength, when the voices in his head were telling him he was weak. And what about Deanne? What logic was there in a feeble man like *him*, winning the hand of a prize like *her*? And the wealth he'd obtained...*and Angela*? He'd been given every desire of his heart, and more. He'd always had the unmerited favor of God—it's just that when you hold up one piece of a puzzle at a time, it's hard to see the whole picture. *And we know that all things work together for good to those who love God, to those who are the called according to His purpose.* That's what the Bible said—even the newly revised versions.

He felt Deanne's touch, feather-light, reaching out to assure herself he was there. She leaned against his arm. *Undeserved love.* Praise God Almighty! Peter took her wrist, kissed her fingertips and let go. He slipped his palm computer from his pocket and with the light emitting from the diode, wrote an e-mail to those who were praying. He needed to let them know of Angela's home going.

WORD HAD gone out on chat lines circling the globe. Dozens of people stood like ghosts in the foggy damp that Friday morning. They had arrived throughout the night and were given candles by the orphans of St. Basil's—who suspended the use of "Universal Church" in light of the occasion.

Buddy's corpulent body billowed through the clouds as he moved about, sprinkling holy water. He paused, spreading his cape like white wings, then he raised his hands and made the sign of the cross: "Réquiem æternam dona ei, Dómine." Eternal rest grant unto her, O Lord. "Et lux perpétua lúceat ei." And let perpetual light shine upon her. "Requiéscat in pace." May she rest in peace. "Amen."

Wispy clouds streamed along the ground keeping visibility down to a few dozen feet. Those in back could hear the priest's recital, but the mist made it hard to see. They were wrapped in shrouds of vapor, visible one minute, invisible the next, save for their candles which flickered in the fog, forming iridescent halos in their hands. A dense murkiness saturated the air. Somehow, the somber mood seemed fitting. The dawn's purple haze kept unwanted eyes from observing the Christian rite.

Father Bloom blessed the ground and the tiny casket while reciting Scripture. He would have read from a Bible if he'd had one, but he'd officiated at so many funerals he knew the words by heart. The passage was from John, chapter eleven. Buddy spread his arms: "'Jesus said unto her, I am the resurrection, and the life: he that believeth in me, though he were dead, yet shall he live. And whosoever liveth and believeth in me shall never die...'"

PETER AND Deanne remained hidden behind the false wall over the coupling of the trailer for most of the two days it took to reach the border. Peter's disguise had been taken from him, and Deanne's was still on the floor of the motel. They couldn't risk being recognized. The same over-zealous Homeland Security operative who'd somehow missed seeing Hank's truck, took charge of the manhunt, vowing to bring the murderer to justice. Never mind that he himself had fired the gun that killed Bob, he added Bob's death to the list of charges against Peter, who now also stood accused of killing a government agent in his desperate attempt to escape. The search was intensified with APBs broadcast on every frequency. Security was exponentially high and all points of exit were being heavily monitored.

Unless Hank could show good reason for leaving the country, it was a sure bet he'd be turned back at the border. From the narrow confines of their limited space, Peter e-mailed his mentor and friend, Bill Best, and explained the dilemma. Bill called in a favor from another old friend, Santos Hurrea, a Mexican-American Bill had nurtured in the faith. The man ran an import and export business out of Las Cruces. A few e-mails back and forth between Bill and Santos allowed for the empty trailer to be filled with goods to be shipped into Mexico. The waxed and polished semi known as Baby headed for Oaxaca City complete with customs documentation and bill of lading.

THE SUN was a lemon drop in the sky, shimmering in rippled waves of heat. The wind scattered dust across the ground. A tumbleweed rolled down the road, chased by the pages of a newspaper. The air was so dry, it parched the throats of those taking it in.

The truck wheezed to a stop. They sat at the edge of the Mexican frontier. One last hurdle and they were home free. Hank looked out upon the line of cars and trucks. Off to the side were a half-dozen Customs and Immigrations vehicles as well as two cars bearing the gold eagle of Homeland Security.

The Mexican sun baked the aluminum, turning the trailer into an oven. Peter and Deanne sat on the floor, trying to remain motionless. One accidental kick of the metal wall would produce a rumble like thunder and alert people as to where they were hiding. Darkness surrounded them, a darkness black as coal—the absence of color, the absence of light. Peter felt Deanne's hand slip into his, her palm moist, her pulse quickening. They worked at keeping their breathing slow and even. Peter felt a trickle of sweat rolling down his chest and the thump, thump, thumping of his heart. The truck lurched forward and stopped again with a *hissssssss* and a *wheeeeeeze*.

Peter heard voices and, somewhere off in the distance, the barking of dogs. The truck tipped as Hank swung his door open and stepped down. Still the feisty protector and defender, Killer began *yip, yip, yipping*.

The voices carried into the trailer, and though muffled, Peter could make out what was being said.

"Keep that dog of yours in the truck."

A door slammed. "Come on, give me a break. It's all right there on the bill of lading. I have a schedule to keep."

"Just pull it up over there."

"But..."

"We have to check every vehicle leaving the country."

"You're gonna drag everything out of this rig, only to put it all back in?"

"Just pull it up over there."

Peter felt the brakes release and the tires bounce as the truck lurched forward. The wheels rolled for what seemed like a block and then came to another stop. He squeezed Deanne's hand. The sun scorched the roof overhead. He didn't know how much more of the hot oven either of them could take.

Now it felt like they were backing up. The truck came to an abrupt halt. The back of the trailer opened with a *screeeech*. He heard the—*puftt, puftt, puftt, puftt, puftt, puftt*—of a forklift pulling pallets from the trailer, bringing them onto a loading dock, one by one, until the trailer was empty.

"There. You satisfied? Just consumer goods, strictly wholesale."

Peter heard footsteps walking through the trailer pounding the walls with a baton. Someone else was under the truck tapping the bottom. He held Deanne's hand to his heart, his breath caught in his throat. *Oh, Lord, protect us.* They were almost there. *Please, God.* He jumped back at the sound of a stick hitting the wall beside him, and felt Deanne tremble.

"Want the K-9s for a sniff search?"

"Naw, we gotta clear this backup. Looks like they're already occupied. Poor sap. He'll do time for sure."

Peter heard more tapping on the floor, but this time right underneath him. The sound was muted, a *thud* different from the hollow *ping, ping, ping,* that came from the rest of the truck's bed. The sound stopped. Peter's heart was pounding hard enough to pop the buttons off his shirt. He was sweating up a storm. He heard a grunt and something that sounded like fingernails scratching metal. Suddenly the hatch door began to lift. A beam of light broke around the crack. Peter's heart stopped; Deanne gasped. They scooted back. Peter took Deanne by the hand and slowly stood, raising her with him. *Oh, Lord. After all this, why now?* Peter's heart was pounding, his hands drenched in sweat.

The man, of obvious Mexican descent, with a broad brown face and dark mustache, held the lid above him. The light streaming through the hole in the floor reflected off the gold badge on his shirt. He set the door aside and turned on a flashlight, shining the beam directly into Peter and Deanne's eyes. *Busted!*

The man clicked his flashlight off and brought a hand up, making the sign of the cross. *What???* Then he grabbed the hatch door and stooped down, fitting it back in place.

Peter and Deanne waited, hearts pounding, expecting a dozen

pistol-carrying officers to pull them from their hiding place at any moment. But it didn't happen. Instead, they heard the pallets being put back onto the truck and a forklift slamming against the wall that hedged them in. They heard Hank rev the engine and, with a shudder and a rumble, the truck pulled away.

For a moment they stood there, holding each other in disbelief. Deanne couldn't seem to stop quaking. Peter shook his head. *Thank You, Lord.* He wondered if he'd ever learn to trust God completely. Hadn't happened yet, but that was the nature of man—*wasn't it?* He took comfort in knowing his namesake, Peter, one of those closest to Christ, had at one point been bold enough to say, "Though I should die with Thee, yet will I not deny Thee," and then, paralyzed with fear, later reversed himself and denied his Lord three times. Faith was such a fickle thing.

Peter sat down, pulling Deanne with him, to avoid their being thrown off balance as the truck bounced over bumps in the road. He felt the sweat and the grime and the soreness in his bones. He was travel-weary, and he ached, and his seat was numb from sitting on the hard floor, but when Deanne lay her head on his shoulder, all his aches and pains dissolved. He was *free.*

EPILOGUE

NESTLED DEEP within the emerald green jungle of the Serra Madre del Sur, there's a place that time forgot, a place where eagles soar and butterflies dance, a place where men live in industry and harmony, thanking God for what they have, praying only for a blessing on the coffee harvest and perhaps a little corn. It is a place unto itself, isolated from a world gone mad.

This day the sunset blazed in three-dimensional hues of violet and ochre and crimson and blue. Peter and Deanne stood on the precipice of a cliff between two outcrops of granite, overlooking the vista of the Pacific Ocean. They were holding hands to strengthen each other, thankful for the haven they'd found. Posada was a place of respite for the weary soul. The surf pounded the rocks below, surging in and out, sucking and pulling against the tide, the ocean rolling in a timeless undulation of translucent green.

Deanne brought a hand up to shield her eyes. A wreath of flowers was woven into her hair, another looped over her arm—symbols of the delicate life Angela had lived. She had been a flower, an unopened bud plucked from the King's garden and bound into heaven's bouquet. How did the saying go? Only the good die young?

They looked out across an expanse of water shimmering with flecks of gold. They had come to acknowledge God's sovereignty and grace—grace because He'd granted them safe passage, and sovereignty because God's decisions, though difficult to understand, were His alone to make. They stood at the edge of the earth with the wind tousling their hair, breathing the salty brine. They wanted, in some significant way, to release Angela to God. Her time on earth was short, but the imprint she'd left on their hearts would forever remain.

Deanne blinked and curled her fingers, using the back of her hand to wipe a tear from her cheek. Her vision was blurred, but she saw what she was looking for. Two eagles circled far off in the distance, appearing more like tiny specks of dust than the majestic birds they were. They were there everyday, a testimony to the faithfulness of God.

She sniffed and rolled her hand to her other cheek, wiping it as well. She felt the emptiness more than Peter. Or maybe it was just the salt...salty air had a way of bringing tears to her eyes. God had given her Angela to fill the lonely hours of isolation, and had taken her back when she was strong enough to face the world on her own. She took consolation in that. No, she wasn't sad that Angela was free of this world's pain. The sadness she felt was from lack of closure. She'd had to leave Angela with Father Bloom. She hadn't been able to say a final good-bye.

Peter blinked to clear his vision. He was studying the sunset but the glare burned his eyes. The freedom with which the ocean moved left one feeling all was well on planet earth—but it wasn't. With all the technological wonders man had invented to save him time, and medicines to cure his every disease, with education providing the tools to make him rich, and his heart and mind continually seeking after peace—the world was a frustrated mess. Yet here, in this sheltered enclave of primitive poor lived some of the happiest, most selfless, carefree people on earth. *Go figure.*

A squall of wind broke through the trees, causing Peter to tighten his grip on Deanne's hand to keep her from being swept over the side. But she pulled free grasping her wreaths. She saved the one on her arm, tucking it to her breast, but when she took hold of the one in her hair, it pulled apart and went sailing across the ground. Little flowers tumbling in the grass. She stood there, her dress flapping like a flag. And then the gust ceased, stopping as quickly as it had begun. She raised a finger to pull a wayward lock of hair from her mouth and then slipped the remaining wreath from her arm.

The sun was disappearing behind the horizon. Only a small sliver remained, a dab of red on the ocean blue. Deanne held the wreath gently with both hands to keep it from coming apart. A tear rolled down her cheek as she began to hum and then to sing:

God be with you till we meet again,
By His counsels, guide uphold you.
With His sheep securely fold you,
God be with you till we meet again

Till we mee-e-eet—
Till we me-eet—
Till we meet at Jesus' feet
Till we mee-e-eet—
Till we me-eet—
God be with you till we meet again.

She looked up, blinking, clearing her eyes. Now her eagles were circling directly overhead, coasting on the current, their wings spread in majesty—*As an eagle stirreth up her nest, fluttering over her young... so the Lord alone did lead them.* God had taken them through the wilderness and brought them safely home—all but Angela. God bore *her* on *His* wings to a place of waiting on the other side. Deanne's arm dropped back and sprang forward, sending the remaining wreath soaring like a Frisbee over the cliff. They watched as it was picked apart by the breeze, the flowers separating into a cascading myriad of tiny parachutes that floated gently to the ocean below.

Peter took his wife in his arms, bringing his hand around to place it on her tummy, feeling the pulse of new life. He raised his eyes to the heavens. *Thank You, Lord.* He didn't know how much time they had or what the future might bring—nor did it concern him—sufficient for the day was the evil thereof. He would continue e-mailing Bibles for as long as the Lord allowed, and commit the future to Him.

The dusk brought out the stars, pinpoints of light illuminating the darkness. All creation was awaiting a day only God knew, a day set aside for redemption. Until then, man's job was to occupy and wait, not to worry about tomorrow. But every once and awhile, when the night fell and the wind swept over the ocean, Peter heard voices—not so distinct as to say they were real, more like voices echoing in an abandoned theater haunted by ghosts of the past. And if he looked *deep, deep, deep* into the vision, he could see Dickens and a troop of actors on a stage rehearsing their lines.

"Ghost of the Future...I fear you more than any specter I have seen... Are these the shadows of the things that will be, or are they shadows of things that may be, only?...Men's courses will foreshadow certain ends, to which, if persevered in, they must lead...But if the courses be departed from, the ends will change. Say it is thus with what you show me."

And he would smile knowing, that for all the makeup and costumes and special effects it required, the earth was just a stage upon which everyone played a part—an unfolding drama that would continue until the final curtain fell—*because the story had been written by the hand of God, before the world began.*